The Moon's Daughter

Book 1 of the *Moon & Sands* Trilogy

LEENA KAZAK

Copyright © 2024 by Leena Kazak

Cover Design by Artscandare

Map Design by Sierra Trowbridge

Proofread by Ellie of My Brother's Editor and MH Editorial Services

All rights reserved.

No part of this book may be reproduced in any form or by any electronic or mechanical means, including information storage and retrieval systems, without written permission from the author, except for the use of brief quotations in a book review.

This is a work of fiction. Names, places, characters, and events are the product of the author's imagination and are used fictitiously. Any resemblance to reality is purely coincidental and unintentional.

For all the eldest daughters.

*I see you. I see the burden on your shoulders:
carrying everyone and everything.*

I hope you find someone worthy of you.

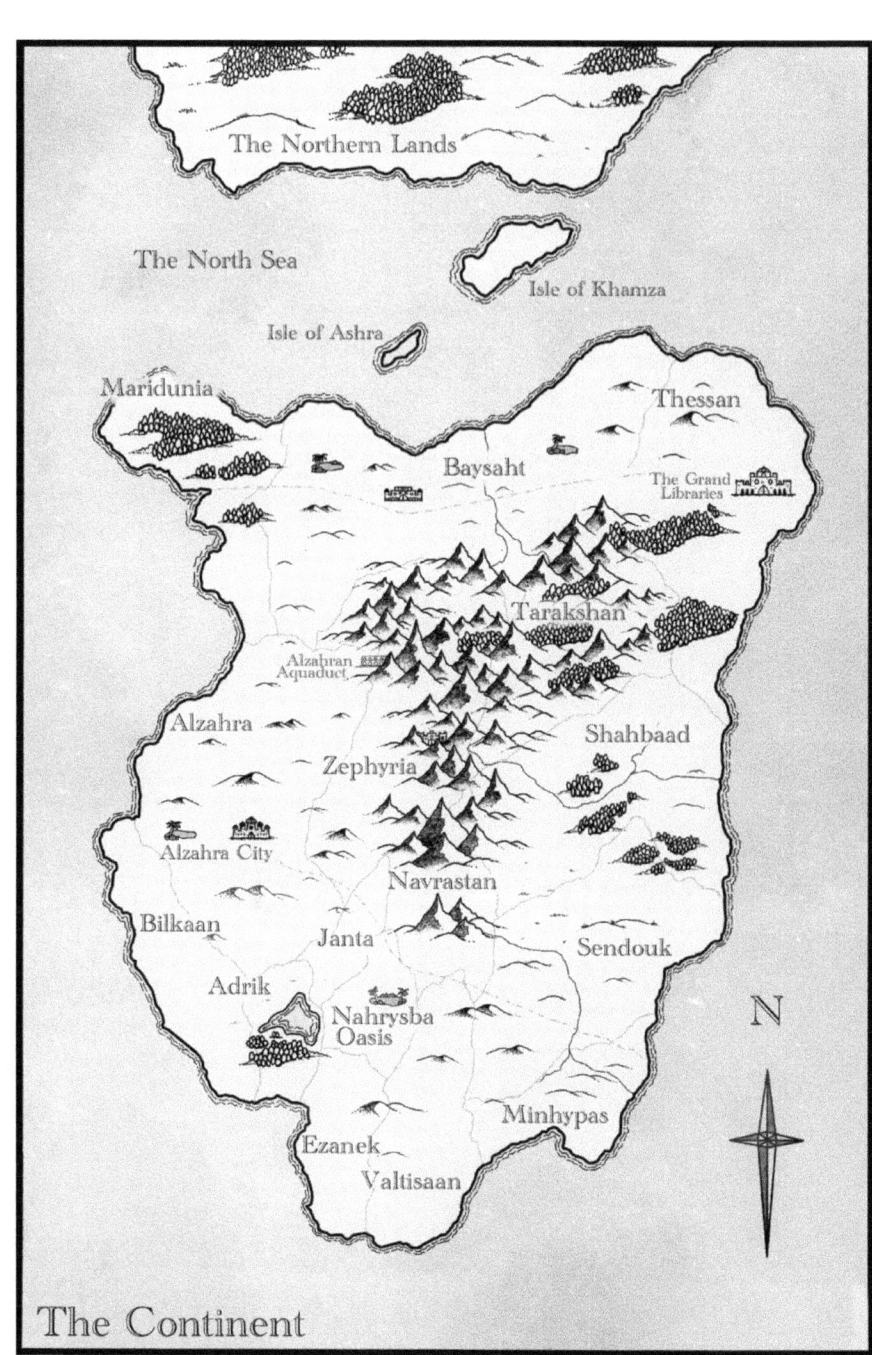

TABLE OF CONTENTS

PROLOGUE
CHAPTER ONE
CHAPTER TWO
CHAPTER THREE
CHAPTER FOUR
CHAPTER FIVE
CHAPTER SIX
CHAPTER SEVEN
CHAPTER EIGHT
CHAPTER NINE
CHAPTER TEN
CHAPTER ELEVEN
CHAPTER TWELVE
CHAPTER THIRTEEN
CHAPTER FOURTEEN
CHAPTER FIFTEEN
CHAPTER SIXTEEN
CHAPTER SEVENTEEN
CHAPTER EIGHTEEN
CHAPTER NINETEEN
CHAPTER TWENTY
CHAPTER TWENTY-ONE
CHAPTER TWENTY-TWO

CHAPTER TWENTY-THREE
CHAPTER TWENTY-FOUR
CHAPTER TWENTY-FIVE
CHAPTER TWENTY-SIX
CHAPTER TWENTY-SEVEN
CHAPTER TWENTY-EIGHT
CHAPTER TWENTY-NINE
CHAPTER THIRTY
CHAPTER THIRTY-ONE
CHAPTER THIRTY-TWO
CHAPTER THIRTY-THREE

PROLOGUE

In the dim recesses of a secluded chamber, a solitary figure sat ensconced before a roaring fire. Shadows draped the room, the flames casting eerie flickers of light and dark across the stone walls. A weathered hand rested on the arm of a high-backed chair, adorned with a ring bearing the insignia of a falcon. Sparse, guttering candles struggled against the darkness, their feeble glow barely illuminating the chamber's farthest corners.

A tentative rapping on the heavy door pierced the silence. The door creaked open, and a voice, quivering with apprehension, addressed the lone figure. "Sire, he has returned."

The seated figure slowly raised a gnarled hand, beckoning the newcomer forward. The door swung open, and a tall, cloaked man strode inside, tracking wet footprints behind him. The fire's glow danced across his handsome features, highlighting sharp cheekbones and a strong jawline, and glinted off his unruly black hair.

The man knelt before the dark-robed figure, a warrior acknowledging his commander.

"Father," he began, his deep voice resonating in the chamber, "the Medjai believe the prophecy will soon come to pass. In Alzahra."

A flicker of interest sparked in the old man's eyes. "Are you certain?" His voice, a low rumble, echoed through the room.

"Undoubtedly," the younger man affirmed. "They are sending *him* there."

The withered figure leaned forward, the light casting sinister shadows across his face. "Alzahra…" he mused, a slow, chilling smile spreading across his lips. "How fitting. The irony is delicious."

"And, Father," the man continued, eyes shining with triumph. "I finally found it." From within his cloak, he produced a small, shrouded object, cradled carefully in his hands.

The robed figure's eyes glowed with greed, tracking every movement with rapt attention. "Show me," he commanded urgently, tightly clutching the arms of his chair.

The younger man carefully unwrapped the object to reveal a gleaming orb. Its surface, a mesmerizing silver, sparkled in the sparse moonlight seeping through the chamber's windows.

The robed figure reverently grasped the orb. "With this, we will sculpt a new world!" The air seemed to grow colder, thrumming with the promise of impending upheaval. "Summon the council. We have the orb. Now, we must prepare. Let Alzahra and its unsuspecting princess be blindsided by their fate."

The young man nodded and rose quickly, his cloak swirling behind him as he left the chamber.

Alone once more, the old man's gaze returned to the flames, the orb clutched tightly in his grasp. He saw not just the fire, but the future—a future where Alzahra bent to his will. In the heart of the flames, he saw his victory, a world reshaped beneath the shadow of his throne.

CHAPTER ONE

"Shit!" Layna exclaimed as she dodged the oncoming blade, narrowly avoiding her opponent's sword. The air was heavy with the scent of jasmine, mingling with the dust stirred up by the duel.

"Such language, dear sister," Soraya chided, her simple burgundy tunic contrasting with Layna's armor. "Unfit for the future queen of Alzahra, don't you think?"

Layna's retort came with a flurry of aggressive strikes, her thick braid swinging behind her. "You'd curse too if you weren't so infuriatingly good with that left hand!"

Their swords danced in the setting sun. Despite the intensity of their duel, Layna laughed when Soraya feigned a dramatic stumble, her younger sister returning a quick wink in response.

The sword fight raged on, a blur of steel, as the sisters darted between the practice dummies scattered across the grounds, each fighting fiercely for the upper hand. In a swift move, Soraya skillfully disarmed her sister and tackled her in a playful pin. Their laughter rang out across the training grounds, signaling the duel's end.

Covered in dust and scrapes, they headed back to the palace. As they walked, Soraya noticed the dark circles under her sister's eyes. "Did you have another nightmare?" she asked softly. Her thick brows knit together.

"No," Layna quickly responded, "not last night." She glanced away, worrying her lip between her teeth. After a beat, she added, "Are you sure I can't persuade you to attend the dinner tonight?" Layna schooled her features into a mock pout. The evening's event was a grand dinner in honor of Prince Nizam of Baysaht, her latest suitor.

Soraya shook her head, her chin-length curls bouncing lightly. "I'll pass this time, dear sister. I must tend to my plants. And you know these formal banquets don't suit my temperament," she replied airily, softening her words with a gentle smile.

Layna sighed, wiping residual sweat from her brow as they walked. "Well, at least Burhani won't be there. That'll be a welcome break."

"She doesn't return until next week," Soraya responded, rolling her eyes. "Then she'll resume her role as a soul-sucking tendril of darkness in our lives."

Layna chuckled before adding, "I heard they're serving stewed lamb at dinner tonight. Your favorite." She looped her arm through Soraya's as they ambled along the stone pathway, passing rose bushes in alternating shades of pale pink and deep blue.

Soraya gave her an amused smile. "Nice try." She paused to inspect a rosebush with withered leaves, frowning slightly as she examined it.

Layna sighed in disappointment but knew her sister too well to press further. Their parents, King Khahleel and Queen Hadiyah, had long since given up on coaxing Soraya into the formalities of court life.

Soraya, with her vibrant spirit and unconventional approach, had always danced to her own rhythm, preferring the freedom of the gardens or the solace of her books over royal events.

Layna, however, had always adhered to the carefully choreographed steps laid out for her since birth, her life a series of predetermined motions within the royal dance of duty. It was exhausting, but it was the role she had been born to play.

Still, she admired Soraya's independence, even if it meant facing the dinner alone.

As they reached the palace, the sisters parted with a quick goodbye, and Layna continued to her chambers to prepare. Inside, her handmaid, Tinga, dressed her in an intricate emerald gown with sheer, billowing sleeves that cuffed delicately at her wrists. Teasing and fussing with her hair, Tinga styled it into a loose braid draped over Layna's shoulder, adorning it with pins and jewels that sparkled in the torchlight.

Tinga, a middle-aged woman with sharp brown eyes and a tight bun, frowned at a scratch on Layna's jaw as she dusted it with powder. "Another scrape," she muttered, clicking her tongue. "Are you a princess or a bandit?"

The princess responded with a sheepish smile, accustomed to Tinga's motherly fussing. "Have you learned anything else about Prince Nizam?" Layna asked while Tinga painstakingly lined her eyes with kohl.

The handmaid clicked her tongue again. "Stay still." Layna waited as Tinga tinted her lips and cheeks with rouge before finally meeting Layna's gaze in the mirror. "Nothing new. Just that he seems different and open-minded. And handsome. I already told you."

Layna reflected on the parade of suitors she'd encountered, none of whom had sparked any real interest. They had ranged from, at best, dreadfully boring, to painfully misogynistic at worst.

Yet, as she stared into the mirror, adjusting the delicate fabric of her gown, she hoped tonight might be different. Maybe, just maybe, Prince Nizam would prove more than yet another name in a long list of suitors.

There was an inexplicable shift in the atmosphere tonight, distinct from the countless other dinners she had endured. Each of those evenings had been orchestrated by her father's council, a tedious parade of suitors—princes, generals, and newly minted kings—each presented as part of a calculated effort to secure a strategic alliance for Alzahra.

But tonight promised something different, something she couldn't quite place. Rumors preceded Prince Nizam's arrival, painting him as a prince not just of royal blood, but of charm and intelligence, a man who defied typical royal conventions.

And, if the whispers among the servants held any truth, he was remarkably handsome. Would he live up to his reputation?

Princess Layna descended the grand staircase and entered the dining hall. Ornate chandeliers hung from the vaulted ceilings, casting a golden light over the throng of guests. The long dining tables were made of imported polished mahogany and adorned with fine linens. Crystal vases overflowed with vibrant flowers from the palace gardens—jasmine, roses, and lilies. The table settings gleamed under the chandeliers, with meticulously polished silverware placed next to fine porcelain plates.

The dining hall resonated with lively conversation, punctuated by the melodious clinking of silverware. However, as Layna moved through the crowd, she sensed an undercurrent of worry beneath the surface cheer. Whispers and fleeting glances hinted at concerns, likely fueled by rumors of growing tensions with Zephyria, a powerful neighboring kingdom that had long cast envious eyes toward Alzahra.

Zephyria had always been a silent rival, their interactions marked by concealed motives and diplomatic maneuvering. And since King Jorah ascended the throne thirty odd years ago, relations had deteriorated even further. Their shared history was a complex dance of unspoken threats and strategic positioning. However, until recently, Zephyria had refrained from overt aggression, but now, the fragile peace seemed on the verge of unraveling, threatening to plunge the kingdom into chaos.

Her parents, King Khahleel and Queen Hadiyah, presided over the festivities with regal poise. As she made her way to the royal table, Layna momentarily brushed aside her concerns and chose to immerse herself in the evening's celebrations. The anticipation of meeting Prince Nizam quickened her pulse, drawing her thoughts away from the kingdom's troubles. For now, she embraced the excitement of the evening, letting herself be swept up in the prospect of meeting the much-talked-about prince.

Layna quickly climbed the stairs onto the raised dais and joined her parents at the royal table. A hushed excitement swept through the hall, and all eyes turned to the entrance. Moments later, the doors swung open, heralding the arrival of Prince Nizam. Flanked by his court, the prince entered with a confident grace that commanded the room.

He stood tall and fair, with sandy blond hair neatly parted and slicked to the side, attractively framing his striking features. His bright green eyes surveyed the hall until they landed on the royal family. Dressed in a finely embroidered cream-colored tunic that highlighted his broad shoulders and trim build, he strode forward.

Layna felt a flutter of attraction as their eyes met. Tinga's information had been correct.

He was indeed *quite* handsome.

As he approached the dais, Prince Nizam bowed deeply, his voice resonating through the hall as he expressed his gratitude for Alzahra's hospitality. Turning to Layna, he offered a respectful nod, their eyes briefly locking again.

The prince gestured grandly toward the entrance. A flock of servants entered carrying several wooden trunks. The hall fell silent as they carefully placed the offerings before the royal family.

"Esteemed King Khahleel, I bring gifts from Baysaht in honor of Princess Layna," Nizam announced, gesturing toward the display.

The first trunk was opened to reveal fabrics in every imaginable shade of green, from the palest mint to the deepest forest green.

Luxurious silks and velvets spilled out, catching the light and drawing gasps from the assembled guests.

Another trunk contained an array of jewelry—necklaces, bracelets, rings, and anklets, each more exquisite than the last, all featuring green stones ranging from jade to peridot to emeralds, winking under the chandeliers' bright light. A third trunk held an assortment of perfumes and oud, the dark green bottles shimmering like rare jewels.

Finally, a smaller chest contained different types of fruit, their green hues vibrant against the dark wood. Apples and pears from Minhypas, renowned for its bountiful gardens, and grapes from Sendouk's famed vineyards, known across the continent for their exquisite flavor. Prince Nizam had gone to great lengths, coordinating with distant kingdoms, to secure such prized produce for the princess.

Layna's eyes widened, a soft gasp escaping her lips as she took in the extravagant gifts, each reflecting a level of detail that left her speechless. The thoughtfulness, more so than the material value of the gifts, touched her heart.

"I was informed of the princess's fondness for this color," Nizam admitted, addressing Layna with a sheepish, yet charming, smile.

Her heart warmed, and she found herself smiling back. "You are indeed well informed. Thank you, these gifts are beyond generous."

Her father, usually stern and reserved in formal settings, nodded in approval. "Your gifts are received with great appreciation, Prince Nizam. They reflect the generosity of Baysaht."

As the servants carefully repacked the trunks, the hall buzzed with whispers and admiring glances toward the prince. Layna felt respect blooming in her chest for the suitor who had gone to such lengths to honor her in front of her people.

Layna hardly tasted her food all evening. She stole furtive glances at Prince Nizam, who was engaged in conversation with her father and Lord Ebrahim, the senior adviser on Alzahra's council. Snippets of their dialogue reached her ears. Her father was assessing Baysaht's resources and the strength of its army. Baysaht, it seemed, would make a strong ally with its silver mines, fertile lands, and an imposing army of five hundred thousand well-armed soldiers.

As the evening progressed, Layna found herself increasingly drawn to the prince. Each time their eyes met, he would gift her a smile, sending her heart into a flutter of excitement.

After the meal, Nizam cleared his throat. "King Khahleel, might I request the honor of a stroll in the gardens with the esteemed princess?" he asked, his eyes flitting briefly to Layna before returning to the king. The request was unconventional, especially before a formal courtship was established, and sent a ripple of surprise through the hall.

King Khahleel's initial frown was smoothed by Queen Hadiyah's prompt and enthusiastic approval.

"Take two guards with you, Layna," her father commanded, his stern gaze piercing through her. Though typically progressive, he seemed displeased by the bold request given their large audience.

"Yes, Baba." Layna nodded, surprised and grateful he had agreed at all. Her heart raced as she rose. Her hand lightly brushed Nizam's as they stepped through the side doors into the moonlit gardens. Under the serene moonlight, a familiar calm washed over her. The moon's soft glow had always filled her heart with peace, and tonight was no different. Its gentle light steadied her nerves.

The quiet gardens felt like a world away from the dining hall's lively noise. Walking side by side, they strolled along the stone pathways in comfortable silence, the mandatory guards maintaining a respectful distance, allowing a semblance of privacy under the watchful moon.

Nizam spoke first. "You have a beautiful kingdom. Its beauty is surpassed only by its princess."

Layna felt her face warm, a telltale flush spreading from her neck to her cheeks. "Thank you. Your words are too kind. Tell me, what is Baysaht like?"

Nizam's eyes lit up. "Baysaht is a land of contrasts—harsh deserts and lush oases. It's challenging, but there's a beauty in its resilience. Much like sword fighting, I suppose."

"A comparison to sword fighting?" Layna smiled at him, her fingers playing with the sleeve of her gown. "Do you also partake in the art?"

"I do, though I must admit, I've heard tales of your skills. I'm certain you could best me," he joked with a wide smile.

"You flatter me. My sister Soraya is the better swordswoman between us." Layna ducked slightly under a low-hanging branch, and Nizam steadied her with a gentle grip on her arm.

Their conversation meandered from politics to art to their childhoods, and Layna found herself genuinely engaged. Unlike previous suitors who were preoccupied with Alzahra's resources, Nizam seemed genuinely interested in Layna herself. He inquired about her hobbies, favorite foods, and leisure activities, seemingly keen to understand her as a person beyond her royal duties.

The prince also shared his own experiences, recounting stories about his travels. "In Minhypas, I was mesmerized by the incredible gardens," he shared, his eyes alight with excitement. "And in Thessan, the Grand Libraries hold more knowledge than one could explore in a lifetime."

"I'm jealous you've been able to travel so much. It's always been a dream of mine," Layna remarked, looking up at him as they passed a trickling water fountain. "Have you ever visited the Northern Lands?"

"No," he chuckled, "my travels haven't taken me *that* far." The prince paused beside a blooming rose bush, carefully plucking a pale pink rose and presenting it to Layna. She winced internally—her sister would be furious if she found out—but accepted the gesture with a warm smile.

As they neared the end of their walk, Nizam turned to her, his eyes soft and a gentle smile playing on his lips. "I really enjoyed our walk. I must confess, my visit wasn't just about a political alliance. I was curious about you, the beautiful sword-fighting princess, and now, I find myself enthralled."

Layna's heart thrummed at his directness. "Your company has also been a pleasant surprise. How long do you intend to stay in Alzahra?"

Nizam's gaze lingered on her. "For a week's time," he replied softly, a hint of regret in his voice. "After that, my duties call me home."

They stood silently for a moment, the moonlight bathing the gardens in a gentle glow. In the tranquility of the night, their eyes met and held, a wordless understanding passing between them, one that promised new beginnings.

One of the guards subtly cleared his throat, discreetly signaling it was time to return. With embarrassed smiles, Layna and Nizam slowly made their way back to the dining hall. There, amidst the soft glow of the chandeliers, they bid each other goodnight.

CHAPTER TWO

Shining beneath the resplendent early morning sun, the proud kingdom of Alzahra basked in its glow. Vast deserts dominated much of the land, transitioning seamlessly into beautiful sandy beaches along the western coast. Scattered villages emerged where the land was kinder, and to the north, the harsh desert landscape softened into cooler, rocky mountains.

At the heart of the kingdom was Alzahra City, its capital, home to the grand royal palace, a jewel amidst the sands. Its stone walls shimmered under the sun's caress. Around the palace, the air was cooler, whispering hints of the gardens within, a marvel of innovation within the arid desert.

Beyond the palace gates lay an expansive courtyard, centered around a majestic fountain. To the right and left, winding paths beckoned toward the lush gardens that wrapped around the palace like a brilliant green wreath.

The palace itself stood tall and proud, its stone walls rising to meet the clear sky, punctuated by sparkling domes and towering minarets. On one of its many towers, a secluded balcony was adorned with flowering vines, their blooms cascading over the edge in a colorful waterfall.

Inside, Princess Layna navigated her chambers in a frantic whirlwind of indecision. She flitted between wardrobes and mirrors, each gown pondered and then quickly cast aside atop a growing pile on her bed.

After considerable deliberation, she finally settled on a shiny silver abaya, a long and billowing garment that cinched tightly at her waist. She left her hair loose, dark waves flowing down her back and framing her face, regretting her stubborn insistence that Tinga only prepare her for formal events. Finally ready, the princess hurried to the breakfast room.

She found her family, along with Prince Nizam and Lord Ebrahim, already seated at the long table. As she entered, Nizam rose respectfully. She bowed before sitting beside Soraya, who greeted her with a knowing smile and a wink, already privy to the previous night's developments. Layna had shared the details of her walk with Nizam the night before.

Layna surveyed the multitude of dishes spread across the table before settling on a plate of delicately arranged pastries and a pot of strong, aromatic coffee. "Prince Nizam," she said, smiling brightly, "may I offer you some of our traditional pastries? They're freshly made this morning. And perhaps some coffee?" She reached for the pot with practiced poise.

"That would be lovely. Thank you." He smiled, gratefully accepting the offered plate. "Your hospitality is unmatched," he added appreciatively as she poured him a cup of coffee.

Layna beamed, her heart somersaulting in her chest.

As they savored breakfast, Queen Hadiyah broke the comfortable silence. "Prince Nizam, we've heard much about your homeland. We would love to know more about your family as well."

Nizam paused mid-bite to respond. "Of course, Your Majesty." He hastily chewed and swallowed before responding. "My father, King Amnaar, is a devoted ruler. He and my mother, Queen Nissa, are loving parents. I'm truly blessed. I also have two younger sisters, Yasmirah and Yasminah. They keep the palace alive with their mischief." A fond smile crossed his face, but it faded as he continued. "My father has been recovering from a stomach illness." A shadow passed over Nizam's features. "He's mostly fine now, but his recovery has been slower than we'd hoped. It's why I must return to Baysaht after only a week's time—to continue overseeing the kingdom while he rests."

Soraya leaned forward, eyes slightly narrowed. "Queen Nissa can manage the kingdom for a short time while you're away, no?"

Khahleel coughed into his coffee, while Hadiyah raised her eyebrows at Soraya in warning. The younger princess tilted her head, looking at her parents inquisitively, not quite understanding their concern.

Nizam shifted uneasily in his chair, his gaze darting briefly to his lap. "My mother is not quite involved in ruling matters," the prince finally said. "Things are a bit different in Baysaht."

Soraya opened her mouth to inquire further, but Lord Ebrahim interjected, expressing warm sentiments for King Amnaar's recovery. The room fell silent, the atmosphere turning solemn as the group absorbed Nizam's words.

"Lord Ebrahim," Nizam said, turning to the senior adviser. "I understand you have a daughter. She has not joined us?"

"Yes, I do." Lord Ebrahim smiled broadly, his eyes crinkling behind his spectacles. "Her name is Burhani. She is currently in Janta working to secure a trade agreement. It's her first diplomatic mission. I don't expect her back for another week or so."

Nizam nodded appreciatively. "If she is anything like her father, she must be quite skilled at diplomacy."

Soraya exchanged a furtive grimace with Layna, who struggled to keep her laughter in check.

"She is an avid learner. Burhani is very bright," Lord Ebrahim said with pride. "Just like our Layna here." He smiled warmly at Layna, running an affectionate hand over her head.

"Lord Ebrahim gives me too much credit," Layna said with a grin. "He's spent countless hours teaching me over the years, mostly because I drove my tutors to the brink of madness." Everyone laughed, the sound echoing warmly through the room. After a beat, Layna turned to her father. "Baba," she said brightly, "Soraya and I were planning to take Prince Nizam on a tour of the city today."

Her father, more relaxed in this informal setting, nodded his approval. "An excellent idea," he concurred. "It would be good for Prince Nizam to experience our culture firsthand."

The palace stables buzzed with activity. Ready to venture into Alzahra City, Layna had changed into lightweight trousers and a short-sleeved tunic, her sword belted securely at her waist. Her horse, Qamar, a majestic Arabian mare with a glossy white coat and a shimmering mane, greeted her with a soft nicker. Layna adjusted Qamar's saddle with practiced ease, tenderly stroking her mane, whispering words of fondness.

Meanwhile, the stablehands prepared a robust, noble bay horse for Prince Nizam. As they equipped the steed with saddle and bridle, it stood patiently, ready to tread the streets of Alzahra City.

Soraya had gracefully bowed out of joining them, citing an urgent need in the palace greenhouse. Layna saw through the flimsy excuse and felt a surge of gratitude. She was excited to spend the day alone with Nizam.

"No guards?" Nizam asked warily from atop his horse, his head tilted slightly and eyebrows knit together.

"No, we'll be alright," Layna reassured with a smile, urging Qamar forward.

As the pair rode away from the palace, her pride shined through as she guided him through the vibrant streets. Each turn revealed architectural marvels and historical sites, rich with the city's storied past.

Trotting along the cobblestone streets, Layna described the ancient Alzahran Aqueduct, an impressive feat of engineering that had stood for centuries. She explained how it channeled water from the distant northern mountains where rainfall was more abundant to sustain the city. A sophisticated network of pipes ensured every building and residence in the capital had running water.

"We've been trying to court some engineers from Valtisaan to further modernize the city and perhaps even the villages," Layna mentioned as they ventured deeper into the city. "But we've had no success so far. The Valtisaani are very secretive about their methods."

"They've always been that way," Nizam agreed. "But even more so now with the new king."

Next on the tour was the Moon Temple. Centuries ago, the moon was worshipped by the people of Alzahra and across the continent. Over time, the world evolved, and the ancient practices gradually faded. Now, the temple stood as a historical monument, preserved by a few dedicated priests and priestesses. While it rarely saw genuine worshippers, it remained an important piece of Alzahra's history.

Their ride soon brought them to the heart of a seasonal harvest festival, a yearly celebration that transformed the city with color, music, and laughter. The streets were decorated with red and gold banner flags, fluttering above the bustling crowds. The aroma of spiced foods and sweet treats permeated the air, as vendors called out to passersby with offers of delicacies and handmade crafts. Dancers moved in synchrony to the rhythm of drums and flutes, their vibrant red costumes swirling around them like shimmering clouds.

Nizam watched in awe, his gaze darting from one spectacle to the next, pure fascination etched across his features. Layna couldn't help but smile. "I'm surprised to see you so taken aback," she teased gently, eyes sparkling with mirth.

He turned to her with a broad smile. "Amazed would be the right word," he admitted. "In Baysaht, we have festivals, but they tend to be more ceremonial. But, moons, this"—he gestured broadly at the scene before them—"is refreshingly vibrant. It's beautiful to see such uninhibited joy and celebration."

Their conversation flowed easily as the crowd parted around them, many of them waving to Layna, who smiled and waved back.

"I must admit, I'm shocked you roam the city without an escort of guards," Nizam remarked, shielding his eyes from the bright sun as their horses trotted along, the sounds of the festival fading behind them.

Layna smiled conspiratorially. "Soraya and I used to sneak out of the palace as teenagers. Baba was always furious when we managed to elude our guards. But once we began sword fighting lessons, I think he worried less. He's tripled the city patrol because of us, though he'll never admit it. Officially, it was for 'public safety,'" she explained with a grin.

"And your citizens? Please don't take this the wrong way, but they don't seem...in awe of you," Nizam noted, his brows furrowed. "When I leave my palace, my guards clear a path and keep the people at bay. It would be chaos otherwise."

Layna thought for a moment. "I never realized it was odd. Perhaps because the citizens see me so often? I host a monthly assembly open to the public, so I interact with many of them regularly."

"That's fascinating." Nizam gently nudged his horse closer to hers, allowing their legs to brush lightly as their mounts trotted side by side.

Layna's cheeks flushed. Each stride sent a ripple of awareness through her, the light pressure pleasant where Nizam's leg brushed against hers.

"I was surprised to see Lord Ebrahim at breakfast," Nizam commented. "It's rare for council members to dine with the royal family in such informal settings."

"Lord Ebrahim *is* part of our family," Layna replied with a soft smile. "He's been advising Baba since before I was born. In many ways, he's like a second father to me."

"Then, you are truly blessed," Nizam said. "And with Burhani, you have another sister."

Layna's smile faded slightly. "Burhani came to live at the palace three years ago. Lord Ebrahim brought her here after her mother's death. I'm not certain he even knew about her before that."

Nizam's eyebrows shot up. "*Oh.* That must have been quite an adjustment." Noting Layna's pensive silence, he did not press further.

As the sun dipped lower, painting the sky with hues of orange and pink, Layna and Nizam journeyed back to the palace.

Their horses slowed to a halt at the stables, an amiable silence wrapped around them. Nizam helped Layna dismount, and the prince and princess returned to the palace together.

As Layna retired to her chambers that evening, the day's excitement lingered in her mind. A gentle knock broke her contemplation. Soraya rushed in, and Layna's smile broadened as her sister sat beside her on the bed. Layna grasped her hand in gratitude. "Thank you. I had the most incredible day with Nizam."

Soraya flashed a cheeky grin and squeezed Layna's hand. "I don't know what you're talking about," she teased, her brown eyes twinkling with mischief. "I truly *did* have an emergency in the greenhouse. Tell me more about him."

"Honestly, I feel such a strong connection to him already. He's charming, polite, smart, and so handsome! I could drown in his beautiful green eyes all day," Layna confided with a dreamy smile. "And he seems to care about me—just *me*, not the future queen."

Soraya listened intently, a knowing smile playing on her lips. "It sounds like he sees the real you," she remarked softly.

The younger princess was quiet for a moment, her expression contemplative. Layna recognized that look. "What's on your mind, Soraya?" she prodded gently, tilting her head to catch her sister's gaze.

Soraya hesitated. "I don't want to put a damper on your excitement, Layna. I truly am so happy for you," she began, choosing her words carefully.

"But?" Layna prompted.

"But…perhaps take some more time before deciding. It's only been two days, after all. And Baysaht—their culture seems quite restrictive of women." Soraya paused, weighing her next words. "Compared to your previous suitors, I agree that Nizam seems like the perfect match. But you need more time to understand him better and see him clearly—not just through the lens of these initial feelings."

"I know it seems rushed," Layna said. "But it just feels right. I can't explain it. Do you remember the stories Mama told us as children? I think she was right that some souls meet before ever setting foot on this earth, and then they recognize each other when they meet again. I feel that way with Nizam."

Soraya snorted. "Mama also told us stories about the monstrous Sun Slayer who'd come and steal us away if we didn't go to sleep."

"Soraya, I'm serious!" Layna exclaimed, swatting her sister's arm. Frowning, she narrowed her eyes as the younger princess broke out in a fit of giggles.

Huffing in annoyance, her gaze drifted as she considered Soraya's words. "Yes, you're right about Baysaht's customs. And you're right to remind me to be cautious. But Nizam seems different. I've been open with him about our customs, and he actually seemed impressed," Layna defended. "Still, I'll take my time and learn more about him. Thank you for caring so much." She squeezed her sister's hand in gratitude.

Soraya enveloped her in a tight hug. "Goodnight," she said. "Sleep well. And without nightmares." Layna gave her a strained smile, her eyes darting to her lap.

After Soraya left, Layna lay awake for hours. The prospect of exploring what lay ahead with Nizam filled her with hope. He was a strong match for her kingdom *and* someone she felt genuine attraction toward.

But Soraya was right. While Layna was already picturing her future with Nizam, what vision did *he* see for them?

In the days that followed, Layna and Nizam spent hours together every day, their time interrupted only when Layna was called to council meetings or when King Khahleel sought Nizam's counsel on Baysaht's resources. Between casual strolls, earnest discussions, and shared meals, each encounter deepened their understanding of one another.

One sunny afternoon, Layna practiced her archery on the training grounds. Her hair was braided, with loose strands fluttering around her face in the gentle breeze. She wore a white sleeveless tunic and fitted trousers, both made of breathable fabric suited to the desert heat. A wide leather belt held her quiver, and sturdy boots protected her feet. As she drew her bow, sunlight glinted off the silver embroidery on her tunic.

The princess released arrow after arrow, each finding its mark with precision. The sound of footsteps broke her concentration, and she turned to see Nizam approaching.

"You never cease to amaze me, Layna," he marveled, handing her a skein of water. She gratefully accepted, gulping down the cool liquid.

"You've seen nothing yet. Archery is just one of many skills we pride ourselves on in Alzahra."

Nizam stepped closer, a playful gleam in his eye. "I've been learning a new form recently. May I show you?" he asked hopefully.

"Yes, of course." Layna handed him the bow and stepped aside.

However, instead of demonstrating himself, Nizam gently pulled Layna back by the fabric of her tunic and positioned himself behind her. "It'll be easier if I guide you through it," he murmured in her ear, sending a cascade of shivers down her spine.

Before Layna could respond, his arms encircled her, his hands guiding hers to the correct position on the bow. The warmth of his body seeped through her training clothes, enveloping her in a cocoon of heat.

Layna's heart raced, her focus scattered by their sudden closeness. His scent surrounded her—a subtle blend of citrus and earth. His breath brushed her ear as he explained the stance, his words a soft whisper amidst the pounding of her heart.

Despite her attempts to focus, Layna was keenly aware of every point of contact between them—the firmness of his chest against her back, the gentle pressure of his hands guiding hers, the shared warmth radiating between them.

She loosed the arrow, but it veered wildly off target and bounced off a nearby stand of weights. A nervous chuckle escaped her as they stepped apart. Nizam frowned slightly at where the arrow had landed.

The moment was fleeting, yet as they separated, Layna struggled to compose herself. "Thank you for showing me. I'll have to practice a bit more," she said with a smile, her heart still fluttering. "Are your sisters also interested in archery and sword fighting?"

Nizam didn't respond immediately. "Yes, they are," he finally said. "But it's been a challenging journey. Baysaht has only recently begun to adopt a more progressive stance on women participating in such activities. It took time, but my father has finally come around." He sighed deeply. "We still need loads more progress. Having a strong queen like you would move mountains."

Layna placed her bow aside and moved to a nearby bench, its wooden frame warm from the afternoon sun. Nizam followed, sitting close beside her.

"What are you thinking?" he asked, his green eyes appraising her with concern.

"Nizam," Layna began slowly, "Baysaht has never had a queen as its ruler. The crown only passes through the male line. And your mother, though she is your father's queen, isn't involved in the kingdom's management." She paused, letting her words sink in. "But *I* will rule Alzahra one day, just as you will rule Baysaht. How will we manage ruling two kingdoms? And will the people of Baysaht accept me?"

"I'm glad you brought this up," he said, meeting her gaze, "and I understand your concerns. But I believe leadership must transcend traditions. Forging new paths is critical. Otherwise, Baysaht will remain stuck in the past." He reached out, lightly covering her hand. "Baysaht may have never had a queen with true power, but I think it's well past time for new traditions to take root."

His gaze drifted to the horizon. "In practice, I imagine we'll divide our time between Baysaht and Alzahra. Of course, I would never interfere in your sovereign decisions over your kingdom. I hope, though, you might rely on me for counsel, as I would rely on you." He leaned back, casually draping his arm over the bench, inching closer to Layna. "We'd need strong councils in both kingdoms to manage affairs in our absence. But with careful planning and communication, I see no reason why we can't make it work."

His words painted a picture of a partnership of equals. "Imagine the message we'd send to our people and the world," Nizam added. "A united front, blending the strengths of both cultures, leading by example. Honestly, I can't picture anyone else as my queen. Only you, Layna."

Layna was at a loss for words. She could only smile at him, her full lips quivering slightly, her eyes suddenly damp. Nizam pressed a tender kiss to her forehead. They gazed out at the horizon together, their future laid out before them.

The days rushed by despite Layna's wish for time to slow down. On the eve of Nizam's return to Baysaht, a creeping melancholy took hold of her heart. Their time together had been perfect. There was an unexpected joy in finding someone who understood her in ways she hadn't dared imagine.

She had always known her duty as future queen meant making a strategic match, but finding a true companion seemed like a distant dream. Her connection with Nizam stirred hopes she had never allowed herself to nurture.

Guided by the moon's soft light, Layna walked to the palace gardens, mindful of any watching eyes.

Nizam had asked her to meet him there.

The cool, fragrant air, perfumed with the scent of jasmine and roses, wove a sweet aroma into a night Layna wished would last forever. She followed the winding paths, humming with the gentle buzz of insects, to a secluded gazebo.

As she approached, Layna saw Nizam waiting. The moonlight cast a soft glow around him, highlighting the green in his eyes and making them sparkle like emeralds. He looked every bit the prince in his elegant white tunic.

He closed the distance between them, his movements graceful and deliberate. As he took her hands in his, Layna felt her heart leap, each beat echoing in her ears.

"Layna," he murmured, his gaze fixed on her, "I wish I had the words to express my heart. I know it's only been a week, but somehow, it feels like my soul knows yours." Gently, he guided her to sit beside him in the gazebo.

"Nizam," she whispered, moonlight illuminating her face, "I'm embarrassed to admit that you have thoroughly won me over, perhaps from the very first night you arrived." Nizam smiled at her, eyes warming at her confession.

She turned to face him, curiosity coloring her tone. "I've been wondering about something. How did you know my favorite color was green?" Her eyes searched his for the story behind his thoughtful gesture.

Nizam's expression softened, his eyes misting with a distant look. A small, wistful smile tugged at his lips. "I saw you years ago at the Grand Summit of Monarchs. Your first Summit, I think. I was only twenty-three. You were maybe seventeen or eighteen. On the first day, you wore a dark green abaya that sparkled with jewels in the sunlight. The next day, it was a simple moss-colored gown. And on the final day, you looked like a goddess in a white abaya, but even then, your belt was encrusted with emeralds."

He paused, a shy smile on his lips. "I was utterly captivated by your beauty. You were always with your father, and I lacked the courage to approach you then," he admitted, glancing away. "During the trade discussions, Zephyria's emissary made a snide remark about Alzahra. But before your father could respond, you angrily chastised the man, who was likely decades older than you. Your fire impressed me then, and I can see it burns brightly even now."

Layna listened, surprise and delight swirling within her. This revelation felt like uncovering a secret page from her own history.

"You remembered me from then?" Her voice was low in the night and filled with wonder. "I'm sorry, I don't recall seeing you." She gently squeezed his hand.

"Yes, I remembered you. How could I not? You left such a mark on me, even from afar. I promised myself that if destiny gave me another opportunity, I would seize it. When Alzahra was recommended among suitable kingdoms by my council, it was my second chance. To finally speak to the fiery girl in green."

The depth of his admission, the idea that she had unknowingly left such an impact on him years ago, rendered her momentarily speechless.

It felt like fate.

In the quiet of the gazebo, under the starlit sky, she simply watched him, warmth blooming in her chest. They sat in comfortable silence, the night alive with the subtle sounds of the gardens.

Nizam cradled Layna's cheek with a feather light touch. "Layna," he murmured, "may I kiss you?"

Her heart raced, every part of her screaming a silent yes. His question hung in the air.

Breathless, she nodded.

Nizam leaned in slowly, giving her a moment to retreat, but she remained still, eyes slowly fluttering closed. Their lips met in a tender kiss, his lips soft and warm as they moved against her own. It was over far too soon, and as they parted, Layna's breath escaped in a soft gasp.

"I'll see you in the morning," Nizam whispered softly. His voice was a tender caress, carrying the hope of what was to come.

Layna could've sworn she felt her fingertips tingling.

Layna stood in the courtyard alongside her sister and parents, the stone floor warmed by the early morning sun. Despite the day's brightness, a shadow dimmed her smile as they gathered to bid Prince Nizam farewell.

Carriages and horses were lined up neatly by the fountain, awaiting their prince for the journey back to Baysaht.

Nizam stepped forward to address King Khahleel. "Your Majesty," he said, grasping the king's hands in gratitude, "I cannot thank you enough for your unparalleled generosity during my stay."

"Prince Nizam, your visit has been a blessing to us. Your thoughtful gifts and the spirit of friendship you've extended are deeply appreciated. Alzahra will remember your visit fondly," Khahleel replied warmly.

Nizam hesitated, his eyes briefly finding Layna before returning to the king. "If I may be so bold…might I request a lock of Princess Layna's hair?"

The courtyard fell into hushed anticipation, every eye on King Khahleel, whose expression remained unreadable.

Layna held her breath.

Then, with a measured tone, Khahleel said, "I am honored by your regard for my daughter. I would be glad to consider it on your *next* visit, should our discussions of alliance progress."

Though a glimmer of disappointment crossed Nizam's features, he accepted the king's decision with a gracious nod. The ritual token would have formally cemented their courtship.

Nizam bowed deeply to Queen Hadiyah and Soraya, offering each a respectful smile. Then, turning to Layna, he paused, the distance between them charged with unspoken words.

"I'll write to you as soon as I return to Baysaht," he promised softly. "And I swear, it won't be long before I see you again."

CHAPTER THREE

In the wake of Nizam's return to Baysaht, Princess Layna found herself immersed in wistful daydreams. The palace, with its sprawling gardens and sun-kissed halls, echoed with the silent melody of her hopeful heartbeats. Memories of Nizam's warm smile and their moments together played like a sweet refrain in her mind.

She envisioned letters, sealed with Baysaht's regal emblem, arriving and weaving the start of a blossoming relationship. Daydreams painted pictures of a life where love and duty walked hand in hand, transcending the mere politics of a royal marriage.

Yet as days turned into weeks, her initial excitement gave way to a gnawing uncertainty.

The eagerly anticipated letters did not arrive.

Each visit to the couriers' quarters, once a source of hopeful joy, became a daily ritual of disappointment. The servants, initially enthusiastic, began casting sympathetic glances in her direction, their silence speaking volumes.

On one particular visit, Layna nearly ran into Burhani, who stood just outside the door with a cruel smirk on her beautiful face. Unlike her father, Burhani had deep ochre skin, piercing blue eyes, and waist-length black hair that she often wore in a tight braid. Lord Ebrahim had never revealed her mother's identity, but it was evident from Burhani's striking features that she was Navrastani.

"Still no letter, Princess?" Burhani sneered, arms crossed over her chest. "I wonder what kind of impression you made. It's a shame I wasn't here to see it."

Layna tensed at the jibe. "Good day to you, Burhani," she replied tightly.

"Good day, indeed," Burhani chortled, her full lips curled in a mocking smile. "Must be difficult, no? Waiting on a letter that never arrives."

Layna took a deep breath. "Your company is *always* such a pleasure, but I have duties to attend to. I'm sure you do as well."

Burhani chuckled. "Of course, Princess." She didn't budge, forcing Layna to walk around her.

Fists clenched tightly at her sides, Layna quickly walked away. Burhani's voice followed her down the hall. "If you do get a letter, be sure to let me know! I'd love to hear what the elusive Prince Nizam has to say."

Layna gritted her teeth, Burhani's words cutting deep. Still, she kept her back straight as she gracefully walked away, frustration and sadness clamping around her heart like a vise.

Behind her, Burhani watched with a satisfied smirk.

Weeks stretched into months, and the vibrant colors of the palace gardens faded as the cooler season arrived. Layna's heart, once uplifted by the promise of Nizam's letters, now felt heavy, anchored in bleak dejection by his silence.

This period of waiting, of hope turned to disappointment, marked a profound change in Layna. The innocence of first love gave way to a more guarded heart. Now viewing the world through a lens tempered by realism, she dismissed the tales of love and chivalry that had once captivated her.

She threw herself into her duties with newfound determination, focusing wholeheartedly on the welfare of Alzahra and its people. Her painful heartache forged a stronger, more resilient queen-to-be, one who understood the price of personal desires in the face of royal responsibilities.

Soraya, ever perceptive, noticed the shadow that had fallen over her sister. One quiet evening, as they sat in Layna's chambers, Soraya reached for her hand. "He doesn't define your worth, Layna," she murmured softly. "In a few months, you'll meet plenty more suitors at the royal ball. Besides, I didn't like him much anyway."

Layna knew her sister was right, yet the sting of rejection was sharper than any sword. Had she been too naïve to believe in a fairytale ending? Was the connection with Nizam merely a fleeting wisp of romance, destined to dissipate? She couldn't fathom why the seemingly smitten prince had made no further attempts at courtship.

If nothing else, Layna yearned for closure.

Despite the months-long silence, the princess was too proud to write to Nizam herself. While she was usually unbothered by breaking societal norms, her pride held firm in this situation. She would not make the next move. Her father's council informed her that Nizam had safely returned to Baysaht and was actively ruling alongside King Amnaar.

The information served as a bitter reminder. If Nizam had wished to continue their courtship, he had every opportunity to do so. His silence was a clear message—he simply didn't want to continue what he began in Alzahra.

Instead, he haunted her thoughts like a persistent ghost. This realization was painful, but Layna knew she must accept it and move forward with her dignity intact.

Perhaps, she told herself, this was for the best. Her mother had always cautioned her about entanglements of the heart. In moments of solitude, Layna often reflected on her mother's lessons. Queen Hadiyah had always emphasized the delicate balance between personal desires and royal duties.

"A heart in love can be a vulnerability for a queen," her mother once said, her voice laced with decades of wisdom.

As they walked through the gardens one evening, Queen Hadiyah spoke of destiny and duty, her words floating on the gentle breeze. "My dear Layna," she began, her eyes reflecting the moonlit sky, "there is something you must understand about the path you walk as future queen. Your role, your very destiny, might have been written in the sands of time long before you were born. Your heart, while your own, is tied to the fate of Alzahra. The choices you must make may not always align with the desires of your heart."

"But isn't love important, Mama? Can't it guide my choices as queen?" a young Layna asked, her eyes wide and filled with hope yet untrampled.

Queen Hadiyah stopped and took Layna's hands. "Love is a powerful force, my child, one that can inspire and empower. But as queen, your first duty will always be to your people. The luxury of following your heart is not yours to claim."

Layna felt a strange emotion, a wave of sadness mingled with something foreign, realization dawning that her destiny was not hers to shape.

As queen, she would be powerful yet, in many ways, tragically powerless.

"The crown is not just a symbol of power; it is a promise to our people. A promise that may require sacrifices your heart might not be prepared to make."

In the quiet hours of the night, Layna stood on her balcony, gazing at Alzahra City. Rooftops stretched out for miles, and in the distance, she could just barely discern the high walls that protected her beloved city. One by one, lights flickered and winked out as her people settled into sleep.

Layna glanced up at the moon, hanging brightly in the star-speckled sky. The cool breeze carried a soothing touch, as if the moon itself was wrapping her in an embrace, offering comfort for her wounded heart. As she felt its gentle light on her skin, a chord of deep peace strummed through her, vibrating outwards, spreading to her fingertips and toes.

She closed her eyes, feeling the familiar calmness settle over her.

The moon whispered secrets of resilience and freedom, beckoning her to the world beyond the palace walls. *One day*, she thought wistfully. Under the moon's soothing aura, Layna felt a shift within her, a new strength emerging from the ashes of heartache.

With each passing day, her resolve grew stronger. She found release in sword fighting. The training grounds became her sanctuary, where she could cast off the mantle of royalty and be her true self. Under the swordmaster's guidance, she honed her skills, each session pushing her limits.

But it was during the night, under the moon's glow, when Layna truly found her strength. She preferred these solitary training sessions, where the silvery light seemed to imbue her with sharper focus and greater stamina. The moon's presence somehow made her feel powerful. In these moments, her sword strokes felt more fluid, her movements more graceful, as if she were part of the night itself.

Her sparring sessions with left-handed Soraya, once challenging, now saw Layna emerging as the clear victor. Even when she managed to persuade some of the palace guards to train with her, there was a noticeable difference in her prowess.

As the months passed, and the illusion of love with Prince Nizam faded into distant memory, Layna emerged stronger and more grounded in her identity. Her path was not about finding love or approval from a suitor.

She was the future queen, and she needed to prepare for her destiny.

One evening, under the moon's watchful gaze, Layna practiced her swordplay alone on the training grounds. Eyes blazing, she repeatedly struck the wooden practice dummy. She circled her motionless opponent, her sword trailing in the sand. Catching her breath, she again furiously attacked the wooden figure with renewed energy.

"I must say, one would be wise to never cross you," a deep voice drawled from behind her. Panting, Layna paused mid-step and spun around, her eyes locking onto an unfamiliar man before her.

He stood tall, his broad shoulders pulled back in confidence. Clad in simple attire—a plain black tunic and loose-fitting trousers—he melded with the night. A large sword hung casually at his hip. His tunic stretched taut over his muscled chest and biceps, the fabric practically straining to contain his strength.

This intruder was positively lethal. Intense hazel eyes pierced through her, unsettling in their directness. The breeze ruffled his unruly dark hair, and the stubble shadowing his jawline gave him a raw, masculine edge.

For a moment, Layna found herself taken aback, her composure wavering under his scrutiny. She felt an inexplicable vulnerability, as though he could see past her royal façade to the woman hidden beneath.

Yet, as quickly as it came, the feeling was replaced by a surge of annoyance. Who was this stranger who dared intrude upon her solitude?

Her warrior instincts kicked in, and Layna tightened her grip on her sword. She squared her shoulders and firmly planted her feet, preparing for any threat.

The man noticed her change in stance and had the audacity to smirk.

With narrowed eyes and a voice sharp with irritation, she addressed him. "Do you often sneak up on others in the night like a scurrying mouse?"

The stranger's smile broadened. "My sincerest apologies, Princess. I didn't mean to *scurry*. I'm Prince Zarian of the Nahrysba Oasis." He continued to smirk at her, oozing arrogance, as if she were the punchline to a joke that only he understood.

To make matters worse, he might have been the most handsome man she had ever seen, which only made her hate him more.

"*Prince* Zarian?" Layna arched an eyebrow as her gaze trailed over his simple attire. "I wasn't informed of your arrival." She tightened her grip on her sword. Her emotional turmoil with Nizam had left her wary of strangers, especially princes.

Unbothered by her appraisal, he stepped closer. "I'm not one for grand entrances and formalities. I prefer a more subtle approach." He took another step closer. "Again, I'm sorry for startling you," he added, extending his hand in greeting.

He didn't seem very apologetic.

"Don't flatter yourself," Layna retorted hotly, still simmering with annoyance. "You didn't startle me." She swiftly sheathed her sword and angrily strode past Prince Zarian and his outstretched hand.

Fuming, Layna marched through the palace corridors until she reached the east wing. Pausing outside her parents' chambers, she fell into a familiar childhood habit. She and Soraya had always found a thrill in eavesdropping, a remnant of their more mischievous days. The door was slightly ajar, and she could hear the hushed, urgent voices of King Khahleel and Queen Hadiyah.

Straining to listen, she caught fragments of their conversation—whispers of a "prophecy" and the "Medjai," but the details eluded her. These words sparked a vague memory dancing at the edge of her thoughts, but it was too indistinct to grasp. Brushing it aside, she focused on her immediate concerns.

Layna pushed open the heavy door and barged in. Her parents looked up, eyes wide, surprised by her abrupt entrance.

"Why is Prince Zarian of the Nahrysba Oasis here?" she demanded, words tumbling out in a flurry of frustration. "And why was I not informed? Is he another suitor?"

Her parents shared a brief glance before her father cleared his throat. "No, my dear, he is not a suitor. Prince Zarian is here as an adviser on matters of state and defense. His arrival was meant to be discreet."

Hadiyah's eyes softened as she looked at her daughter. "We didn't want to burden you further, especially after…recent events," she added, acknowledging Layna's heartache.

Layna's shoulders slumped slightly, the weight of confusion and suspicion mingling with her emotional fatigue. "But we don't have a formal alliance with the Oasis," she said, the fire of her anger fading into a flicker of curiosity. "Why would their prince come here?"

"King Tahriq, Zarian's father, and I are old friends," Khahleel explained, casting a meaningful glance at Hadiyah. "With tensions rising with Zephyria, I thought we could benefit from his expertise in palace security and other crucial matters."

Layna nodded slowly. Who *was* this Prince Zarian, and what role was he to play in Alzahra?

"Layna," her father continued, his voice softer than usual, "Prince Zarian is an esteemed guest. I expect you to extend the hospitality that befits your upbringing. Remember, you are destined to be queen, and part of that destiny is learning to master your emotions."

Layna bowed her head slightly. Despite the gentleness in his tone, the reprimand stung, reminding her of the heavy responsibilities on her shoulders. "Yes, Baba," she acquiesced quietly.

After leaving her parents' chambers, a whirlwind of thoughts clouded Layna's mind. Eager to gossip about Prince Zarian's arrival, she set off to find her sister.

Layna traversed the palace, her footsteps echoing through the vast corridors. She checked Soraya's usual haunts—the palace greenhouse, the library, even the quiet alcove in the gardens where her sister often escaped with a book—but she was nowhere to be found. *That's odd*, Layna thought. *Where could she be?*

With a sigh, Layna headed back to her chambers. As she passed through to the private balcony, the cool evening breeze carrying the scent of night-blooming jasmine, her gaze drifted to the training grounds below. There, under the soft light of torches, she saw a solitary figure practicing with a sword.

It was Prince Zarian.

In the dim light, he moved with a captivating grace and ferocity. His tunic lay discarded, revealing a muscular, well-defined physique. The torches cast a warm glow over his tanned skin, highlighting the contours of his muscles and the sheen of sweat that already glistened on his back.

Layna's eyes traced the curve of his biceps, each movement accentuating the strength in his arms. Her eyes followed his every thrust, the sword an extension of his arm. She was reluctant to admit, even to herself, that he was incredibly skilled.

She caught sight of a tattoo on his left pectoral. The ink, a rich, deep black, stood out starkly against his sun-kissed skin. The tattoo was a circular design, and at its center, a crescent moon was cradled within the sun. Thick black whorls branched out in symmetrical designs until just below his collarbone.

An unexpected feeling stirred within her, a mix of intrigue and something more primal. She watched, transfixed, as Zarian executed a series of complex maneuvers, his body moving with a rhythm and assurance that spoke of years, perhaps decades, of training.

Mouth suddenly dry, Layna swallowed deeply and tore her eyes away from the prince. She stepped back from the railing, the image of Zarian's fluid movements etched in her mind. The night air felt uncomfortably heavy on her skin.

Returning to her chambers, she prepared for bed, her mind a tangle of confusion and questions. She tossed and turned as sleep eluded her. Zarian's impressive display, his strange tattoo, and the sculpted strength of his body consumed her thoughts.

The next morning, Layna quickly dressed and headed to breakfast. She greeted her parents and Burhani before sitting beside her sister, swiping a pastry from Soraya's plate. Her younger sister rolled her eyes.

A few minutes later, Lord Ebrahim and Prince Zarian entered, deep in conversation. The two men fell silent as they walked in, but Layna could have sworn she heard Lord Ebrahim mention something about the Medjai.

"Welcome, Prince Zarian," King Khahleel said, standing to greet him. "We are honored and look forward to your stay here." Turning to the table, he explained, "Prince Zarian will be providing counsel on palace security and other defense matters."

"Thank you, King Khahleel," replied Zarian, nodding his head. "The honor is mine."

Lord Ebrahim made introductions as they were seated. "This is my daughter Burhani, and these two ladies are Princesses Layna and Soraya," he said, gesturing around the table.

"It's a pleasure to meet you, Burhani and Princess Soraya," Zarian greeted. Turning to Layna with a smirk, he added, "Princess Layna, I believe we've already met." Layna smiled tightly and busied herself with her plate.

Soraya looked inquisitively at her, but Layna gave her a meaningful look. *Later*, she conveyed silently with raised eyebrows. She nabbed another pastry from Soraya's plate, prompting a deep sigh from her sister.

"You certainly have an impressive appetite," Zarian said to Layna with a teasing smile, nodding at the pile of pastries on her plate. "Do you always start your mornings by raiding your sister's breakfast?"

Soraya snorted, quickly covering her mouth with her hand, but Layna caught the sound and glared at her.

Turning back to Zarian, Layna shot him a withering look. "It's only fair. She always takes the best ones."

Burhani leaned closer to Zarian and loudly whispered, "Don't listen to her. Princess Layna is just used to getting what she wants." Layna noticed Burhani's eyes lingering appreciatively on Zarian's biceps, the fabric of his navy tunic straining across them.

The princess bristled. "I think Burhani is just jealous of my impeccable taste in pastries."

Burhani opened her mouth to respond, but Soraya quickly interjected. "Prince Zarian, how long are you staying in Alzahra?"

"For as long as I'm needed," he said with a cryptic smile and a wink.

Layna furrowed her brow, ready to press further, but then Queen Hadiyah engaged Zarian in conversation, and the meal continued without further comment.

After breakfast, Layna sought out Zarian in the hallway. "Prince Zarian," she called, quickly catching up as he turned around. "I, um, I wanted to apologize for my behavior last night. I was caught off guard," she stammered, playing with the sleeves of her abaya.

The prince gave her a charming smile, his hazel eyes crinkling at the corners. They were the color of the desert at dusk, reflecting both warm golden sands and deep shadowed dunes.

"It's alright, Princess," he responded, still smiling. "I look forward to getting to know you better." He glanced around the hallway before leaning casually against the wall. "I'm still getting situated in the palace. Perhaps you could show me around?"

"Oh, unfortunately my schedule is quite busy this week. Royal responsibilities and all," Layna said, wringing her hands. "Perhaps Soraya would have time."

"Of course," Zarian agreed, the corners of his mouth twitching. The intensity of his gaze unsettled her, assessing and appraising, as if he was trying to read her thoughts.

She took a steadying breath and straightened her spine, forcing her hands to her sides. "Enjoy your stay," Layna said primly and glided away, head held high.

Zarian lingered, watching her retreat.

CHAPTER FOUR

In the heart of the palace, nestled within stone walls that whispered of secrets, lay a spacious chamber illuminated by the soft glow of oil lamps. Tall, arched windows draped with navy blue curtains allowed slivers of moonlight to dance across the richly woven rugs cushioning the cold stone floor.

Two intricately carved beds stood on opposite ends of the room, their posts reaching toward the high ceiling, each draped with silken canopies that fluttered gently with the night's breeze. Between these beds sat a grand wooden chest filled with treasures and toys, its surface scarred with marks of play and secret pacts.

Curled up on one of the beds lay a slumbering puppy, its fur a shiny coat of shadow. The animal slept soundly, undisturbed by dreams of chases and conquests.

Two figures huddled over a wooden board topped with worn pieces, their laughter echoing softly in the room. The elder, a handsome boy with a crown of dark waves, moved his piece confidently, a sparkle of triumph in his eyes. The younger, his features a mirror of his brother's, was graceful in his defeat, his strategy crumbling under his brother's practiced skill.

Their game was interrupted by a sharp knock, a sound that resonated with authority. The door swung open to reveal their father. His gaze, proud and searching, settled on the elder boy, who sat up straighter under the weight of his father's attention.

"How have your studies progressed, my son?" the father inquired gently.

"I've mastered the latest strategies in warfare from General Harith. And my understanding of our kingdom's history has deepened, especially our alliances and motivations." He looked up at his father, hoping for his approval.

The father nodded, a rare smile tugging at his mouth. "And what of the art of leadership? Have you given thought to how you will wield the power that will one day be yours?"

The elder boy paused, considering his words carefully. "Leadership is not just about strength and command, but about wisdom and understanding. It's about honoring our order." His youthful voice carried a conviction beyond his years.

The father's expression softened. "You have learned well. It is this blend of strength and wisdom that makes a true king."

The younger boy, silent until now, watched with wistfulness. The elder son turned to him with an encouraging smile. "And what about you, brother? Have you not also excelled in your own studies and training?"

The father's attention shifted, albeit briefly, acknowledging the younger son's presence with a fleeting glance, but it was enough to stir a feeling of importance in the younger boy.

"Yes, Father! I've been practicing my swordsmanship and studying the ancient texts on governance," the younger son added.

The father gave a curt nod. "Good. It's important for both of you to be prepared for the future."

As their father exited, the boys breathed freely, the weight of the future momentarily lifted. The elder boy turned to his brother, placing a reassuring hand on his shoulder. "You did well," he praised, an encouraging smile warming his face. "Remember, we both have our paths to follow, but we'll always be brothers."

In the grand hall of Alzahra's royal palace, beams of sunlight pierced the lofty windows, bathing the room with golden warmth. The scent of polished wood and lingering incense infused the air. Soft murmurs of a diverse crowd—farmers, artisans, and merchants—filled the large room.

Though most of the attendees were men, there were a fair number of women present as well. A few women wore the traditional *niqab*, a veil that concealed everything but their eyes, while others chose to cover only their hair, and some chose to not wear any covering at all.

Zarian, standing discreetly to the side, observed the gathering. It had been over a week since his arrival in Alzahra, and each day had revealed a new facet of Princess Layna's personality. After her stilted apology, she had still remained cautious and distant. Throughout the week, she seemed busy with her royal duties, though Zarian had a sneaking suspicion she was avoiding him.

Nevertheless, it was clear at least *some* of her duties were genuine—today's assembly was a testament to her dedication to her people. She personally hosted these monthly meetings, giving the citizens of Alzahra a platform to voice their concerns and ideas directly to their future queen.

His gaze was drawn to Princess Layna as she entered the hall. Dressed in a simple olive-green abaya, she moved with a commanding grace. Her long, dark hair fell loosely around her shoulders, and a simple banded crown sat on her head. Despite himself, Zarian noticed her brown eyes were lined with kohl today, appearing even larger than usual.

As Layna moved through the crowd, greeting her people with a genuine smile and kind words, Zarian admired her ease in interacting with them. Unlike other royals, she seemed humble and sincerely concerned about the well-being of her people.

She seemed like a good person.

A shard of guilt scraped at his conscience, but Zarian quickly silenced it.

"Good morning, citizens of Alzahra," Layna greeted. "It's heartening to see so many of you here today. Together, we can ensure Alzahra continues to thrive, even in these challenging times."

The chatter gradually hushed as Layna spoke. All eyes focused on her, and it was evident she was deeply respected by her people.

On the raised dais, the large throne dwarfed Layna as she sat down. The assembly began, and a farmer in a sun-bleached tunic and weathered hat was the first to step forward, the lines on his face deepened with worry. "Your Majesty, I'm not exactly sure why, but the mirsham fruit crops are dwindling. We fear this will affect our livelihood."

The mirsham fruit, resembling a small sun with its bright yellow skin, was a marvel of the Alzahran desert. It grew on the resilient

Dhara tree, which had adapted to the harsh climate, drawing sustenance from underground water reserves.

The fruit also held medicinal properties, used by locals in revitalizing drinks and healing concoctions. During the sweltering summer months, mirsham juice, served with a dash of spices, was a traditional and popular refreshment.

Layna addressed the farmer by his name. "Khaleeb, I understand your concerns. The mirsham fruit is vital to Alzahra's trade." She paused to gather her thoughts. "Let us explore sustainable farming practices and see how Princess Soraya and the royal agronomists can assist. Alzahra's prosperity is tied to your success."

The farmer bowed deeply. "Thank you, Princess. Your support means everything."

Next, a tall, lean merchant stepped forward. He bowed respectfully. "Your Majesty, recently I've spotted several unfamiliar figures near the city outskirts. Their cloaks are too heavy for our climate, and they conceal their faces. Their behavior is suspicious. They could be Zephyrians."

Layna's eyes narrowed slightly. "I appreciate your vigilance. We will look into this immediately. Alzahra's security is our highest priority."

She caught the eye of a palace guard at the back of the hall. He stepped forward, quickly jotting down details with a grave expression.

Layna thanked the merchant with a grateful smile. "We rely on the eyes and ears of our people. You have done a great service to Alzahra today." The merchant straightened, his chest puffing with pride, and returned to his seat.

The meeting continued with Layna addressing a variety of issues, from market regulations to festival preparations. Each concern was met with empathy, intelligence, and a deep understanding of her people's needs.

However, the atmosphere shifted when a foreigner approached. He stood out among the local Alzahrans with his attire—a long, dark coat over a fitted vest and slim trousers, distinctly Minhypan in style.

He was tall and imposing, with a stern countenance that seemed out of place in the congenial gathering. His black hair was neatly slicked back into a tight bun, revealing sharp, angular features. Shrewd gray eyes surveyed the room with an air of superiority.

Though his voice was thick with the Minhypan accent, a distinct edge of displeasure was apparent. "I am visiting Az-Zahra on business. I heard this kingdom to be *bohat khoob*, magnificent. *Liken*, it did not live up to its reputation," he said, waving a dismissive hand. A murmur rippled through the hall, attendees exchanging glances, their expressions ranging from surprise to displeasure at his blunt assessment.

Layna bristled at his insult but maintained her composure. "I am here to listen and address any concerns you might have," she stated firmly. Zarian caught a fleeting glimmer of anger in her eyes, but it vanished quickly.

"To start, the market district is completely *jaahil*. The stalls are poorly arranged, causing unnecessary congestion. Where is the orderly structure? We pride ourselves on this in Minhypas," the man boasted.

Zarian scowled. The foreigner's attitude grated on his nerves. His fingers flexed for his sword, but he clenched his fists tightly instead.

Layna listened attentively, her features schooled with practiced neutrality. "I appreciate your feedback. We value the organic growth of our markets, but I'll certainly consider your suggestions for improvement."

Undeterred, the foreigner continued, "*Aur*, the public water fountains are not well maintained. In Minhypas, public amenities are a symbol of the city's health. Here, they are *nazar andaaz*, or *kaise*—uh, neglected."

"I'll ensure our maintenance teams give them the attention they deserve," Layna replied.

The Minhypan man grew increasingly agitated. "Upon my arrival, I was subjected to an excessive inspection at the city entrance. *Bakwaas*! Such treatment for visitors—*bohat* unusual *hai aur* insulting *bhi hai*."

"Given the current political climate, we've implemented heightened security measures at all entry points. It's a necessary step to ensure the safety of Alzahra City and its visitors," Layna explained calmly.

The man's expression soured further. "I can understand the need for security, *liken itni* scrutiny seems too much. *Aur ab*, I find it hard to believe that an *aurat*, a woman," he sneered, "will be able to address my concerns."

At this last insult, Zarian, who had been simmering quietly, finally let his anger boil over. His jaw tightened, a familiar sense of duty stirring within him. Before Layna could respond, Zarian stepped forward angrily. "Such disrespect will not be tolerated," he rebuked, eyes blazing with icy rage.

The Minhypan man's eyes widened, and he stepped back hesitantly. Before he could protest, Zarian gestured to the palace guards and had the man escorted out of the hall.

Layna watched the scene unfold, lips pressed into a thin line and fingers drumming impatiently on her tightly crossed arms, though she remained silent.

The assembly continued, but the earlier warmth had evaporated. Attendees exchanged uneasy glances and shifted in their seats. Layna handled the remaining queries with grace, but the incident had clearly affected the mood in the hall.

Once the session concluded, Layna quickly sought out Zarian, her jaw clenched and fists tightening with each step. "Prince Zarian," she snapped, fire burning in her eyes, "your actions were unacceptable. You undermined my authority and made me appear weak in front of my people."

Zarian was taken aback. Despite being a full head shorter than him, Layna was somehow still intimidating with her blazing eyes and accusatory finger pointed at his chest. "Princess, I didn't mean to offend you. I only intended to protect your honor," he explained.

"That's not your decision to make, nor is it your honor to protect! I'm perfectly capable of handling such situations myself. I don't need your protection."

Zarian was silent for several heartbeats as he carefully assessed the princess. He finally spoke, "I apologize. I overstepped. I'm not accustomed to princesses being such formidable figures. It won't happen again."

Layna observed him closely. Her eyes softened slightly at his apology, though he could still see her lingering frustration in her stiff posture. "Ensure that it doesn't. As future queen, it's crucial that I'm seen as a strong leader, not a defenseless damsel."

Zarian nodded. "Understood, Princess."

After her confrontation with Zarian, Layna retired to her chambers, seeking a moment of peace. Standing on her balcony, she gazed restlessly into the distance, her mind abuzz like the fluttering raithbees that frequented the palace gardens.

Her mind replayed the morning's events, particularly the encounter with the Minhypan man. His condescension had ignited a scorching anger within her. She huffed, fingers absently tracing the grooves in the stone on the balcony railing.

Equally confounding was Zarian's intervention. Her fury at him had been so intense, it felt like her blood was crackling in her veins. Now that the fire of her anger had dimmed, a small part of her felt flattered by his chivalry. It was a delicate balance, being a strong, independent leader while navigating the patriarchal undercurrents of royal diplomacy. Zarian's actions, though outwardly protective, had highlighted this struggle.

She sighed, her frustration mingling with her conflicting feelings about the prince. There was an enigmatic quality about him that Layna couldn't decipher. It both drew her to him, yet also put her on edge.

Around him, she often found herself angry, embarrassed, nervous, or a disorienting combination of all three. She felt like the vulnerable girl she once was, stuttering and uncertain, instead of the strong queen she needed to be.

Layna gazed past the palace gardens to the streets of Alzahra City. She needed to clear her head. A ride through the city seemed like the perfect escape.

The princess changed into her riding gear and headed to the palace stables. The gentle nickering of horses and the soft rustle of straw underfoot helped ground her runaway thoughts. With practiced motions, she brushed Qamar's mane and secured the saddle.

The soft patter of footsteps invaded her sanctuary. Turning, her heart sank as she saw Zarian approaching, determination clear on his handsome face.

"Princess Layna," he greeted, stopping in front of her. "I've been looking for you. I wanted to apologize again for earlier."

Layna studied him for a moment before deciding he seemed genuinely remorseful. "Your apology is noted, Prince Zarian," she replied coolly. "I would love to discuss further, but I'm about to take a ride through the city."

Zarian's eyes lit up. "May I join you? It's been days since I've ridden Najoom. He'll be eager to stretch his legs."

Layna faltered for a moment. Memories of Nizam, sharp and unbidden, flooded her mind, stirring a sense of déjà vu so intense she nearly refused outright.

Yet, something in Zarian's earnest gaze swayed her.

"Very well," she said, still wary. "Would you prefer for guards to accompany us?"

"I think the two of us will manage just fine," he quipped with a lazy grin. Layna turned quickly and finished saddling her horse.

Unlike her white mare, Zarian's mount, Najoom, was an enormous stallion, with a lustrous ebony coat that absorbed the sunlight, giving him an almost otherworldly appearance. The stallion angrily pawed at the ground, his eyes flashing. The stablehands were reluctant to approach him, yet Zarian saddled him with ease, his movements calm and assured.

Mounted on their steeds, they set off, leaving the palace behind. As they ventured deeper into the city, merchants called out, advertising their wares from stalls brimming with spices and trinkets. Children darted through alleyways, laughter ringing out as they played. The scent of freshly baked bread and sizzling street food wafted through the air.

As they trotted along the cobbled streets, Layna remained mostly silent. She occasionally gestured toward an ancient building or monument, providing brief explanations. The historical sites, usually a source of pride, were mentioned almost mechanically, her mind replaying memories she wished to forget.

Zarian watched her quietly, refraining from his usual teasing remarks.

They neared the busy heart of the markets and decided to continue exploring on foot. As they navigated the crowded lanes, a stray dog approached, its mottled brown fur scruffy and unkempt. Ribs visible beneath its thin coat, the dog tentatively wagged its tail.

Zarian paused, bending down to extend a hand. With a gentleness that seemed at odds with his warrior's stature, he stroked the dog's fur, whispering words of comfort. The dog leaned into his touch, its initial apprehension melting away under Zarian's soothing voice.

After a moment, Zarian stood and walked to a nearby vendor, exchanging a few coins for a piece of meat. He returned to the dog, his approach slow and deliberate. Crouching beside the stray, he offered the meat with an outstretched hand. The dog, after a hesitant sniff, quickly devoured the food.

Layna watched him, an unexpected warmth spreading through her chest. The simple act of kindness tugged at her heartstrings. For a brief moment, she saw a glimpse of the gentle man beneath his royal title.

Reluctantly, Zarian stood and watched the stray scamper away. He returned to stand next to Layna, but his usual charming smile seemed a bit forced.

As they walked back to the horses, Layna's foot snagged on a raised cobblestone. She stumbled, bracing herself for the harsh impact of the ground.

But the fall never came.

Swiftly, Zarian caught her by the waist and helped her right herself. They were barely a breath apart, her body tense from the sudden jolt, and her heart pounding not just from the near fall. With wide eyes, Layna looked up at him, her breath catching at his proximity, her palms pressed firmly against his muscled chest.

She quickly composed herself, stepping back as a deep flush spread across her cheeks. "Thank you," Layna mumbled, avoiding his gaze.

The proud princess briskly walked ahead, hoping to reach Qamar as quickly as possible.

They mounted their horses and set off again. As the sun began its descent, Layna led them past the markets toward the outskirts of the city. They followed a tranquil, winding path, surrounded by the quieter, rustic beauty of the capital.

The path took them through narrow lanes bordered by old stone walls, where the city's noise faded into a serene hush. The peacefulness was a welcome respite. They dismounted, allowing their horses to graze, as they watched the sun set on the dunes.

"It's beautiful, isn't it?" Layna remarked softly, her gaze fixed on the sprawling desert. "Alzahra has many faces beyond the majesty of the palace."

Zarian nodded, his eyes catching the fading glimmers of light as he gazed at her. "It certainly is. And I find each new facet intriguing." He turned to watch the sunset, jaw tightly clenched, an unreadable emotion passing through his eyes.

As the sun dipped below the horizon, they rode back to the palace in comfortable silence.

Back at the stables, Zarian swung down from Najoom and extended his hand to assist Layna. Ignoring his outstretched hand, Layna gracefully dismounted on her own. Facing him, she quipped, "Formidable princess, remember?"

Zarian raised an eyebrow, his lips curling in an easy smile. "Formidable, indeed. Next time, I think I'll let you test the ground's embrace," he teased with a quick wink. Laughing, he led his horse away, leaving Layna sputtering in shock.

CHAPTER FIVE

After their ride through Alzahra City, Layna embarked on a quiet quest for information. She inquired subtly about the prince from the Nahrysba Oasis, but palace servants and courtiers gave vague answers and noncommittal shrugs.

It was as if Zarian had appeared out of thin air.

Unlike typical princes, Zarian did not care for the pomp and ceremony typical of royal life. For instance, at formal dinners, where others basked in the spotlight, he engaged in quiet conversations in the background.

His tattoo, in particular, intrigued Layna. Among warriors and soldiers, such markings were common, symbolizing allegiance or valor, but on a prince, it was a rarity and a bold departure from royal norms. The ink on Zarian's skin seemed to speak of a deeper commitment, perhaps a personal creed or a significant chapter of his life, making it even more unusual in the context of his royal status.

What life experiences had shaped Zarian into the man he was now? A prince with the markings of a warrior who moved with the ease of a commoner, undaunted by the trappings of royalty.

Layna was convinced that her parents and Lord Ebrahim were not entirely forthcoming about Zarian's purpose in Alzahra. She had overheard them mention the word "Medjai" a few times, always in hushed whispers, and always stopping abruptly whenever she drew near.

But most disconcerting of all was Layna's growing attraction to him. There were quiet, unexpected moments when her thoughts would drift to him unbidden. She would recall a charming smile he had given her at breakfast, one that lit up his face with a warmth that radiated directly into her heart. Or she'd remember his laughter echoing in the corridors, a sound that sent her heart fluttering. These small, innocent moments lingered in her mind, stirring unsettling feelings.

Layna reflected on these thoughts early one morning as she walked through the palace gardens. The air was rich with the fragrance of jasmine and roses, mingling with the subtle scent of dew-kissed grass. Sunlight filtered through the canopy of ancient trees, dappling the stone pathways with golden light.

As she wandered along the winding paths, she came across Zarian. He was meditating in a secluded clearing, sitting cross-legged on the soft earth, eyes closed and hands resting on his knees, palms facing upward. The early rays of the sun caressed his face, casting a gentle glow that outlined his sharp cheekbones.

His breath flowed in a measured, calm rhythm. Layna paused at the edge of the clearing, ready to announce herself, when Zarian's confident voice cut through the silence.

"Hello, Princess. I trust the morning finds you well." His eyes remained closed, a peaceful picture of tranquility.

A ripple of surprise crossed Layna's features. She quickly composed herself, smoothing her expression into one of poised neutrality. "Indeed, it has," she responded, her tone measured and even, as if his awareness of her silent approach was an expected courtesy and not a startling revelation.

Zarian opened his eyes and stood slowly, a faint smile playing at the corners of his mouth. He began to stretch, extending his arms and rotating his shoulders, loosening the muscles that had remained static during his meditation. Layna's gaze lingered on his sculpted biceps and forearms, each muscle corded with prominent veins.

The princess drew a deep breath, forcing her gaze away. Her heart quickened against her will. She despised how her body betrayed her with its involuntary attraction, fighting her resolve to keep him at a distance at every encounter.

Gathering herself, Layna measured her next words. "I find myself curious, Prince Zarian. About the Nahrysba Oasis."

"I think we're at a stage where we can drop the formalities, no?" Zarian teased, his eyes sparkling with amusement. He inhaled deeply as he slowly rotated his neck.

"Alright, fine. Zarian, then. Tell me about the Nahrysba Oasis." Layna tilted her head slightly and crossed her arms over her chest.

"It's my home," he said simply. His gaze trailed over her slowly, taking in her loose hair and dusty pink abaya. He gave her a slow, lazy grin. "You look lovely, by the way."

Layna huffed sharply, her heart somersaulting in her chest. He was distracting her, she was certain of it. "Thank you. But surely you can tell me more."

He finished stretching and came to stand before her. "What would you like to know, Princess?" he murmured, his voice low and deep.

"What can you tell me about the Medjai?" she demanded, her brows furrowed. "I've heard you and Lord Ebrahim whispering about them."

Zarian's expression remained carefully neutral. He paused, considering her question. "What exactly do you wish to know about the Medjai?" he asked evenly, his voice almost challenging.

Layna met his gaze squarely as she pressed further. "Who are they?"

Zarian watched her for a long, silent moment, so long that Layna thought he might not answer at all. Then, a decisive look crossed his face before he finally spoke. "The Medjai are an ancient order. They are keepers of peace, tasked with maintaining the balance of our world. Their allegiance is to the realm itself, not to any one ruler or nation. Except the Oasis, I suppose."

His eyes searched her face intently, though Layna couldn't discern what he hoped to find.

Her mind raced back to a childhood memory, a fragment of a conversation she once overheard with Soraya. They had hidden behind a tapestry, listening to their father speak with a mysterious visitor about the Medjai and some sort of prophecy. Her parents had also mentioned something about a prophecy on the day that Zarian first arrived.

"I've heard rumors about the Medjai and their connection to a prophecy," she remarked casually. "Is there any truth to these tales?"

Zarian again studied her, his expression unreadable. "Prophecies are complex, Princess. They can be both a guide and a riddle."

Layna exhaled sharply in frustration at his continued evasion. "Your tattoo. Is it related to the Medjai?"

A flicker of surprise crossed Zarian's features, quickly replaced by a playful smirk. "Princess—when, might I ask, did you have the opportunity to see my tattoo?"

Layna felt a sudden rush of embarrassment. She had seen it that first evening when he was training, his tunic cast aside, revealing the intricate ink on his skin. "It—it was on the training grounds. You were training. Without your shirt," she stammered, her cheeks reddening.

Zarian's smile broadened as he observed her, but he offered no further inquiry, allowing the moment to pass. "Yes, it's related to the Medjai. It symbolizes a commitment to something greater than myself."

Before Layna could interrogate further, Lord Ebrahim approached. "Princess Layna, your presence is requested in the council chamber."

"Of course, Lord Ebrahim," she agreed. Turning to Zarian, she said, "We'll continue this conversation another time." With that, she followed Lord Ebrahim, her mind still mulling over the enigma of the Medjai and the prince who stood apart from the rest.

As she walked alongside Ebrahim, her thoughts lingered on her conversation with Zarian. His connection to the Medjai, his indifference to royal norms, and his enigmatic tattoo painted a picture of a man who was something more than a prince. The more she learned about him, the more she realized how little she knew.

Layna addressed the senior adviser. "Prince Zarian mentioned the Medjai at the Oasis," she remarked. "There's much I wish to understand about them. They seem shrouded in mystery. Could you enlighten me?"

Lord Ebrahim studied her closely, eyes slightly narrowed behind his spectacles. He ran a hand over his short, white beard before finally responding. "The Medjai have been allies to our monarchy for centuries. Their wisdom and role as guardians have been crucial. Most kingdoms work with the Medjai in some shape or form, but we generally try to limit knowledge of their existence."

Layna listened intently, her thoughts racing. "If the Medjai have been such critical allies, why was I not taught about them in my lessons? It seems like important knowledge for a future queen."

Ebrahim glanced at her, his expression a mix of understanding and regret. "Princess, the Medjai are enigmatic, operating in the shadows to protect the continent. They are secretive about their work, history, and methods. It's a delicate balance—knowing of their existence and influence, yet not fully understanding the depth of their involvement. The decision to keep details discreet was to protect their anonymity and efficacy. However, I agree that perhaps we should have provided you with more knowledge and shared some of their ancient texts from the library."

Layna found his last admission odd. She had spent countless hours in the library but never encountered any texts about the Medjai, which now seemed like a glaring omission in her education.

Had it been intentional?

Nonetheless, she absorbed his explanation, puzzle pieces slowly fitting together in her mind. The Medjai's existence as shadowy protectors and Zarian's presence in Alzahra were somehow intertwined.

"Thank you, Lord Ebrahim. Your insights are always enlightening."

Lord Ebrahim chuckled softly. "It is not my insights, Layna. You've always been intelligent." He patted her head affectionately. "Never doubt your instincts. You have a good heart and a sharp mind. You will find your way as you always have."

Layna smiled. "Thank you."

"I received a letter from General Idhaan, by the way," Lord Ebrahim mentioned as they rounded a corner. "He asked about you, as usual. He wanted to know how your sword fighting is progressing."

Idhaan had been her first instructor in her teenage years. He was eventually promoted and stationed far from the palace. Yet he never failed to check up on his favorite pupil.

"I'll have to write to him and let him know I can best Soraya now!" Layna said, prompting a shared laugh between her and Ebrahim.

They arrived at the council chambers and took their seats at the round table. The chamber, with its high vaulted ceilings, large windows, and ornate tapestries, was abuzz with the low murmur of the advisers gathered around the massive table.

Layna's heart sank at the sight of Burhani. As if sensing her presence, Burhani's eyes flicked up, her gaze narrowing as she glanced between Layna and Lord Ebrahim. Burhani pursed her lips, a shadow of irritation crossing her face that she didn't bother to mask.

As Layna settled into her seat, her gaze swept across the council members, each representing a crucial pillar in Alzahra's governance. The council was a diverse assembly of wisdom and strategy, guiding the kingdom through times of peace and conflict alike.

There was Lord Varin, the master of war. A short man with broad shoulders, he had spent decades serving Alzahra's military. As the commander of the kingdom's forces, he was responsible for its defense. Though Alzahra had enjoyed prolonged peace, the growing tension with Zephyria thrust Varin back into the limelight, shifting his focus from theoretical strategies to actively preparing for the looming specter of war.

Lady Mirah, the master of coin, was a woman of sharp intellect and shrewd economic insight. Her expertise in trade, finance, and economic policy had steered Alzahra through seasons of scarcity and abundance alike. She managed the kingdom's treasury, ensuring that its resources were allocated wisely.

Next to her sat Lord Saldeen, the master of internal affairs. His jurisdiction covered the well-being of Alzahra's citizens and the running of day-to-day operations. From maintenance and infrastructure to law enforcement and public health, Lord Saldeen's domain was vast.

And, of course, Lord Ebrahim, the senior adviser with decades of service, was the keystone of the council. His vast knowledge spanned across all aspects of the kingdom's affairs. He oversaw the council's deliberations, ensuring every decision was made with the kingdom's best interests in mind.

King Khahleel, with Queen Hadiyah by his side, presided over the meeting, his expression grave. "The tensions with Zephyria continue to escalate," he announced.

Lord Ebrahim unfurled a map across the table, tracing the boundary line. "Reports indicate that Zephyria has been amassing troops along our eastern border. They have also been turning away more and more caravans from our agreed trade routes. Their intentions are unclear, but we must be prepared for any eventuality."

Lord Varin spoke next. "We must strengthen our defenses and consider a show of force. Zephyria respects strength. Alzahra cannot appear weak."

Queen Hadiyah interjected, "While we must protect our kingdom, we should also explore diplomatic channels. War is costly, not just in resources, but in lives."

The room hummed with a chorus of agreements and dissenting views, a mixture of strategy and caution.

Listening closely, Layna keenly felt the weight of her future responsibilities. She had been trained in the art of warfare since adolescence, but the stark realities were evident in the council's deliberations.

"My lords, my ladies," Layna spoke up, standing to address the council members. "Let's not abandon hope for peace. Perhaps an envoy to Zephyria could provide clarity on their intentions. It may avert unnecessary bloodshed." She paused to gather her thoughts.

"We should also strengthen our resources for healing should conflict arise. I suggest we ask Princess Soraya and her greenhouse attendants to increase the cultivation of medicinal plants. It could be vital in supporting our army's healing needs."

Her suggestion was met with thoughtful nods around the table. However, Lord Varin seemed less receptive, his expression one of thinly veiled displeasure.

King Khahleel looked at his daughter with pride. "Wise counsel, Layna. Lord Ebrahim, arrange for an envoy to meet with Jorah and his heir. But we will also prepare our defenses, as Lord Varin suggests." He turned to address his daughter. "And, Layna, speak to Soraya about the medicinal plants."

As the council meeting moved toward its conclusion, Layna whispered in Lord Ebrahim's ear, "I thought King Jorah had never taken a wife. How, then, does he have an heir?"

"Indeed, your understanding is correct," Lord Ebrahim responded, adjusting his spectacles. "Jorah has never married. However, several years ago, he made a surprising declaration, naming a young man called Azhar as his heir. This was done without any explanation." He paused, letting the information sink in before continuing. "Jorah's heir has been removed from the spotlight, never attending formal events or entertaining royal visits. The general consensus is that Azhar is Jorah's illegitimate son. Though Jorah has never publicly acknowledged Azhar as his blood, he has granted him significant power and authority."

Layna mulled over this information, along with the looming threat of Zephyria, as the council meeting ended. The possibility of war cast a dark cloud over her heart.

"Layna," Lord Ebrahim said, interrupting her musing. "Burhani and I are having lunch today to celebrate her success in Janta. Would you like to join us?"

Layna glanced between them, catching Burhani's faint frown and the simmering intensity in her eyes. "Thank you for the invitation, but I'm afraid I have other matters to attend to," she replied with a polite smile. Burhani exhaled, her tense shoulders relaxing, though she did not bother acknowledging Layna.

Exiting the council chambers, the weight of her destined crown felt heavier than ever.

As Layna left with Lord Ebrahim, Zarian's gaze lingered on her retreating figure. The first time he saw her, she was practicing her swordplay on the training grounds, her aggression and skill evident even from a distance. Her fierceness had intrigued him, so different from the usual demureness he associated with princesses.

Her fiery anger remained vivid in his memory, the flare of indignation in her eyes, upset at feeling scrutinized. Despite her fury, he was drawn to her raw, unfiltered emotions. Against his better judgment, he found himself increasingly provoking her with teasing remarks, hoping to peel back her royal façade and reveal the woman beneath.

Yet, beneath his attraction, Zarian felt a deep respect for her. He recalled how she had presided over the assembly with a remarkable blend of empathy and diplomacy. It was clear she wasn't just fulfilling a ceremonial role; she was genuinely invested in the well-being of her kingdom and its people.

Her hands-on approach was impressive. Unlike other royals who relied heavily on advisers, Layna availed herself to her subjects. She wielded her position with a sense of responsibility and care.

Then there was her reaction when he questioned her about his tattoo. The delicious blush that colored her cheeks when she'd revealed her observation of him was a moment of unintended intimacy. Her almond-shaped eyes had widened, a soft flush spreading across her face as she quickly turned away, flustered. It was a glimpse into her vulnerable side, one she tried desperately to conceal. Despite his better judgment, Zarian wanted to strip away her barriers to truly see *her*.

His thoughts turned to his mission, casting a shadow over his contemplation. It was concerning that she knew about the prophecy, though he'd have to gauge the depth of her knowledge.

Despite his attraction to Layna, Zarian couldn't afford to let his personal feelings interfere. He had never struggled so much to remain detached. Instead, he found himself doing the complete opposite and constantly flirting with her. The pull was irresistible.

His role as a Medjai, in protecting the balance, was a burden he had carried since adolescence. Zarian reflected on his journey that led him to Alzahra.

In the scorching heat of the Nahrysban desert, a young Zarian faced the relentless trials of Medjai training. His instructor, a hardened warrior with eyes like polished steel, was a man of few words, but each carried the weight of centuries of tradition.

"Focus, Zarian! Anticipate, react, survive!" his instructor bellowed as Zarian navigated grueling exercises designed to push him beyond his limits.

The training was not just physical, but mental and psychological as well. Zarian learned to endure extreme temperatures, trekking barefoot across burning sands, honing his body to withstand thirst and fatigue. He practiced combat in blinding sandstorms and learned to use his other senses when sight failed him.

"Your enemy is not always seen, but felt," his instructor said as Zarian learned to fight blindfolded, relying on intuition and the subtle cues of wind and sand.

Equally brutal were lessons in strategy and tactics. He studied ancient texts by moonlight, memorizing the histories of kingdoms and the intricacies of court intrigue. He was taught the art of diplomacy and deception, skills as crucial as swordsmanship for a Medjai.

"Remember, your mind is your greatest weapon. Use the element of surprise. Never let your enemy see you," the instructor often reminded Zarian, stressing the importance of cunning and intelligence.

Zarian also underwent spiritual training, meditating under the sun's morning light, learning to quiet his mind and connect with the deeper currents of the world.

His instructor often spoke of the weight of their duty, "As Medjai, we are the unseen guardians. Our sacrifice is silent, our battles unknown, but our resolve must be unwavering."

As the training intensified, his body, mind, and spirit melded into a singular force, a weapon tempered by will and discipline. He learned to endure pain without flinching, to face fear without faltering.

"You must be prepared to do whatever it takes," his instructor warned, his voice as hard as the desert rock. "Guarding the balance is our ultimate duty."

Those words were etched into his mind, a constant reminder of the path he was destined to follow.

Zarian's mind journeyed back through time, the memories of his rigorous training vivid and unyielding. The years blurred together, a tangle of discipline and commitment and loneliness.

Then a few months ago, everything converged in a pivotal moment.

Zarian listened intently to the Medjai elders as they spoke of the signs that had already come to pass and the one still to come. "The birth of a girl under the moon's blessed light, the rare celestial alignment on the eve of the equinox, and now the impending eclipse," Zanjeel, the head elder recounted, his weathered, stern face grave.

"Each sign has unfolded as prophesized," another elder added. "The Daughter of the Moon is among us. The time has come for us to return to Alzahra."

His father, King Tahriq, turned his attention to Zanjeel. "And what of the earthly moon?"

"It is hidden, safely ensconced far beyond the reach of those who would seek to misuse its power," Zanjeel assured. "By the moon, it will remain undisturbed until the end of days." The head elder continued, "Prince Zarian, you must—"

"Protect the princess," King Tahriq interjected quickly, earning a sharp glance from Zanjeel. "I will send an envoy to inform King Khahleel of your arrival." Tahriq placed a hand on Zarian's shoulder. "Ensure the prophecy is fulfilled, my son. And if her powers threaten the balance...then neutralize her.

"I will not fail, Father," Zarian vowed, bowing his head, his fingers twitching slightly. Out of the corner of his eye, Zarian saw a shadow flicker near the window, *but when he turned his head, it was gone. It was merely an errant play of light, the fire's dancing flames casting shapes into the chamber's corners.*

King Tahriq placed a firm hand on Zarian's shoulder. "Remember, as Medjai, we value the balance above all. Protect the princess and earn the trust of her father. Ensure the prophecy comes to pass. Guard the balance from anything and anyone that may threaten to destroy it."

Zarian glanced at the head elder, who stood tense with his lips set grimly, before turning back to his father and accepting his mission.

Now, under the vast sky, he reflected on his journey. From the intense training of his youth to this moment of destiny, his path had been clear.

But now, as he watched the stars, Zarian felt conflicted about what path *he* wanted to walk.

Sighing, he shook off these thoughts and reminded himself of his duty. He needed to focus on the path laid out for him by fate.

What he wanted was irrelevant.

CHAPTER SIX

In the lush gardens of the palace, the air was fragrant with blooming gardenia. The distant sound of water from the fabled springs melded with the soft laughter and chatter of a royal visit. Such visits, though rare due to the secret nature of their order, occasionally became essential.

This particular visit aimed to forge a trade agreement with a coastal kingdom, securing valuable resources—chief among them, pearls and spices.

The setting sun cast its golden warmth over the gardens, highlighting the anticipation of an impending game. The elder brother stood with a commanding grace, his loyal dog by his side, tail wagging. His younger sibling, though equally handsome, perhaps even more so, stood next to him with hunched shoulders, his eyes darting nervously between their guests and the ground.

As they gathered to explain the rules of the traditional game—a test of teamwork and strategy—the excitement among the princesses from Maridunia was palpable.

"It's all about precise teamwork and learning your partner's skills," the elder brother explained, his voice carrying across the garden and catching the attention of

the two visiting princesses. He gestured toward the playing field, where pairs of hoops were set into the grass at varying distances, with a rack of mallets standing nearby. "Each team's player must hit the ball through a hoop. But to advance, their partner must jump the same distance. Choose your hoops wisely—the first team to reach the far side wins."

"I wish to be on your team," declared the younger princess boldly, her eyes sparkling as she stepped closer to him.

The elder princess elbowed her sister before quickly adding, "As the eldest, I would be better matched with you. It would be an honor to learn from the future king."

An awkward silence descended over the group. The younger brother, feeling the familiar sting of being overshadowed, offered a tight smile, his discomfort thinly veiled.

The elder cast a quick glance his way. "The game's spirit is in its partnership," he interjected smoothly, "and as much as I appreciate your requests, it's only fair that we draw lots to decide the teams."

The princesses exchanged hesitant looks but eventually nodded in polite acquiescence.

The lots were drawn, and fate, with a hint of irony, paired each brother with a princess. The younger brother's partner, though initially disappointed, quickly masked her feelings with a courteous smile.

As they took positions at opposite ends of the field, the game commenced. The elder brother's team moved with ease, their coordination evident in every maneuver. The younger, however, found an unexpected rhythm with his partner, their initial awkwardness giving way to a surprising synergy.

The game progressed with laughter, playful taunts, and the thrill of competition. The match ended with the younger brother's team claiming a narrow victory. All *four players bore easy smiles, recounting the game's highlights with shared pride and admiration.*

As the sun dipped below the horizon, casting long shadows across the garden, the younger brother felt proud of his achievement, however small. The game provided a rare moment of recognition, a fleeting sense of importance.

Yet, as the evening drew to a close, the princesses again lavished praise upon the elder for his skill and leadership. The younger brother's earlier triumph dimmed, and the familiar sense of being overlooked settled back upon him like a well-worn cloak.

After the princesses departed to their guest chambers, the brothers were left alone in the garden.

"You played well," the elder brother offered, hands stuffed in his pockets, attempting to bridge the gap widened by circumstance and birthright.

The younger brother met his gaze, a complex mix of gratitude and resentment swirling in his eyes. "So did you," he finally replied, as the barrier built from years of living in the shadow of a destiny not his own grew ever taller.

Princesses Layna and Soraya strolled leisurely through the palace gardens. The air was perfumed with fragrant roses, and a gentle breeze whispered through the leaves.

"I've started organizing the greenhouse for increased production of medicinal plants," Soraya shared, her eyes bright. "We're focusing on plants like *zakhmin* for wound healing, *bukhra* for fevers, and *motchuplant* for sprains. It's a small step, but it'll help our soldiers if it comes to war."

"That's excellent," Layna encouraged, looping her arm through her sister's. "Your knowledge of plants could be vital. I'm so glad you're taking charge of this."

"It feels good to contribute," Soraya admitted. "To use my passion for something so crucial. And the greenhouse attendants are incredibly dedicated. They've been working tirelessly to prepare." Soraya poked Layna in the side, a playful smile on her lips. "So how is avoiding the mysterious Medjai prince going?"

"I'm not avoiding him." Layna frowned, brushing a stray leaf from her shoulder.

"You weren't at breakfast again this morning," Soraya pointed out as they paused to admire a row of rosebushes. "I had to eat all my pastries by myself."

"I had some things to take care of," Layna replied. She pursed her lips as they continued walking.

"It's for the best anyway," Soraya sighed. "Burhani kept finding excuses to touch him. A hand on his shoulder here, a brush on his forearm there. It was quite nauseating, actually."

Layna's jaw tightened. She pulled her arm free from Soraya's and toyed with the hem of her tunic.

As the sisters rounded a bend, they came upon King Khahleel and Prince Zarian deep in conversation. The king, spotting his daughters, beamed with fatherly pride.

"Ah, my daughters," he exclaimed, gesturing toward Layna and Soraya. "Zarian, I was just telling you about them. The shining jewels of Alzahra. Layna is as sharp with her mind as she is with her sword. And Soraya, my talented free spirit, has a heart as vast as the oceans."

"Baba, *please*," Soraya groaned dramatically, rolling her eyes as her father chuckled.

"It's an honor to know them, Your Majesty," Zarian said with a small smile.

An adviser approached quickly and whispered urgently into the king's ear. With a nod to his daughters and Zarian, King Khahleel excused himself, leaving them in the quiet of the gardens.

Soraya seized the opportunity. "Prince Zarian! I've heard much about you from Layna, but please enlighten me—how do you manage the responsibilities of both a prince and a Medjai?"

Zarian cast a knowing smile at Layna, a hint of satisfaction lighting his hazel eyes. Layna felt her cheeks warm and glanced away, worrying her lip between her teeth.

The prince chuckled lightly. "It's a life of balance. One must navigate the duties of royalty while upholding the role of the Medjai." He leaned casually against the tall hedge. "But keep this Medjai business between us, hmm? It's a bit of a secret," he whispered conspiratorially.

"You have my word," Soraya exaggeratedly whispered back. Then in a normal tone, she added, "Do you ever find time for leisurely pursuits in all that balancing?"

"Occasionally," Zarian admitted, a hint of amusement in his voice.

"Then you must join us for a game," Soraya declared, clapping her hands in excitement. "It's a tradition of ours. Right, Layna?"

Layna shifted uneasily, her posture tensing. "Zarian has important duties he must attend to and—"

"I'm at your service, Princess Soraya," Zarian interrupted. "What game did you have in mind?"

"A game of Alzahran croquet," Soraya announced. "It's much-loved here in the palace. And it's Layna's favorite."

"We have a similar game in the Oasis," Zarian replied, crossing his arms over his chest as his mouth curled into an easy grin. "What do you say, Layna? Will you indulge me?"

"Er, alright," Layna agreed. "Let's play. It'll be refreshing."

The trio moved to a lush clearing where a croquet set lay ready. Each player had to hit wooden balls with a mallet through hoops embedded in the course, requiring both skill and careful judgment.

Layna rolled her eyes as Zarian selected his mallet with exaggerated care. He caught her expression and flashed her a charming smile. She pursed her lips and resisted the urge to smile back.

"Let the game commence, and may fortune favor the skilled," Zarian declared, eyes twinkling with playful challenge.

"I await with bated breath to see your talents," Layna retorted sarcastically, rolling her eyes again.

Zarian smirked. "Careful, Princess," he quipped, leaning in slightly, "your eyes might get stuck like that. But I suppose they'd look lovely regardless."

"I—it's your turn!" Layna hastily said.

Zarian laughed lightly. He positioned himself on the course, aimed with precision, and struck the ball which smoothly sailed through the hoop.

"Quite the impressive start," Layna remarked, her competitive spirit igniting.

"It's a matter of foresight and accuracy," Zarian responded, stepping aside for Layna's turn.

Layna focused on her target, her form precise and controlled. With a clean hit, the ball arced through the hoop, mirroring Zarian's expertise.

"Did you accurately foresee that?" she jested.

Zarian chuckled approvingly. "You are indeed a formidable opponent, Princess."

Soraya was next, her technique less polished but brimming with zest. As she swung, her shot veered off slightly, yet her laughter and bright smile infused the game with a joyful, carefree energy.

The match continued, a blend of strategic precision from Layna and Zarian, along with Soraya's more spontaneous plays.

As they approached the final hoop, the scores were close, with Zarian slightly ahead. Yet, in a surprising twist, the prince's final shot veered off course and missed the hoop entirely.

Layna smirked as she prepared for her final shot. "Seems even Medjai can falter at crucial moments," she teased, glancing playfully at Zarian.

Zarian huffed a laugh, a hint of mock frustration in his smile. "It appears so, Princess. Let's see if you can seize this opportunity."

Focusing, Layna took a moment to assess the angle, keen to take advantage of the unexpected turn in her favor. Her stroke was precise, and the ball rolled through the hoop, securing her victory.

Zarian nodded in approval, a satisfied smile tugging at his lips. "Nicely done, Princess. Your victory is well-deserved."

Layna beamed, a slight blush on her cheeks. Her heart was racing and not just from her win.

"Well done, Layna!" Soraya congratulated. "Aren't you glad you decided to play?"

As they bent to gather the croquet equipment, Zarian's hand brushed against Layna's while reaching for the same mallet. The brief contact sent a whisper of electricity through the princess. Their eyes met, lingering for several heartbeats.

Layna straightened first, offering Zarian a tentative smile. "Thank you. I think you skipped a security briefing to indulge us, so I appreciate your time."

"The pleasure was all mine, Princess." He took the mallet from her hands. "Though I insist on a rematch in the near future."

Layna laughed and readily agreed. With the game concluded, the princesses and Zarian went their separate ways.

As the sisters returned to the palace, the charged tension in the gardens gave way to the tranquility of Layna's chambers. Reclining on the canopied bed, surrounded by plush pillows, the sisters basked in the golden light of the setting sun filtering in through the open balcony doors.

"So," Soraya began, a teasing lilt in her voice, "You and Prince Zarian seemed quite *in tune* during the match."

Layna let out a soft sigh, her gaze drifting toward the window. "Soraya, it was just a game."

"Was it?" Soraya raised an eyebrow, a playful smirk on her lips. "The way you two looked at each other, it was as if the whole world faded away. And that final shot of his…I'm certain he let you win."

Layna shook her head. "Zarian is a skilled player. I doubt he would just *let* me win."

"What about his comment about your lovely eyes?"

"He's just a shameless flirt, that's all," Layna insisted, crossing her arms.

"Please, dear sister. It's clear he has a soft spot for you. He doesn't give Burhani or anyone else a second glance. There's definitely something there."

Layna sighed deeply, worrying her lower lip. "Even if there is—I'm just not ready to trust again. Not after Nizam."

"I understand," Soraya murmured, her tone softening. "But Layna, not everyone is like Nizam. Just don't close off your heart completely." Before Layna could respond, Soraya glanced at the clock and stood abruptly. "I should go."

Layna looked up in surprise, narrowing her eyes slightly. "Where are you off to in such a hurry?"

Soraya paused at the door and glanced back at her sister. "Just a little errand. I remembered something about the new plants. Nothing to worry about."

Layna watched as Soraya slipped out of the room, her steps light and purposeful. She wondered about Soraya's true destination but knew better than to pry. Her sister would tell her when she was ready.

Left alone, her thoughts drifted back to Zarian and his deep, intoxicating voice and his easy smile. Despite her reservations, she couldn't deny their chemistry.

And from what she'd observed so far, Zarian was undeniably kind and intelligent, though occasionally a touch arrogant. She hated that she found even his arrogance attractive. Perhaps Soraya was right, but was she ready to take that leap of faith again?

In the fading light of day, Zarian retreated to a secluded part of the palace gardens. He navigated the familiar path with ease, his mind replaying the events of the croquet match.

As he reached a particularly shadowed alcove, a cloaked figure emerged from the darkness. Zarian relaxed slightly and gave a subtle nod of acknowledgment.

"Jamil," Zarian greeted, his voice low. The figure pulled back his hood, revealing a tanned, boyishly handsome face framed by a mop of dark hair falling into his green eyes. A thin white scar ran down the left side of his face, from cheekbone to jaw.

"You look like you just lost a game of 'Desert Shadows,'" Jamil teased, a game from their youth where they would sneak and hide in the desert, training their stealth.

Zarian chuckled. "Some things never change. You always had a knack for finding the best hiding spots."

"And you were always too focused on the mission, even back then. Speaking of which, how goes your current endeavor? You seem...distracted. It's unlike you."

Zarian sighed. "It's more complex than I anticipated. The princess...she's extraordinary. Determined, intelligent, stubborn." He sighed again. "Beautiful."

Jamil's expression softened. "And what of the prophecy? Does she suspect her role?"

"She's asked me about the prophecy, but I don't think she realizes its full extent," Zarian admitted.

Jamil nodded, his expression turning serious. "Be cautious, brother. Our reports indicate rising tensions in the region. Zephyria is mobilizing, and we cannot afford any distractions." He continued, his angular face grave. "There was an incident in the Grand Libraries of Thessan. Two senior librarians were found murdered weeks ago, their throats slit. Several Medjai texts are missing."

"Why didn't we hear of this earlier?" Zarian questioned, instantly alert.

Jamil shrugged. "Our man in Thessan is missing. Likely dead," he speculated. "When he didn't attend his briefing, the king sent Rohaan to search for him. That's when we learned about the librarians."

Zarian's face clouded with concern as the gravity of the situation dawned on him. "Someone is searching for the orb."

"And they may have already found it." Jamil's face was heavy with implication. "We dispatched groups of Medjai to search for the orb and the attacker, but whoever it was, he hid his tracks well. And some of our men didn't return. We must prepare for the worst," he added solemnly. "You must keep a vigilant eye on the princess."

Zarian's gaze hardened, the Medjai in him responding to the urgency in Jamil's words. "I will. Are you returning to the Oasis?"

Jamil shook his head. "No. Your father instructed me to remain here should you need my help. Saahil is with me. He'll relay any updates."

Zarian nodded in understanding.

"Remember, Zarian," Jamil cautioned, his voice surprisingly gentle, "our duty is to the balance. Personal feelings…they have no place in this. You know what you might have to do. I'm sorry." He placed a comforting hand on Zarian's shoulder.

Zarian did not respond. As Jamil disappeared into the night, he remained alone, his thoughts a swirling mix of duty, destiny, and an unwanted emotion he tried to suppress.

CHAPTER SEVEN

Layna stood alone in the vast expanse of the Alzahran desert. Above her, the night sky was a mural of glimmering stars, the moon hanging low and full, casting a silver glow over the sandy dunes.

As she gazed upward, the moon began to change, slowly engulfed by a creeping shadow. The desert around her came alive, the sands stirring and forming patterns that danced with a life of their own.

The shadow concealed the moon, and the sky turned a deep, blood-red. Layna spun around frantically, fear constricting her lungs, as the desert sands rose up around her. She searched for an escape, for help, but found nothing.

She was utterly, helplessly alone.

The rising sand formed the shapes of ancient warriors and terrifying, legendary beasts. They encircled her, red monstrous eyes glowing ominously.

Layna bolted upright in bed, her heart pounding so hard she feared it might burst from her chest. Outside her window, the moon hung heavy, a silent sentinel in the night sky. Cold sweat dripped down her back, her thin nightgown clinging to her like a second suffocating skin.

With concerted effort, she drew deep steadying breaths, attempting to rise above the terror.

Breaths finally slowing, she reclined back, the moonlight bathing her in its light. She had experienced this nightmare since childhood, but recently, it had become a frequent nocturnal visitor, each time leaving her trembling with fear. Each awakening felt like emerging from a harrowing ordeal that blurred the lines between dream and reality.

Eventually, her heartbeat settled, and she drifted to sleep once more.

As the days slipped into weeks following the croquet match, vivid nightmares continued to haunt Layna in the stillness of the night, and the ghostly echoes resonated during her waking hours. They followed her like a persistent shadow, a lingering dread she couldn't escape.

Amidst the daily demands of royal life, it was Zarian's presence that offered brief moments of distraction from her fears. Layna noticed their paths crossed more often, but she couldn't tell if *she* was the one unconsciously seeking him out or if *he* was deliberately looking for her.

She remembered a particular instance in the corridors when she hastily rounded a corner and had collided squarely with Zarian's muscled chest. He had caught her by the waist, steadying her with a gentle firmness that sent a shiver down her spine. His hands had lingered a heartbeat longer than necessary, a featherlight caress, but Layna was surprised to find that she didn't quite mind. His apologetic smile had been infuriatingly charming, leaving her both annoyed and secretly thrilled.

Another time, she covertly observed him from a balcony. A young servant had stumbled, scattering a stack of linens across the floor. Zarian knelt beside the flustered boy, helping to quickly gather the linens, his attitude devoid of the condescending and haughty attitude often exhibited by nobles.

To make matters worse, the prince's presence in Layna's life became increasingly pronounced after her father requested Zarian's attendance at council meetings. These sessions, once a refuge where Layna could immerse herself in the kingdom's affairs, now became another place she couldn't escape him. Zarian's astute observations only intensified the tangled web of emotions Layna felt toward him. Each meeting, she found herself inadvertently seeking his opinion, his deep voice resonating with a quiet authority that both excited and frustrated her.

On one occasion, she arrived early to the meeting but stopped in her tracks at the sound of Burhani's uncharacteristically sweet voice. Through the doorway, she saw the perpetual source of her torment batting her eyes at Zarian, inquiring about the Oasis with a coy smile. From what Layna could tell, Zarian kept his responses formal and polite, yet an irrational jealousy still twisted her insides, burning through her veins with startling intensity.

And then there was Zarian's growing rapport with Soraya. After breakfast one morning, her sister had insisted on a spontaneous horseback ride through the desert, and to Layna's surprise, he had readily agreed. Watching them return, laughing and sharing stories, Layna couldn't help but appreciate his willingness to indulge her sister.

Layna was immersed in these thoughts during an early morning training session on the quiet grounds when the sun was just peeking over the horizon. Clutching a heavy weight to her chest, she performed deep squats, feeling the familiar burn in her thighs before rising smoothly with each repetition. As she finished her set, she went to put the weight down, but her grip faltered unexpectedly. She lost her hold, and the weight plummeted toward her foot.

With a sharp yelp of surprise, Layna jerked back just in time, narrowly avoiding several broken toes. Her hasty movement threw off her balance, and she careened backward, landing awkwardly on the dusty ground with a loud thud. "Fuck!" she exclaimed, gasping as she sat there catching her breath.

"That's quite the mouth on you, Princess," a deep voice drawled from behind her.

Layna whipped her head around, eyes locking on Zarian who leaned nonchalantly against the gates of the training grounds, arms crossed casually over his broad chest.

Her mouth gaped as she took in his relaxed posture. How long had he been watching her?

Flustered and speechless, Layna scrambled for a sharp response. "Must you always sneak up on me?" she finally snapped, her eyes narrowed.

Zarian's smile widened. He straightened and strolled over, extending a hand to help her up. The princess waved it away angrily, avoiding his gaze. "I'm quite content here, thank you," Layna huffed, cheeks burning with embarrassment.

He studied her for a moment before, to Layna's surprise, he sat down across from her, his black trousers gathering dust as he crossed his long legs. His unwavering gaze captured her attention. Today, he seemed more serious, his usual flirtatious demeanor subdued.

Layna's eyes traced the contours of his chiseled cheekbones and the strong line of his jaw. The bridge of his nose was slightly crooked, the only flaw marring his otherwise perfect features. As her gaze drifted lower, she noticed the buttons of his tunic were undone, revealing the upper edge of his tattoo. Flustered, she quickly looked away.

"You were talking to Burhani yesterday after the council meeting," she blurted out, not quite meeting Zarian's eyes as she worried her lower lip between her teeth.

Zarian quirked a half-smile. "I was." His gaze drifted to her lips before trailing over the long column of her neck. "She was telling me about her visit to Janta."

The prince didn't offer up any more information. His piercing eyes were fixed on her, making her feel like prey stalked by a mighty lion.

Her nerves fluttered under his intense scrutiny, and she quickly asked, "Are you feeling okay? You seem…off."

He didn't respond immediately, intently studying her face as if trying to memorize it. Hunger and something else swirled in his eyes, something Layna couldn't place. She blinked, and it was gone, replaced by the lazy grin that haunted her dreams when she didn't have nightmares.

"I'm flattered by your concern, Princess," he teased.

Layna rolled her eyes. Her gaze drifted to her lap as her fingers traced lines into the sand. "The royal ball is in a few days."

"I heard," Zarian replied, not taking his eyes off her. "Are you looking forward to it?"

"Honestly," Layna exhaled deeply, "not particularly." Zarian regarded her curiously, head tilted slightly as if puzzling her out. "I wish I could simply enjoy the festivities, or better yet, not attend at all like Soraya. But I'm expected to mingle with dignitaries, uphold our alliances, and, of course, dance with potential suitors all night."

As she finished, Zarian's jaw tightened, and his eyes darkened for a brief moment. In his lap, his fists clenched and unclenched before he gripped his knees.

Layna noted the shift, a fleeting crack in his usual composure, and felt a flicker of satisfaction. Typically, Zarian maintained a tight rein on his emotions. It was gratifying to see his composure waver, if only for a moment. Perhaps she wasn't the *only* one wrestling with frustrating feelings.

"I see," Zarian murmured. "It can be difficult trying to fulfill the roles we were born into. But you, Layna, handle it with such grace." He flashed her an easy grin, adding, "Just limit the swearing to the training grounds and you'll be fine."

His laughter rang out as Layna huffed and swatted his arm.

"It's not that funny!" she exclaimed. He laughed even harder, a genuine, joyful sound that washed over her. She had the distinct impression that very few people had seen him so unguarded, so *happy*.

Warmth pooled low in her belly, his laughter cracking the wall around her heart, until her irritation slowly melted into a chuckle.

Soon, she was laughing too, head thrown back, hands clutching her stomach.

The breeze carried their laughter away into the depths of the desert, immortalizing the moment within the eternal, infinite sands.

As their laughter slowly faded, their eyes locked. Zarian looked at her as if she were the answer to every question he'd ever asked, the embodiment of every secret, silent wish. Her cheeks flushed, and she glanced down at her lap when she no longer felt bold enough to hold his gaze.

Slowly rising to his feet, Zarian dusted off his trousers before extending a hand, which Layna accepted gratefully this time. He carefully replaced her weights, and Layna was surprised to find that, for once, she didn't mind his help.

Together, they made their way back to the palace, side by side.

Later that day, Layna helped her mother with the royal ball preparations. The annual ball was not only a cultural celebration, but a political gathering where alliances were subtly forged and reinforced. The guest list was a carefully curated mix of local nobility and distinguished royal visitors. Every detail, from floral arrangements to menu selection, was meticulously planned to showcase Alzahra's splendor and hospitality.

After finishing preparations with her mother, Layna returned to her chambers to finalize her outfit. She entered to a scene of organized chaos—gowns and abayas in every imaginable shade covered her bed and sofas, each paired with matching jewelry, meticulously arranged by Tinga.

A gold-sequined gown that glimmered like streams of sunlight called to her. Tinga zipped her up, her eagle-sharp eyes scrutinizing the gown for any pulled threads or missing sequins.

Layna was examining her reflection in the mirror when Soraya entered. "Layna," she began, brows furrowing, "you look as beautiful as the dawn itself, but…" She paused, searching for the right words. "This gown doesn't quite reflect *you*. Don't you think so, Tinga?" She turned to the handmaid for support.

Tinga clicked her tongue. "None of that, little princess. This gown is perfect," she chastised and walked away, busying herself with packing away the other dresses, the white streaks in her bun glinting in the light.

"Do you really think so?" asked Layna, turning toward her sister. "I was rather fond of it." She looked back to the mirror, worrying her lower lip between her teeth.

Soraya moved toward the bed and quickly grabbed another gown before Tinga could reach it—one of deep, midnight-blue silk, its fabric rich and lustrous like the velvet night sky. "Try this on," she urged, holding the gown up to Layna. "This color will suit you better. Mysterious and radiant, like the night itself."

There was a moment of hesitation as Layna considered her sister's words. Reluctantly, she eased out of the golden gown, its fabric cascading to the floor in a pool of liquid sunshine. She delicately stepped into Soraya's choice, and her sister quickly zipped her up.

Layna turned to face the mirror. She marveled at the transformation. The gown clung to her form, accentuating her silhouette with an ethereal elegance. The neckline was deeper than she typically wore, a daring plunge that highlighted the delicate contours of her shoulders and collarbones.

The fabric was adorned with a constellation of intricate embroidery, each thread shimmering subtly as if woven with strands of moonlight. Silver sequins flowed like rivers of stars, converging and diverging along the hem and cuffs where the embroidery thickened, mirroring the night sky where stars gathered in glittering clusters.

Soraya gazed at her sister with a satisfied smile. "Moons, you look absolutely dazzling! Like a queen of the night, powerful and untouchable."

Tinga ambled over, carefully folding a teal gown, and peered into the mirror, her eyes appraising. She gave a curt "hmph" and retreated to the mountain of dresses.

"That means I'm right," Soraya declared triumphantly. She added casually, "What color should I wear?"

Layna's eyebrows shot up. "You're actually attending?"

Soraya gave a noncommittal shrug. "I thought it might be interesting this time." Layna eyed her sister suspiciously, but before she could probe further, Soraya stepped closer and continued admiring the gown, delicately tracing the luxurious fabric. "Perfect. This plunge accentuates your beautiful neck. Zarian won't be able to tear his eyes away."

Layna shot her a mild glare, a blush creeping up her cheeks as she quickly glanced at Tinga to see if she had overheard. Crossing her arms and shifting on her feet, she stammered, "Soraya, please, that's not…I mean, we're just…" Her eyes darted away as she struggled to find the right words, but her heart somersaulted at the thought. "Focus on the ball, not on Zarian," she finally admonished half-heartedly, trying to hide the smile tugging at her lips.

CHAPTER EIGHT

Under the silvery gaze of the moon, Alzahra City awoke to a night of enchantment with its annual royal ball. The palace transformed into a masterpiece of splendor and magic. The gardens, a centerpiece of the festivities, were bedecked with sparkling lanterns, their golden light casting a warm glow on stone paths lined with blooming jasmine and roses.

The sweet fragrance of flowers mingled with the spicy scent of incense. In the heart of the gardens, a magnificent fountain, illuminated by submerged lights, became a twinkling wonder, as the water danced rhythmically to the tunes of the traditional drumbeats echoing across the grounds.

In the grand ballroom, crystal chandeliers hung from the high ceiling, each a constellation of glowing lights. Servants flitted about like butterflies carrying trays of refreshments and appetizers. Musicians, dressed in billowing trousers that cuffed at the ankles and long embroidered tunics, were perched on a raised dais, skillfully coaxing their instruments to fill the hall with rhythmic sounds of drums, flutes, and harps.

A lavish banquet table stretched across one side of the room, piled high with delicacies. Heaping platters of spiced lamb and chicken sat alongside bowls of tabbouleh and trays of warm, fluffy pita bread.

But it was the dessert table that was the true masterpiece. Smaller in size but no less grand, it was artfully arranged with mountains of sweets. There were trays of luqaimat, golden, crispy dumplings drizzled with date syrup, along with freshly baked pastries and cakes. The crown jewel of the dessert table, and Layna's favorite, was a magnificent arrangement of kunafa. This classic dessert, made of thin, noodle-like pastry soaked in sweet syrup, was layered with creamy, soft cheese and baked to a perfect golden brown.

From a quiet corner of the ballroom, Zarian watched Layna make her entrance.

Moons, she was gorgeous.

The sight of her stole the breath from his lungs. Clad in a gown of midnight blue that glittered like the night sky, she moved with a mesmerizing grace, as if the very moon had descended to grace the earth. The embroidery on her dress caught the light with every step, casting a glow that seemed to emanate from within her. Tonight, she wore her hair down in loose waves, a shining silver tiara nestled atop her head.

Mouth suddenly dry, he resolved to watch her closely throughout the evening, attempting to persuade himself that his motives were purely related to his mission.

As Layna crossed the ballroom's gleaming marble floor, her gaze landed on Zarian. For a moment, she was left breathless by how strikingly handsome he looked. His tunic, a deep shade of midnight blue, was embroidered with intricate silver thread that shimmered under the light. The soft glow of the chandeliers highlighted his hazel eyes, and his inky black hair appeared only *slightly* unruly.

It only intensified Layna's urge to run her fingers through and tousle it.

Steeling her nerves, Layna approached him, her heart fluttering slightly.

"Zarian," she greeted, her voice mostly steady despite the frenzied raithbees in her stomach.

Zarian's eyes smoldered, his gaze slowly trailing down her body. "Princess, you look breathtaking," he remarked, his voice low. "And in blue, no less. It seems we have a penchant for matching colors tonight." He gave her a playful smile, subtly gesturing toward his own deep blue tunic that complemented Layna's gown.

Layna felt a blush warm her cheeks at Zarian's attention. "Thank you. You look quite handsome yourself." Her fingers toyed with the sleeve of her gown. "Have you seen Soraya this evening? I seem to have lost track of her."

He shook his head, his hair catching the light. "I'm afraid not. If I find her first, I'll let her know you're looking for her."

"Thank you. I should go check on our guests," Layna trailed off as she surveyed the room. Turning back to Zarian with a final nod and a small smile, Layna excused herself and crossed the ballroom.

The room echoed with soft conversations, the clinking of glasses, and gentle strains of music as Layna scanned the crowd for key guests.

First, she approached Lord and Lady Rashad, influential landowners whose support was crucial for maintaining Alzahra's agricultural prosperity. With a warm smile, she thanked them for their dedication to the kingdom's well-being. Their conversation was pleasant, with Lord Rashad praising Princess Soraya's recent initiatives to modernize farming techniques, which had led to higher yields of mirsham fruit.

Moving on, Ambassador Zara from Bilkaan caught Layna's eye. She was engaged in an animated conversation with Lord Varin. As Layna's gaze lingered on the master of war, she noticed the well-worn fabric of his formal tunic, distinctly out of fashion compared to the luxurious garments worn by his peers. It struck a chord of sympathy within her.

The Varin clan, once among the wealthiest and most influential families in Alzahra, had suffered greatly after a series of disastrous business ventures orchestrated by his father. These ill-fated decisions not only depleted their vast fortune but also tarnished the family's reputation, compelling his father to flee Alzahra in shame and his mother to take her own life.

It was a dark chapter in the Varin history, one that Lord Ebrahim had once shared with Layna, highlighting the resilience and honor Lord Varin displayed during those difficult times.

Despite his family's troubles, Lord Varin had risen through the ranks of the military, eventually being appointed to Khahleel's council. His journey from disgrace to distinguished service was nothing short of remarkable, though it appeared that the Varin family's lost fortunes were unlikely to be reclaimed.

Layna's attention shifted as the music transitioned to a livelier rhythm, and the palace dancers began a classical performance. They wore vibrant costumes of deep reds and shimmering golds, sparkling with every graceful movement. Bells jingled on their hips with each undulation, adding a rhythmic chime to their fluid motions.

As Layna admired the dancers, a deep voice interrupted her focus.

"Princess Layna, might I have the honor of this dance?" The speaker was Prince Kareem of the coastal kingdom of Maridunia, known for its vast ports and thriving trade. He stood with shoulders squared, chest puffed out, and hand extended.

Layna faced him. He was a handsome man, with close cropped brown hair and bright, ocean-blue eyes. "Of course, Prince Kareem. I would be delighted," she replied with a courteous smile, loosely grasping his offered hand.

"Your kingdom's hospitality is as legendary as its beauty, Princess," Prince Kareem said as he guided her across the dance floor. "I am enchanted by Alzahra's charm."

"Thank you. Maridunia's prosperity and its ports are equally renowned," Layna trailed off absently, her words diplomatic yet distant. Her attention was elsewhere, as she sensed a pair of eyes fixed upon her.

Glancing over Prince Kareem's broad shoulder, she caught sight of Zarian. He was watching them intently from the edge of the dance floor, arms crossed over his chest and jaw clenched tightly. His gaze was predatory, and it sent an unexplained thrill through her.

Trying to refocus on her dance partner, Layna continued politely, "Maridunia's strategic location must be a boon for trade."

"It is indeed," Kareem affirmed, trying to maintain her interest. "We seek to expand our alliances, and a connection with Alzahra would be most beneficial."

Layna smiled politely, aware of his underlying implication. "Speaking of alliances, congratulations on the recent weddings of your two sisters," she deflected smoothly.

The music shifted to fast-paced, rhythmic drumbeats, and Layna released Kareem's hands, swaying her hips in time with the music. She danced the traditional dance of her ancestors, arms outstretched and flowing gracefully, while her partner clapped in time with the beats.

The song ended, and she thanked Prince Kareem and excused herself, her thoughts dominated by the enigmatic Medjai watching her intently.

As the evening progressed, several other princes requested dances with her, all eager to nurture a potential alliance with Alzahra, including Prince Kamal from Sendouk and Prince Malik of the mountainous kingdom of Tarakshan.

During each dance, Layna's responses were polite but distracted. Her thoughts were elsewhere. Zarian, regardless of his own conversations, seemed to always have his attention fixed on her. His gaze was a constant presence, stoic and unyielding, a silent sentinel observing her every move.

Layna was dancing with Prince Malik, whose hands wandered just enough to make her uncomfortable. Twice, he had brushed her hair back over her shoulder, his hand lingering on her neck. His other hand alternated between caressing her waist and lower back, sending unwelcome shivers down her spine.

The music shifted to a slower, more intimate melody, and Layna saw Burhani approach the dance floor. Draped in a breathtaking red gown with high slits showcasing her long legs, Burhani glided gracefully toward Zarian. Layna watched as she leaned in, her voice syrupy sweet, "Zarian, would you honor me with this dance?"

Zarian hesitated, his eyes briefly flicking to Layna before accepting Burhani's hand with a courteous nod.

Jealousy knifed through Layna's heart. It was hardly fair, given how many dance partners she had entertained, but seeing Burhani with Zarian deeply agitated her.

As they danced, Burhani's melodic laugh rang out, capturing her attention. Layna watched as she subtly invaded Zarian's space as they moved together across the floor.

Layna stumbled, drawing a concerned look from Prince Malik. "Are you alright, Princess?" Malik asked, holding her upper arms to steady her, his thumbs brushing the sides of her chest.

"Yes, apologies, I just lost my footing," Layna replied with a forced smile, taking a step back from him. She struggled to focus, her gaze repeatedly drifting back to Zarian and Burhani who were deep in conversation.

As the final notes of the song faded, Burhani's hand lingered on Zarian's arm. The prince smiled politely and gently extricated himself from her grasp. With a courteous bow, he stepped away and into the crowd.

Burhani stood alone, her forced smile failing to hide the slight drop of her shoulders.

After Layna left to speak with important guests, Zarian watched her be courted by various princes. Each dance she accepted sent a searing wave of jealousy through him. He watched her glide across the floor, her laughter and smiles reserved only for her dance partners, feeling a dull ache in his chest each time their hands touched hers.

Lips set grimly, he watched as the handsy Prince Malik traced idle circles on Layna's lower back, his fingers venturing lower with each pass. She was stiff, angling herself away from him as her eyes darted around the room, clearly uncomfortable with his touch.

Rage surged within him, his fingers flexing for his sword. Why had he left it in his room? Only the thinnest thread of self-control and a lifetime of discipline kept him from storming over and breaking Malik's legs.

Malik brushed Layna's hair back over her shoulder, his fingers lingering to caress her neck. *Sleazy fucking bastard.* Zarian was going to kill him.

He was debating whether to slice off one of Malik's hands or both when a soft voice interrupted his spiraling thoughts.

"Zarian, would you honor me with this dance?"

He turned to find Burhani standing before him, bright-eyed and smiling, her red gown shimmering under the chandeliers' light. Zarian hesitated, glancing back at Layna and Malik before taking Burhani's offered hand.

"Of course," he replied with a polite smile.

As they joined the other couples on the dance floor, Burhani drew closer, her hand resting lightly on his shoulder, fingers gently tracing the fabric of his tunic.

"I've been enjoying your presence at the council meetings," she gushed. "Your advice on the political climate is brilliant."

"Thank you," Zarian responded, keeping his tone carefully neutral. Burhani's interest in a romantic relationship was clear, and he did not wish to lead her on. "The entire council's insights serve well."

Burhani laughed loudly, attracting attention from nearby guests. "You're always so modest. Your leadership is invaluable."

He offered a restrained smile. "I appreciate your confidence."

As they continued to dance, Burhani leaned in slightly, her chest brushing against his. "We have much in common, you know. We're both outsiders here."

Zarian's shoulders tensed. "It's a blessing," he said, his stubborn eyes fixed on Layna over Burhani's head. "Our different perspectives can be quite useful." When he looked back at Burhani, he noticed her smile had dimmed. His brow furrowed slightly as a whisper of guilt crept in.

"Are you from Navrastan?" he asked, refocusing on her as they glided across the marble floor.

"Originally, yes. But my mother and I moved to Thessan when I was quite young," Burhani said quietly, glancing away.

"Do you miss it?" Sympathy threaded its way through him. She tightened her grip on his shoulder and sighed.

"Terribly," she replied with a half-smile, her red lips matching her dress. "I was studying to be a scholar of the Grand Libraries." Her eyes dimmed, and her smile faded into a wistful curve.

"Tell me more," Zarian requested, twirling her gracefully. Drawing her back, he put a bit more distance between their bodies.

"It was always just Mama and me. But she fell ill a few years after we came to Thessan. The doctors were baffled. It was slow, she was sick for years. And then, one day she was just gone." Burhani bit her lip and inhaled shakily. "A few weeks later, Ebrahim came. Mama had written to him before she passed. He brought me here."

"I am so sorry, Burhani," Zarian said quietly.

Burhani shrugged. "It's alright." As the song ended, her hand lingered on his arm.

"Thank you for the dance," he said with a soft smile, gently removing his arm from her grasp. "It's been a pleasure."

Her smile faltered briefly before she masked it with a gracious nod.

With a respectful bow, Zarian stepped away, his eyes finding Layna, still dancing with Prince Malik.

Needing a moment to quell the rising tide of envy, Zarian walked to the refreshment area.

"Some wine, Your Majesty?" asked the barkeep from behind the counter.

Zarian eyed the pale liquid for a beat. "Just water for me, thank you," he replied quietly. As he took a sip, Soraya approached him with a radiant smile.

"Zarian!" she greeted. "Enjoying the festivities?" She glanced down at his glass. "No wine? You can relax for one night!" Soraya reached past him and plucked a flute off the counter.

He returned her smile, albeit wryly. "I don't drink. And yes, I am enjoying the festivities. Though I suspect you had a hand in the striking color coordination between your sister and myself," he insinuated, arching an eyebrow.

"Oh, I merely suggested the color. Any resemblance to your outfit is purely coincidental." Soraya gave him a disarming smile, her brown eyes twinkling with mischief.

Zarian chuckled. "By the way, Layna is looking for you."

Soraya's expression softened. "I'll find her soon. But you really must ask her to dance before one of these lackluster princes sweeps her off her feet."

Zarian forced a smile, a muscle ticking in his cheek. "None of them hold a candle to her." His eyes slid back to Layna on the dance floor with yet another partner.

"That's for certain," Soraya agreed, following his gaze.

Zarian turned back to the younger princess and stepped closer. "And Soraya, in your own pursuits…tread carefully," he advised quietly. Her eyes widened briefly before she composed herself, giving him a small nod as she departed.

Returning to the outskirts of the dance floor, Zarian struggled to maintain his resolve. Seeing Layna in the arms of other men was unbearable. He needed to feel her hand in his, to experience the connection that seemed to spark whenever she was near.

Finally, unable to resist any longer, Zarian made his way through the crowd.

During a brief pause between dances, Layna retreated to a quiet corner of the ballroom. She gratefully accepted a glass of wine from a passing servant, savoring a moment to catch her breath.

Her reverie was broken by Zarian's approach. She watched as he stalked toward her, a man on a mission, his hazel eyes glinting in the light. Coming to stand before her, his posture was strangely stiff, his jaw slightly clenched, an intensity radiating from him that was impossible to ignore. He inhaled deeply, closing his eyes for a beat. His shoulders relaxed slightly before he offered his hand.

"May I have this dance, Princess?" he requested, his deep voice resonating through her.

She tentatively clasped his hand, feeling the cool touch of his fingers as he intertwined them with her own. Unlike the other princes, Zarian's palm bore the rough calluses of a warrior.

He guided her to the floor, leading them into the first steps of the dance, their movements quickly falling into a smooth rhythm.

"Did you enjoy your dances with the other princes?" he asked, his tone seemingly casual, though Layna could see the fire burning in his eyes. "Did any of them spark your interest, perhaps?"

Layna watched, transfixed, as a muscle feathered in his cheek.

He's jealous.

Layna reveled in the thought. She couldn't resist teasing him. "Prince Amir of Minhypas was particularly charming," she said, eyes sparkling mischievously. "He's quite the dancer."

Zarian's jaw tightened further, along with his grip on her waist. Her gown billowed as he twirled her away with a swift motion, then pulled her back quickly into his strong arms.

"And you? Did you enjoy dancing with Burhani?" Layna asked breathlessly, her palms braced against his muscled chest.

Zarian gave her an easy smile and arched his eyebrow. "Would it bother you if I did?" Layna frowned and looked away. He twirled her again, then drew her back into his arms, her back pressed flush against his chest. "I think you'll be relieved to know that I didn't," he murmured in her ear.

As they continued to dance, the world around them faded into a dimmed hush.

"You move with the grace of a warrior, Princess," Zarian remarked softly. A pleasant shiver ran up her spine as he traced patterns on her lower back.

"I *am* a warrior. And you dance with a precision that speaks of more than just courtly training."

Their gazes locked, and the desert itself held its breath.

"Perhaps," Zarian conceded with a faint smile. "But true understanding lies beyond the steps of a dance."

Layna's heart quickened. "Just understanding, or something more?"

Zarian's smile widened, guiding her through a twirl. "Do you *want* more, Princess?" he murmured, his voice a velvety whisper.

A breathless laugh escaped her, and she averted her eyes as a furious blush warmed her cheeks.

As they danced, the space around them seemed to shrink, leaving them cocooned in their own private world within the crowded ballroom.

"You read people well," Layna noted, her eyes twinkling in the chandelier light. "Is that a skill you learned in the royal court of the Oasis or in the company of the Medjai?"

"Perhaps a bit of both. But I find you equally enigmatic. You hide your true self behind your royal façade. I think you wish for something more. What do you seek?"

Layna sighed softly, eyes downcast, as she absentmindedly stroked his shoulder. "Freedom, I suppose. To explore the world beyond Alzahra, freedom from my responsibilities." She gave him a small, dejected smile.

For a moment, Zarian looked at her with what seemed like pure longing. He said nothing, but tightened his hold on her waist and hand, drawing her closer to him.

As the music swelled, the electricity of their connection seemed almost tangible. Each glance, each touch, ignited sparks that danced invisibly in the space they shared.

"Princess," Zarian said as the song ended, "this has been perfect. Thank you."

Layna met his eyes, her breath catching. "Yes, quite perfect," she managed to reply, feeling a familiar warmth spreading through her. As the final notes died away, they reluctantly stepped apart.

As the evening continued, Layna finally caught sight of Soraya. She was on a balcony that overlooked the ballroom, radiant in a flowing gown of vibrant burgundy. She stood partially concealed in the shadows, and for good reason—she was in close company with a young nobleman.

Engrossed in their own world, Soraya and the young man shared soft laughter and quiet conversation. Layna noticed Soraya's bright eyes and the gentle tilt of her head as she listened to him, the subtle way their hands brushed against each other.

Sisterly concern radiated in her chest. She knew Soraya to be a free spirit, but this was more serious. Who was this nobleman, and what were his intentions? Layna felt a pang of worry, but there was also a part of her that felt happy for Soraya, seeing her so evidently smitten.

She made a mental note to seek out Soraya later, to gently probe and offer support. For now, she allowed her sister this moment of hidden joy and turned her attention back to the ball.

Later in the evening, as the music softened and the crowd thinned, Queen Hadiyah pulled Layna aside to a quieter corner of the ballroom.

"Were any of the princes promising?" her mother asked with a tight smile, the faint creases around her eyes deepening.

"Not particularly," Layna replied, her shoulders tense. Her mother studied her for a moment then turned her to face the ballroom.

"Observe," the queen advised, her arm heavy across Layna's shoulders. "Alliances form not just in council chambers but here, amidst dances and smiles."

Layna saw a prominent duke from a neighboring kingdom in animated conversation with a high-ranking military officer from Alzahra. Their laughter and hearty handshakes were the seeds of a budding military alliance, likely to be solidified in the coming days.

Nearby, merchants conversed with the minister of trade, potentially shaping future economic policies and trade agreements.

A hushed conversation nearby captured Layna and Hadiyah's attention. A group of well-dressed courtiers were whispering about the latest rumors surrounding Zephyria. Layna leaned in slightly, trying to covertly listen.

"I hear Zephyria has been forging new alliances," one courtier said quietly, a thin, wiry man with long blond hair. "King Jorah has secured pacts with Ezanek and Valtisaan, increasing his military strength significantly."

"If that's true, it could tip the balance of power," another added. "Jorah has always had his lecherous eyes on Alzahra, but with Ezanek's naval fleet and Valtisaan's superior weaponry..."

The conversation trailed off as they noticed Queen Hadiyah's gaze. The group dispersed quickly after that, leaving mother and daughter to ponder the implications of what they had just overheard.

A knot of worry formed in Layna's stomach. Zephyria's growing power was a major concern. She saw the same apprehension reflected in her mother's eyes.

"We'll worry about that later," her mother said stiffly. "Layna, each word, each gesture here carries meaning. One day, *you* will nurture these alliances and decipher these silent conversations." Taking Layna's hands, she added, "I see so much of myself in you, but you have a fire I never had. You will be an exceptional leader. Alzahra is lucky to have you."

Layna smiled softly but remained silent, her shoulders slumping under the weight of her duty.

As the hour grew late and the remaining guests began to disperse, Layna left the ballroom. She had only made it a few steps when she heard the rapid patter of footsteps behind her. Turning, she saw Zarian quickly approaching.

"Might I escort you to your chambers?" he offered, his voice hopeful in the quiet of the hallway. The corridors were deserted, many of the palace servants tending to duties in the ballroom.

After a brief hesitation, Layna nodded. The soft glow of lanterns illuminated their path, casting gentle shadows around them.

They walked together, shoulders occasionally brushing, as the echoes of the royal ball faded behind them. Deep in thought, Layna's lips pressed together, a faint crease appearing between her eyebrows. Despite their time together, she realized how little she truly knew about the man beside her.

"Is there something on your mind?" Zarian asked, his voice a deep hum that washed over her pleasantly.

"Will you tell me about your family?" She looked up at him as they walked through the dimly lit hallways. "Do you share a close bond with your parents?"

Zarian's expression shifted, and a muscle feathered in his cheek. "My father and I—it's complicated." He inhaled deeply, forcing his shoulders to relax as his fingers twitched slightly at his sides. "I haven't always agreed with his decisions. At one point, things were awful between us. I barely spoke to him." Zarian sighed and pinched the bridge of his nose. "It's better now, but his expectations are a weight I constantly bear." He smiled sadly at Layna. "I'm sure you can understand."

Layna nodded. She, too, deeply felt the burden on her shoulders.

"And your mother?" she ventured cautiously.

A shadow darkened Zarian's features. "I never knew her. She passed before my second birthday."

"I'm so sorry," Layna murmured. "The loss of a parent must leave a void that never truly fills." She reached out, touching his arm gently. "Do you have any siblings…or someone special back home? Someone who is to you what Soraya is to me?"

Zarian stiffened. His throat bobbed as he swallowed deeply. "I have—I had a brother," he finally replied. The prince remained quiet for several heartbeats before speaking again. "Sometimes, I envy your bond with Soraya. You are incredibly lucky to have such unwavering love and support."

Layna saw the change in his demeanor, the haunted look in his eyes and the stiffness in his shoulders. She wanted to ask more about his brother but sensed a deep-seated pain behind his carefully chosen words.

Zarian continued, "However, I do have a close friend named Jamil. We've been through much together. He's like a brother to me."

They turned a corner, the silence somber in the space between them.

He straightened his posture and took a deep breath. Raking a rough hand through his hair, he returned it to the disheveled mess that Layna loved. His shoulders relaxed slightly, and he gave Layna a half-smile, though it didn't quite reach his eyes.

"Were you perhaps inquiring about a romantic entanglement?" he teased, studying her with playfully narrowed eyes.

Layna's cheeks warmed under his gaze. "No, that—that wasn't my intention," she stammered, thrown off by the sudden change in his mood.

She watched him closely, searching for the emotions he kept tightly locked away beneath his flirtatious mask.

Let me in. Stop distracting me, and let me in.

Zarian chuckled. "To answer your unasked question, while most princes focus on forming alliances through marriage, my path has been different. My duties as a Medjai have consumed all my time."

"That sounds incredibly lonely," she commented softly.

"Perhaps," he conceded with a shrug, "but it gave me purpose and clarity. It taught me to observe beyond the surface. To see that sometimes, a harsh exterior guards a vulnerable heart."

Her gaze locked with his, and Layna feared he could see into her very soul.

"Perhaps. But some lessons are learned through experience, not just observation," she said, her thoughts drifting to past hurts.

"Life can be a cruel teacher, Layna, but you're one of the strongest people I know. You are kind and selfless and *good*." He tore his eyes away sharply, hands clenching and unclenching. For a fleeting moment, Layna glimpsed raw agony in his expression before he managed to conceal it.

His sincere words took her by surprise. Blinking rapidly, she turned her face away as well, her eyes suddenly damp.

They reached her chambers, and she turned to bid him goodnight, but the words evaporated in her mouth as their eyes met again. He was looking at her intently, with so much longing and *want*, that Layna felt laid bare before him.

In the soft glow of the torchlights, he reached out tenderly, his touch featherlight, and brushed his fingers against her cheek before tucking an errant curl behind her ear.

Eventually, she found her voice, a soft whisper in the night. "Thank you, Zarian. For your words and for this evening."

Zarian bowed slightly. "It was my honor. And I thank you. It's rare I find someone interested in my life…if you could call it that." The vulnerability in his voice pierced the barriers around her heart, filling her with a warmth she had never felt before, a desire to soothe, to console, a desire to *love*.

He hesitated for a moment before bringing her hand to his lips. He pressed a lingering kiss to the back, the sensation sending a current of electricity through her.

"Sleep well, Princess," he murmured, his voice a quiet whisper.

CHAPTER NINE

The sun beat down on the crowded marketplace as the younger brother meandered aimlessly through the colorful stalls. As he walked, his attention snapped to a young girl around his age. She stood a few paces away, her gaze fixed firmly on him, a bright smile on her lips.

Confused, he approached her, managing a somewhat awkward, "Hi."

"Hello," she responded warmly, her smile broadening as she extended her hand. "I'm Mila, General Harith's niece. I'm visiting for the summer months."

The young prince blinked, slightly taken aback, but shook her hand. "It's nice to meet you, Mila. I'm—"

"I know who you are! My uncle has told me much about you. And I saw you training yesterday," she continued, eyes twinkling with admiration. "You were quite impressive, even from afar."

His cheeks flushed with pride, and a wide smile spread across his face. He offered to show her around the marketplace. As they strolled past various stalls, he pointed out his favorite spots, sharing bits of both history and gossip. Mila laughed easily at his jokes, her delight clear and contagious.

When Mila's stomach rumbled, they both burst into laughter—hers tinged with embarrassment, his with joy. He bought lunch—tangy fire-roasted chicken legs atop soft flatbread, caramelized onions, and fried pine nuts. They ate standing, licking the delicious juices off their fingers, smiling and savoring each bite.

Eventually, their walk led them back to the palace as the sun dipped below the horizon.

Mila turned to him with a smile. "Thank you for being my guide," she said sweetly, eyes earnest. "Perhaps, I'll see you tomorrow?"

He nodded, his heart full.

She bid him goodnight with a soft smile and an awkward half-hug, half-pat on the back. As she walked away, his smile faltered, and he stood there, frozen, watching her disappear into the night.

She had called him by his brother's name.

As dawn broke over the palace, Layna awoke with a conflicted heart. She lay in bed, drowning in thoughts of Zarian, practically suffocating with *want*. The feel of his hands on her waist, the gentle caress on her cheek, his lips on her hand.

An inferno of desire raged within her, and it roared to be sated.

Despite her efforts to maintain a distance, he had found his way into her heart. He saw her—not the crown princess, but the woman beneath who longed for freedom.

But as the first rays of sunlight breached her private chambers, icy needles of reality pierced through desire's hazy embrace.

Her heart was not free to choose love. She had known and accepted this her entire life. Her marriage was destined to be a strategic alliance, essential for Alzahra's prosperity and welfare. Her gut twisted painfully. Had she jeopardized all chances of an advantageous marriage last night?

Layna dressed quickly and made her way to Soraya's chambers.

Soraya looked up from her bed, still dressed in her nightgown, as her sister entered. "Is everything alright?"

Layna took a shaky breath. "No," she whispered, her voice trembling.

"What happened?"

The elder princess trudged across the room and sat next to her sister, cocooning herself in the sheets.

"It's Zarian. I'm drawn to him in a way I can't explain. It scares me. We've been growing closer," she confessed, her face marked with grief. "But it's not a path meant for me."

Soraya leaned in, her voice gentle, placing a hand on Layna's shoulder. "But that sounds like the beginning of something beautiful. Why resist it?"

Layna flung the sheets aside and stood. She paced the room, wringing her hands together. "It's my duty to Alzahra. I am the future queen. My marriage must serve the kingdom. Not my heart."

"Why wouldn't a match with the Oasis be beneficial?" Soraya inquired, her brows furrowed.

Layna sighed, her gaze drifting. "The Nahrysba Oasis wasn't on Lord Ebrahim's list of suitable kingdoms," she explained, voice rife with frustration. "And from what I remember of my lessons, the Oasis is a modest kingdom with few resources. I think their focus must have been on developing the Medjai."

"Have you managed to learn more about the Medjai?"

Frowning, Layna shook her head. "Only what Lord Ebrahim reluctantly shared—that they are our allies and a secretive order dedicated to maintaining balance. Whatever that means." A memory flickered in her eyes as she added, "Do you remember the assassination of the tyrant Khyrain in Valtisaan? It was years ago. Nothing was ever proven, but rumors say it was the work of the Medjai."

"Really?" Soraya sat up straighter. "That doesn't seem right. The Medjai can just remove a sovereign monarch without repercussions?"

"Lord Ebrahim didn't seem concerned," Layna reasoned. "After all, they've been our allies for centuries, and Khyrain *was* a brutal king. His people suffered greatly—poverty, lawlessness, trafficking, all were rampant."

Soraya frowned, crossing her arms.

Layna shifted the conversation back to Zarian. "I don't know what to do. I wish I could change how I feel."

"Love and duty don't need to be exclusive, Layna. You can find a way to have both. Marrying for love doesn't mean neglecting your duty. You can benefit the kingdom in other ways."

The elder princess shook her head, sighing deeply. "It's not that simple. Our kingdom's future might depend on a powerful alliance. Especially with a war looming over us. My feelings for Zarian are a luxury I can't afford."

"I wish you could follow your heart," Soraya lamented. "But I understand the weight of the crown. I'm sorry you have to carry it alone."

Layna smiled sadly. "Thank you for listening." She stopped pacing and returned to sit beside her sister. "Let's not wallow in my depressing circumstances any longer. I think *you* have much to tell me. I saw you with someone at the ball."

Soraya's eyes widened, a blush creeping onto her cheeks. "Er, yes. His name is Almeer. It's still fairly new, but it feels…perfect."

Layna studied her sister. Soraya's eyes sparkled with a joy reminiscent of starlight. "Just be careful. The heart is a fragile thing. Who is he?"

Soraya hesitated for a moment, then sighed softly. "Almeer is from Zephyria," she revealed, her voice brimming with defiance. "He's a junior diplomat, here on a temporary mission. He arrived months ago. We met by accident in the gardens."

Layna's eyes widened. "Zephyria? But with the current tensions—"

"I know," Soraya interjected quickly, "which is why I've kept it a secret. If word got out, it could complicate the already tense situation."

"Does he know who you are?" Layna asked, concern coloring her voice.

Soraya nodded. "He does, and he understands the need for discretion. That's why we meet in secret." Her expression softened. "He's kind, Layna, and he listens. With him, I feel like just Soraya, not a princess who doesn't meet expectations. It's a freedom I never knew I needed."

Listening to her sister's self-deprecating words, Layna's heart clenched. She gently grasped Soraya's hand. "I understand, but please be careful. Not just because of the politics, but for your own heart."

"I will be. I promise." Soraya pulled Layna into a tight embrace. When they pulled back, she added, "I think you should go find Zarian."

Layna nodded, and with a heavy heart, she left Soraya's chambers.

The soft, early morning light filtered through the sheer drapes of their private chambers. King Khahleel and Queen Hadiyah sat close together in their bed.

The royal ball was a clear success, each detail executed to perfection, but it was the developments between their daughter and Prince Zarian that now consumed their thoughts.

Hadiyah leaned into Khahleel, her dark hair loose around her shoulders. "I fear Layna is growing too close to the Medjai prince…far too close," she whispered, her forehead etched with worry. "Their dance strayed near the bounds of propriety, did it not?" The queen looked thoroughly scandalized, a flush of indignation creeping up her neck to her cheeks.

Khahleel sighed deeply. "I have observed the same," he admitted, his gaze fixed on the morning light. "Yet, I have held my tongue."

"Should we not dissuade her? Or perhaps rebuke Zarian for overstepping his bounds?" Hadiyah pressed.

Khahleel shook his head. "No. Zarian has proven himself trustworthy and honorable." The king paused. "I like him," he said matter-of-factly.

"But what of Layna's duty to forge a strong alliance through marriage? I have been preparing her for it her entire life."

Khahleel faced his wife, his hand reaching out to lovingly caress her cheek. "My heart does not feel inclined to push her in that regard," he confessed, his voice heavy with a father's love. "Her destiny, intertwined with the prophecy, will already place upon her burdens far beyond her choosing. Should we begrudge her this sliver of happiness as well?"

Hadiyah looked into Khahleel's eyes and found there the same compassion that healed her heart all those years ago. The weight of destiny and duty was a constant shadow over their family, and the thought of Layna facing her path without the comfort of love was painful.

"I don't like it. The council will not be pleased," Hadiyah sighed. "But, perhaps, you are right."

Khahleel nodded. "Let us offer our guidance, but also trust her judgment. Layna is strong, wise beyond her years. She will navigate these waters with the grace and dignity that has always defined her."

Before dawn, Zarian awoke, his mind a tempest of emotions. The ball had ignited something deep within him. He could no longer deny that Layna completely owned his heart. Yet, the weight of his secrets—his mission and the prophecy—loomed over him.

He was drawn to her, enraptured by her strength and heart, but there were parts of him she could not know, secrets he must guard. She desired him now, but what would happen when she discovered his true purpose in Alzahra?

Would she still feel the same?

Standing by the window, he looked out over the palace grounds, awash in the dim pre-dawn light. The tranquility contrasted with the tempest raging within him. The peaceful morning mocked him with its serenity as he wrestled with his desires. He was a Medjai, sworn to his duty, yet his heart rebelled, yearning for something achingly, tantalizingly beyond his reach.

With a sigh, Zarian dressed and headed to the training grounds, hoping physical exertion would help clear his mind.

The grounds were deserted at this early hour, a silent stage awaiting its lone performer. Zarian began his routine, each movement precise and deliberate. As he swung his sword, he replayed the night's events—Layna's laughter, the closeness of their bodies, his lips on her soft skin.

But with each thrust and parry, he forced himself to focus on his duty. He was here to protect Layna, ensure the prophecy was fulfilled, and guard the balance, not to indulge in feelings that could cloud his judgment.

And if she threatened the balance, what would he do then? He couldn't stomach the thought, pushing it far from his mind.

When he looked at her, it wasn't the future queen or the foretold Daughter he saw, but the headstrong, vulnerable woman who had captured his heart.

He saw the fire in her eyes when she was angry, the beauty mark on her collarbone, the embarrassed blush that often graced her cheeks.

Lost in these reflections, he continued his training.

He was in the *moharib* stance, knees bent and sword aimed at the sky, when he heard soft footsteps approaching. He paused, turning toward the sound, his heart quickening as he recognized Layna's silhouette in the early morning light.

Approaching cautiously, Layna watched Zarian train, a mighty lion in human form. Her eyes drank in every detail—the sculpted cut of his muscles, the wind tousling his hair, and the sun glinting in his hazel eyes. She closed her eyes for a heartbeat, etching the image into her memory forever.

Hearing her footsteps, Zarian halted his practice, acknowledging her with a smile. "Princess," he greeted.

Layna stopped before him, eyes downcast.

"Zarian," she began slowly. "I must apologize. My behavior last night…it wasn't appropriate. I can't allow personal feelings to cloud my judgment. I have a duty to my kingdom."

She looked up and saw a flicker of pain cross his eyes, quickly concealed behind a mask of impassivity. He inhaled deeply as if gathering his strength.

"You have nothing to apologize for, Princess," he said quietly, his gaze fixed on the dusty ground. His voice wavered slightly as he spoke. "I am the one who overstepped. I am bound by the creed of the Medjai, and I cannot let my feelings interfere either." He took a steadying breath. "I will remain professional going forward."

Layna managed a sad smile. "Thank you. That's all I can ask."

She turned and walked back to the palace, alone.

Watching her leave, a cutting sense of loss wrapped itself around Zarian's heart. Her words echoed in his mind, a bittersweet symphony of what could have been and what must be.

He watched as she receded into the distance, each step taking her further and further away from him. His heart constricted tightly in his chest, and his eyes burned. *It's just sand*, he tried to convince himself.

Blinking rapidly, he returned to his practice. Zarian's movements carried a new intensity, each fearsome strike a release of his pain. He had to keep his focus, not only for his mission, but for Layna as well. Protecting her from his own heart was now a part of his duty.

The path of the Medjai was one of sacrifice.

And so, as Layna surrendered to her duty, so too would he.

After all, she had already made the choice for him.

CHAPTER TEN

In the shadowed embrace of rugged terrain, where the desert's sandy whispers met the stoic silence of rocky, majestic mountains, a young man found himself at the crossroads of destiny. The land here was harsher, more unforgiving than the oasis he had fled, its beauty as perilous as the secrets it hid.

With only the moon to guide his weary steps, he collapsed near an outpost, the weight of his choices bearing down like the storm clouds overhead. As consciousness slipped from his grasp, the last thing he saw was a group of armored riders approaching, their shadows merging with the night.

He awoke on the carpeted floor of a dimly lit room, the air heavy with the scent of burning wood. At the room's center sat a weathered figure, clad in dark robes.

"You've wandered far from any known path," snarled the figure. "I am known to execute trespassers."

The young man struggled to his feet. "So be it. I have left nothing behind worth returning to." The bitter words scraped like shards of glass against his bone-dry throat.

The dark figure's eyes narrowed, sensing untold stories in the young man's lack of concern for his life. "And what would you seek here, hmm? Sanctuary? Or perhaps...revenge?"

The question hung in the air.

The young man's silence spoke volumes.

The dark figure leaned forward, firelight casting fleeting shadows across his lined face. "I can offer you both," he promised, a slow, cunning smile spreading across his angular features. "But allegiance comes with a price. Serve me, and you shall have your sanctuary...and, perhaps in time, your revenge."

The young man's heart pounded. Here was a chance to redefine his destiny, to carve a path where he was not overshadowed by a legacy he had grown to resent.

"I will serve."

The kingdom of Zephyria unfurled in rugged splendor under an overcast sky. Here, the terrain was harsh, with jagged peaks clawing at dark clouds that perpetually gathered overhead. The air was cooler, scented with rain and pine, a cool contrast to its arid neighbor.

Jutting from this brooding landscape stood the Zephyrian castle, a monstrous fortress of stone and iron, its sharp towers piercing the fog.

In the castle's highest tower, Azhar stood alone. His chambers were sparsely decorated, save for walls adorned with fearsome weapons and the mounted heads of several unlucky animals. The dim light of dusk cast long, eerie shadows, intensifying the grim, vengeful presence of the trophies. The only luxury was a large desk, covered with scattered parchments and maps in organized chaos.

With cold hazel eyes, Azhar gazed out a narrow window at the darkening sky, as rain sluiced against the glass. With one final look, Azhar turned and made his way to King Jorah's council chambers.

The council chamber was a cramped room, dominated by a long, dark wooden table where Jorah and his advisers were already seated. The low murmur of discussion ceased as Azhar entered, leaving only the rhythmic sound of rain against the windows.

"Ah, my son," Jorah greeted with a rare smile. "Join us. We were just deliberating on Alzahra."

Azhar took his seat, his eyes scanning the maps spread out before them, detailing Alzahra and Zephyria, the contentious border highlighted.

"We must tread carefully," an adviser said. "The eclipse approaches, and with it, the prophecy. Our timing must be precise."

Azhar spoke, his voice a low rumble. "Have the astronomers determined the exact timing of the eclipse?"

"Not yet," responded Lord Ebric, adjusting his spectacles. "But they are tirelessly studying the stars for signs."

Lord Garrisman, the kingdom's war general, spoke next. "Sire, we are meeting with envoys from Ezanek and Valtisaan tomorrow to discuss our joint strategy."

Jorah's eyes shone with glee. "Outstanding, Lord Garrisman. These alliances are pivotal. We will tighten the noose around Alzahra."

Garrisman bowed slightly. "I cannot take all the credit, sire. Azhar's information was instrumental in fostering the deal with Valtisaan."

Jorah nodded, a look of pride on his face. "I expect no less from my son. Well done, Azhar."

Azhar ignored Jorah's praise, his mind racing. "We need to draw more of Alzahra's soldiers away from the palace. I know just the thing. We'll send a message—something personal. And then when we finally strike, the palace will be near defenseless."

The council murmured in agreement as Azhar explained his plan, an idea taking root. Jorah nodded. "Proceed with caution, Azhar. Let the shadows be our allies until the eclipse reveals our path."

As the meeting adjourned, Azhar felt a surge of anticipation. In the dark game of war and prophecy, he would finally have his revenge.

After the council disbanded, King Jorah retreated to his chambers. His quarters offered a sweeping view of the rugged landscape below. Jagged mountains framed the horizon, their peaks piercing the shadowy sky. Rolling hills dotted with tall, ancient trees stretched beneath the twilight, while a silver river wound through the valleys, catching the last glimmers of the sun's rays.

The familiar smell of burning wood greeted him. His joints creaked loudly as he settled into his high-backed chair with a weary sigh. The fire crackled softly in the hearth, casting a warm glow that did little to dispel the chill of solitude that was his constant companion.

Jorah contemplated the journey that had led him here. The first time he heard the prophecy of the Daughter of the Moon, it had come from an adviser recently returned from Thessan. At the time, Jorah dismissed it as a fanciful legend, a story spun by zealots clinging to the shadows of the past.

But then Azhar entered his life, dropped at his feet by fate's hand, and corroborated the tale. The young man, with his dark past and seething hatred, had unknowingly filled a void in Jorah's life. There was a kinship in their shared experiences of abandonment, forming a bond stronger than the usual ties between king and ward.

In Azhar, Jorah saw a reflection of his younger self—hurt, spurned, and driven by a desire to prove himself against the world's scorn. Surprisingly, he found not just a tool for his ambitions, but someone he genuinely cared for, a son in all but blood.

Jorah's thoughts turned to the war. The prophecy, once a tale he scoffed at, was now a beacon guiding him toward his fate.

It was only fitting that now, decades later, he would take both Khahleel's daughter and her power.

CHAPTER ELEVEN

After the royal ball, weeks crept by like the painfully slow crawl of a sahrabeetle. Princess Layna sat solemnly among the council, struggling to concentrate on the discussions that would determine her kingdom's fate.

As always, her eyes disobeyed her and drifted to Zarian.

He sat across the table, a stoic statue. They had maintained a cautious distance, their interactions strictly professional. A shadow had fallen over him, woven from the same dark fabric that shrouded her own heart.

Layna forced herself to focus on the council's deliberations. The envoy and his entourage sent to Zephyria never returned, and despite Alzahra's suspicions of foul play, there was no evidence to implicate Zephyria. In the end, the council ultimately blamed desert bandits for the disappearance.

To make matters worse, their scouts had confirmed what Layna and Hadiyah overheard at the ball: Jorah had secured military alliances with Valtisaan and Ezanek.

King Khahleel's brow furrowed in concern. "We must prepare for the worst."

Queen Hadiyah added, "I will write to my father in Shahbaad. Our allies in Bilkaan must also be informed. Their naval fleet could secure our coast."

Lord Saldeen spoke next, "Has there been any word of potential proposals since the royal ball? An alliance with a powerful kingdom at this juncture could provide much-needed resources. It might even deter Zephyria from escalating matters."

An awkward silence descended upon the council chamber, threatening to crush Layna under its heavy weight.

No word had come from any kingdom.

She swallowed deeply, her palms sweating, eyes fixed on the table as she felt the council members' sharp gazes boring into her.

"There has not," said Lord Ebrahim quietly. He cleared his throat. "And who can blame them? Alzahra is on the brink of war. It would be a steep risk for any kingdom. It does not reflect on Layna. Our princess is beyond reproach," he added firmly, glancing around the room, his gaze lingering on Burhani.

Layna appreciated his support, but the words rang hollow even to her own ears. She glanced at Zarian from beneath her eyelashes. Like her, he was focused on the table, unable to meet anyone's gaze.

Lord Varin spoke next. "If we cannot gain new allies, then we must consider a show of force. A display of our military strength could dissuade King Jorah. Let us not forget, a decade ago, Zephyria encroached upon our northern border. Their thirst for power has only intensified."

King Khahleel's response was swift and sharp, cutting through the room like a blade. "We prematurely engaged Zephyria then, based on your decisions," he retorted, his eyes hard. "We lost several hundred men in a conflict that could have been avoided. We will not repeat the mistakes of the past. Zephyria has not actually done anything yet. We will not be the ones who start this war."

Lord Varin's expression darkened, displeasure shadowing his features, but he held his tongue.

Taking a steadying breath, Layna stood to give her update. "I have news from Princess Soraya. She has increased the cultivation of healing herbs to support our army's needs. We have abundant stores."

Lord Ebrahim nodded. "A prudent move. Well done, Princess." From her periphery, Layna saw Burhani roll her eyes before she stood to give her own update.

"If I may," Burhani began smoothly, "the trade agreement I secured with Janta is bearing fruit. They've agreed to send additional food stores for our soldiers as an advance for later shipments of goods."

"Wonderful," said Lord Ebrahim. "It will help boost morale."

"Yes, and it strengthens our relationship with Janta," Burhani added triumphantly. "Prince Zarian helped me write the request." She smiled brightly at the prince, who responded with a curt nod.

Layna simmered with jealousy but forced a smile. "That's excellent news, Burhani. Well done."

"Thank you, Princess Layna," Burhani replied, arching an eyebrow. "We must *all* do our part to support the kingdom."

As the meeting progressed, another piece of news was brought to light—Prince Nizam's father had passed, making Nizam the new king of Baysaht. Layna felt a jolt at the mention of his name. Intrusive memories of their brief, poignant connection stirred a mix of nostalgia and pain.

Lord Ebrahim added, "Baysaht has historically remained neutral in regional conflicts. It will, indeed, be interesting to see whether King Nizam will uphold his father's legacy of neutrality or choose a side in the conflict."

Zarian, observing quietly, noted the subtle changes in Layna's expression. At the mention of Nizam's name, her eyes dimmed and a deep crease formed between her brows. She quickly schooled her features into impassivity, but it was too late. It was evident. There was a history between them. Queen Hadiyah's quick, concerned glance toward her daughter confirmed his suspicions.

A slow-burning jealousy took root within him, though he could not explain to himself why. It manifested as a constricting tightness in his chest, his mouth involuntarily settling into a grim line.

As the council meeting ended, King Khahleel turned to his daughter. "Layna, with the threat of the impending war, you might be a target as future queen. Prince Zarian will be your new instructor. There is much you can learn from his expertise in swordfighting."

Hadiyah pursed her lips and glanced away, her hands clenching into fists on the table.

Layna warily met Zarian's gaze. "I understand, Baba. I'm ready to learn."

Zarian nodded. "I will train you to the best of my abilities, Princess," he promised. It was a struggle to keep his voice firm and professional.

As they exited the council chamber, their eyes met for a moment, a silent, tortuous exchange. Then, both princess and Medjai turned away, each stepping back into their respective roles.

The weight of the kingdom's fate clung to Layna's shoulders. As she stepped onto the moonlit training grounds, she took a deep breath, ready to transition from princess to warrior. The moon cast a serene light over her, enhancing her focus.

Her dark linen pants rustled gently as she stretched, the cool breeze caressing her bare arms. Light armor hugged her form-fitting shirt, her sword strapped to her waist.

Zarian soon joined her, wearing a sleek, black tunic and loose-fitting trousers. "Hello, Layna," he greeted.

She offered him a tight smile, her nerves thrumming with anticipation.

"You're already quite adept with the sword," Zarian noted as he stretched out the muscles in his arms and thighs. "First, we'll spar.

That'll help me gauge your skills and decide on the best approach for your training."

She nodded and unsheathed her sword. In the silvered light of the moon, Layna and Zarian faced each other, brown eyes meeting hazel, swords in hand. As they circled, the measured rhythm of their footsteps on the cool earth was the only sound in the night air.

Layna struck first, a quick thrust Zarian blocked easily.

As their blades clashed, Zarian's movements were fluid and precise, unlike Layna's fierce, aggressive style. The resounding clang of metal echoed under the star-speckled sky. Layna's breath escaped in short bursts, her chest rising and falling rapidly as she tried to focus.

Each parry and thrust brought them closer, igniting a tension that neither acknowledged, yet Layna felt keenly. Zarian clenched his jaw tightly, and Layna's knuckles were white as she gripped her sword with sweaty palms.

Their duel was punctuated with moments of stillness, filled only with the sounds of their breathing. In these fleeting pauses, their eyes met and held. Layna tried to read his expression, but he remained impenetrable, a stone fortress made flesh.

In a moment of respite, Layna demanded, "Who are you, really?"

Zarian returned her steely stare. "I am a prince, a Medjai, and now your trainer."

Frustrated, she channeled her emotions into the next bout, lunging with a series of aggressive strikes, each blow more forceful than the last. Zarian parried her thrusts effortlessly, barely breaking a sweat. His movements were practiced and controlled, a sharp contrast to the fury driving hers. Their swords clanged loudly in the night, mirroring her mounting frustration as she struggled to gain the upper hand.

He gave her a wide, teasing smile.

"You know, Layna, you don't need to be the best at everything."

Layna aimed her sword for Zarian's arm, but he easily deflected it with his own.

"What do you mean?" Layna panted. "I know that." She thrust her sword at his chest this time, and again he easily blocked her strike.

"Are you sure? You seem quite upset that you're not winning," Zarian teased. With a skilled motion, he knocked her sword out of her hand, and it landed on the ground with a dull thud. He took a step back and grinned at her.

Layna's anger flared. She wanted to wipe the arrogant smirk off his face.

And she knew exactly how to do it.

She quickly retrieved her sword and resumed her stance.

"I'll admit you're quite skilled," she said casually, lunging at his chest again. "Almost as good as Bilzayn." Zarian's smile faded quickly, though he still easily evaded her sword.

"Who is Bilzayn?" His sword crashed against hers, this time with more force.

"My last instructor. I miss him," she said wistfully. Zarian was silent. A muscle feathered in his cheek. Layna panted as she struggled to block his strikes. "He said I was his favorite pupil, so strong, so motivated—" Layna paused, ducking to avoid Zarian's sword. "And so beautiful."

Her words hit their mark. Zarian's jaw clenched so tightly she thought his teeth might crack. His eyes flashed dangerously, and she could practically feel the jealousy radiating off him.

She felt powerful, and it was intoxicating.

"I learned so much from him. He had a very *hands-on* approach." Layna smirked as she watched Zarian's composure crack before her eyes.

With a low growl, Zarian swiftly crouched and swept Layna's legs out from under her. Her sword fell to the sandy earth. In the next heartbeat, he had pinned her to the ground, their bodies pressed closely together.

"Is this hands-on enough for you, Princess?" he demanded, his voice low and angry in her ear.

Instinctively, she bucked her hips and pushed at his chest. "Get off me!"

He groaned, a deep rumble in his chest. His eyes snapped shut.

"Stop. Squirming," he bit out through clenched teeth.

Layna writhed harder, but he captured her wrists in one large hand, locking her arms above her head and covering her legs with his own.

She had no choice but to lay still, breaths coming in heavy gasps. Their faces were inches apart, eyes locked in a fiery gaze.

He braced himself on one forearm, and she sucked in a deep breath, filling her lungs, her chest heaving against his. Zarian's eyes drifted down to Layna's parted lips. He inched closer, the space between them narrowing to a sliver.

Layna froze, heart pounding frantically in her chest. His eyes were stormy, desire and rage swirling in their depths.

He edged even closer still, his lips just a hair's breadth from hers. Layna's eyes fluttered closed in anticipation, breaths quickening with each passing second. Her lips parted slightly.

And then his weight on her was gone.

Confused, she opened her eyes to find him towering over her. After a long, charged moment, he extended his hand and helped her up, his firm grip leaving goosebumps in its wake.

"The first rule of Medjai combat," he rasped, his voice rough like gravel, "is to never let your emotions best you. Control is paramount."

"Are you telling me or yourself?" Layna snapped, still panting. A strange mix of emotions twisted through her—desire, anger, frustration. She was angry that he had pinned her so easily, upset that he didn't kiss her, and mad at herself for even *wanting* him to.

Zarian tore his gaze away. He rubbed the back of his neck but didn't immediately respond. Stepping back, he put a professional distance between them.

"Tomorrow, we'll focus on strength training and building stamina," he finally said, crossing his arms over his chest.

"Fine," Layna said stiffly. She sheathed her sword and left the training grounds, her back straight and shoulders squared despite the ache in her muscles and the turmoil in her heart.

As she walked to her chambers, Layna's thoughts were consumed with Zarian. The memory of his powerful body atop hers wreaked havoc on her senses.

The fresh night air cooled her anger but did nothing to temper the desire and frustration coursing through her. Every nerve was alight, her fingertips and toes tingling with electric anticipation.

She had barely closed the door to her chambers when it burst open behind her. Tinga barged in, practically shaking. Her eyes, wild with panic, darted frantically around the room.

"Tinga, what's wrong?" Layna asked, eyebrows furrowed in concern.

"Where were you just now?" Tinga questioned urgently, rushing forward and gripping Layna's arms. "Where were you?"

"Tinga, you're scaring me. What happened?" Her handmaid's grip only tightened, shaking her slightly. "I was training on the grounds! With Prince Zarian." Layna's voice rose along with her increasing concern.

"Prince Zarian?" Tinga repeated, seizing Layna's face and tilting it toward the lantern light, her eyes scanning intently before checking her neck and wrists.

"Yes, Baba asked him to train me in sword fighting. That's where I was," Layna explained, her confusion mounting. "*What* is going on?"

Tinga studied her closely, her hawk-like gaze seemingly finding what it was searching for in Layna's face. The older woman took a deep breath, and her shoulders relaxed slightly.

"Nothing," she finally said, her voice strained. "I will oil your hair tonight. Go take a bath. You smell like a desert bandit."

Layna wanted nothing more than to collapse into her bed and drown in memories of Zarian's body covering her own, but Tinga's strange, frantic demeanor compelled her to listen.

Less than thirty minutes later, she sat in front of her mirror, her skin scrubbed to a rosy pink and the pain in her muscles soothed to a dull ache.

Tinga poured a generous amount of rose oil into her hands and began massaging it into Layna's scalp. The princess studied her handmaid closely in the mirror, but she seemed entirely focused on her task.

Tinga eventually broke the silence. "I had finished my tasks for the day and was heading to bed. I passed through the private balcony—the one that connects this tower to the main palace. The one that overlooks the training grounds."

Layna's heart stuttered in her chest. She eyed Tinga warily in the mirror, who finally met her gaze. Her face was impassive, but a strange mix of emotions flickered behind her eyes that Layna couldn't decipher.

"It…it wasn't what it looked like," Layna explained, her voice small.

"It *looked* like he was forcing himself on you!" Tinga replied angrily, raking her nails against Layna's scalp. "I was ready to shout for the guards, but then he let you up."

"No! No, he would never hurt me. He was training me, like Baba asked him to," Layna responded, eyes wide as she held Tinga's gaze in the mirror. She grabbed Tinga's oil-slicked hand, squeezing it tightly in reassurance.

"I have seen you train, Princess, and it has never been like that," Tinga said firmly. "Unless he was training you for his bed."

"Tinga, please," Layna pleaded, her cheeks reddening in mortification. "It's not like that. I promise, he wasn't taking advantage of me."

Tinga studied her closely, her fingers digging into Layna's skull. "Princess, if you ever feel threatened, you *must* tell me," she demanded.

"And what would you do?" Layna asked, her lips quirking in a tentative half-smile. She reached behind her and gently squeezed Tinga's arm.

Her handmaid remained stone-faced. "I would spike his drink at dinner with *neendakhi*. The little princess grows it in the greenhouse, did you know? The infirmary healers use it to put patients to sleep before major procedures." She looked away, thinking for a moment. "For a big man like him, I'd need a fair amount. He'd fall into a deep sleep within the hour. I'd bind his hands and feet while he slept, then separate him from his manhood."

Layna gasped, her blood growing colder with each word. She looked at Tinga in the mirror with growing concern, but her handmaid had a distant look in her eyes.

"Getting him out of the palace would be difficult, but not impossible. I still need to think on that. But then, I would bury him alive in the desert, so his final moments were nothing but terror and sand."

Layna was pale, dread coiling in her belly. "Tinga, did some—"

The handmaid abruptly cut her off before Layna could voice her fear. "You said 'It's not like that' with Prince Zarian. Then, tell me, what is it like?" She resumed massaging Layna's scalp, rubbing her fingers in tight circles.

Eyeing her closely in the mirror, Layna hesitated. "I like him," she finally admitted quietly. "But he isn't a powerful match for Alzahra. And he has his own path. I can't be with him."

"Hmm," Tinga mused, grabbing a wide brush and dragging it through Layna's long waves. "Then, Princess, you are playing with fire. You will get hurt."

Layna looked down at her lap, silent in her sadness. Tinga tugged at her hair, forcing Layna to meet her sharp eyes in the mirror.

"Or perhaps that fire will burn through the ropes that bind you."

CHAPTER TWELVE

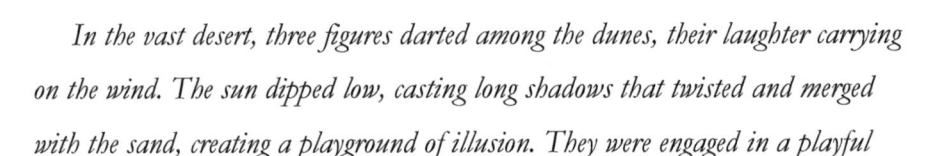

In the vast desert, three figures darted among the dunes, their laughter carrying on the wind. The sun dipped low, casting long shadows that twisted and merged with the sand, creating a playground of illusion. They were engaged in a playful game, a test of stealth and strategy.

The youngest, a boy with fire in his heart, moved across the sand with silent steps. He had never won, always outmaneuvered by his older companions who seemed to blend with the desert itself, vanishing into thin air only to reappear when victory was theirs.

But today felt different. Today, he was close, so close to claiming a victory that would prove his worth.

Just as he was about to close in on his target, a servant's voice shattered the silence.

"Young Master! Your father wishes to see you immediately," the man called, his voice echoing across the sands.

The elder brother and their companion emerged from their hiding place, far from where the youngest stood. They did not see him. As they walked toward the servant, a large black dog bounded up to his brother, placing its paws on his shoulders in a display of affection reserved only for him. "Easy, Sultan!" The boy buried his hands in the dog's fur, laughing as he enthusiastically licked his face.

Hidden within the dunes, the youngest watched, a feeling of numbness creeping through his limbs. He chose not to follow them back to the confines of the palace.

Instead, he remained in the desert, letting time slip through his fingers as stars claimed the sky. In the solitude of the sands, with only the desert as his witness, he was invisible and alone.

Hours passed before anyone came to look for him.

In the far recesses of the palace library, Zarian found Soraya absorbed in a tome on ancient irrigation methods. Tall shelves lined the walls, brimming with books, their spines a riot of colors and textures. Streams of golden sunlight pooled on the richly patterned rugs through large, arched windows.

Soraya looked up, her eyes brightening. "Zarian! It's always a pleasure. Layna, however, is elsewhere at the moment." She gave him a playful smile, marking her page and setting the book aside.

"I appreciate that, Soraya, but actually, I came to speak with you." Zarian sat down across from her at the table. "How are your plants? And the stores for the war efforts, are they sufficient?"

Soraya beamed. "The plants are thriving, thank you! The new irrigation techniques are showing promising results." Before Zarian could respond, Soraya added, "How are the training sessions with my sister? Has she been keeping up with your strict regimen?"

Zarian's expression softened. "She's progressed very well over the last few weeks. She is very dedicated."

Soraya smiled knowingly. "It sounds like you're quite impressed with her," she teased, her smile widening at Zarian's brief, unguarded look of affection.

"She is exceptional," he admitted with a small smile.

A comfortable silence fell, broken only by the soft rustling of pages and Zarian drumming his fingers on the table.

Soraya broke the silence. "I always enjoy our conversations, but you seem to have something else on your mind."

Zarian hesitated before nodding. "You're quite perceptive. I wanted to know, well…what can you tell me about your sister and Nizam?"

Soraya's eyes widened. "Layna mentioned him to you?"

"No," Zarian confessed, "His name came up a few weeks ago in a council meeting. Layna's reaction was…telling. I sensed a history between them. I can't seem to get it off my mind." His gaze was earnest and open as he braced his arms on the table and leaned forward.

Soraya smirked. "Was her *reaction* telling or were *you* obsessively watching her every move despite your vows of professionalism?"

Zarian chuckled and dramatically clutched his chest. "Please, Soraya, have mercy on me. Don't leave me in the dark."

Relenting, Soraya sighed, her smile fading as she responded. "You're right. Nizam and Layna's connection was brief but profound. He visited Alzahra a few months before you arrived. Layna thought she had finally found a suitor who was both a love match *and* a powerful alliance. Things seemed perfect between them. Layna was smitten. But, for some reason, he didn't continue their courtship. He didn't even send a single letter. His rejection shattered her heart. It's why she was so standoffish when you first arrived. She thought you were a suitor."

Zarian's expression grew pensive. "I see," he murmured, deep in thought.

Soraya leaned forward and rested her chin on her hand. "Give her time, Zarian," she implored softly. "Layna is so committed to her duties that she forgets her own happiness isn't a betrayal. She sees love as a complication." Soraya gave Zarian a comforting look, one he returned with a tight smile. "And I think, perhaps, you should also rethink your own priorities."

In the silence that followed, a spark of jealousy quickly spread within him like untamed wildfire. His fingers twitched, and he clenched his hands into tight fists. The idea that Layna had once harbored such deep feelings for another man unsettled him more than he cared to admit.

He inhaled deeply, forcibly relaxing his hands. Soraya was right. He was also complicit in the distance between them. After the ball, when Layna sought him out and apologized for crossing a boundary, he had also chosen the path of duty over desire. He had cloaked his feelings in responsibility, prioritizing his role as a Medjai above his heart.

It was a choice he now deeply regretted.

If offered a second chance with her, if she was willing to explore their relationship, he vowed to seize it without hesitation.

Halting his spiraling thoughts, Zarian asked, "And what of your own 'complication,' if I may?"

Soraya's face lit up, radiating with the soft glow of a woman in love. "Oh, I'm very happy, Zarian. Almeer makes everything brighter. But…" she paused, brow furrowed. "I try not to think too far ahead. The present is complicated enough."

Zarian asked gently, "And do you feel safe with him?"

"Absolutely, yes," she reassured, nodding fervently. "My Almeer is the gentlest soul. He's shown me nothing but kindness and respect."

"I'm glad to hear that, Soraya," Zarian said, nodding. "If you ever need anything, you can always come to me. Our families are bound by duty, but I hope you consider me a friend as well."

"Thank you, Zarian." Soraya smiled warmly. "That means a lot to me. Truly."

As the early morning light warmed the palace gardens, Princess Layna strolled amidst the dew-kissed blooms. Her conversation with Tinga weighed heavily on her heart, revealing the pain beneath her handmaid's tough exterior. Layna had broached the subject a few times, but Tinga always deflected and quickly changed the subject.

Sighing deeply, Layna reflected on the past few weeks. She had thrown herself into intense training sessions with Zarian, each encounter leaving her more conflicted than before.

Under the moon's watchful eye, Zarian taught her the ways of the Medjai. She learned to harness her inner strength, channeling it through her blade with precision. He demonstrated various grips for her sword and how to block attacks from every direction.

Layna improved remarkably in her swordplay, her movements becoming more fluid and confident. She still couldn't best Zarian, his experience and sheer strength always prevailing, but the thrill of the challenge and the push to exceed her limits drove her forward.

Each week, Zarian introduced a new skill. He taught her how to use the environment to her advantage, turning the terrain into an ally, showing her how shifting sands could destabilize an opponent or how the sun's glare could momentarily blind an adversary.

He never pinned her again, yet she found herself yearning for it with every session, a hopeful anticipation simmering beneath her focus.

Occasionally, Layna would deliberately falter in her stance, just to feel Zarian's firm, steadying touch as he corrected her. His fingers would linger a moment too long on her arm or waist, each touch leaving a trail of goosebumps. She craved those moments, though she'd never confess it even under the threat of torture. Sometimes, she caught a suppressed smile on his face, though he never revealed if he suspected her tactics.

As Layna walked, her mind replayed their recent sessions—the sound of swords clashing, Zarian's hands on her skin, the intensity in his eyes. It ignited a tempest of feelings in her she wasn't yet ready to face.

She was a princess, destined to rule Alzahra, bound by duties and expectations. Her heart wasn't free to chase love, especially with someone like Zarian, whose own path was also set in stone.

Yet, the more she tried to suppress these feelings, they clawed their way back, stronger each time.

Her rational mind reminded her of the alliances to be formed, the kingdom to be led. But her heart, rebellious and untamed, yearned for something else, something that whispered of freedom and love.

At night, she lay awake, tossing and turning, Zarian always dominating her thoughts. She imagined exploring those feelings, abandoning the restraints of her title to just be Layna, a woman capable of love.

But with each dawn, reality set in with the golden rays of the sun. Layna would don her princess's mantle, steeling herself for another day where duty outweighed desire. Each meeting with Zarian, each brush of their hands, tested her willpower. She clung to her role as future queen, using it as a shield to guard against her emotions.

It was a constant struggle, an inner turmoil that drained her. She knew she was walking a tightrope, one as thin as a single strand of hair, where one wrong step could devastate not just her, but her entire kingdom as well.

She could not fall.

Zarian prepared for bed, having just returned from his training session with Layna. He poured a glass of water from the pitcher by his bedside and gulped down the soothing liquid.

He slid under the cool sheets, his body still thrumming with residual energy. As he did every night, he replayed the moment from their first session when he had her pinned beneath him, her soft curves pressed against him, both anger and desire swirling in her beautiful brown eyes.

It was a lapse in his control, a moment of weakness he regretted, yet he regretted not kissing her even more.

After his conversation with Soraya, he had carefully weighed his priorities again and again, and each time, Layna emerged at the top. His mission, his father's expectations, his duty to the Medjai—all dimmed under the light of her smile.

But Layna had been clear about her dedication to her kingdom. His heart constricted painfully in his chest as he recalled when she came to apologize after the royal ball. The sadness and resignation in her eyes tormented him.

As the night deepened, he succumbed to a restless slumber.

The moon kept its watch over Alzahra, over a prince and princess whose destinies were becoming ever more intertwined.

CHAPTER THIRTEEN

In the blistering noon sun, the training grounds were a scorching inferno of sand and stone. The elder brother emerged from the shadow of the palace to find his younger sibling navigating a grueling obstacle course.

The task was to swing across a series of bars, each spaced just out of comfortable reach, demanding precise leaps and iron grips. The sun turned the metal bars into searing rods, but the younger brother persevered, hands desperately clenching and unclenching to maintain his hold.

With each attempt, his raw, bleeding hands slipped from the heated metal, sending him crashing to the ground. His palms were a mess of burst blisters and chafed skin. Still, he picked himself up again and again, driven by a fierce need to conquer the course.

The elder brother, watching with growing concern, stepped forward. "Stop," he implored. "You've pushed yourself enough for today. You can try again tomorrow."

But his words fell on deaf ears. The younger brother, consumed by the challenge, focused entirely on the taunting bars.

On the next attempt, his grip faltered again, his weakened hands unable to hold on. He fell heavily, sending a cloud of dust into the air. The elder brother rushed to his side, grabbing his arm to help him up.

With a grunt, the younger brother angrily knocked him aside and stormed off. Left alone in the dust, the elder brother watched his sibling walk away.

Zarian and Layna walked through the palace halls on their way to the council chambers. Layna listened intently as he explained the virtues of meditation.

"Clearing your mind is invaluable," he explained. "In battle, clarity and calmness can be as decisive as the sharpest blade."

Layna's focus, however, was abruptly shattered as they rounded a corner. She stiffened, her eyes wide, and grabbed Zarian's arm tightly. At the corridor's far end, a seemingly innocuous cluster of servants bustled about.

Without explanation, the princess quickly shoved Zarian down a side hallway and in through the first door she saw. It creaked open loudly, revealing a storage room. Dust motes danced in the sliver of light from a small window, illuminating stacks of old decorations and rolled-up rugs.

Layna swiftly shut the door, pressing her back against it. Her hands were planted firmly on Zarian's chest, feeling the solid muscle beneath, while his hands steadied her hips.

The sudden intimacy of their position left her breathless. The heat of his body sent a surge of desire through her. His scent—sandalwood mingled with spice—enveloped her senses, making it difficult to think coherently.

"Layna," Zarian whispered, his voice low as he scanned the room, eyes adjusting to the darkness. "I don't mind in the slightest, but this is quite bold of you. Has something changed your mind about us?" He refocused his gaze on her, his voice sounding almost hopeful in the dark. His deft fingers traced winding patterns along her hips and waist.

"I—no, not at all," Layna hastily replied.

Zarian's hands stilled, and a glimmer of disappointment—almost devastation—crossed his features. But it vanished swiftly, replaced by his customary lazy grin.

"Then why, Princess, are we hiding in here?" he drawled, the timbre of his voice dropping as he placed his hands on either side of her head, effectively trapping her between his muscular arms.

An involuntary shiver ran through her. His proximity was intoxicating. She swallowed deeply, struggling to regain control over her heart.

"I was avoiding those servants," Layna explained awkwardly. Zarian raised an eyebrow. "They work in the couriers' quarters. And they—well, they pity me. I used to visit there quite often, and well, it's a long story," she rambled uneasily, his face just inches from hers.

"I see," he said slowly, his eyebrows shooting up in almost comical disbelief. "Layna, if you wanted more time alone with me, you need only ask."

Layna huffed and pushed at his chest, putting distance between them.

"That's not it," she snapped, cheeks flushing. "I think they're gone now. Let's just get to the council chambers." She cracked the door open, checked the hallway, and hurried out. Zarian followed close behind, a wry smile on his face.

As Layna and Zarian arrived at the council chambers, an air of solemnity had already settled thickly over the room. The usual pleasantries were conspicuously absent, replaced by a tension that weighed heavily on everyone.

Lord Ebrahim wore a grave expression. "My lords, my ladies," he began uneasily. "We face a predicament. King Jorah has sent a marriage proposal."

Queen Hadiyah leaned forward. "A proposal? For Layna, I presume? On behalf of his heir?"

Ebrahim hesitated, his eyes flickering to Layna and King Khahleel before returning to the queen. "No, my queen. The proposal is from…King Jorah himself."

The chamber plunged into stunned silence. Even Burhani was at a loss for words, her mouth parted in shock. Across from Layna, Zarian sat rigidly, murder flashing in his eyes. His jaw clenched tightly, a vein pulsing in his forehead as he tightly gripped the arms of his chair. He looked angrier than Layna had ever seen him.

Layna's eyes blazed as she fought to keep her own outrage in check at the insulting proposal.

King Khahleel's face reddened with anger. He pondered for a heart-stopping moment, the weight of his daughter's future and his kingdom in the balance.

Then, with a voice like thunder, he boomed, "No! Never! This will never happen!" He slammed his fist on the table, startling the council members. "Does that fool think I will sell my daughter? Let there be war! Let that dog bring whatever he can! I will raze his entire kingdom to the ground!"

A heavy silence enveloped the room. Layna's fiery gaze swept over the council and landed on her mother. Queen Hadiyah was white as a sheet, her usual composure replaced by an unreadable expression. Layna couldn't quite discern the emotion in her mother's eyes—was it shock, fear, or something else?

In that moment, Layna recalled her mother's many lessons about the burdens of leadership, memories pouring cool water over the smoldering fire of her anger. As future queen, her reactions needed to be measured, even in the face of such blatant disrespect.

Taking a deep, steadying breath, Layna reined in her emotions and turned to her father, who was still seething with rage.

"Baba, while your anger is justified, we must consider all our options," she advised calmly. "As much as we abhor this proposal, we must not let emotions cloud our judgment. Our kingdom's future is at stake. Let's at least discuss it."

Khahleel turned sharply, his eyes blazing. "No, Layna! *I* am still the king. My answer is no." He faced the council. "Do not respond to the proposal. Instead, send fifteen thousand more troops to our eastern border. That should show them where Alzahra stands." He took a breath. "If that bastard wants a war, I swear by the moon and sun, I will give him a war!"

Queen Hadiyah, her voice a whisper, reached out in a bid to soothe the tempest in her husband. "Khahleel, please, try to contr—"

Yet her plea dissolved into the thick air as the king dismissed her gesture, rising so abruptly his chair screeched a loud protest on the stone floor. The room constricted further as he stood, a towering figure of fury.

"There will be no further discussion on this matter!" he bellowed. "He could not have you, Hadiyah, so now he seeks to take my daughter? *Never.* I will not entertain such an outrageous proposal!"

His raw declaration, a revelation veiled in decades of silence, reverberated through the chamber, leaving a palpable shock in its wake.

The king stormed out, his heavy footsteps resonating with rage. The council members sat frozen. Some exchanged furtive glances, acknowledging a truth long suspected but never spoken, while others awkwardly stared at their laps, avoiding the queen's gaze.

Shocked, Layna sat motionless, still as a statue. Was King Jorah's hostility rooted in a spurned interest in her mother? The implications shook her to her core.

Following the king's abrupt departure, a heavy silence settled over the room. Queen Hadiyah, with a resigned sigh, addressed the council.

"We shall reconvene tomorrow. For now, let us reflect on this development." She rose gracefully, her expression a mask of regal composure, though Layna could see the worry in her eyes.

As the council members dispersed, Layna remained seated. She glanced at Zarian, their eyes meeting before he stood abruptly. His footsteps echoed, each one a sharp, angry staccato, as he left the room.

Layna tried to focus on her tasks throughout the day, but her thoughts remained heavy. She hadn't seen her mother since the explosive council meeting that morning. The queen had been conspicuously absent around the palace.

Her heart ached for her mother's comfort and wisdom. The idea of marrying Jorah was abhorrent. Yet, wasn't her duty to her people paramount? She had the ability to avert the war and to save countless lives. Could she, *should* she, sacrifice her own happiness for the greater good?

It was time to speak to her mother.

Determined, Layna navigated the palace corridors. Reaching her parents' quarters, she knocked softly on the heavy door. When there was no response, she slowly pushed it open. Hadiyah was alone, seated by a window overlooking the gardens, lost in thought.

"Mama," Layna began tentatively, "are you alright?" When the queen didn't respond, she continued. "What Baba said in the council meeting…is it true?"

Queen Hadiyah sighed, turning to face her daughter. "It's true, Layna," she said softly, her eyes reflecting a past, long buried. "As you know, before I was your father's queen, I was Shahbaad's only princess."

A distant look came over Hadiyah as she told Layna of a grand dinner in her homeland, where she first met Prince Jorah.

The grand hall of Shahbaad glowed with the light of a thousand candles, the flickering flames casting a golden sheen over the assembled nobility. At the center stood a young Hadiyah, dressed in her finest silk gown. Her hair, a cascade of dark brown waves, was adorned with jewels that sparkled with every movement.

Then there was Prince Jorah. His entrance had been nothing short of regal, his tall, lean frame moving with a confidence that effortlessly parted the sea of guests. His features were sharply defined, a sculptor's dream, with an aquiline nose and shrewd, piercing eyes. Those eyes found Hadiyah across the room, locking onto hers with an intensity that drew her to him. On his finger, a silver ring bore the falcon sigil of Zephyria, its wings spread wide in conquest.

As they dined, Jorah was the epitome of charm and wit. He spoke eloquently of the future, of an alliance that would bring their kingdoms into a new era of prosperity. But it was not his words that captivated Hadiyah; it was the way he looked at her, as if he had been searching for her for an eternity.

In the months that followed, their courtship was a whirlwind of stolen moments and shared dreams. Jorah was attentive, sharing stories of his travels, painting vivid pictures of distant lands and cultures, igniting in Hadiyah a curiosity and desire for adventure.

During a private walk in the gardens, under a canopy of stars, Jorah took her hand, sliding off his ring and pressing it into her palm. "A promise," he said softly, "of a future together."

"We courted for a year. I...I loved him," Hadiyah continued, eyes downcast. "But my father decided a union with Khahleel of Alzahra was a stronger match. It tore at my heart, but I did my duty."

She paused, her gaze drifting to a portrait of King Khahleel. "And in doing so, I found a truer love with your father. Khahleel showed me a depth of kindness and compassion that I hadn't known with Jorah."

Hadiyah sighed. "All these years, I emphasized the importance of a strategic marriage to you. My hope was to shield you from the heartache I endured with Jorah." Her mother smiled at her sadly.

Layna listened intently, her mind racing with questions. "Do you think Jorah was always this evil? Or did losing you change him?"

Her mother shook her head. "I often wonder about that myself, Layna. Was the man I knew just a façade, or did heartbreak twist him into the man he is today? I don't know. But I do know his proposal now is not about love or even politics. It's about revenge."

Layna took her mother's hand. "Thank you, Mama, for sharing this with me. Understanding the history helps, even if it doesn't change our situation."

Hadiyah nodded, squeezing her daughter's hand. "We must be cautious. Your father's anger is understandable, but we must think strategically. This is a game of chess, not sand rugby."

Layna nodded in agreement. Glancing toward the clock, she realized it was nearly time for her training with Zarian. Rising from her seat, she embraced her mother tightly before excusing herself.

After the council meeting, the day passed in a blur of briefings with security advisers, but nothing had managed to quell Zarian's simmering rage.

In one meeting, he snapped at a junior adviser for a minor oversight in the palace security log, his voice harsher than intended. The young man recoiled, eyes wide, and Zarian had to grit his teeth to refrain from apologizing.

As he walked through the halls, his fingers kept clenching and unclenching into fists, tension visible in the rigid set of his shoulders. Passing servants and guards gave him a wide berth.

Now, as he approached his chambers, the council meeting replayed in his mind, the ridiculous proposal fueling the fire of his anger. The hours had done nothing to lessen his fury, and he knew he needed to release it before it consumed him.

Inside his chambers, he hastily scribbled a coded note for Jamil. The words were brief but urgent.

With the note securely folded, Zarian slipped out and headed to the palace gardens. He strode with purpose to a secluded spot and concealed the note under a large rock, confident Jamil would find it on his nightly rounds.

As Zarian left the gardens, anger swirled unchecked within him. His fury was directed at King Jorah for daring to propose such a humiliating union.

But another part, a part he was reluctant to acknowledge, was directed at Layna for even considering the thought of marrying the old tyrant. The thought of her sacrificing herself, playing the dutiful princess to avert a war, ignited a fierce protectiveness in him. But alongside that protectiveness was a sense of betrayal he didn't fully understand.

She doesn't owe me anything, he reminded himself. *I have no right to her.*

Still seething, Zarian arrived at the training grounds, fists clenched as he watched Layna approach.

"Princess," he greeted tightly. "Shall we begin?"

Layna nodded distractedly, lost in her own thoughts.

As they began sparring, Zarian's movements were intense, his instructions sharp, his usual patience replaced with an acrid urgency. Each parry and thrust were an outlet for his anger and frustration.

Their swords clashed, echoing across the grounds. Zarian was aggressive in his strikes.

He swiftly disarmed Layna, sending her sword flying. Zarian swept her legs out from under her, sending her crashing to the ground before pinning her beneath him, his weight pressing her into the earth.

But unlike the first time, there was no moment of charged tension or lingering gazes. He quickly rose, resuming his stance.

As Layna stood, brushing off the dust, Zarian watched her with piercing intensity. His voice, when he finally spoke, dripped with bitter sarcasm.

"If you plan to rule Zephyria, you might want to improve your technique," he mocked, the corners of his mouth curving into a sardonic smile. "At this rate, you'll hardly impress King Jorah."

The words hung in the air. For a moment, Layna stood in shock, seemingly taken aback by the venom in his voice.

Her eyes narrowed and her shoulders stiffened as if bracing for a blow. She drew a sharp breath.

"Perhaps," she retorted, her voice surprisingly steady, "but, luckily, I have you to teach me." Her chin quivered slightly, and Zarian felt like camel dung scraped off an old, worn boot.

But then the violent tide of his anger rose up once more and pulled him back under. He was powerless against it. His fury crushed the pang of regret that had bloomed in his chest and forced the apology back down his throat.

Layna took a deep, steadying breath and retrieved her sword. As they resumed sparring, she attempted to use the techniques he had taught her, but Zarian gave her no quarter. His defense was impenetrable, his attacks relentless. Twice more, she found herself pinned and released, each time rising with mounting frustration.

"You're supposed to train me, not dominate me!" Layna exclaimed, her temper flaring as she angrily picked herself up off the ground yet again. Furious and clearly done with their lesson, she stormed off toward the gardens, leaving Zarian standing alone.

As she strode away, Zarian watched for a heartbeat and then, against his better judgment, quickly followed her, his restraint no match for his anger.

He jogged slightly to catch up with her furious pace and caught her arm, roughly twirling her around to face him, his eyes alight with icy rage.

"How can you even *consider* marrying King Jorah?" he growled. "You'd be nothing but a puppet, a fucking plaything for him!"

Layna met his gaze fiercely. "I have to do what is necessary for my kingdom," she countered. "It's my duty." She tried to wrench her arm away, but he pulled her closer, fingers digging into her skin, his iron grip unyielding.

"There has to be some limit to duty!" he snapped.

"And what of *your* duty, Zarian?" Layna shot back bitterly. "Aren't you prepared to do whatever it takes to uphold your vows to the Medjai? Why do you even care who I marry?"

In that moment, the last shred of Zarian's self-restraint snapped.

He pulled her into a deep, searing kiss, pouring into it all the words he couldn't say, all the emotions he couldn't express. The kiss was a meeting of passion and desperation, a silent confession of his feelings.

Then, he pulled back abruptly, releasing her arm. "Shit, Layna, I'm sorry, I shouldn't have—"

But Layna cut him off, seizing his face and drawing him back into a kiss that was even deeper. She tangled her hands in his hair, pulling him closer, their lips fused together.

Their kiss deepened, and Zarian gripped her hips, pulling her flush against him. He guided her backward with deliberate steps, lips never parting, until he pressed her against a secluded hedge, hidden from prying eyes.

The force of their kiss escalated with each breath and each touch. Layna's hands raked through Zarian's hair and down his muscled back, holding him close, feeling the raw strength beneath his tunic.

Zarian firmly grasped her chin, angling her mouth as his lips grew more demanding, his free hand tracing patterns along her side. He nipped at her lower lip with his teeth, gently tugging, then soothed it with his tongue. Her hands clutched his shoulders tightly, her chest heaving against his as their lips moved in a fierce, passionate rhythm.

She was the scorching desert heat, burning through his veins.

She was the first sip of cool, clear water after a lifetime of thirst.

She was everything.

Zarian was lost in her kiss, and he never wanted to be found. He wanted to drown in this moment forever, tasting her, feeling her, only her.

Only her.

Moving closer, he pressed his leg firmly between Layna's thighs. The unexpected contact elicited a loud moan from her, a sound that pierced through the haze of his desire.

A sound that brought him back to his senses.

Reluctantly, he broke their kiss, and the pair slowly parted, gasping for breath, foreheads pressed together. Zarian searched Layna's face, seeking answers to questions unasked.

The world around them slowly came back into focus—the buzzing insects, the distant sounds of the palace, and the inescapable weight of their duties.

Zarian gazed at Layna, his eyes tracing the contours of her face with tenderness. Her rosy lips were swollen, her chin and cheeks marked by his rough stubble. He reverently tucked a lock of hair behind her ear, his touch lingering on her skin. Leaning down, he gently pressed another chaste kiss to her lips.

With a deep, resigned sigh, he trailed his thumb across her cheek in an unspoken apology. Layna leaned into his touch, pressing his hand against her warm cheek.

"Where do we go from here, Layna?" he murmured, his voice a soft whisper of hope.

Layna's eyes held his, a storm of emotions swirling within them. Zarian thanked the moon that regret wasn't one of them.

"I don't know," she admitted. "I truly don't know."

CHAPTER FOURTEEN

In a dim, busy tavern in Ezanek, a hub of clinking glasses and murmured conversations, the elder brother sat alone, drumming his fingers on the table. His cloak was drawn up around his face. He inhaled deeply and winced; his nose still had not fully healed.

The tavern was a favorite among locals and travelers alike, its walls adorned with old weapons and shields. The air was thick with the smell of spiced meats and ale, and the hearth cast a warm glow over the worn tables.

He had been waiting for hours, anxiety mounting with each passing moment. Their mission was to gather intelligence on the smuggling of stolen weapons—a matter that threatened the balance of power in the region. His role was dual: to ensure the mission's success and to oversee his younger brother, a task that weighed heavily on him. Tensions between them had been high, even more so than usual.

His younger brother had left earlier to follow a lead. Now, his prolonged absence was a source of concern. Deciding enough time had passed, the elder brother stood and headed to the door, the heavy thud of his boots echoing in the quiet moments between conversations.

Stepping into the cool night air, he headed east in search of his brother. The sounds of the tavern faded behind him, replaced by the quieter, sinister whispers of the city at night.

As he approached an alley, a disturbing noise caught his ear—a muffled struggle, desperate and panicked. Quickening his pace, he turned the corner and was met with a scene that chilled him down to the marrow in his bones.

His brother, who he fought alongside, who he sought to protect, who he loved, was upon a woman, attempting to ruck up her skirts with one hand while stifling her cries with the other.

The elder brother stood frozen for a heartbeat before fury overtook him, a blazing red-hot anger that scorched his veins. Rushing forward, he roughly yanked his brother back, sending him stumbling into the wall. The woman seized the opportunity and fled, her rapid footsteps echoing her terror in the night.

"What the fuck are you doing?!" the elder brother roared, the fury in his voice reverberating through the alley. "Where is your honor?!"

The younger brother, recovering from the initial surprise, straightened slowly.

"Please, brother," he scoffed, brushing off his clothes with exaggerated nonchalance. "Have you not had your fair share of dalliances on these missions? I merely seek some entertainment." He turned and watched the fleeing woman. "A shame. She was a feisty one, too."

The elder brother hauled back and punched him squarely in the mouth, knocking him to the ground.

"I have **never** *taken a woman against her will," he seethed, his words a low growl in his chest as he glared down at his brother.*

The younger man spat out a mouthful of blood, calmly wiping his lip and rising to his feet, unfazed by his brother's rage.

"How else do you expect me to find companionship with the shadow of the future king looming over me?" he snarled. *With a dismissive shrug, he pushed past his elder brother. "I have obtained the intelligence. We can leave,"* he declared, *as if the altercation was just a minor inconvenience.*

The elder brother watched him walk away. The divide between them had never been more apparent, and it was well past the point of repair.

Layna awoke conflicted, memories of the prior night flooding her mind. Their kiss had been perfect—his full lips pressing against hers, the heat of his body, the safety of his embrace. Electricity had crackled through her veins, coursing from her lips to her fingers.

She quickly dressed and joined her family for breakfast. Zarian was notably absent, his empty seat a glaring reminder of the previous evening. Lord Ebrahim and Burhani were also missing, for which Layna was grateful.

King Khahleel and Queen Hadiyah sat quietly at the table. The king periodically cast concerned glances at Layna, while Hadiyah maintained a composed demeanor, her occasional touch on her husband's arm a quiet gesture of support. Despite her father's tirade at the council meeting, it appeared her mother bore no resentment.

The usual morning chatter was replaced by a heavy silence, each member of the royal family lost in their own thoughts.

Layna absentmindedly picked at her food. Soraya observed her sister with concern.

The younger princess said, "These palace walls feel stifling lately. Let's escape for a day, Layna. A ride in the desert might clear our minds."

Layna met Soraya's gaze, appreciation softening her solemn expression, a ghost of a smile touching her lips.

"That sounds wonderful. Some space to breathe would be welcome."

Hadiyah nodded, her eyes shadowed. "It's a wise idea."

King Khahleel looked at his daughters with affection. "Go, Layna. Find some peace. I'll manage the council and address…the matters at hand."

Layna's smile deepened as she looked around the table at her family. "Thank you. A ride through the desert sounds lovely."

As breakfast ended, the sisters planned their outing, their conversation filled with a lightness missing since the royal ball. For a few hours, they could escape the burdens of duty and politics and reconnect with the simplicity of their childhood.

Layna wore a lightweight navy tunic over her trousers, the breathable fabric ideal for the desert heat. At her waist, she fastened her sword. Soraya wore a vibrant orange tunic, as radiant as the fiery desert sun. She, too, strapped her sword to her side. Both sisters wore white turbans, ready to shield their faces from swirling sands.

Layna's white mare, Qamar, stood quietly ready for the journey, awaiting her command, while Soraya's steed, Sirocco, a spirited chestnut stallion, nickered impatiently, eager for the ride ahead.

Mounted on their horses, the sisters shared an excited glance. The air was warm on their skin as they led their horses through the busy streets, past the lively markets, until the city gradually gave way to the quiet outskirts, where the vast expanse of the desert unfolded before them in an endless sandy sea.

At the city's edge, the guards recognized the princesses and offered respectful bows before quickly clearing the way through the checkpoint.

With subtle nudges, they urged their horses into a brisk gallop. The vast desert beckoned, an open canvas where they could shed the weight of royalty and taste the freedom beyond the palace.

Hooves kicked up clouds of sand as the horses effortlessly traversed the dunes. Layna felt a rush of exhilaration as Qamar responded to her cues, the mare's pace quickening. The wind whipped through Layna's hair, and she tilted her face to the sky, savoring the feeling of liberation, even if just for a moment.

Beside her, Soraya and Sirocco matched their pace, the stallion easily keeping up with Layna's mare. Together, they crossed the desert, the endless dunes stretching out around them.

The ride was cathartic. The rhythm of her horse's gallop freed her mind from the tangle of duty and desire. For these precious minutes, she was not a princess torn between love and obligation.

She was simply Layna, riding alongside her sister, embracing the beauty of her homeland.

As the horses slowed to a trot, Layna opened up to Soraya.

"We crossed a line," she revealed, eyes focused on the horizon. "Zarian and I…it's complicated. I feel so drawn to him, but so conflicted. I know I should uphold my responsibilities, but when I'm with him, I don't remember anything else. I feel protected. It's a relief from always having to be strong."

"It's okay to let yourself depend on someone, even as queen," Soraya replied softly.

Layna sighed. "When I was in his arms, I felt precious." Her gaze was distant, lost in the memory of their kiss. "With him, I can let down my guard and be myself. I don't have to be the perfect princess."

She paused, her brown eyes reflecting the desert sun. "But our duties bind us, Soraya. How can I think of my own happiness when Alzahra's future rests on my shoulders? And with a war approaching?"

Soraya reached between their horses, taking Layna's hand in a comforting grip. "Maybe it's not about choosing between love and duty, but finding a way to balance both."

Their conversation continued as they came upon a small oasis, a hidden gem amidst the dunes. It was a special place, one they often escaped to in their younger years. Modest in size, the oasis was a pocket of lush greenery, a secret haven that held many of their childhood memories.

The oasis was ringed by a small cluster of palm trees, their fronds whispering in the desert breeze. At its heart lay a tranquil pool, crystal clear, reflecting the azure sky above. Purple and yellow wildflowers dotted the greenery.

They dismounted, tying their horses to a tree, and stretched their legs.

"I know it's been difficult, but I'm glad you've opened your heart again. After Nizam, I worried you might close yourself off completely," Soraya said gently, looping her arm through her sister's.

Layna exhaled slowly, eyes lingering on the horizon. "It wasn't intentional. I tried to keep him at a distance, yet somehow, he found a way into my heart. Now, I can't picture my life without him."

Soraya smiled sympathetically. "Sometimes, the heart knows better than our minds. You can't control who you fall for." Then, the younger princess hesitated and gave Layna a sheepish smile. "Actually, I wasn't entirely forthcoming about our picnic today."

A few paces away, stepping into the clearing was Almeer.

Almeer's features weren't striking at first glance, but the more Layna looked at him, the more she saw his appeal. He stood slightly taller than her, with dark brown hair falling to his shoulders in loose waves. He was a slim man, the straight lines of his body accentuated by his typical Alzahran attire—a simple tunic and loose-fitting trousers. His skin was tanned, and his gray eyes, though darting nervously, held a genuine warmth.

Layna watched him closely as he hesitantly approached, his hands fidgeting at his sides.

"Your Majesty," Almeer greeted. He reached out to shake her hand, then switched mid-motion and bowed deeply instead.

"It's a pleasure to meet you, Almeer," Layna welcomed with a wide smile. "Soraya speaks of you often. But please, call me Layna."

They sat down, the soft breeze carrying the scent of desert wind around them. The picnic was simple—delicate sandwiches with roasted meats and crisp vegetables, along with savory pastries filled with spiced cheese and spinach. For dessert, there were buttery shortbread cookies dusted with sugar and a selection of ripe fruits, including dates, figs, and mirsham fruit.

Soraya led the conversation with her usual playful energy, teasing both Layna and Almeer about their various quirks—Layna's competitiveness and Almeer's picky eating—drawing laughter and groans in equal measure. In turn, Layna and Almeer joined forces, poking fun at Soraya's own peculiarities.

Once Almeer seemed more comfortable, Layna donned the mantle of protective sister and asked about his family in Zephyria.

"I have a younger brother named Bashir. He's quite the opposite of me—more adventurous and less inclined toward diplomacy," Almeer shared with a chuckle. "We're close, though. He has a knack for finding trouble, but his heart is always in the right place."

Layna smiled and continued with her questions. "What was the diplomatic mission that brought you to Alzahra?"

"My delegation came to meet with Lord Farhan, the minister of trade, to discuss new routes. But as tensions between Zephyria and Alzahra escalated, our talks became strained, and eventually, there was nothing left to discuss." Almeer paused, a pensive expression on his face. "My companions returned home, but I chose to extend my stay a bit longer." He and Soraya shared a soft smile.

"It must be quite difficult to leave my sister," Layna teased. "Where have you been staying?"

"At a small inn near the palace," Almeer explained. "It's modest but comfortable. And so far, the city guards have respected my diplomatic status, but I'm not sure how much longer that will last."

Layna nodded thoughtfully. "And how did you and Soraya first meet?"

Almeer looked at Soraya. His eyes shone brightly with what could only be love. "It was in the palace gardens. Soraya was there, a vision of dedication among her plants. She's incredible." Soraya flushed at his praise.

As Layna observed them, a much-belated realization dawned upon her. Had Soraya always felt overlooked living in the shadow of a crown princess? Was that why she shied away from formal events where the spotlight was always, inevitably, shining on Layna?

Soraya had always been there for her, always understanding, never voicing any resentment at being eclipsed by Layna's role as future queen. She had consistently been Layna's pillar, offering unwavering support without a hint of envy.

But here, with Almeer, Soraya shone brightly, a rare gem, her own unique qualities appreciated and cherished.

"Eventually, I must return to Zephyria," Almeer added, disappointment marring his features. "But I find myself delaying the journey. There's something about Alzahra that makes it hard to leave." He looked at Soraya with an affectionate smile.

Layna could clearly see the happiness radiating from her sister.

Here was a love that defied odds and expectations. A glimmer of hope bloomed in her chest, a thought that perhaps there *was* a way for her to balance the desires of her heart with the duties of her crown.

After enjoying their picnic, Layna and Soraya bid farewell to Almeer and rode back to the city. Nearing the busy city center, they decided to take a detour through the vibrant markets.

Stalls lined the streets, each one overflowing with goods ranging from exotic spices to handcrafted jewelry. The air was filled with the rich aromas of street food and the lively chatter of vendors and shoppers.

One section of the market was particularly renowned—the textile quarter. Here, the stalls were draped with fabrics, hallmarks of Alzahran craftsmanship. Silks shimmered in the fading sunlight, velvets in deep, luxurious colors piled high next to stacks of finely woven linens, their textures begging to be touched.

As they wandered, Soraya purchased a delicate scarf, its fabric light as air, dyed in shades of deep blue and sparkling silver reminiscent of Almeer's homeland.

Layna, meanwhile, was captivated by a collection of colorful bandanas. One called out to her—it was a deep teal which she thought would complement Zarian's hazel eyes. On a whim, she bought it.

The elderly shopkeeper was honored to have the princesses in her stall and initially refused their payment. Still, they pressed the coins into her wrinkled hands, leaving her with a grateful heart and a story to tell.

As they returned to the palace, the sisters basked in the warmth of the setting sun, hearts content with the simple pleasures of the day and the comfort of each other's support.

As the first light of dawn crept through his curtains, Prince Zarian lay awake, the memory of his kiss with Layna vivid in his mind.

He chose to skip breakfast. Facing Layna in front of her family, with the memory of their kiss so fresh, seemed an impossible task. He feared his eyes would betray him, and his years of training to master his emotions would crumble under the weight of a single glance from her.

He'd rather face a pit of venomous cobras. Again.

His day was spent in a state of distraction, overseeing palace guards and holding meetings with security advisers, yet his thoughts constantly wandered back to Layna. For all he knew, he might have assigned every guard to the same post.

As the sun set, painting the sky in shades of orange and purple, the thought of finally seeing Layna at their training session quickened his pulse.

Their situation was complex, but he could no longer deny his feelings. Whatever challenges lay ahead, his heart was firmly intertwined with hers. In her arms, Zarian felt a completeness he had never known.

He refused now to live without it.

But first, he had to meet with Jamil for a brief update. Changing into his training attire, Zarian set out, eager to conclude the meeting quickly so he could see Layna.

After returning to the palace, Layna expressed her gratitude to Soraya for the wonderful day. The respite had been much needed.

With a lighter heart, she quickly dressed for her training session, securely tucking the teal bandana into her vest.

Heart thrumming with hope, she headed to the training grounds with a newfound optimism, eager to share Soraya and Almeer's story with Zarian. Their love had kindled a flame of hope within her.

Maybe, just maybe, she and Zarian could carve out a path forward together.

However, she was disappointed to find the training grounds empty. Frowning, she scanned the area expecting to see him walking toward her. After several minutes of waiting, she grew concerned—he had never been late.

She headed to the nearby gardens in search of him, a labyrinth of beauty and tranquility. It seemed the perfect place to find a quiet moment with him and present her gift. *Maybe he'll kiss me again*, she thought wistfully.

Moonlight bathed the gardens in a soft glow, casting fleeting shadows across the stone pathways as Layna traversed the winding paths. It was a humid night, strange for the season, and the air felt heavy on her skin.

She passed the rose trellises, hoping to glimpse Zarian's familiar silhouette among the vines. Finding no sign of him, she continued her search, heart quickening with anticipation.

She paused by a fountain, the gentle splash of water offering a moment of peace, but not the man she sought.

Layna walked through the flowers a while longer until hushed voices from a secluded arbor caught her attention.

Frowning, she moved closer, recognizing one of the voices as Zarian's. Concerned, she crept forward with the light, silent steps he had taught her and concealed herself behind a hedge. Her heart pounded as she strained to hear their conversation.

Zarian was speaking with a cloaked figure, their conversation laced with urgency. "The prophecy, Zarian! You must remember your purpose here." The man jabbed a finger into Zarian's chest. "Your involvement with the princess is dangerous. It clouds your judgment! It compromises the mission."

Layna's breath caught. The prophecy? Her mind raced with questions. Who was this shadowed man with Zarian?

Zarian responded in a hushed whisper, too low for Layna to hear.

"That doesn't matter! Remember your training. The princess is the key. You were brought here to protect the Daughter of the Moon, not ravish her! You're jeopardizing everything!" The cloaked man took a deep breath. "It's good she trusts you, but maintain your distance. I must return to the Oasis—Saahil never made it back on his last trip. I'll return when I can."

A chill ran down Layna's spine as she listened to the hushed conversation. The revelation struck her like a tempest—*she* was the subject of this mysterious prophecy?

Confusion and doubt swirled within her, mingling with a growing sense of betrayal. Why had Zarian never mentioned this? Who was this cloaked man? She had just begun to lower the walls around her heart, but now felt exposed and deceived.

Crouched in the shadows, disbelief, anger, and a clawing betrayal warred within her. She tried to piece together fragments of past conversations, whispers of a prophecy she had never understood.

But nothing had prepared her for this revelation.

Were the moments they shared—the intimate conversations, their passionate kiss, the quiet understanding—real, or just a part of his duty to some mission?

She had opened herself up to Zarian, shared her deepest hopes, believing in their genuine connection. Had he been manipulating her emotions for some prophetic agenda this entire time? Layna grappled with her feelings, torn between the man she thought she knew and the one ensnared in secret plots.

She quietly retreated from her hiding spot and trudged back to the training grounds. Flinging herself onto the dusty floor, she cradled her head in her hands, struggling to keep her tears at bay. How could she reconcile the man she felt so strongly for with the one shrouded in secretive discussions about her fate? How could he have held her, kissed her so intimately, while harboring such deep secrets?

To him, was she merely a mission?

A blistering anger began to burn inside her. She had been a fool to entertain the possibility of a future with him. The realization struck her with bitter clarity—she did not truly know who Zarian was.

Minutes later, Zarian arrived at the training grounds, his steps hurried. He saw Layna, her huddled figure silhouetted against the moonlight.

"Layna, what is it?" he asked, his voice laced with concern as he drew closer.

She lifted her head, revealing the storm brewing in her eyes. The silence stretched between them like a chasm. Then, in a hoarse whisper, she said, "I heard your conversation in the garden."

The words hung in the air, heavy with unspoken accusations. The blood drained from Zarian's face.

"Layna, please, let me explain," he implored, stepping closer.

"I don't want to hear any more of your lies!" Layna snapped, her temper boiling over as she shot to her feet. "Was that your spy? The prophecy, the secrets, your duty…you're a liar, Zarian. You pretended to care just to get close to me!"

Zarian's pale face was a canvas of pain—remorse, despair, and an unexpected vulnerability.

"Layna, please," he begged, his voice raw, barriers stripped away. "Yes, I came here because of the prophecy, to protect you, the 'Daughter of the Moon.' But I didn't know how deeply you would affect me. My feelings for you are real, Layna, as real as anything I've ever felt."

His words hung in the air between them, but she only gave him her silence.

"Layna, I never expected any of this to happen." He inched closer, his hand outstretched as if approaching a wild, untamed mare.

"Expected what?" she raged, eyes blazing with fury. "To play with my heart while you hide behind your duty? How can I trust anything you say?"

"I understand why you're upset," Zarian pleaded, taking another step toward her. "But I swear on my honor, I care deeply for you. I would never betray you, Layna. Please, you must believe me." He reached out, hoping to bridge the gap between them.

Layna recoiled. "Believe you? Never again. You're just another prince with hidden agendas. Stay away from me!" She spun on her heel, leaving Zarian standing alone.

Returning to the palace, she rushed through the corridors. Her mind was a whirlwind of betrayal, confusion, and the painful sting of yet another wound to her heart. Her sister, she knew, would understand.

She found Soraya in her chambers. Soraya looked up, immediately noticing the agony etched on her sister's face.

"Layna, what happened?"

Soraya's voice broke through the tsunami of Layna's thoughts, but the words felt distant, muffled by the overwhelming tide of emotions within her. Layna's legs gave way, and she collapsed, a sob escaping her lips. The dam of composure she had so carefully constructed over the years burst.

Soraya was by her side in an instant, wrapping her arms around her sister. Layna clung to her as she sobbed uncontrollably, tears cascading down her cheeks. Soraya held her tightly, whispering words of comfort, her presence a steady anchor amidst Layna's despair.

Gradually, the sobs subsided, replaced by a hollow emptiness. As Layna's tears dried, Soraya gently helped her stand, leading her to the bed. There, she sat with Layna, a silent guardian in the quiet aftermath of her sister's heartache.

"I overheard a conversation," Layna began hoarsely. "Zarian and a stranger, talking about a prophecy—'The Daughter of the Moon.'

They think *I'm* at the center of it, and that's the real reason he's here. I'm his mission. He's been lying to me this entire time."

"That sounds ominous. But Zarian—he doesn't strike me as someone with bad intentions," Soraya reasoned.

Layna took a deep breath, her emotions still raw. "I confronted him," she confessed. "I accused him of betrayal, of using me. I said very harsh things."

"I understand why you reacted that way, especially after Nizam. But Zarian has always seemed genuine. Maybe there's more to this than we know."

"How can I be sure?" Layna shook her head, frustration clear in her face. "He pretended to care about me to benefit himself."

Soraya gently squeezed her sister's hand. "I think you should focus on the prophecy first. That'll help you understand your role in all this, and perhaps, also about Zarian's purpose here."

"But how can I ever trust him again?" Layna questioned, wiping away an errant tear.

"Take small steps." Soraya gently squeezed her sister's shoulder. "Learn about the prophecy, understand its implications, and maybe it'll help you understand Zarian and his motivations."

Layna pondered her sister's words, the storm inside slowly settling into a cautious resolve.

"You're right. I need to know why they think I'm this 'Daughter of the Moon.'"

Soraya nodded, her expression serious. "And I'll be here, every step of the way. We'll figure this out together."

"Lord Ebrahim once mentioned Medjai texts in the library," Layna mused, her brow furrowing. "But I've never seen them. Have you?"

"No." Soraya shook her head. "And I practically live there."

The sisters exchanged a look. They knew what needed to be done.

"We should search the library," Layna decided, a new determination lighting her eyes.

"Tomorrow," Soraya added gently. "Tonight, we rest."

Layna reluctantly agreed. As they talked into the night, she felt a sense of clarity emerging from the chaos of her thoughts.

She might not have all the answers, but she had a direction.

CHAPTER FIFTEEN

The elder brother stepped into his father's study. The walls were lined with shelves filled with ancient scrolls and books. A large desk dominated the room, cluttered with maps and parchments. The air was thick with the scent of incense. Sunlight filtered through the high windows, casting a warm glow over the plush carpets.

He approached his father cautiously. "Father," he began, his voice heavy with worry, "I have concerns about my brother. His heart—it has become hard. I want to help him, but I don't know how."

His father looked up with a resigned expression. He sighed deeply, the weight of his crown evident in the lines of his face. "I am not surprised. The boy killed his mother, after all."

"Father, please," the elder brother implored. "It was a tragedy, but you cannot blame him. Women often die in childbirth."

His father's face contorted with anger as he rose from his seat. "I will hear no more!" he thundered, his voice echoing off the stone walls. "You dare defend him? After he robbed us of her light? His birth was a curse upon this family."

The elder brother recoiled at his father's fury, the rebuke cutting deeper than any blade. The gap between them, cleaved by grief and blame, seemed insurmountable.

Silently, he turned away from his father, the king's harsh words still echoing in his ears. He felt a profound sadness, not just for the loss of his mother, but for the chasm between him, his brother, and their father.

The elder son walked out, his steps measured and heavy, the door closing behind him with a final click.

He sank bonelessly against the cool, stone wall as grief made its home in his heart.

In the seclusion of his quarters, Zarian stood by the window, his silhouette framed against Alzahra's starlit sky, a kingdom now as familiar as the lines on his palm.

The night was still, but his mind was anything but.

His role here had been clear—to protect Princess Layna and ensure the prophecy came to pass, and if needed, protect the balance by any means necessary. His gut twisted painfully as he recalled his father's parting words.

Neutralize her.

The first time he saw Layna, she was a vision of strength and beauty on the training grounds, her sword furiously swiping through the air. Her spirit had captivated him, a flame that burned bright and fierce.

There was a resilience in her beyond physical strength. Her attitude was a blend of defiance and self-protection, a shield she wielded as deftly as her sword. Zarian had been amused, and yet, enraptured by her. He sensed that behind her tough exterior, she was safeguarding her heart, perhaps from past hurts or the heavy expectations placed upon her as crown princess.

Zarian sat on the edge of his bed. It was large and stately, befitting a guest of his rank, with a solid wood frame. The bedspread was rich with hues of deep blues and golds. But the room, for all its comforts and elegance, was a gilded cage, confining him with his own abrasive thoughts.

He sat with his head cradled in his hands. Layna—with her guarded heart and her fierce independence—captivated him.

She was no longer his mission.

Layna was the woman who owned his soul.

She had swept away the grief and pain that had taken root inside him and claimed his heart as her home. He longed to tell her how deeply he felt for her, how her every laugh healed something he hadn't known was broken.

But she would refuse to believe him, and he couldn't blame her. Could he ever bridge the chasm his duty had created?

Regret suffocated him.

Their dance at the royal ball was a turning point. As they moved together, the moonlight seemed to cast a spell over Layna. Her movements were graceful and fluid, and in her eyes, Zarian was lost. The rest of the world faded away, leaving only the two of them in their moonlit sanctuary. He had felt a profound connection, a pull toward her that eclipsed his duty.

Training with her had only deepened his feelings. Recalling the moment he pinned her beneath him, he couldn't escape the intensity that had surged through him.

He didn't want to.

The physical closeness had ignited a fire within him, a smoldering heat that he struggled to keep at bay.

With each session, he grappled with his growing feelings. When he was close to her, guiding her movements, feeling the warmth of her skin, he was acutely aware of the line he was treading. It was a dance of restraint and desire, one as dangerous as their sparring.

Despite her dedication to her own duty, he knew that she, too, craved his presence and touch. He had struggled to conceal his smiles when she would deliberately falter stances that had given her no difficulty earlier.

Then, there was their kiss, the moment his discipline had faltered under the weight of his desire. That kiss had unraveled him, laying bare the depth of his feelings.

Sleep had eluded him as he replayed that moment over and over in his mind, frustration and longing and *want* churning within him like a raging sandstorm.

Again and again, his mind came back to his father's warning about "neutralizing" Layna if she lost control. It haunted him. The thought of harming her was unbearable. Impossible. Unfathomable.

He'd let the world burn first.

Before meeting Layna, Zarian had merely gone through the motions of life, fulfilling what was expected of him, blindly carrying out what was commanded of him. But now, his heart yearned for something more, a different path—one he could walk alongside her.

But Layna's trust was broken. Her words echoed in his mind, a reminder of the pain his secrets had caused.

How could he protect her when she saw him as an enemy? He had lost both her trust and respect.

It was a bitter draught to swallow.

Zarian let out a deep sigh. The path ahead was rife with uncertainty, but his resolve was clear. He would protect Layna, and perhaps, in time, find a way to mend the trust that had been broken.

In the quiet of the night, with the moon as his witness, Zarian made a silent vow.

He would stand as the shield against any storm that threatened Layna. For her, he would walk through fire.

To hell with the balance.

CHAPTER SIXTEEN

Late at night, while the palace slept, Princesses Layna and Soraya crept down dimly lit corridors to the palace library. The high ceiling loomed ominously in the darkness, shadows dancing in the moonlight streaming through the large windows. The familiar, musty scent of old books permeated the air.

With only a lantern to light their way, they navigated through the towering shelves, eyes scanning for any clue about the Medjai or the prophecy.

As they ventured further, past shelves containing histories of kingdoms and volumes of ancient poetry, into the seldom-visited depths of the library, Soraya noticed a peculiar outline on the floor near the back wall, concealed beneath a thick rug. Exchanging a knowing glance, the sisters rolled the rug aside, uncovering a trapdoor.

Together, they hefted the heavy door, its hinges protesting loudly in the stillness of the library. A narrow staircase spiraled downward, beckoning them into the shadows.

Hand in hand, the princesses descended into the darkness.

At the bottom was a large hidden room, a sanctum of forgotten knowledge. Rows upon rows of dusty books and scrolls lay in wait, their secrets untouched. The sisters pushed forward, determined to find answers.

As they explored the shelves, Layna's eyes were drawn to a section where a symbol similar to Zarian's tattoo was inscribed on several aged spines.

"Soraya!" she called, her voice echoing in the chamber. "Come, look at these!"

There were manuscripts, bound in leather and adorned with intricate symbols, along with several old, yellowing scrolls.

They sat at a nearby table and poured over the writings. Layna felt the pieces of her past slotting into place—the overheard conversation from her childhood, whispers of a prophecy, and now, her current predicament with Zarian.

One scroll contained a detailed sketch of what appeared to be an orb, its surface shimmering with white filigree. An ominous sensation washed over Layna as she examined it, a chill running down her spine and a sense of foreboding that clung to her heart like a shadow. Though it was warm in the hidden chamber, her skin erupted in goosebumps. With shaking fingers, she rolled up the scroll and placed it aside.

Another text, frayed at the edges, caught her attention. She carefully unfurled it, revealing a script that seemed to dance in the lantern light. The text was written in an ancient dialect, but Layna, well-versed in the old tongues, began to read aloud:

"When darkness seeks to engulf the lands,
The Daughter will rise amidst the sands.
With heart, pure, and courage blinding bright,
She shall wield the ancient, moonlit light.
In her wake, attacking shadows will flee,
Only, then, will the realm be safe and free.
Beneath the night of shadow's embrace,
The eclipse will reveal her true face.
In this hour, the heart's choice shall bear its weight,
Deciding the course of future and fate.
In her hands, the power to mend or maul,
Her will must be steady, lest darkness enthrall.
For if the Daughter's control slips from hand,
She will wreak havoc across the sands.
Should she be blinded by her bright light,
Daughter, fear the earthly moon's hidden might."

As Layna recited the ancient words of the prophecy, they seemed to wrap around her like a cloak woven from the threads of time itself.

The words burrowed their way into her very soul.

Soraya gazed thoughtfully at the worn script. She turned to Layna, her sister's pale face illuminated by the soft light.

"It's strange," Soraya mused, her voice a gentle murmur in the quiet chamber. "This was written long before our time, but it's about *you.*" The younger princess paused. "Your nightmares…it all makes sense now."

Layna nodded silently, her eyes still fixed on the faded parchment.

Soraya continued, "You've always faced your responsibilities with such grace and strength. But this prophecy," she paused, searching for the right words, "it's like a path set out for you, one that's been waiting since the stars first aligned." She placed a reassuring hand on Layna's shoulder. "I've seen you grow, confront challenges, and make difficult choices for Alzahra. But no matter what the prophecy holds or what destiny demands, you are not alone."

Layna covered her sister's hand with her own, her mind abuzz with the implications. This wasn't just a tale from the past; it was a living, breathing part of her reality.

But was she really the Daughter of the Moon? What did the prophecy mean? What would happen to her during the eclipse?

As the sisters continued to read, they found references to the Medjai, described as guardians of balance and protectors of sacred knowledge. Soraya peered over her sister's shoulder.

"Zarian must know more about this. You should talk to him."

Layna considered her sister's words. Despite her warring emotions—anger, mistrust, and betrayal—she knew that she needed to unravel the tangled threads of the prophecy.

And for that, Zarian was the key.

Taking a deep, steadying breath, Layna wrapped her sister in a tight embrace before ascending the stairs and leaving the library.

Determined, she navigated the silent, shadowed hallways. Despite the late hour, Layna instinctively knew the prince would still be awake—their last conversation must haunt him the way it did her.

The council chambers were deserted. She received no response when she knocked on the door to his guest quarters, and the training grounds were empty.

Layna hurried along the palace corridors, heading to the rooftop terrace where he sometimes meditated. Her heart pounded with a mix of nerves and resolve. She reached the narrow, spiraling staircase, her footsteps echoing on the ancient stone as she climbed.

Pushing open the heavy door, she emerged onto the large terrace. The full moon cast its silvery light across the space, highlighting two stately pillars that stood like guardians. Beyond them, the city unfolded—a mosaic of rooftops and streets that faded into the vast desert stretching to the horizon.

At the terrace's edge, near one of the pillars, Zarian stood alone, his silhouette stark against the starlit sky. He was staring at the moon, lost in thought. He turned as she approached, his eyes widening in surprise.

The tension between them was thick, the air charged with unspoken words. Layna took a deep breath and stepped closer.

"Prince Zarian," she began, eyes fixed just above his shoulder. "I owe you an apology. I reacted harshly and with anger. A princess must always be composed, and I was not." Her words were stilted, coated in a cutting formality.

"Layna, I'm deeply sorry you learned about the prophecy that way. I waited too long to tell you." He tried to meet her gaze, willing her to see the truth in his eyes, but Layna refused to look at him. She walked past and slowly sat on the ground.

As she looked up at the moon, Zarian came to sit beside her.

Layna took a deep breath and squared her shoulders. "Soraya and I found texts about the prophecy and the Medjai. Tell me why you're here and my role in all of this," she pleaded, hating the vulnerability in her voice. "Just tell me the truth."

Zarian looked into her eyes, his own swirling with regret, affection, and perhaps, a sliver of hope.

In a quiet whisper, he said, "The prophecy warns of an era marked by turmoil—a time when the very fabric of our kingdoms will be tested. The Daughter of the Moon is the key."

Layna felt a chill run down her spine. "And you're saying that... *I* am this Daughter? How do you know for sure?"

"Your birth coincided with a rare celestial alignment, deeply connected to the lunar cycle. This event was prophesized to mark the arrival of the Daughter of the Moon. It happens only once in centuries."

Layna shook her head. "That could just be a coincidence."

Zarian leaned closer. "Tell me, Layna, do you not feel an intrinsic connection to the moon? Has it not been a source of peace and strength for you? Does it not call to you through your dreams?"

Layna absorbed his words in disbelief, realization washing over her in a frigid wave.

She had never told him about her nightmares.

"The eclipse," she said. "When is it supposed to occur? What will happen to me?"

Zarian sighed and shook his head. "The elders believe it will occur soon. But the texts don't specify exactly what will happen, only that it's the final event in the prophecy's fulfillment. They think you'll receive powers of some kind, but I don't know for sure."

Layna felt a haunting chill settle into her bones. She gazed at the moon, steadfast in the sky, its pale light casting a glow over them.

After a moment of silence, Layna turned back to Zarian. "We found a sketch, some type of orb. I felt…strange when I saw it. Do you know about it?"

A flicker of recognition crossed Zarian's features. "Yes. The Orb of Al'Qamzain. Medjai legends say it emerged from the sacred springs of the Oasis under the darkness of an eclipse, imbued with powers from the moon itself. It was hidden by the first generation of Medjai to protect it from those who would misuse its power."

Zarian hesitated before adding, "Our intelligence suggests someone is trying to locate the orb. More alarmingly, it might already be in the wrong hands." He drew in a slow, deliberate breath. "The orb has significant power over the Daughter of the Moon. Whoever possesses it likely has ill intentions toward you."

Layna's expression clouded with worry, the crease between her brows deepening. "Does my father know about the prophecy?" she finally asked.

"Yes," Zarian nodded. "Years ago, an envoy from the Medjai came to Alzahra. He shared our belief that you fit the criteria." He paused, closing his eyes and tightly pinching the bridge of his nose. "I only learned of this months ago, before I was tasked with coming here. The elders had kept your identity a closely guarded secret before then."

Layna's eyes widened, a memory flickering to life. "That's what Soraya and I overheard about the Medjai and a prophecy when we were children. We were eavesdropping from behind a tapestry in Baba's office."

"Your father has known of your destiny for years," Zarian explained. "I imagine it's why he's insisted on rigorous training. He wanted you to be prepared, even if the full scope of the prophecy was unclear."

Layna absorbed this new piece of her history. Her father had been preparing her for this role her entire life, without her ever realizing the true reason.

Another question occurred to her. "Why are there ancient Medjai texts here in Alzahra? Shouldn't they be safeguarded in the Oasis?"

"The first generation of Medjai were guardians not only of the Oasis, but of sacred knowledge as well," he replied, his fingers tracing idle patterns on the cool terrace floor. "They believed it was too risky to keep all their ancient texts and artifacts in one place. The danger of such treasures being discovered and misused was too great. So, they spread the artifacts and texts about prophecies across the realm. They aren't just within Alzahra, but hidden in many different locations."

"*Prophecies?*" Layna asked incredulously. "There's more than one?"

Zarian forced a strained smile and said, "Yes, there are several prophecies—and supposedly a handsome Medjai guarding each one." Layna remained stone-faced, and his smile slowly faded. He sighed, glancing away. "Truthfully, even I don't know how many prophecies there are. The Medjai cherish their secrets, even from their own."

"And what is your role in all of this? Are you even a prince?" she questioned, tightly hugging her knees to her chest.

Zarian straightened. "Yes. My lineage as a prince and my role as a Medjai are deeply intertwined. My father is also a Medjai. He instilled in me the understanding that our royal duty extends beyond the throne—it's a commitment to the balance."

Layna was silent, processing the new information Zarian had revealed.

Shifting his eyes to his lap, Zarian took a deep, steadying breath. His face contorted, as if it pained him to utter his next words.

"Layna, there's one thing your father doesn't know. The elders fear the unknown. We don't know what will happen during the eclipse, but if you threaten the balance in any way…I'm supposed to stop you. By any means necessary."

Layna gasped sharply, her eyes widening as his confession stole the breath from her lungs. The blood drained from her face, and she recoiled from him as if he had slapped her, her body instinctively putting distance between them.

"But know this," he continued quickly, "I would *never* harm you. No matter what happens. No matter what power you wield. No matter how you wield it. My feelings for you are *real* and true."

The princess studied him warily. "And what exactly is it that you feel for me?"

Zarian held her gaze, intense and unyielding. "Every moment with you, Layna, I have to remind myself to breathe," he confessed, his heart in his words. "You are the answer to a prayer I must have made in my dreams. I've tried to suppress how I felt for months, but at the royal ball…watching you with the other princes, the jealousy that ran rampant through me made it impossible to keep lying to myself. I wanted you and only you. I still do."

He continued, his voice hoarse, "Before I met you, I was content with my path. Not happy, but content. I've questioned *everything* since meeting you." He took a shaky breath, hazel eyes glistening in the moonlight, willing her to see the sincerity in his heart. "Layna, you are the most incredible person I've ever met. It torments me night and day that I wounded you so deeply. Please, give me a chance to earn back your trust."

Layna was silent, her eyes brimming with unshed tears. She blinked, and one escaped, tracing a wet path down her cheek. Zarian's hand wavered, as if he wanted to reach out and wipe it away, but he clenched it into a fist and kept it at his side.

"I…I need time to understand all this. To understand my role, the prophecy, and…what you and I are to each other."

Zarian nodded. "I'll be here when you're ready."

CHAPTER SEVENTEEN

The relentless sun beat down on the sprawling training grounds as the eldest brother engaged in a grueling regimen of combat exercises. He was tall, his muscles well-defined from years of rigorous training, and he moved with precision and power. Stubble darkened his jaw, lending him a handsome ruggedness that drew many admiring eyes. Again and again he struck the training dummy, the determined thud of his fists the only sound in the heavy silence.

His concentration was broken by the hurried approach of his closest friend, his boyishly handsome face red with exertion. Frantic gestures accompanied a torrent of words, each one a hammer blow to the elder brother's heart.

Without hesitation, he sprinted, dread slithering in his veins and winding around his heart, sweat dripping down his back. Bursting into his father's chambers, he confronted him, his voice raw with emotion.

"Father, what have you done?"

His father, seated behind a massive desk, regarded him with a calm, resigned gaze. "I did what I had to," he replied simply, steepling his hands. "No longer is he a stain on our order."

Anguish and disbelief warred within the elder brother. "It wasn't his fault! You failed him as a father," *he jabbed an accusing finger,* "and I—I also failed him." *Without waiting for a response, he stormed out of the chamber.*

Returning to his room, he found utter chaos. His belongings were scattered, curtains torn, furniture overturned, drawers emptied haphazardly.

But it was the sight above his bed that halted him in his tracks, a sight so horrendous it froze the very air in his lungs.

There, nailed by the ear to the wall, was the head of Sultan, his beloved dog. Its lifeless eyes stared back at him in accusation, as dark blood dripped onto his pillow.

He collapsed to his knees, a silent scream of horror welling up inside him.

Nestled within the verdant Nahrysba Oasis, the throne room was a marvel of ancient craftsmanship. Carved from the heartstone of the Oasis itself, the walls told tales of the Medjai ancestors, shimmering under the caress of sunlight that danced through the lattice windows.

The room was suffused with the delicate scent of jasmine and myrrh, mingling with the cool hint of the Oasis's waters, carried in by the gentle breeze. At the room's heart stood the throne, a masterpiece forged from desert ironwood.

King Tahriq sat immersed in discussion with his council. "Is there any news on the location of the orb?" he questioned, gazing down at his council. "Or about the Medjai that have gone missing?"

"No, Your Majesty. We are still awaiting news." His senior adviser spoke with urgency. "But recent reports from our scouts bring troubling news. The unrest in the regions bordering Alzahra grows more pronounced." He hesitated, his hands fidgeting at his sides. "I know we have waited to gauge the situation, but we've found evidence suggesting that...your younger son is actively involved."

King Tahriq's expression darkened. The adviser paused, carefully measuring his words. "Also, there has been a disturbing discovery—Saahil's body was found at the edge of the Oasis. His throat was slit, similar to the Thessani librarians. We have no proof, but..." the adviser trailed off.

The room grew colder with each word, the implications settling over the room like a shroud.

Tahriq's knuckles turned white as he gripped the armrests of his throne.

"You were right. We should have acted sooner," he admitted, his voice quiet. "I never should have let him live. To think that he would go to such lengths." The king sighed deeply, his shoulders tensing as he struggled to contain his mounting rage.

Another adviser interjected hesitantly, "Your Majesty, perhaps the time has come to inform Prince Zarian. His brother will inevitably head to Alzahra. He must be prepared for what may come."

King Tahriq's countenance darkened at the suggestion, his mind casting back to a day long past, etched in the chambers of his heart with shame and regret. He remembered Zarian's outburst, the raw pain when he learned of his brother's banishment. The memory of his steadfast son's voice cracking under the weight of betrayal haunted him.

"No," Tahriq said firmly, the command slicing through the air. "Do not inform him." Reopening old wounds would ignite a fire that could consume what little peace remained in his son's heart. "Instead, send three of our most trusted men to Zephyria. End this."

It had taken ages for Zarian to recover from the loss of his brother, and he was never the same. A new, fierce anger had taken root inside him, always simmering just beneath the surface. Tahriq couldn't bear to inflict any more pain on him.

Another adviser knocked on the heavy door before entering quickly. "Sire, Jamil has returned." Tahriq waved him in.

Jamil approached and bowed deeply. "Your Majesty," he began. "As you know, Ezanek and Valtisaan have aligned with Zephyria. Their combined forces now significantly surpass Alzahra's army. And to make matters worse, King Jorah proposed marriage to Princess Layna. King Khahleel was furious and sent troops to their border in response. It appears war is imminent."

King Tahriq's concern deepened. Turning to his advisers, he asked, "How many men can we send to Alzahra?"

"After considering those on active missions, perhaps a little over 10,000," the adviser responded after a moment of calculation. "The rest are too scattered across the continent to return in time."

"Then send the orders. We must do what we can," Tahriq commanded. He watched his advisers depart.

As the room began to clear, Tahriq's gaze fell upon Jamil, who also stood to leave.

"No, Jamil, you remain," the king ordered.

The others filed out, leaving only Jamil standing before the king.

King Tahriq considered his next words carefully. "Tell me of Zarian," he began, his voice quieter. "Do you foresee any obstacles in his path?"

The silence that followed was thick, the very air awaiting Jamil's response. Tahriq's gaze, sharp and penetrating, fixed on the younger man, expecting a straightforward answer. The moment of hesitation spoke volumes, a silence that whispered of secrets.

Tahriq's patience snapped.

"Jamil!" Tahriq's voice was a sharp crack, echoing off the walls. "Remember where your loyalty lies. The Medjai and your oath come first—not your friendship with my son. Speak plainly."

Chastened, Jamil met the king's angry gaze. "Your Majesty," he said, this time with a clear sense of resolve, "Zarian has developed feelings for Princess Layna. He will protect her, perhaps die for her—but I fear he prioritizes her safety over the balance. If she becomes a threat, I worry he won't be able to neutralize her."

Tahriq listened, his expression unreadable.

Love, a perilous distraction, often spelled death for a Medjai.

"Keep a close watch," the king finally said, his voice low. "And remind Zarian of his first duty—to our order. To the balance."

"Yes, Your Majesty," Jamil said, bowing deeply.

He stood to exit the chambers when Tahriq spoke again, "Jamil. Speak of this to no one." The young Medjai nodded in understanding and excused himself.

Tahriq remained seated. He sighed deeply, pinching the bridge of his nose.

Tahriq trudged through the palace corridors, his heavy footsteps echoing off the stone walls. His shoulders sagged under the weight of his crown, tension knotting his muscles.

He reached a pair of imposing double doors, emblazoned with the emblem of the Medjai, a crescent moon cradled within a blazing sun. With a nod, the two guards swung the doors open, revealing the sacred chamber of the elders.

The chamber was sparse, with towering ceilings and high windows framing a stone floor. Flickering torches lined the walls, casting a warm, dancing light. One wall was etched with the names of all the elders since the first generation of Medjai, the earliest inscriptions faded by time's hand.

The elders served until death, after which the remaining members would select a replacement. The current elders were a blend of middle-aged and old men, their names still crisp upon on the wall: *Zanjeel, Hilder, Munta, Zarqi, Kussaam, Jameer,* and the youngest elder at only fifty years old, *Bowrain.*

In the center of the room, an enormous fire blazed, illuminating the weathered faces of the seven elders seated at a long table at the back. Tahriq stepped forward, bowing respectfully.

"I have come to give my report."

The head elder, Zanjeel, an old man with a long, silver beard and eyes sharp like a hawk, waved him forward. "Proceed, Tahriq. We are eager to hear your account."

Tahriq detailed the latest developments about Zephyria's mobilization, the search for the orb, and the missing Medjai.

When he finished, Zanjeel leaned forward. "And what of Zarian? Does he still think his mission is to *protect* the princess?" the elder scoffed, his demeanor dripping with disapproval.

A flicker of hesitation crossed Tahriq's face, but he quickly masked it. "Zarian will do what is needed when the time comes," he said smoothly, meeting their gazes with unwavering conviction. "He is dedicated and has proven himself time and time again. He is a good man."

"A *good man* does not make a good leader. You have sheltered him too much," Zanjeel rebuked sharply. The fire crackled loudly in the center, sparks flying in every direction. "We have disagreed with your decisions regarding *both* your sons over the years. Our goodwill is limited. Do not test us further."

Tahriq clenched his fists at the reprimand but remained silent.

Another elder, Hilder, interjected, "I've said this before, but this business with the Daughter of the Moon has dragged far too long. We should have taken care of this decades ago, the way your great-grandfather handled the Sun Slayer." He looked dismissively at Tahriq, disdain etched on his face.

"The Sun Slayer was an unknown peasant girl, not the *crown princess* of a powerful kingdom!" Tahriq defended, his voice rising in the stark chamber. "This matter is different. We need Alzahra's support. And with her powers manifesting so late, there's a good chance she won't survive the eclipse at all."

"Still—" Hilder began.

"The kingdoms work with us *for now*," Tahriq interrupted, his features grim. "They will no longer do so if we begin assassinating their heirs."

"Tahriq is right," said Zanjeel, placing a hand on Hilder's shoulder. Turning back to the king, he continued, "Keep us informed."

Tahriq nodded and turned to leave. As he approached the massive doors, Zanjeel's voice rang out once more. "Oh, and Tahriq!" he called. "Keep a vigilant eye on Zarian."

Tahriq hovered by the door. He nodded, his knuckles white.

CHAPTER EIGHTEEN

Under the cool expanse of a starlit sky, the elder brother tread quietly across the sandy training grounds. He had just returned from chaos-stricken Valtisaan, and his steps carried the weight of his weariness. The soft murmur of sand beneath his boots accompanied him as he sought out his younger sibling.

He found him sitting against a low wall sharpening his dagger, the rhythmic sounds of metal scraping against stone filling the night air.

"Brother," he called softly. The sharpening stopped abruptly. There was a lengthy pause, the silence stretching so long he feared there would be no response at all.

Then, finally, his younger brother spoke without sparing him a glance, "Returned from your latest mission, have you?"

The elder brother exhaled slowly, the tension in his broad shoulders visible even in the dim light.

"You'll be going on your first mission soon enough," he said, fists clenching and unclenching at his sides. "But I wanted to talk to you about something else."

The younger brother rose with a theatrical groan and faced his brother, defiance oozing from his every pore.

The elder brother's eyes were serious as he spoke, "I've completed recon in Valtisaan. After the removal of the king—"

"You mean assassination," the younger brother interjected sharply.

Undeterred, the elder brother pressed on. "Valtisaan needs support now, someone to ensure the kingdom remains stable through the transition. You could serve on their council." He paused, considering his next words carefully. "I could talk to Father—"

"You wish to send me away?" his brother cut him off again, his voice heated. The accusation hung heavy between them, the night air thick with unspoken grievances.

The elder brother sighed deeply. "Just hear me out," he tried again, "this is a chance for you to step out of my shadow. A chance to hold a position of power and truly make a difference. Is that not what you desire?"

The younger brother's eyes glinted with rage. "You know nothing of what I desire," he spat. "I don't need your pity or your handouts. I will carve my own path. Without your help." His words dripped with acrid bitterness as he began to walk away.

He brushed past, and the elder brother caught his arm. "Wait—"

The younger brother whirled around, his fist connecting sharply with his brother's face. The sound of bone crunching under impact shattered the night's calm. The elder brother staggered backward, hand flying to his nose as blood poured between his fingers.

A brief flash of remorse flickered in the younger brother's eyes, quickly replaced by steely resolve as he turned and strode off into the desert night.

Azhar stood before the mirror in his dimly lit chambers, his reflection a dark silhouette against flickering candlelight. His mind spiraled with the latest news from his spies. Zarian, the epitome of Medjai discipline, and the crown princess grew ever closer, a connection he could only view through the lens of bitter envy.

A cold smile played on Azhar's lips. His estranged brother, always the paragon of virtue, was captivated by the Daughter of the Moon.

How ironic.

It was a chink in Zarian's armor, one Azhar was keen to exploit.

The idea that his brother might find happiness and love, luxuries that had always eluded him, gnawed relentlessly at his heart.

It was time to put his plan in motion. He dressed meticulously for the operation, layers of dark, reinforced fabric hugged his muscular frame, while leather bracers shielded his corded forearms.

At the stables, his tempestuous black steed, who Azhar had not bothered to name, awaited. Powerful and restless, it paced the confined space, hooves stamping the ground with loud thuds. Muscles rippled beneath its glossy coat, nostrils flared wide, exhaling sharp snorts that cut through the air.

Riding through Zephyria's mountainous terrain, his thoughts were consumed with vengeance. Ever since learning of his brother's feelings for the Daughter of the Moon, Azhar had been haunted by a dark obsession. The idea of claiming the princess, the jewel of Alzahra wrested from his brother's grasp, became a fixation that fanned the flames of his resolve.

His mind wandered back to his last covert visit to Alzahra, where a glimpse of the crown princess on her balcony had captured his attention. Hidden in the shadows, he observed her, her long brown hair cascading down her back. The sight of her glowing skin, practically shimmering in the soft moonlight, had given life to a new hunger within him, a desire to *take*.

He imagined countless scenarios, each designed to break his brother's spirit. Perhaps he'd brutally ravage the princess while forcing his bound brother to watch. Or maybe he would torture her, covering her creamy skin in thousands of small, shallow cuts before plunging his knife into her heart, all while his brother witnessed the cruelty, unable to stop him.

Azhar's thoughts grew increasingly twisted as the hours passed during his journey. Jagged mountains gave way to rocky terrain, and then the vast expanse of the desert was upon him. He deftly guided his steed through the ever-changing landscape, the horse's hooves kicking up clouds of sand as they progressed.

Finally, Azhar reached the Zephyrian camp at the border. From a distance, he observed the restless soldiers, their constant pacing and anxious glances betraying their impatience after weeks of idle waiting.

The encampment sprawled with tents and makeshift structures. Soldiers gathered around fires, sharpening weapons and discussing strategies in hushed tones. Azhar rode through the camp with quiet authority, his presence commanding attention. He dismounted, leaving his horse with a foot soldier.

The men gave him a wide berth, conversations halting as he passed. Known for his volatile rage, even the bravest soldiers hesitated to engage him.

His reputation was not unfounded; just two weeks prior, Azhar noticed a young soldier struggling to light a fire. Without a word, Azhar had taken the flint, striking it with efficiency. The sparks caught quickly, igniting into a roaring blaze. Before the soldier could express his gratitude, Azhar viciously grabbed his arm and held it within the flames.

The smell of burning flesh, disgustingly potent, permeated the air. The soldier's screams of pain echoed through the camp. No one dared intervene. Eventually, Azhar released him, his arm a smoldering mess of melted flesh.

"If you cannot master a simple fire, you are of no use on the battlefield," he snarled, flinging the man to the ground, ignoring his pitiful sobs.

Azhar moved toward the edge of the camp. As the fires flickered behind him, casting long shadows across the desert floor, he blended into the darkness.

Tonight, his actions would set the course for the impending war, a declaration that would reverberate through the halls of Alzahra.

Azhar, a silent desert shadow, slipped across the border. He easily located his target, the tent of the top general, the information from his source precise.

Inside, the general was alone. It was an oversight that would cost him dearly.

Azhar approached silently from behind, a wraith in the dim light, and with a swift, deep slash, slit the general's throat. The body crumpled to the ground with a muffled thud, blood pooling rapidly.

Azhar knelt next to the body and continued his work. Brutal, efficient, and devoid of emotion. He moved quickly, completing the gruesome task with a chilling detachment.

Afterward, the desert shadow returned unseen to the Zephyrian camp, his silhouette a dark blur against the starlit desert. The head general greeted him. Wordlessly, Azhar thrust a heavy black bag into his chest.

Glancing inside, the general sucked in a sharp gasp, wide eyes darting to Azhar's stoic face. He quickly regained his composure and assured, "I will ensure this reaches the palace. You need not concern yourself further. I have prepared the finest tent for your rest tonight. Is there anything else you need, sire?"

Azhar's expression darkened, a sinister edge creeping into his voice. "Yes. Bring a woman to my tent," he commanded, his tone leaving no room for questions. "Fair-skinned with long brown hair. Make sure she's there within the hour."

The head general bowed deeply. "As you wish, sire." He turned sharply on his heel and hurried away, the bag leaving a trail of dark droplets on the ground behind him.

The next morning, Azhar remounted his horse, his mind consumed with thoughts of Alzahra's princess. The woman from the night before was nothing more than a mere diversion, a pale substitute for the true object of his obsession. The cool morning air did nothing to quell his twisted desire.

Upon his return to the castle, King Jorah summoned Azhar to his chambers. The king's chest swelled, and his eyes gleamed with approval.

"You have served me well, my son. I could not have hoped for a better heir," Jorah declared, his voice laden with a warmth reserved only for his adopted son. "Your actions propel us closer to victory. Our gift has already been dispatched to the princess."

"Father," Azhar began, sensing an opportunity. "Let me go to Alzahra alone. I'll take the orb and return with the princess. You need not expose yourself to unnecessary danger."

The king regarded his adopted son with a calculating gaze. "Your zeal is commendable. But this task requires control and precision," Jorah finally said, his posture stiff. "We will go together. Under your protection, no harm shall befall me. The orb's power is immense, and it requires a firm hand to wield it—my hand. If all goes to plan, I will use it to control her. Besides, there is a reckoning I have long awaited."

Azhar stared at Jorah, silent and still, a muscle feathering in his cheek.

"But make no mistake, your role is crucial," Jorah added quickly. "Your courage and resolve have not gone unnoticed. Upon our success, whatever your heart desires will be yours."

Azhar's expression remained unwavering. "I desire the princess," he asserted, his voice a low rumble. "For myself."

Jorah's brow furrowed. "Azhar, my son—*I* need the princess to harness her power once the prophecy is fulfilled," he explained. He paused for a moment, his mind racing. "But after I destroy Alzahra and control the continent, then—then you shall have her."

The promise was a hollow one, and they both knew it. Yet, it was a bargain struck in the shadows of ambition and vengeance. Though Jorah loved Azhar like a son, *this* was the one concession he could not make.

"You've done well. But now, you must rest. The war will escalate from here," Jorah continued. "We must stand ready, my son. Ready to deploy every shred of our cunning, every ounce of our strength. I need you at your peak."

Azhar met Jorah's gaze with cold, hazel eyes. "I understand," he responded. "I will be ready."

Jorah departed, leaving Azhar to the silence of his chambers. He contemplated how the war would progress. Alzahra would undoubtedly retaliate, and the war would officially begin.

Yet, in the depths of his cold heart, the thought of Layna, a prize to be claimed, provided a twisted sense of anticipation.

CHAPTER NINETEEN

In the heart of the Alzahran desert, Layna stood under a starry sky, the full moon casting its glow across the sands. She watched as a creeping shadow slowly engulfed the moon, turning the sky a deep, blood-red. The desert came alive around her, sands morphing into the shadowy forms of warriors and beasts. Encircled by this ominous spectacle, Layna's heart pounded with fear, her escape blocked by the encroaching figures.

Amidst the chaos, a voice whispered, "Rise, Daughter! Rise!" The spectral warriors and beasts bowed down before her.

As the moon emerged from the shadow, bathed in a new, radiant light, Layna felt an immense power surge through her. Raising her arms, the desert sands obeyed her command, swirling violently around her.

The earth beneath her trembled, resonating with her newfound might, until a large chasm split open beneath her bare feet. Layna plummeted into the gaping divide, enveloped in an all-consuming darkness, her sight swallowed by the abyss.

The princess jolted awake with a strangled gasp, her heart hammering a painful rhythm against her ribcage. The dream had never extended that far before.

She rushed to the washroom, splashing cold water on her face, trying to erase the lingering terror. Layna stared into the mirror, droplets trickling down her pale face, her mind replaying her dream's terrifying new development.

As the first light of dawn broke over the horizon, painting the sky in shades of orange and pink, Layna returned to her room. A steely resolve settled over her. She needed answers, and she knew exactly where to start.

Layna found her father in his private office in the west wing. The spacious study, its walls lined with towering bookshelves, centered around a large mahogany desk cluttered with parchments and inkwells. Oil lamps ensconced within the walls cast a warm glow over the room.

A grand tapestry depicted a battle where mythical creatures and warriors clashed under a pitch-black sky. Emerald and sapphire dragons soared above, their scales shimmering in the moonlight, while below, the armored warriors fought their enemies with glinting swords.

Near the tapestry, an arched window offered a view of Alzahra City, sunlight casting shadows on the polished stone floor. A few potted plants, a personal touch from Soraya, added a bit of greenery to the otherwise austere room.

King Khahleel sat behind his desk, his shoulders slumped.

"Baba," Layna called as she entered.

Khahleel looked up but did not seem surprised to see her. He sighed deeply and cradled his head in his hands.

"Layna," he said softly, "I spoke with Zarian. I'm sorry I didn't tell you." His eyes glistened with unshed tears.

Layna nodded, her heart heavy. With slow steps, she came to sit across from him.

"Why did you keep this from me?" she asked quietly.

He looked away, shame coloring his features. "When the Medjai first came with their prophecy, I couldn't bring myself to accept it. Even after they showed me the ancient texts, I thought they were just religious fanatics." He took a breath, steeling himself. "I remember hearing you and Soraya giggling behind the tapestry. My mischievous, carefree girls. The thought of you shouldering such an immense burden was unthinkable."

Layna's eyes widened, and a faint smile touched her lips. "You knew we were there?"

Her father's eyes softened. "Yes, I always knew. You two were never as sneaky as you thought. Hearing your laughter, so full of innocence and joy, made it even harder to accept that one day you would face such a heavy destiny."

"But then your nightmares began, and I knew the prophecy must be true. I tried to prepare you, to strengthen you, but a part of me still hoped it was just a tale." Khahleel paused and met Layna's eyes. "That hope shattered when the Medjai returned months ago, saying the time was imminent. They promised to send someone to protect you. I agreed, believing it was the best path forward."

"And they sent Zarian," she said flatly.

"Yes, they sent Zarian," Khahleel repeated, observing her closely. "He is one of their best. And their prince. I trust him. He has been honorable thus far."

Layna remained silent, conflicting emotions fighting for dominance in her eyes. The truth of Zarian's betrayal lingered on the tip of her tongue, but she couldn't bring herself to voice the words.

"Thank you, Baba," she finally said quietly. Rising to her feet, she left the office, resolved in her quest to uncover more answers.

Behind her, Khahleel buried his face in his hands, his shoulders shaking with sorrow.

Next, she sought out her mother. She found Queen Hadiyah in the palace gardens. When Hadiyah saw her daughter, she pulled her into a comforting embrace. Layna allowed herself a moment of vulnerability and sobbed quietly, tears soaking the sleeve of her mother's gown.

"You were born for greatness, my child," Hadiyah whispered. "Whatever destiny awaits, know that I am here."

Hadiyah led her to a bench. Layna rested her head in her mother's lap while Hadiyah gently stroked her hair.

"When your father first told me of the prophecy, I wanted to deny it, to shield you from such a fate. But deep down, I knew it was true."

She paused, her gaze distant as she recalled a memory. "It was a summer night, much like this one. I was watching you play in the gardens after dusk. There was torchlight, of course, but it was quite dark. The shadows were long, and it is easy for a child's imagination to run wild. A stray dog wandered into the gardens. It must have seemed monstrous to your young eyes."

"You were terrified, Layna. Before I could comfort you, you took off running, your little feet barely touching the ground. The dog ran after you, and I quickly followed. But then, you reached a moonlit clearing, just over there." Hadiyah pointed at a nearby spot, lost in her memory. "Your transformation was instantaneous. Under the light of the moon, your fear evaporated. You stopped running and faced the animal. There was no panic in your eyes, only calm resolve. You stood your ground, and the dog stopped and eventually wandered away."

Hadiyah's eyes met Layna's again, her expression one of awe. "It was as if the moon's light had given you courage far beyond your tender years. I knew then that you were special, destined for greatness beyond even a queen's reign."

"Layna, I have witnessed your growth, your resilience, and your spirit. You will be remarkable, my daughter. You *are* remarkable."

Layna listened, her mother's words sinking in. "Thank you, Mama," she said softly, kissing her cheek. "Your faith gives me strength."

Her next destination was clear in her mind, the final piece in her quest for answers. With a deep breath, Layna stood and left the palace gardens.

Her steps were purposeful as Layna sought out Lord Ebrahim. She found him in his office. Without preamble, she scraped back a chair and faced the man she considered her second father.

"Lord Ebrahim, tell me about the Nahrysba Oasis. How did the Medjai come to live there?" she demanded.

The adviser fixed his gaze on the princess for what seemed like minutes.

"Certainly, Layna," he finally replied, his eyes sharp behind his spectacles. "The Nahrysba Oasis has a rich history, steeped in lore. Legends tell of a wandering tribe, lost and desperate, led to a sacred spring by a divine sign."

"As the tribe flourished, they became guardians of the Oasis. Over generations, this guardianship transformed into a sacred duty. The community that emerged was deeply connected to both the land and the energies that pulsed beneath it. The springs of Nahrysba are said to be blessed, abundant with unusually pure and healing water—a manifestation of this sacred connection."

"As the community grew, they became known for their wisdom and strength. They were fierce protectors of their land. From these early inhabitants arose the Medjai, a noble order of warriors. The early generation of the Medjai recorded their knowledge in scrolls that were passed down through generations."

The senior adviser paused and gave Layna a knowing look. "Based on your questions tonight, I suspect you have finally found the texts about the prophecy." The princess confirmed his assumption with a small nod.

Layna gathered her thoughts. "In the texts we found, there was mention of an eclipse. But nothing detailed what exactly will happen. Do you know?"

Ebrahim sighed deeply. "The truth is, we do not know. The prophecy speaks in metaphors, leaving much to interpretation. Unfortunately, the specifics elude us still." His expression softened. "I understand how frustrating this must be for you, especially now, when clarity seems most crucial. But as for what will happen during the eclipse, we are all, in a sense, in the dark."

Layna was quiet for several heartbeats, worrying her lip between her teeth.

"You should have told me," she finally said.

"I am so sorry, Layna," he whispered, eyes filled with regret. "I wanted to, I truly did. I mentioned it to your father several times, but in the end, I heeded his command."

Layna sighed and placed her hand over his. "Thank you." She inhaled deeply, closing her eyes for a beat. Her heart battled against her mind. She opened her eyes and hesitantly asked, "I...I also wanted to know more about the Oasis's current resources." She sucked in a sharp breath. "Would an alliance with the Nahrysba Oasis benefit Alzahra?"

Ebrahim looked at her knowingly, a sad smile curling his lips.

"The Oasis is already allied with Alzahra through the Medjai. King Tahriq would gladly provide us with whatever aid he could. A formal alliance would not bring additional military or economic power to Alzahra."

Layna's gaze dropped to her lap.

"But, Princess," he added gently, "a formal alliance would not *harm* Alzahra's position either."

Layna met his gaze, but before she could respond, the door burst open. A junior adviser rushed into the room.

"My Lord, Your Majesty," he exclaimed, his voice strained with panic, "there is urgent news—Zephyria has...there has been an incident!"

Lord Ebrahim and Layna stood quickly.

"Gather the council immediately," Ebrahim commanded.

In the council chamber, a heavy silence hung in the air, each member bracing for news that could change the course of Alzahra's history.

"We have been attacked." Lord Varin's voice angrily resonated through the chamber. "A covert force from Zephyria infiltrated our eastern borders and committed an act of unspeakable brutality against General Idhaan, our top general at the eastern front."

The blood drained from Layna's face.

Lord Varin paused, allowing the council to absorb his words. "We received word this morning that Idhaan's body was found in his tent...without his head."

Shocked gasps echoed through the council chamber.

Lady Mirah, her face a mask of horror, interjected, "What evidence do we have of Zephyria's involvement?"

Before Lord Varin could respond, the junior adviser, still visibly shaken, stepped forward.

"My Lady, we received a parcel from Zephyria. Addressed to Princess Layna." He swallowed hard, struggling to maintain his composure. "Inside was General Idhaan's head. It was accompanied by a note, declaring it a 'wedding gift' for the princess."

Another collective gasp rang out as a flurry of revulsion swept over the council. Layna's hand flew to her mouth, her eyes wide with horror. Her heart pounded wildly against her chest as she struggled to keep her tears at bay.

The grotesque message left the council in stunned silence.

Lord Varin, his face contorted with anger, slammed his fist onto the table. "This is a declaration of war! We have no choice. We cannot—we *will* not hold off any longer!"

Layna felt a cold shiver travel down her spine as the terror of Zephyria's message embedded itself deep within her. The gruesome delivery of General Idhaan's head, a man she respected and cared for, left her feeling nauseated.

King Khahleel's expression was grim as he commanded, "Prepare our forces. The time for diplomacy has passed. Zephyria will answer for this heinous crime."

"What about his family?" Layna asked quietly, turning to her father. Khahleel rested an affectionate hand on her head.

"I will see to it that they are cared for," he promised. "His wife and daughters will want for nothing."

The council members murmured their agreement. Lord Varin clenched his jaw tightly.

Zarian glanced at Layna with concern before settling his gaze on Lord Varin. "Were there signs of struggle in any other tent besides General Idhaan's?"

"No," Lord Varin said, eyes shifting from Khahleel to Zarian. "There were no other disturbances reported."

"And this tent," Zarian pressed, "did it have any distinctive markings? Anything indicating it belonged to the top general?"

Varin hesitated before responding. "Er, no. All our tents are identical. There was nothing to indicate its importance. Perhaps Zephyria's assassins scouted the camp first and gathered intelligence. I'll instruct the men to conduct nightly sweeps going forward."

The room fell into silence as Zarian's questions highlighted the peculiar precision of the attack.

Zarian turned to King Khahleel. "We must also fortify our defenses, especially here at the palace. If Zephyria's operatives were bold enough to strike at a military general, they might target the royal family next."

"As always, your advice is sound, Zarian. Ensure the palace defenses are strengthened. We cannot afford any vulnerabilities."

Zarian nodded. "I will coordinate with the guards."

Lord Varin's eyes were hard as he spoke again. "We'll plan the strike meticulously. Zephyria will learn that treachery comes with a high price."

The king gave a solemn nod. "Proceed with caution, Lord Varin. We must act swiftly but wisely. Alzahra's security is paramount."

CHAPTER TWENTY

In his father's office, the elder brother sat alone, the hollow chamber lit only by the moon's scattered rays. His shoulders were drawn tight, head cradled in his hands. His beard had grown out, framing a haggard face marked with dark circles and gaunt cheeks. A perpetual headache throbbed behind his eyes.

The door creaked open, and his father entered with heavy footsteps, lighting a lantern. He turned and gasped, seeing his son in his chair.

"My son. I did not know you had returned." With slow, cautious steps, the king sat across from him, as if afraid of startling a skittish animal.

The elder brother remained motionless, a statue paralyzed by grief.

"How did your mission in Sendouk fare?" his father asked softly.

Again, there was no response, the oppressive silence bearing down on them.

He tried again, "My son, please. You've not been yourself since your broth—"

"The Gundaari," his son interrupted abruptly without looking up. "Why do we work with them?"

"I—what?" his father asked, eyebrows furrowed in confusion.

"The Gundaari," the elder son bit out through clenched teeth. He finally looked up at his father, disgust and anger swirling in his bloodshot eyes. *"They use children in their dealings. Why do we work with them? We should have eliminated them ages ago."*

"It is complicated," his father sighed. *"Our order demands much from us. Oftentimes, we must do things we dislike for the greater good. Yes, the Gundaari are vile criminals, but they have unique access to information. We use that information to protect the balance on a larger scale. It helps us save countless lives. But worry not. Their time will eventually come."*

"How do you live with yourself?" The son's face morphed into a sneer, disdain dripping from his every pore.

"It is my burden to bear," his father answered sharply, eyes narrowed. *"And, one day, it will be yours. I may be the king, but even I must answer to the elders."*

He was met with silence.

The father tempered his tone slightly and added, "I see you've been frequenting the taverns again. I can smell the ale on you. It's unfit for the future—"

His son shot to his feet, swaying slightly before furiously sweeping his arm across the desk. Papers, ink pots, and quills flew through the air, scattering like leaves in a violent storm. Ink spilled from fallen pots, and a large black stain spread across the intricately-patterned rug.

His father sat motionless. Grief-stricken eyes followed his son as he stumbled to the door and left without a backward glance.

In the wake of Zephyria's harrowing attack and the gruesome "gift" sent to Layna, a blanket of worry descended over the palace.

The shift resonated deeply with the princess. Each day unfolded in the same dreary pattern: she would awaken from restless sleep marred by nightmares, dress in silence, sit through council meetings focused on war strategies—her gaze carefully avoiding Zarian's—and flit about the palace like a ghost.

Her relationship with the Medjai prince had returned to being strained and formal. Still grappling with feelings of betrayal, Layna maintained a stubborn distance. Their training sessions, too, had halted while Zarian focused on preparing the guards and fortifying the palace's security.

The prince had approached Layna several times, apologizing and attempting to mend the chasm between them. Each time, he was met with harsh words and a sharp rebuff. On his third attempt, Layna had drawn her sword. He took the hint and ceased his efforts after that.

She clung to her anger like armor, squashing any softer emotions that surfaced. Layna reminded herself daily of his lies, using them as a shield to guard her heart.

Late one afternoon, Layna lounged on Soraya's bed, a deep furrow creasing her forehead. Soraya sat cross-legged on the floor, agricultural drafts and greenhouse designs strewn haphazardly around her.

"I think you should talk to him," Soraya ventured, engrossed in her work.

Layna exhaled sharply. "Did you miss the part where I said he came here to *kill* me?"

"Yes, that was bad," Soraya admitted, looking up at her sister. "But that was before he knew you! He would never harm you now." Soraya raised an eyebrow. "And why haven't you told Baba about that? He would've executed Zarian by now."

Layna's silence was telling.

"You still want to be with him," Soraya guessed. "And you're struggling to keep ignoring him."

"He lied to me," Layna replied lamely, crossing her arms.

"So did Baba and Mama," Soraya countered. "For *years*. It seems you're holding him to a different standard."

"It's not the same," Layna retorted. "They were trying to protect me—"

"So was Zarian," Soraya cut in gently.

"*No*, he was protecting the prophecy! He's been lying since he came here and pretended to care about—" Layna broke off, her breaths shallow as she avoided her sister's knowing gaze.

Soraya moved to sit beside her on the bed, her expression one of understanding as she grasped her sister's hand.

"Layna, I know you're hurt, but I think some of your anger might be mingling with older wounds. At least speak with him?"

Suspicion clouded Layna's features. "Did he put you up to this?"

"No. But he's not himself either. It's absolutely killing me that my two favorite people in this palace are so miserable. He's devastated about hurting you, Layna. He's really fallen for you. And a handsome man like Zarian…" Soraya trailed off. "He could have his pick of the women on this entire continent. Burhani certainly doesn't hide her interest in him. Do you want to see him with *her*? And those scribes who loiter around the grounds while he's training the guards—surely you've noticed? And—"

"You've made your point," Layna snapped, irritation flashing in her eyes. "I wonder if all those women would still want him if they knew he was a lying, murderous Medjai."

Soraya sighed and returned to her greenhouse designs.

CHAPTER TWENTY-ONE

"We have successfully executed a strike against Zephyria's forward base," King Khahleel announced. "The operation disrupted their supply lines and inflicted significant damage."

"Our scouts report confusion in their ranks," Lord Varin added. "It's a temporary setback, but we must press our advantage."

"What measures are we taking to prepare for their counterattack?" Layna asked.

"We're sending more soldiers to the border and deploying additional scouts," Lord Varin replied.

Zarian stood next. "The Oasis is mobilizing a force of 10,000 men. They will join the Alzahran army." A murmur of approval swept through the chamber.

"It's quite noble of your kingdom to assist us, Prince Zarian," Burhani said loudly. "Especially with no formal alliance between Alzahra and the Oasis." Layna tensed at the thinly veiled jibe.

Zarian thanked Burhani and shifted the discussion toward palace security, a matter that had become alarmingly pertinent. The prince had been working closely with the palace guards to fortify the palace.

"We've enhanced surveillance around the perimeter and installed hidden sentries at strategic points," Zarian explained. "We've also conducted drills to prepare for a siege. My goal is to ensure the guards are prepared for any scenario."

Layna listened, reluctantly impressed by Zarian's thoroughness, but troubled by the necessity of such measures.

As the meeting adjourned, her father placed a reassuring hand on her shoulder. "You're doing well, Layna," he murmured with a soft smile.

Later that evening, Layna was studying various maps in her chambers when the door suddenly swung open. Soraya burst in, tears streaming down her face.

"Soraya, what happened?" Layna exclaimed, moving to console her sister.

Through loud sobs, Soraya's words came out in a rush. "The palace guards...they've arrested Almeer! They think he's a spy, Layna! The minister of trade found it strange that he stayed behind after the trade talks halted. They've thrown him into the dungeon! He's been there since morning!" As Soraya finished, fresh tears began flowing anew in a torrent of distress.

Layna's eyes widened before she quickly composed herself. She pulled Soraya into a protective embrace, gently rubbing her back.

"Don't worry," Layna consoled. "I'll handle this. Stay in your chambers. I'll return as soon as I can."

With a reassuring squeeze to Soraya's shoulder, Layna left her room. She needed to act quickly and discreetly.

The fate of an innocent man and her sister's happiness depended on it.

In the quiet of his quarters, Zarian sat alone. His mind methodically revisited the new safety measures around the palace.

Then, as it often did, his mind wandered to Layna. His chest ached as he thought of her. She could barely stand to look at him, let alone speak to him.

A sharp rapping on his door jolted him out of his thoughts. His body tensed as his head snapped toward the sound, eyes narrowed in suspicion.

He opened the door slowly. His eyes widened in surprise.

It was Layna.

"May I come in?" she whispered urgently.

Zarian stepped aside, quickly scanning the corridor before quietly closing the door behind her.

Inside, Layna anxiously paced the room, wringing her hands together. "May I sit?" she finally asked, gesturing toward his bed.

"Of course," he replied, watching her closely as she sat down. She had not spoken to him in weeks. What brought her to his chambers at this late hour?

As she settled onto his bed, Zarian lost control of his thoughts. He should have thrown himself at her feet, begging once more for her forgiveness, but the sight of her here, in his private space, was intoxicating, igniting something primal within him.

He yearned to bridge the gap between them, to lay her back gently on his bed and express his feelings in a way words never could. He imagined capturing her lips with his, feeling the softness of her body pressed against his own, losing themselves in a moment of passion.

But his daydream was abruptly cut short as Layna cleared her throat, tethering him back to reality. Guilt washed over him for letting his mind wander, especially when she was so clearly distressed.

"What happened?" he asked.

"It's Soraya," Layna said, her voice strained. "She's in a secret relationship with someone—a Zephyrian diplomat. The palace guards suspect him of being a spy and arrested him this morning."

"I see," Zarian said slowly. "That's quite the predicament."

"I can't intervene directly," she continued. "It would cause a scandal, perhaps political uproar. Jorah may even retaliate against Almeer's family. I didn't know who else to turn to."

"I'm glad you came to me," Zarian said gently. He cautiously added, "Do you think Almeer might actually be a spy?"

"The thought crossed my mind. But after meeting him…I don't think so. He seems genuinely in love with Soraya."

Zarian considered her words. "Let me think about how to handle this. We can't compromise the palace's security or cause unnecessary panic."

Layna nodded, a tentative smile gracing her lips. "Thank you, Zarian."

In the dead of night, Zarian slipped silently through the palace corridors toward the dungeon. He wore a dark, close-fitting tunic and trousers, blending seamlessly with the shadows.

A few corridors away, he carefully positioned a small sack filled with marbles. Hidden in an alcove, he waited for the right moment, then tossed a stone to knock over the sack. The marbles scattered loudly across the stone floor, rolling in every direction.

The guards, startled by the sudden clatter, left their posts to investigate the commotion.

Zarian seized the opportunity.

He found a disheveled and weary Almeer in a dimly lit cell. The young nobleman looked up in surprise as Zarian approached.

"Don't panic. I'm a friend of Soraya's," Zarian whispered, observing Almeer's tense shoulders and fearful gaze.

Almeer's eyes widened, a spark of hope flickering within them. Zarian quickly set to work on the lock, his skilled fingers manipulating the pins with a long needle. With a soft click, the lock yielded, and the cell door swung open.

Quietly, they crept out of the dungeon, Zarian leading Almeer through a labyrinth of corridors. They eventually reached a side entrance that emerged into a secluded part of the gardens, where the darkness of night offered cover.

Zarian spotted Jamil, Layna, and Soraya waiting in the shadows, anxiety and apprehension written on their faces. As Zarian and Almeer approached, Soraya rushed forward and embraced Almeer tightly.

With stiff shoulders, Zarian took measured steps toward Jamil. His friend's boyishly handsome face was a picture of fury—brows drawn together tightly, lips pressed into a thin, hard line, jaw firmly clenched. His arms were crossed over his chest, and his narrowed eyes fixed a cold, penetrating glare on Zarian.

Layna watched the two Medjai from a distance. Jamil stood stiffly. His angrily whispered words carried an edge of accusation, a tension that clashed with Zarian's calm demeanor. He repeatedly jabbed a finger into Zarian's chest, growing more forceful with each word.

Zarian met Jamil's anger with a measured calmness. He reached out slowly, placing a hand on his friend's shoulder. Jamil paused, his expression softening slightly, and after a deep breath, he gave a reluctant nod.

Turning away from Jamil with one final word, Zarian approached Layna.

"We don't have much time before the guards change shifts. Jamil will escort Almeer to the Oasis," he told her, his voice low and deep in the night. "The Medjai will protect him and ensure he isn't a spy. It's the safest place for him right now, far from both Alzahra and Zephyria."

Layna nodded, her eyes on Soraya and Almeer, who stood, hands entwined, sharing a sorrowful goodbye.

Zarian followed her gaze. "After the war, maybe they'll be reunited."

Layna turned to Zarian, her hands finding his. He looked down at their joined hands. Layna couldn't quite decipher the emotion that passed through his eyes, but it looked something like disbelief.

He squeezed her hands gently, as though needing the touch to convince himself she was truly there.

"Thank you," Layna said. "I know this wasn't easy for you, choosing between your duty and helping me. I'm eternally grateful, more than I can express."

Zarian's eyes darkened as he looked down at her.

"I no longer feel conflicted, Layna," he confessed, his deep voice washing over her. "I am yours." He glanced at Soraya and Almeer, then back at Layna, his eyes filled with meaning. "The rest is for you to decide, Princess."

Before Layna could respond, Zarian signaled to Jamil, a subtle nod indicating it was time for them to head out.

Layna walked Soraya back to her chambers. After tucking her in, she nestled beside her sister in the large bed. With gentle, soothing motions, she rubbed Soraya's back, whispering words of comfort until soft sniffles melted into the steady breaths of sleep.

Yet, sleep refused to claim Layna.

Her thoughts wandered to Zarian. He had risked everything—his standing with the Medjai, his duty, even his trust with Jamil. Zarian had chosen *her*, placing her sister's happiness above the rigid codes that governed his life. The magnitude of his decision weighed heavily on her.

Hours passed by as Layna stared at the shadow-dance on the ceiling cast by the moonlight. The quiet of the night offered no comfort, her mind a whirlpool of thoughts about duty, love, and the uncertain future that awaited them all.

Zarian's words echoed in her heart. *I am yours.*

Eventually, exhaustion overcame her, pulling her into a restless slumber. But Zarian found her even in her dreams—his bright hazel eyes, the gentleness of his touch, the silky softness of his unruly hair.

I am yours. I am yours. I am yours.

CHAPTER TWENTY-TWO

In the heart of the Alzahran desert, under a canopy of stars that stretched infinite and eternal, Layna stood alone. The full moon bathed the sands in silver, casting long shadows across the tall dunes. An unnatural chill swept through the air. The stars dimmed as a creeping shadow enveloped the moon, staining the night an ominous red.

The sands beneath Layna's feet began to whirl, forming towering figures of fearsome warriors and beasts. Encircled by this spectral army, her heart raced, breath catching as the figures advanced, their forms growing more defined, more threatening with each second.

Amidst the menacing growls of the beasts, a voice, clear and resonant, cut through the chaos.

"Rise, Daughter! Rise!" it commanded. The warriors and beasts halted, bowing in submission to the princess.

Layna felt an awakening, a surge of energy that coursed through her veins. She lifted her arms toward the blood-red moon, and the sands rose high, swirling into a maelstrom of power around her. An unearthly radiance emanated from her, her eyes glowing with a piercing white light, mirroring the brilliance of the moon itself.

Beneath her, the desert sands heeded her call, but it was Layna herself who transcended earthly bounds. She flew up in the night sky, her silhouette outlined against the moon. Her loose gown billowed like wings, swirling in a tempest of her own making. The wind wove through her hair, lifting it in a wild, majestic halo.

Gazing down, Layna's heart clenched with a sudden rush of fear as she realized her towering height.

She began to plummet. The sands parted below to reveal a dark, gaping abyss, ready to engulf her in its shadowy depths.

The chasm yawned wide, its darkness so complete, so absolute, that it swallowed the very light of the moon. Her descent was timeless, an eternal fall through layers of oblivion that absorbed every thought, every fear, every hope.

Layna felt herself dissolving, her very essence unraveling, the darkness seeking to claim her completely.

Yet within her, the spark of power grew brighter still.

Layna jolted awake, shallow breaths escaping in sharp gasps, her nightgown clinging to her sweaty skin. Her heart pounded fiercely, lingering dread twisting around her lungs in an ice-cold vise.

Soraya stirred beside her. Her sleepy eyes crinkled with concern as she fixed on Layna's pale, distressed face.

"Layna?" she rasped. "Was it the dream again?"

Nodding, Layna tried to steady her breath. "Yes," she managed. "It felt more real than ever."

Soraya moved closer, wrapping an arm around Layna's trembling shoulders.

"They're coming more often now, aren't they?"

Unable to trust her voice, Layna nodded again.

"It must mean the time is near," Soraya mused softly. "Perhaps, you should tell Zarian. He might understand what it means."

Layna forced a smile. "I'm fine, really," she reassured, her voice cracking. She cleared her throat. "It was just a dream, after all."

Soraya studied her for a moment. Eventually, she nodded though concern still clouded her gaze.

"Alright," she conceded softly, "but promise me you'll talk to Zarian?"

"I promise," Layna affirmed.

Soraya gave her sister's hand a final, comforting squeeze before laying back down.

Layna stood, borrowed a robe, and walked back to her own chambers as the early morning light began to seep through the palace corridors.

Once inside, she let out a deep breath, as if trying to physically expel her fear. Her movements were mechanical as she quickly bathed.

She approached her wardrobe and selected a simple white abaya. As she tightened her belt and pinned back her hair, Layna's reflection in the mirror showed a princess ready to face the day.

But behind her poised exterior, the echoes of her nightmare remained, a reminder of the prophecy that haunted her both day and night.

In the council chambers, Zarian sat rigidly, lost in memories of the previous night. His heart swelled as he recalled Layna seeking him out, trusting him to help her sister. When she had thanked him, he was certain he glimpsed affection in her eyes—something that had been absent for weeks. Hope flickered within him, a fragile belief that perhaps, at last, she had forgiven him.

But then he remembered Jamil. His partner's words, sharp and disappointed, echoed in his mind. Jamil had been incensed, not just at Zarian's dangerous actions, but at being dragged into a situation that jeopardized their mission.

Jamil's anger was understandable. Unwavering loyalty to the Medjai had been beaten into them since childhood. Yet, in that moment with Layna, her distress and his need to protect her eclipsed all else.

His musings were interrupted as Layna entered the council chambers, radiant in a flowing white abaya, her hair pinned away from her beautiful face. The sight of her stirred an emotion so strong that the prince was hesitant to give it a name.

As Layna took her place at the table, Lord Varin stood, clearing his throat before delivering a report on a recent border skirmish. A Zephyrian detachment had ventured dangerously close to Alzahran soil. Alzahra's sentinels fired a warning shot—an arrow ablaze, intended to halt the advance. But instead of retreating, the Zephyrians responded aggressively, initiating a clash that quickly escalated into a full-blown skirmish.

The Alzahran soldiers mounted a disciplined defense, and after a lengthy exchange of arrows and swords, their counterattack eventually led to the Zephyrians' retreat.

"We lost fifty men," Lord Varin stated grimly.

Lord Ebrahim leaned forward, a deep frown on his face.

"Lord Varin, I've heard reports that Zephyria has amassed even greater numbers at our border. Ezanek and Valtisaan have sent several platoons of soldiers. Were you aware of this?"

Varin's eyes widened slightly, and his mouth opened and closed.

"Yes, I was aware," he finally said, crossing his arms tightly over his chest. "It is under control. I have already passed orders to our generals."

The master of war quickly introduced a new topic of concern.

"Our guards arrested a suspected spy yesterday, but somehow, he has already escaped. He was a Zephyrian diplomat who arrived months ago as part of a trade delegation. Curiously, he chose to remain here even after his party returned home."

Zarian spoke up. "I will investigate among the guards and find out what happened."

Lord Varin seized the opportunity. "Was not Prince Zarian tasked with bolstering our palace security?" he demanded sharply. "How, then, did our guards falter so grievously under his tutelage?"

Before Zarian could respond, Layna sharply interjected. "Would Lord Varin hold himself accountable for a soldier's desertion or misjudgment in battle?" she rebuked coldly. "Perhaps your attentions are divided, given your oversight in failing to inform the council of critical enemy movements."

Lord Varin was momentarily speechless.

"I apologize, Prince Zarian. We are grateful for your counsel," he reluctantly said. His posture remained rigid, defiance etched in the set of his shoulders and the stubborn tilt of his chin.

Zarian was taken aback by Layna's fierce defense, his mouth parting slightly.

The meeting moved on to a few brief updates, but Zarian's thoughts remained fixed on Layna's intervention. When the council adjourned, he approached her with a playful glint in his eyes.

Recalling an earlier exchange between them, he said, "Your actions today were unacceptable. You undermined my authority and made me appear weak. I am fully capable of handling such situations." He offered her a slow, tentative smile.

The moment hung between them.

Zarian held his breath.

Then, for the first time in what felt like weeks, Layna threw her head back and laughed with pure joy, a sound Zarian hadn't realized he'd been desperate to hear. An affectionate smile tugged at his lips as he watched her.

After a brief pause, he added, "Princess, there's something I've been wanting to discuss with you. Somewhere private, if possible."

Layna thought for a moment. "I know just the room," she murmured, grasping his hand on a whim.

Layna led him through the palace's maze of corridors, steps quick and silent. They ducked into an unassuming room. The forgotten chamber was sparse and unused, with high ceilings and narrow windows that let in beams of sunlight.

Once inside, Zarian collected his thoughts. "I've come to suspect Lord Varin's loyalties may not be as they appear. He's been overly eager for war with Zephyria. I'm not sure what his motivations are, but my instincts tell me something is wrong." He paused for a beat. "It's suspicious that the Zephyrian assassin knew exactly which tent housed Alzahra's top general."

Layna's expression hardened. "I've felt the same," she confessed. "His insistence on conflict has been troubling, and his failure to report the additional troops at the border seems deliberate."

Together, they brainstormed a plan to uncover the truth.

"We'll need to monitor his communications discreetly," Zarian suggested. "And perhaps follow his movements."

After they finalized their strategy, Layna hesitated. "There's something else I need to tell you. My nightmares—they're becoming more vivid and extending farther each time."

She described the latest dream in detail—the desert under a blood-red moon, swirling sands and mythical creatures bowing before her, and finally, her own figure, rising high above the ground, powerful and commanding, before plunging into the gaping abyss.

Zarian listened intently, his brows furrowed in concern. "The eclipse must be imminent. But don't worry. I won't let anything happen to you."

Layna gave him a small smile. As they fell into a comfortable silence, she became acutely aware of their closeness. He was watching her intently, his eyes burning with intensity. She could feel the heat radiating off his body.

"Zarian," she said softly as she looked up at him, "thank you again for last night. For helping Soraya."

"Of course, Princess. As I said, I am yours. If you'll have me," he murmured, his voice, low and deep, washing over her like a warm caress.

"Please don't say things like that," she whispered, molten desire shimmering in her brown eyes.

"And why not?" he whispered back, taking a step closer.

"It makes me want to kiss you. And I'm tired of fighting it." She drew a deep breath, as if summoning the strength to resist him.

He said nothing, his gaze smoldering as he inched closer, leaving only a sliver of space between them.

Layna hesitated for a heartbeat, then twined her arms around him and buried her face in his neck. Zarian's strong arms encircled her waist, holding her tightly against him.

After a moment, she tilted her head back to meet his gaze. She breathed in his scent, a heady mix that was distinctly Zarian—sandalwood mingled with a subtle hint of spice. Her heart raced as she felt the hard planes of his body against her own soft curves.

He lowered his head, his lips hovering just inches from hers. Gently cupping her face, his thumbs stroked her cheeks with a tenderness that sent her heart into a flutter.

She waited, breathless, for him to close the final gap, to claim her lips as he had done before.

But he didn't.

Instead, he nuzzled her nose, pressing his forehead against hers. He breathed her in, letting her scent envelop him as if he wanted to etch every detail into his memory.

Impatience simmered inside her, her lips aching to be reunited with his. But instead of kissing her, he traced the curve of her cheek with his nose, slowly drawing it up to her temple. His touch was reverent and feather-light, as though he feared she might disappear if he held on too tightly.

Layna couldn't wait any longer. She grabbed his face and crushed her mouth to his in a searing kiss, their lips colliding with desperate need. A rough, throaty groan rumbled from him—a sound thick with equal parts relief and desire, as if her kiss had finally answered his silent, unspoken plea.

Zarian's grip tightened, pulling her closer as his lips finally claimed hers with a demanding passion. Layna yielded beneath him with delicious sweetness.

The kiss deepened, eliciting a low moan from Layna. Her mouth moved against his with mounting urgency, lips parting slightly to urge him closer. His hand threaded through her hair, possessively holding her to him.

Layna savored his taste, their mouths dancing together in a primal rhythm. The sensation of his lips moving against hers, the gentle tug as they explored each other, was mesmerizing, sending waves of desire cascading through her.

She tangled her hands in Zarian's dark locks. His hands traced the curve of her waist, drawing her closer against him, until she swore she could feel his heartbeat against her chest.

The world fell away, leaving only the two of them. All worries of the present and uncertainties of the future dissolved into nothingness. Layna melted into him, her breathless sounds filling the air.

Suddenly, the loud sound of laughter—servants, likely, passing through the corridor—shattered their bubble of privacy.

Startled, they broke apart.

Layna's cheeks glowed with a soft blush, breaths deep and uneven. She lingered in the sensation, her eyes remaining closed just a beat longer.

"I should return before my absence is noticed," she finally murmured, opening her eyes.

Zarian gently tucked a stray strand of hair behind her ear before taking her hand, his gaze never leaving hers. He kissed each fingertip with a tenderness that sent pleasant shivers through her. Layna's heart fluttered, every nerve alive with the touch of his lips on her skin. Her lips parted as she pressed her thighs tightly together.

Zarian's eyes slowly traced the contours of her body, lingering before meeting hers again. A slow, lazy grin spread across his face. Heat flared within her, and she felt as if she'd burst into flames at any moment.

"Do I have your forgiveness, Layna?" he murmured, the deep timbre of his voice setting her nerves alight.

"Yes," she breathed, eyes hooded and lips slightly parted as she watched him. He pressed an open kiss to her palm, his tongue flicking against her skin just enough to weaken her knees.

"And we can start afresh?" he continued, watching her closely as his lips brushed over her wrist, where her pulse fluttered wildly beneath his touch.

Layna nodded, unable to form words.

Zarian chuckled, a low, velvety sound that rumbled in his chest. "I should start some inquiries on Varin," he said. His fingers traced a slow path down her neck.

"Mhmm," Layna managed, her voice too shaky to trust.

He traced her collarbone, and her knees buckled. He laughed lightly as he steadied her.

Zarian pressed a sweet kiss to her forehead. "Go," he whispered. "We've been in here for a while now."

With one last longing look, Layna reluctantly left the room.

The setting sun cast long shadows on the cobblestone streets of Alzahra City. Through the dwindling clamor, past merchants closing their stalls, Lord Varin made his way home. His run-down manor, a sad contrast to the palace's opulence, awaited him, far removed from the prosperity that once defined his family's name.

The Varin estate, once a symbol of wealth and influence, now stood as evidence of their fallen status. The paint on the ornate wooden door was chipped and faded, the garden overrun with weeds. As he pushed open the gate, its creaking hinges sounded as weary as Varin felt.

Inside, the house was dimly lit, the sparse furnishings a daily reminder of the luxuries his father was forced to sell. Portraits of the once-proud family hung askew on the walls, their faces gazing down upon a legacy tarnished by poor fortune and ill-fated decisions. Most of them had fled Alzahra in shame.

Seated in the drawing room, his thoughts soured as he dwelled on the day's council meeting. The princess's rebuke lingered in his mind, her words burning his pride like acid.

"To question my actions, as if I were a mere foot soldier," he muttered. "That foolish girl flaunts her affection for the prince like a badge of honor." He poured himself a glass of ale, taking a deep swig of the amber liquid. "She'll be on her knees soon enough."

His family's misfortunes had hardened him, stripping away any semblance of loyalty to the crown. The shame of their reduced circumstances, the whispers of pity and derision, and Khahleel's lack of financial assistance, all fueled his resolve.

"Betrayal?" he scoffed quietly, gazing at the flickering candlelight. "No, it's survival. They are nothing more than stepping-stones back to my rightful place."

Varin felt no remorse as he contemplated his actions. *Let them scorn me*, he thought with a grim smile. *When the time comes, I will rise above them all.*

His mind drifted back to the pivotal moment that changed his fate.

Night had fallen heavy over the Varin estate. In his chambers, the feeble light of a single candle flickered, casting shadows that danced across his worn bedding.

Alone, Varin prepared for sleep, finding no comfort in his evening rituals.

As he left the washroom, a presence in the room, silent as the night itself, announced itself with a sharp blade pressed against his throat. Varin froze, his blood running cold.

The man behind him was a shadow, his breath a dark whisper against Varin's ear.

"Tell me, Lord Varin," the voice said, low and dangerous, "how do you enjoy being the source of pity and derision? The kingdom laughs at you."

Terror gripped him, yet a spark of anger flared deep within. "Who are you?" he hissed, attempting to mask his fear.

The man chuckled, a hollow sound, as if the life had been wrung from it. "A friend," he said mockingly, "or perhaps your only chance to regain what you've lost. A chance to restore your family's name and claim the power you seek."

Varin, despite the blade at his throat, found himself listening, a desperate hope kindling within him. "What do you want?" he demanded.

"Your loyalty," the man replied. "And in return, I offer you the chance to strike at the heart of Alzahra. A chance to reclaim your honor. And your wealth."

The proposition was tempting: an escape from the mire of his current existence. Yet, the risk was immense. It required the betrayal of his kingdom and his people.

And, if caught, the price would be his head.

Varin's gaze hardened as he weighed the intruder's words against the heavy silence of the room. "And if I accept? What do you require of me?"

The shadow's response came with an air of casual malevolence, as if he were discussing the weather instead of high treason. "Merely two tasks," he murmured, his voice like silk as the blade's edge pressed ever so slightly against Varin's skin. "First, use your influence to sway the council toward war with Zephyria. Shatter their cherished peace."

Varin's breath caught at the audacity of the demand, but the man continued unfazed. "Second, I require information. Regular updates, particularly about the crown princess. Her actions, her plans, anything unusual. You have access, Lord Varin. Use it."

The blade withdrew, but before Varin could turn around, the man melted into the shadows. Varin was left alone, the weight of the decision pressing down on him. Would he dare align with this mysterious figure and gamble everything on the promise of power and wealth?

The night stretched on, and Varin sat in the darkness, contemplating the crossroads before him.

But in his heart, the choice had already been made.

In the royal greenhouse, Soraya found peace among the vibrant blooms and lush foliage. At night, the greenhouse transformed into a magical escape, illuminated by flickering lanterns that made the leaves and petals shimmer as if imbued with their own inner light.

The air was always fresh, brimming with the earthy scent of soil and the subtle perfume of flowers. For Soraya, it was a haven where her troubles melted away, if only for a while.

Lately, her visits had become more frequent, each trip an effort to escape her sorrow since Almeer was forced to flee. She cherished the memories of their time together—his inquisitive gaze when he asked about her plants, the gentle timbre of his voice as he told her of his life back home, and the comfortable warmth of his embrace.

A single tear escaped, tracing a path down her cheek, quickly wiped away. She resolved to remain strong until they could be reunited, drawing strength from the peace her greenhouse provided.

As she tended to a *silpharoon* plant, her thoughts drifted to Layna and Zarian. Despite her own sadness, Soraya was happy for her sister who was finally exploring the possibility of love with the prince. Zarian brought Layna a joy she hadn't seen in ages.

Glancing at the old clock near the glass door, Soraya realized it was almost time for her nightly visit to Layna's chambers. Recently, they spent nights playing card games, another pastime from their childhood. She knew it was Layna's way of comforting her, though it no longer lifted her spirits as it once might have.

Then, an idea sparked in her mind.

She left the greenhouse and headed to the council chambers, where she found Zarian alone, absorbed in the maps and documents spread before him. His brows were knit together in concentration, and a quill was clenched between his teeth. Normally, she might have teased him about it, but her heavy heart stifled any playful remark. He glanced up as she entered, taking the quill from his mouth, concern replacing his focus.

"Zarian," Soraya greeted softly, "I'm joining Layna for an evening of card games. She can be quite competitive, as you know." They shared a small smile. "If you have some time for leisurely pursuits, we'd love for you to join us."

Zarian gave her a grateful smile. "It would be an honor. Thank you for the invitation."

Together, they walked through the palace corridors, the silence between them comfortable. Soraya's steps felt a little lighter, even if her heart still ached for Almeer.

CHAPTER TWENTY-THREE

A weary figure sat alone. The private chambers, spacious and adorned with fine artifacts, spoke of a lineage that had ruled the land for generations. Tall, arched windows draped with richly embroidered curtains framed views of the sprawling oasis and the desert beyond, the sands glowing under the moon's silvery light.

A solemn adviser entered, breaking the heavy silence. "Your Majesty, our trackers have located him in Zephyria. Shall we send three men and…finish this?"

The king sighed, fatigue settling deeply into the lines of his face as he pinched the bridge of his nose. "No," he finally responded, his voice laced with a heavy sadness. "Leave him to his fate."

The adviser cautiously added, "Shall I inform the young master?"

The king's response was sharp, a swift command born of a father's protective instinct. "No! No, do not tell him," he said firmly, his gaze distant. "He would seek him out, attempt to bring him home. He cannot see the boy is past saving."

The adviser bowed silently and retreated, leaving the king alone with his regrets.

In the heart of Zephyria, the night held its breath. The castle, a ruthless fortress of stone and ambition, stood imposing against a backdrop of jagged mountains.

Silent as a shadow, Azhar crept through the cold corridors. He arrived at Jorah's chambers. The faint glow of flickering candles cast dancing shadows across the walls. The old king sat upright in his large bed, his gaze fixed on a small trinket box in his hands.

Jorah delicately pinched a lock of wavy, brown hair between his fingers, lifting it close to his face. With a deep breath, he inhaled its scent, eyes closing as he allowed the illusion of a faint fragrance to envelop him, drenched in reminiscence and melancholy.

As Azhar entered, the king carefully placed back the lock of hair, setting the box aside. "Come, my son, what brings you here at this hour?"

Azhar approached and sat on the bed. Slowly, he clasped Jorah's frail hand within his own. "You took me in when I had no one. When I had nothing," Azhar began, his voice low, eyes downcast. "I am indebted to you. For as long as you live."

A smile tugged at the corners of Jorah's lips. "You have served me well, my son. It has been an honor to have you in my life," he remarked, love evident in the warmth of his voice, as he placed a hand on Azhar's shoulder.

"It's been an honor for me as well. But now, consider my debt fulfilled," Azhar said, his voice flat.

Confusion flickered across Jorah's face, a question forming in his eyes.

But it was too late.

In one swift, merciless motion, Azhar drew his dagger across the king's throat. Crimson blood spurted from the gash, splattering Azhar's face and staining the rich linens.

Azhar watched, emotionless, as Jorah's life ebbed away, the king's hands clutching futilely at his wound, pitiful confusion clouding his eyes.

With the same cold detachment, Azhar retrieved the orb from its hidden spot in Jorah's chambers, its surface gleaming in the candlelight. Without a backward glance at his adopted father's lifeless body, he exited the chamber, disappearing as silently as he had arrived.

The following morning, Azhar wasted no time in consolidating his power. After Jorah's body was discovered by a panicked servant, he immediately summoned the council. He stood before them, not as the heir, but as the man who would lead them through the war ahead.

In the solemn assembly, Azhar's posture was a study in contrasts. Clad in traditional mourning blacks that draped heavily over his shoulders, he stood with a quiet dignity, his head bowed in mock reverence for his murdered father. Yet, the defiant set of his jaw and his calculating gaze spoke of his newfound power.

His voice carried a subtle tremor as he declared, "Alzahra stands accused of the most heinous betrayal against our kingdom. They have assassinated our king. My father."

A stunned silence blanketed the room.

"My heart is heavy with grief, but I must do my duty. I must guide Zephyria through these dark times," he continued, his gaze sweeping across the room, meeting the eyes of each council member in turn. "I vow to avenge my father's death and to continue in the pursuit of his ultimate goal—the destruction of Alzahra."

One by one, the council members rose from their seats, their movements deliberate. They knelt before Azhar, heads bowed in allegiance.

"We pledge our loyalty to you, King Azhar," they intoned, their voices merging into a single declaration of unity.

Azhar stood tall, accepting their oaths with a nod. He was no longer just Azhar, the unwanted stray taken in by Jorah.

He was the ruler of a mighty kingdom.

In shadowed corridors, Lords Garrisman and Ebric talked quietly, far from prying ears.

"Have we any evidence of Alzahra's hand in Jorah's murder?" Lord Ebric whispered. His gaze darted about, vigilant for any lurking eavesdroppers.

Lord Garrisman glanced around before leaning closer. "Does it truly matter? We all know Jorah longed for war with Alzahra. He had been orchestrating it for months. Now, we're merely awaiting confirmation of the eclipse before launching our attack."

Lord Ebric shifted uncomfortably. "Still, without proof can we really—"

Garrisman cut him off with a sharp gesture. "Listen, Ebric. It would be wise for you not to question Azhar's claims too closely. The man is ruthless, perhaps a touch unhinged. Questioning him, especially now, could be *unhealthy* for you."

Lord Ebric's eyes widened behind his spectacles, the unspoken threat hanging between them like a noose. "I understand," he stammered. "We must stand united behind our new king."

Garrisman nodded, a grim smile tugging at the corners of his mouth. "Exactly. Azhar's path is now Zephyria's path. We march to war under his banner, for better or worse."

CHAPTER TWENTY-FOUR

Valtisaan, a city unlike any other on the continent, gleamed under the twilight sky. It was a marvel of modernity and advancement, nestled within the heart of a world that had not quite caught up. The streets were lined with luminescent stones that glowed softly, illuminating the path for travelers and citizens alike. The architecture blended traditional elegance and contemporary innovation, with buildings that soared toward the heavens, their surfaces shimmering with a metallic sheen.

Cloak drawn up around his haggard face, the elder brother tread these illuminated pathways with heavy footsteps.

It had been a year since his brother's banishment. Six months he had spent in mourning, not just for the brother lost to a path of darkness, but for his beloved Sultan, whose absence was a wound on his soul. Six months to grapple with betrayal and loss and guilt.

Six months too long.

Now, he found himself in Valtisaan, the latest stop in a relentless search that had dragged him across kingdoms, chasing shadows and whispers of his brother's fate.

As he walked, the city's advanced marvels blurred into the background, his focus narrowing on the mission that consumed him. Valtisaan, for all its progress and beauty, was just another waypoint in his quest for either a reunion or for closure.

He had just turned a corner when an instinctual wariness halted him in his tracks. The hair on the back of his neck stood as his hand grasped the hilt of his sword. Three cloaked figures emerged from the shadows at the end of the pathway, their forms shrouded in darkness.

"You found me," the elder brother said simply, his voice resigned as he subtly shifted his stance, a lifetime of training coming to the forefront. His muscles tensed, ready to spring into action, while his eyes, sharp and calculating, assessed the potential threat. He stood tall and imposing, a silent challenge to those who dared approach him with ill intent.

The cloaked figures advanced slowly. The man in the center removed his hood, revealing the familiar face of his childhood friend, a companion from a life that seemed a world away. A fresh wound marred the left side of his face, a thin yet deep cut that ran from cheekbone to jaw.

"It's time to return home," his friend said, his voice carrying the weight of an order long delayed. "Your father has given you time to make your peace, but the kingdom needs you now. Your duties await."

"And if I refuse?" the elder brother challenged, his words hanging in the air. His shoulders, though squared in defiance, slumped ever so slightly.

His friend offered a sad smile. "Apologies, brother. Then, we must insist." As he spoke, the two figures beside him closed in.

A deep sigh escaped the elder brother as the fight drained from him. He had known this moment would come. His friend's apology was a small comfort, a balm to the sting of being called back not as a son, but as a prince.

"It's not your fault," his friend reassured him, but the words felt hollow.

Duty called him back, not to the warmth of home, but to the cold embrace of responsibility.

A month quickly passed following a whirlwind of diplomatic and military maneuvers. The assassination of King Jorah sent shockwaves through the region, accusations flying as his heir ascended the throne and hastened the war efforts against Alzahra.

In response, Alzahra had been proactive, dispatching envoys to neutral kingdoms to clear its name from the assassination scandal and to seek additional support. The diplomatic efforts were critical, aiming to ensure that Alzahra was seen as the aggrieved party, unjustly accused and fighting for its sovereignty.

In the shadow of an escalating war, the palace's atmosphere had grown tense, the air charged with constant worry for the future. Layna, bearing the dual burden of leader and sister, had faced one of her most challenging decisions yet. The safety of her sister, paramount in her mind, necessitated drastic measures.

Zarian was pivotal in arranging for Soraya's safe passage to the Oasis. However, the decision was not met without resistance. Though the king and queen were readily persuaded to send the younger princess away under the guise of a royal stay, Soraya herself was much more difficult to convince.

She was reluctant to leave Alzahra and, more importantly, her sister. Soraya had expressed her concerns, grasping Layna's hands tightly within her own. "How can I leave when you need me here?" The thought of being far away, possibly safe but helpless, tormented her.

"I need to know you're safe," Layna had insisted. "It's the only way I can focus on the war efforts. And you can be with Almeer." Eventually, Soraya reluctantly agreed.

Convincing Jamil, however, to ferry another individual to the Oasis proved to be a much more difficult challenge. Initially, he was furious with Zarian and vehemently refused outright. The weight of his previous assistance bore down on him, making a similar task seem daunting. The two had almost come to blows.

In the end, Zarian penned a letter to his father for intervention. Fortunately, by some miracle, King Tahriq was swayed by his son's words and allowed Jamil to bring Soraya to the Oasis.

Their farewell was marked with tight, tearful hugs and unspoken words. As Jamil led Soraya away, Zarian stood by Layna's side as she watched, eyes shining with tears.

In the weeks past, Layna was also increasingly plagued by nightmares. Sleep became a battleground for her fears. Her dreams, vivid and chilling, left her terrified in the dead of night, her skin slick with sweat and her heart racing with unnamed dread.

The eclipse loomed large in her mind. What transformation awaited her? Would it exact a cost she wasn't prepared to pay? Layna spent countless hours in the no-longer-secret library sorting through ancient texts and scrolls. The uncertainty of her fate filled her with dread, a fear that she dared not voice, even to Zarian.

The past few weeks had brought Layna closer and closer to him, their relationship blossoming amidst the chaos that surrounded them.

With Soraya's departure to the Oasis, Layna found herself leaning on Zarian more than ever. He had become her solace. Their relationship, which had begun under the most trying circumstances, had flourished like a resilient desert bloom. The stolen moments they shared became the highlights of Layna's days.

Though the couple attempted to be discreet, Layna couldn't ignore the whispers among the courtiers and the knowing looks from some of the palace staff.

Yet, surprisingly, her parents remained silent on the matter. She had braced herself for a reprimand, or at the very least, a conversation.

But that conversation never came. Layna was grateful for their unspoken approval, or at least their willingness to look the other way.

Before Soraya's departure to the Oasis, she had cheekily gifted Layna a *silpharoon* plant, widely used throughout the continent for its contraceptive properties, a gesture that left Layna both grateful and red-faced.

However, while Layna and Zarian had enjoyed plenty of intimate moments, her Medjai prince still seemed reluctant to cross certain boundaries. If he had noticed the new plant in her chambers or knew of its purpose, Zarian made no mention of it. And so, the bittersweet anticipation of fulfillment left Layna in a perpetual state of frustration and confusion.

Layna dwelled on these thoughts as she made her way to the training grounds where Zarian conducted daily drills for the palace guards. His duties had kept him occupied for the past few days, and Layna's heart ached to see him.

At the edge of the training grounds, the sounds of metal clashing against metal rang out, along with shouts of exertion and the occasional cheer or groan of mock defeat. It was here, among the palace's defenders, that Zarian had found his second home.

His presence was unmistakable, his skill and command drawing the eye of every onlooker. Clad in a lightweight tunic and loose trousers, he was a warrior in his element. A teal bandana was nestled snugly against his neck, a splash of color against a sea of blacks and browns and tans.

His muscular body, sculpted from decades of training, moved with a feline grace. The light sheen of sweat on his skin caught the sunlight, highlighting the contours of his muscles.

His focus was absolute, his sword an extension of his arm, up until the moment he caught sight of Layna in his periphery and turned his head to look at her.

The momentary distraction was enough for his opponent to land a superficial cut on his arm, causing a thin line of blood to flow from the shallow wound. The sparring session halted abruptly, and Layna, unable to conceal her concern, called out to him.

"Prince Zarian," she called, her voice carrying a formal note as she motioned him toward her. Mindful of the onlookers, she added, "Please, allow me to attend to your wound. It's crucial you remain in peak condition to continue training the guards."

Zarian sauntered over, brushing off her worries with his usual charming grin. "It's merely a scratch," he assured her, his smile wide. Layna noted the shadow of fatigue beneath his eyes, and her fingers itched to gently trace along his face.

She quickly fetched the medical kit from a nearby supply bench. With practiced care, Layna delicately cleansed the cut and wrapped a bandage around his muscular bicep.

While her gaze remained intently on his arm, her voice carried a soft, inviting undertone as she quietly asked, "Will you visit me tonight?"

Zarian kept his gaze fixed on Layna's face. "The entire Zephyrian army couldn't keep me away," he murmured, his deep voice laden with promise. He flexed his bicep as her fingers worked over him, drawing a smile Layna struggled to conceal.

"Ensure that it doesn't," she quipped lightly, looking up at him coyly.

She felt the eyes of the guards on them, but couldn't bring herself to care.

After Layna treated his wound, Zarian returned to training. Swords clashed and feet shuffled in the dance of mock combat, but his focus was not quite as sharp.

He parried and lunged with skill, but his reactions were slower, his mind replaying Layna's touch as she bandaged his arm. The warmth of her hands lingered on his skin, her coy smile sending a shiver through him.

They'd been apart for too long.

A light jest from one of the guards shook Zarian out from his thoughts, a reminder that the men were all too aware of his rare lapse in concentration. Zarian managed a small, distracted smile before refocusing.

After training concluded, Zarian reflected on the past few weeks as he went about his day. His connection with Layna had deepened, transforming into something indispensable. Each moment with her was a reprieve from the relentless pressure of his responsibilities. In Layna, he had found both a partner and a source of strength.

Soraya's departure to the Oasis marked a significant moment for them both. For Zarian, it tested his commitment to Layna's happiness, going as far as to involve his father to ensure Soraya's safety. Writing to the king, persuading him to safeguard Soraya, was a difficult decision. As expected, it drew sharp criticism from both King Tahriq and Jamil. But miraculously, his father had agreed.

The gratitude in Layna's eyes and the warmth of her embrace made all dissenting voices fade away. Her safety and happiness were paramount, even if it meant disappointing his father.

In recent weeks, their relationship had grown both emotionally and physically. This growing closeness, their intimate kisses, challenged Zarian's self-control, as he struggled to balance their blossoming bond and the restraint required to honor certain boundaries. He knew Layna was ready, eager even, to consummate their relationship, but he still held himself back.

Zarian's hesitation wasn't born out of a lack of desire—far from it. His first gaze upon the new *silpharoon* plant in her chambers, undoubtedly a gift from her sister, sent his blood rushing south.

Zarian's restraint was caused by the weight of their circumstances. He already knew, deep in his heart of hearts, he would choose Layna above everything. He would face his father's fury and abandon his duties to be with her.

However, he was not yet certain that Layna would do the same. Would she, *should* she, choose him above the responsibilities of her title? Above her people?

His reluctance to cross that final boundary was his armor, protecting them from heartache if their names were not written together in the sands of time. The thought of having Layna so completely, body and soul, only to lose her to a political marriage, was unbearable. This potential torment gnawed at Zarian and kept him awake at night. He doubted he could survive losing her to another.

But moons, did she test his restraint.

One night, she convinced him to remove his tunic under the pretext of comparing his tattoo to a symbol on an old Medjai scroll. She gently traced the black ink first with her fingertips, then with her lips until goosebumps erupted across his skin. The little minx didn't spare a single glance at the tattered scroll she was supposed to be checking. It took all of Zarian's willpower not to throw her onto the bed and give her what she so clearly desired.

Sighing deeply, Zarian's thoughts inevitably drifted to the impending eclipse. The foretold event, shrouded in mystery, loomed over them. It promised change, potentially cataclysmic in its scope.

His heart was heavy with concern for Layna, for what the eclipse might herald for her. The uncertainty was a constant shadow in his mind.

He longed for reassurance that Layna would emerge unscathed, unchanged, and above all, still his. The thought of her suffering a horrible fate he couldn't prevent gripped his heart like a vise, yet amidst his fears, Zarian clung to a thread of hope. He *had* to believe she would be alright, that whatever tempest the eclipse unleashed, they would face the next dawn together.

As the day progressed, Zarian fulfilled his responsibilities around the palace. However, as night fell over the kingdom, the prince prepared for more covert activities. He donned a dark cloak, melding with the night, his steps silent atop the cool marble floors.

Zarian navigated the palace grounds with ease. He intimately knew every secret passage and hidden exit, each mapped out meticulously during his time in Alzahra.

Reaching a secluded part of the gardens, he scanned for any observers. Satisfied, he slipped through a hidden gate among the flowering bushes.

The cool night air greeted him as he stepped into the quiet city beyond the palace walls. In the silver moonlight, Alzahra City transformed into a realm of shadows and whispers, its beauty muted yet somehow magnified in the night. The capital's buildings were bathed in a serene light, casting long, dancing shadows across the cobblestone streets. Zarian looked down, silent as the night itself, as he traversed the rooftops with grace.

Every leaping bound was a silent dance. Wind rushed through his dark locks, a cool caress against his skin, whispering the city's secrets. He became one with the shadows, slicing through the air with the precision of a falcon. The physical exertion, his pounding heart, the rush of adrenaline—it all merged into a moment of pure, unburdened freedom.

The city below sparkled in the moon's silver light. The rooftops provided solace, where Zarian reveled in the solitude of his task, and his identity as a prince, a protector, and a lover faded into the night.

He paused, catching his breath. His thoughts returned to his nightly mission: tracking Lord Varin. Despite their suspicions, his surveillance had revealed nothing but the ordinary comings and goings of a man whose home spoke more of past wealth than present riches.

Perched on a nearby rooftop, Zarian watched Varin disappear into his home.

The hours that followed were a grueling test of patience, the stillness of the night offering too much time for reflection. His thoughts drifted to Layna—her vibrant smile that could light up the darkest rooms, the way her long hair felt when he tangled his fingers in it, and the intoxicating softness of her lips pressed against his.

As the night stretched on, Zarian eventually rose from his post. Hours had passed in a silent vigil, yet there was no sign of intrigue or betrayal. He turned toward the palace.

He had a promise to keep.

In the quiet of her chambers, the moonlight cast a serene glow through the open balcony doors. Layna awaited Zarian's arrival with a heart full of anticipation.

Her room, a spacious haven, was adorned with luxurious fabrics and furnishings. The large, regal bed was draped in silken sheets and a mountain of pillows, while the adjacent seating area boasted three plush sofas and a small table.

The soft glow of candlelight gently illuminated the room. The large double doors to her balcony stood open, inviting the cool night breeze into her private chambers.

A noise from the balcony caught her attention. Layna turned to see Zarian climb over the railing with ease. His arrival, always a spectacle, never failed to leave her in awe. His presence, so commanding and yet so gentle, filled her with a warmth that radiated from her very core. Moonlight illuminated his features, casting shadows that played across his handsome face, highlighting the stubble gracing his jaw and the sharp contours of his cheekbones.

She darted across the room, excitement in her steps, and embraced him tightly. Zarian, strong and sure, captured her in his arms and pulled her close, their bodies drawn to each other like magnets.

The connection between them was instant, an irresistible pull that drew them into a deep, fervent kiss. Layna's hands traced the contours of Zarian's back, longing to memorize every inch of him. When they finally parted, breathless, she whispered, "I've missed you."

"As I have missed you, Princess," Zarian murmured, their foreheads pressed together.

Layna took his hand, leading him to the plush sofa. "Come, let's sit." Chilled mirsham juice and an assortment of snacks awaited on the table, but the true nourishment they sought was each other's company.

They settled on the sofa, moonlight streaming through the open balcony doors. Layna drew closer, tenderly tracing the contours of his face with her fingertips. She frowned, observing the dark circles under his eyes.

"It seems sleep has been eluding you," Layna said, her lips pursed.

Zarian captured her wandering hand, pressing a gentle kiss to her palm. "You appear just as weary," he murmured. His fingers skimmed the line of her jaw to tilt her face toward the light, revealing the subtle signs of exhaustion beneath her eyes.

Layna glanced away, worrying her lower lip between her teeth. "The dreams have been more frequent. Sometimes, twice in one night." Zarian's brow creased with concern as he caressed her cheek.

Seeking to lighten the mood, Layna smiled and offered him juice. "What have you learned about Varin?" she asked.

"Nothing unusual so far," Zarian replied in between sips. "But something still seems off about him. He might know he's being watched."

Layna's expression grew troubled, worry etched deeply in her features. "To think someone so close to us could betray the kingdom. It's a scary thought."

Zarian ran his fingers through her hair, pausing to massage the base of her skull with gentle pressure. Layna's eyes fluttered shut, a delighted groan escaping her lips as she threw her head back, eyes closing at the sensation.

"We might need a new strategy," he remarked. "But don't worry. I'll handle it."

Layna leaned forward, pressing a quick kiss to his lips in thanks.

"Tinga cornered me today after breakfast," Zarian mentioned, his lips quirking into a half-grin. "She was making small talk, but I'm certain she was actually threatening me."

Layna chuckled. "She's quite protective. But she did promise me she won't enter again without knocking first. Don't worry, she'll warm up to you." She tenderly cupped his cheek, her eyes bright as they drank him in, her steadfast, guiding star. "I did, didn't I?"

As the night wore on, Layna rested her head in Zarian's lap, her gaze drifting upward to meet his. His hand gently stroked her hair.

"What do you hope for in the future?" she asked softly. "After the eclipse?"

Without a second's hesitation, Zarian replied, "I hope for us to be together. Truly together. I imagine leaving Alzahra and the Oasis behind, traveling to lands across the continent, perhaps even beyond."

"Beyond the continent?" she echoed, her voice laced with the wonder of dreams long-held but never truly believed.

"Yes," Zarian affirmed. "I've traveled to most kingdoms already on my missions, but I want to experience it again through your eyes. To embrace the beauty and adventure, not as a Medjai, but as someone just *living*. With you."

"But what of your kingdom? Who will rule the Oasis after your father?"

Zarian shrugged, resigned. "Perhaps, my father can name a new heir. Or the noble families could elect the next king, as they do now in Valtisaan."

Layna could hear the undercurrent of sacrifice in his words, the willingness to forsake his birthright for a future with her.

"Is that possible?" she asked, her voice quiet in the night.

"It's unprecedented in the Oasis, but not impossible," Zarian admitted, meeting her gaze. "It would be difficult. Chaotic, even. But I don't see what other choice my father and the elders would have."

Layna absorbed his words, the gravity of his decision sinking in. Zarian's willingness to challenge centuries of tradition for their future together was both awe-inspiring and daunting. It opened a realm of possibilities she hadn't dared to consider, a life of love and adventure, free from the expectations that had always defined them.

After a moment, Zarian softly asked, "And you? What do you see for your future?" His hopeful eyes searched hers, looking for a glimpse into her heart and the dreams within.

Layna hesitated. Her heart knew the answer—it yearned to be with Zarian, to share in the future he envisioned. Yet, uncertainty clouded her thoughts, the weight of her duties and the expectations of her kingdom pressing down on her.

"I—I want to be with you," she began tentatively. "My heart is with you, Zarian. But…" Her voice trailed off, the conflict within her too vast to articulate.

Zarian's fingers stilled in her hair. He slowly withdrew his hand, bringing it to rest limply at his side.

"Have things improved with Jamil?" Layna asked quickly.

Zarian was quiet for several heartbeats, before finally responding. "I haven't seen him in days. He must be delayed at the Oasis. Things are still tense, but we'll get through it. We always do." He took a deep breath. "It's quite late. You should rest."

Layna pouted, not ready for their time to end. Zarian leaned down and kissed her frown into a smile. "Goodnight, Layna. I'll see you tomorrow," he murmured, a tender farewell as he slipped away into the night, leaving Layna to ponder their futures, both together and apart.

CHAPTER TWENTY-FIVE

Layna awoke with a strangled gasp. Another vivid nightmare wrenched her from sleep, leaving her heart racing and her nightgown drenched in sweat. The remnants of the dream crawled over her, inescapable needle pinpricks of dread mercilessly stabbing her skin.

With a deep breath, she pushed the covers aside and started her morning routine. Like every other waking moment, her thoughts drifted to Zarian. The previous night had been a revelation—he had spoken of a future together, free from their duties. In the short time they had shared, Layna realized she couldn't imagine life without him.

But how could she abandon her people, her kingdom, and her family? Her heart clenched painfully in her chest.

As she dressed, her thoughts wandered back several nights, when she had returned to her chambers after a late-night meeting with Lord Ebrahim and her father where they had strategized and counted allies, attempting to anticipate Zephyria's next move.

Returning to her chambers well past midnight, Layna found Zarian waiting for her. He sat against the frame of the open balcony doors, a shadow against the moonlight, knees drawn up in patient solitude. Hearing her enter, he turned, offering her a tired smile.

The sight of him lifted the weight from her shoulders. Zarian shifted slightly, making space for her in an unspoken invitation. Layna closed the distance between them, nestling herself in the space between his knees, her side pressed against his firm chest, her head finding a comfortable spot on his shoulder.

She breathed in sandalwood and spice, and it felt like home.

He wrapped his strong arms around her, cocooning her in his warmth, his fingers tracing gentle patterns on her back. She sighed softly in contentment. They sat in silence, the only sound the gentle rustling of leaves in the night breeze.

Eventually, she broke the silence. "Will you tell me about your brother?" she asked, her voice a soft whisper against his neck.

She felt Zarian stiffen against her. His silence stretched on for minutes, and Layna felt his grip on her waist tighten.

When he finally spoke, his voice was rough, as if coated with gritty sand. "We were inseparable as children. He was always by my side, like my shadow. But my mother died giving birth to him, and my father...he couldn't forgive him for that. Sometimes, he couldn't even bear to look at him."

Layna listened intently, her heart aching for the young boys they once were. "It must've been difficult for him, growing up feeling so unwanted," she murmured.

"It was. And then there was the matter of succession. I was the heir and not him. That brought its own set of challenges. He always felt the weight of my shadow." Zarian trailed off, lost in the what-ifs of a past already immortalized in the sands of time. "I wish things had been different. I should've done more to protect him, to make him feel loved. I—I should have done more."

Layna leaned back slightly and cupped his face, forcing him to meet her gaze. "You were only a child yourself," she reminded him gently. "You did what you could. No one could have asked for more." She traced the hollow of his cheek with care. "Do you know where he is now?"

Zarian let out a heavy sigh. "I don't know. I tried to find him, but he had vanished. And then my father summoned me back to the Oasis. I hope, wherever he is, he's found some measure of happiness. The love he was denied growing up. I hope the wounds of the past have healed." His gaze drifted off into the distance, as if trying to pierce through the night to find his sibling.

Layna's heart ached for Zarian and his lost brother. She squeezed his shoulder in silent support. "He has you, someone out there who cares deeply for him, wishing well for him. That's a form of love too, Zarian. And wherever he is, I'm sure he knows that," she said softly, hoping to offer some peace to the man who held her heart.

Zarian's gaze locked with Layna's, the raw anguish sending a sharp pang through her chest. The desolation in his stare was so profound, it felt like her heart yearned to escape her chest and beat in his, just to share his burden. "I truly hope you're right. Thank you for listening. It means more to me than you can imagine. That I'm not alone."

Layna sat for a moment in the quiet of her chambers, the memory of their conversation lingering like a tender wound. Her heart ached for Zarian—her strong, gentle man burdened with such deep-seated pain. His brother's story had unveiled a vulnerability that Layna had sensed, but never fully grasped until now.

How she wished she could erase the shadows of his past, to fill the gaping void left by years of unresolved grief and guilt.

How she wished she could promise him a future together, days and months and years of unconditional, pure love.

Layna arrived at the council chambers, taking her seat across from Zarian. She offered a small smile in greeting, and he responded with a subtle curve of his lips. They tried to maintain some semblance of discretion in front of the council members, at the very least.

Lord Varin rose first, clearing his throat. "The integration of the Oasis's men with our forces has bolstered our defenses. Their expertise in guerrilla tactics and desert warfare has been invaluable," he said, his eyes flickering between Layna and Zarian.

Lord Saldeen stood next. "Regarding public morale…the people are understandably anxious. We've been circulating stories of our soldiers' bravery and the unique alliance with the Oasis. However, I propose King Khahleel address the people. It would help improve spirits."

"A sound idea," King Khahleel said. "Make the announcement. Lord Ebrahim, prepare the speech."

"Of course. I'll have Burhani draft it. She's made great strides in her lessons," Lord Ebrahim responded, a proud smile on his face. Burhani remained expressionless.

Layna stood next. "Baba, I have my assembly with the people today. It's a chance to address their concerns."

"Excellent point, Layna. Your meetings have always helped bridge the palace and our citizens. It's an invaluable platform, especially now."

Attention shifted back to Lord Ebrahim, who reported, "Our envoys have returned from the neutral kingdoms. Most understand Alzahra's plight, but the combined might of Zephyria, Valtisaan, and Ezanek has made them hesitant to support us openly."

A hush settled over the room, a collective moment of quiet disappointment.

"Except Baysaht," Lord Ebrahim announced. "King Nizam will send 250,000 soldiers."

A murmur of surprise swept the room.

Lord Varin exclaimed, "That's nearly half his forces!"

"Indeed," Lord Ebrahim confirmed with a small smile. "This could very well swing the tide in our favor."

"Did King Nizam ask for anything in return?" Queen Hadiyah asked, glancing at Layna with concern. "A trade treaty or, perhaps, some sort of alliance?

Lord Ebrahim shook his head. "No, surprisingly, he did not. At least, not yet." His eyes, too, darted to the princess.

Layna's expression remained unreadable. The room buzzed with discussion, but she sat still, her gaze distant.

Zarian watched her closely. She had told him of her halted courtship with Nizam. What should have been a moment of unbridled relief, instead stirred a swarm of emotions within him—jealousy, concern, and a protective instinct over Layna.

Baysaht's substantial military support was unexpected. What motivated such a grand gesture?

To her credit, Layna maintained an unreadable façade. Her expression revealed none of the conflict that Zarian knew must be roiling beneath.

The council, buoyed by the news of Baysaht's support, swiftly moved into strategizing. Plans were drawn and logistics debated.

But throughout it all, Zarian's mind was elsewhere.

In the palace's great hall, Layna's monthly assembly had gained new significance. The tension and uncertainty wrought by the war drew an unprecedented number of citizens. Faces of hope, fear, and worry crowded every inch, many standing shoulder to shoulder as seating fell short.

Layna was a vision of dignified grace in her midnight-blue abaya. She had forgone a crown, yet her presence was no less commanding. There was an innate regality to her, her composed posture and sweeping gaze leaving no doubt of her position.

Off to the side, Zarian remained vigilant, his keen eyes scanning the crowd for signs of trouble.

A middle-aged man, worry lining his face, approached. "Princess Layna," he began, his voice clear over the crowd, "we hear tales of the war and of lives lost. How do we hold hope?"

Layna met his gaze. "Your concerns are valid. But let me assure you, we stand united, stronger than we've ever been. Our forces fight not just for land but for the very essence of Alzahra—a belief in peace and justice. Together, we will weather this storm. The Oasis has sent us 10,000 strong, well-armed men," she said, glancing down at Zarian. "Their training and expertise have been vital."

Her words settled over the crowd, offering a flicker of warmth against the chilling fears of war.

No sooner had the man returned to his place, than a woman made her way forward. She wore a deep red scarf over her hair, its ends tucked into the neck of her tunic. Her steps were determined, her face marked with a deeper, more personal anguish.

"Princess," she said, her voice trembling, "my son is a soldier. Each day without word torments me. When will he return home?"

"Your son is a hero," Layna declared. "His bravery is the shield that protects Alzahra. I cannot promise you that fear will not touch our hearts. But know that your son, and every man who stands in defense of our homeland, holds my deepest respect and gratitude. We owe them our continued hope and support."

The woman, eyes brimming with tears, nodded in silent thanks before stepping back.

As the meeting progressed, Layna addressed each concern with grace and wisdom.

Zarian watched, his admiration growing with every word she spoke. In her, he saw a true leader—a beacon of hope for Alzahra.

Yet, he felt a twinge of guilt for the selfish part of him that dared hope Layna would set aside her crown and its burdens and choose a life with him instead.

The first time he witnessed Layna hosting her assembly, he had barely known her. Their interactions were rife with tension, her fiery spirit clashing with his teasing attitude. He vividly remembered the stern rebuke she gave him when he stepped in to defend her against a rude foreigner. Her independence had surprised him, her refusal to be seen as needing protection—a trait that had intrigued and challenged him.

How things had changed in just a few short months—now, Layna sought him out first when she felt vulnerable, finding in him comfort, protection, and solace.

Back then, Zarian could never have predicted that he would fall so deeply in love with her, the Daughter of the Moon. Watching her now, he marveled at the emotions she inspired in him.

As the assembly continued, his gaze remained fixed on her, and a silent vow formed in his heart. No matter what the future held, he was completely, irrevocably hers. In her, he found his home.

He chose her.

He could only hope that she, too, would choose him.

Night had enveloped the city by the time Lord Varin entered his home. The day's events swirled in his mind like a maelstrom—the council meeting, the unexpected news from Baysaht—all played over in his thoughts as he made his way through the dimly lit halls of his residence.

The moment he entered his bedroom, intending to shed the day's pretenses along with his clothes, he was forcefully thrust against the wall, his face pushed into the cold stone, the cold kiss of a blade pressed sharply against his throat.

"What have you learned?" the voice, dark and gravelly with threat, pierced the silence.

Varin laughed bitterly. "You certainly took your time, didn't you? And must we always play this tiresome charade? Have I not proven my loyalty?"

The blade pressed harder, drawing a thin line of blood.

"Yes, yes, I have news," Varin stammered, his earlier confidence evaporating. "Baysaht is sending 250,000 men to Alzahra. It will shift the tide of the war. Our whore of a princess must have spread her—"

The pressure against his throat eased, and then Varin was violently slammed into the wall. He crumpled to the floor.

Dazed and breathing heavily, he struggled to his feet. Varin spun around, his breath catching as he faced a towering figure shrouded in black.

The cloaked man's posture radiated with unchecked rage, his stance rigid, every line of his muscular body spelling imminent threat. The lower half of his face was hidden, but his unruly hair and his hazel eyes, currently blazing with fury, were unmistakable.

A moment passed—a moment too long—before a chilling wave of recognition washed over Varin. It rooted him to the spot, sending a fearful shiver down his spine and turning his blood to ice in his veins.

"Prince Zarian…" he breathed, disbelief and fear mingling in his voice, eyes wide with shock.

Zarian lowered his mask, revealing his face, his every feature taut with barely contained wrath. His voice vibrated with a cold, seething anger that cut through the air, "I had hoped I was wrong about you, Varin."

In the tense silence that followed, Lord Varin scrambled for a lifeline. "Wait, Prince Zarian, please," he pleaded, wringing his hands together. "I can help you! Let me act as a double agent. I'll feed false information to Zeph—"

Zarian's fist silenced him with a solid punch, knocking Varin out cold. The crunch of bone felt satisfying beneath his knuckles.

Varin slumped to the floor, a heap of treachery and failed plots, his grand visions for power and wealth dashed in a single moment.

Zarian stepped over Varin's prone body and exited the house into the cool night. Four trusted members of the palace guard were waiting for him.

"It's confirmed. Varin is a traitor," Zarian rumbled. His hands flexed at his sides. "He's unconscious in the bedroom. Take him to the dungeon." He paused for a moment, his gaze hard and unyielding. "And there's no need to be gentle with him."

The head of the palace guard, Jaffar, nodded solemnly.

"Yes, Your Majesty. Consider it done."

Zarian placed a firm hand on the man's shoulder in gratitude. Without another word, he turned and made his way back to the palace, his steps quick and determined. The night air cleared his head, but not his heart, which still pounded with rage at Varin's crude words about Layna.

Upon arriving, he headed straight to the king's private office where a meeting was already underway. King Khahleel, Queen Hadiyah, Layna, and Lord Ebrahim were gathered, worry blanketing every face.

As Zarian entered, Layna's face caught his attention. Her brows were knit together, and her lips were slightly parted, as if she were about to speak. Her eyes, wide and troubled, searched his face for answers. The sight of her, so beautiful yet so concerned, melted the remnants of his anger, replacing it with a strong urge to comfort.

"What happened, Zarian?" King Khahleel asked, a deep crease between his brows.

"Varin is indeed a traitor," Zarian reported. "He's been feeding information to Zephyria. The guards are bringing him to the dungeon now. Jaffar will begin interrogating him tonight."

A heavy silence fell over the room. King Khahleel's face hardened, the betrayal of a council member a harsh blow.

Layna remained silent, her worried eyes locked on Zarian.

Queen Hadiyah brought up another pressing matter. "With Layna's nightmares becoming more frequent, has the time not arrived to inform the council about the prophecy and the eclipse? They will be blindsided."

King Khahleel, after a moment of consideration, responded decisively. "No. We do not fully understand what will happen. We cannot afford to trust anyone outside of this room."

"Does Burhani know about the prophecy?" Layna asked, turning to Lord Ebrahim.

"No. And I will keep it that way," the senior adviser assured. "We can break the news of Lord Varin's betrayal to the council tomorrow. Perhaps, we'll have more to report after his interrogation."

After the meeting, Layna retired to her quarters. She went about her nightly routine, slipping into a lilac silk nightgown. Despite the late hour, sleep seemed an elusive companion.

As she pulled back her bed sheets, a faint sound from the balcony caught her attention. She approached the balcony doors, hope fluttering within her as she saw a familiar figure climb over the railing, the moonlight casting his shadow into the room.

"Zarian!" Layna's voice cut through the quiet of the night, her face lighting up as if kissed by the sun's first rays. "I didn't expect you tonight. I thought you'd be in the dungeon."

The prince smiled, one that spoke of weariness, but also of an affection that refused to be dimmed.

"I wanted to see you," he said simply, stepping into her room. "The dungeon can wait."

His gaze slowly trailed over her body, lingering on her curves. The moonlight filtered through the pale fabric, outlining her silhouette in a way that left very little to his imagination. Warmth ignited within him, and he swallowed deeply, his mouth suddenly dry.

Layna recognized the hunger in his gaze. She closed the distance between them. "Zarian," she whispered, gently touching his cheek.

"From the depths of my heart, thank you. You handled the matter with Varin for me, just as you promised."

Zarian smiled down at her, brushing back a lock of hair from her face.

"Of course. I am yours." He inhaled deeply, trying to steady his racing heart, but her proximity made it nearly impossible. He could feel the heat emanating from her, and it was wreaking havoc on his self-control.

Layna reached for his hand. "Come," she said softly. "Tell me everything." Zarian followed, settling down next to her on the thick carpet. Layna leaned back against her bed, her nightgown draped tantalizingly over her form.

Zarian struggled to focus as he recounted the night's events, his eyes often wandering over Layna's curves. He was careful to shield her from Varin's venomous words. Layna listened intently, her gaze locked on him.

As Zarian concluded his tale, she sat back in disbelief. "You punched him? In the face?!" Her laughter filled the scant space between them. "Impossible."

Zarian adopted a mock-offended expression, raising an eyebrow in indignation.

"My dear Layna—I am first and foremost a *warrior*," he asserted with playful sternness. "There is no one I haven't bested in a swordfight, including you, in case you've forgotten."

A happy laugh escaped her again, her eyes sparkling with mirth. "Forgive me, my strong, formidable prince. I didn't mean to insult your prowess. Sword fighting is different. It's an art, more of a dance.

I just can't imagine you *punching* someone like in a common tavern brawl. You're the gentlest man I know."

Zarian twirled a lock of her hair around his finger. "You bring out the best in me, Layna," he said softly, his smile slowly fading. "You don't know what I'm capable of."

Layna's smile turned coy, her gaze steady on his. Leaning in, she whispered seductively, "I want to learn *exactly* what you're capable of." She sat up on her knees, moving closer to him, opening her arms in invitation.

Zarian gripped her hips and pulled her close. His usual restraint, worn thin by the flimsiness of her nightgown, threatened to snap under the weight of his desire.

Layna's breath hitched as he held her against his strong form, her hands instinctively rising to rest on his chest.

Zarian bridged the gap between them, his lips soft against hers, moving with a tenderness that contrasted with the strength of his grip. Layna responded in kind, her own lips parting slightly, inviting him deeper into her mouth. His hands tightened on her hips, anchoring her to him, as if he could merge their bodies into one.

Zarian's tongue brushed against hers, a bold stroke that elicited a soft moan from her, the sound swallowed by the depth of their kiss.

His hand traveled up her back to tangle in her long locks, a silent plea for closeness that Layna eagerly answered, her fingers gripping the fabric of his tunic as she pressed her soft curves against the hard planes of his body.

Their tongues dueled, a sweet exploration that sent shivers down Layna's spine. Zarian groaned, a rumbling, primal sound that vibrated through them both. She breathed heavily, her chest rising and falling rapidly against his with a delicious friction. Their breath mingled in the scant space between them when they parted for air, only to be drawn back deeper into the kiss.

Layna, emboldened by their passionate exchange, trailed her hand down Zarian's firm chest, her fingers tracing the ridges of his muscular abdomen through his tunic.

Yet, as she ventured further south, Zarian's reflexes snapped into action. Without breaking their kiss, he firmly intercepted her wandering hand, guiding it back to rest on his neck, his tight grip conveying a silent message.

Layna panted as she pulled away, a frown creasing her brow as disappointment flashed across her features. Her lips parted, poised to voice her frustration, but Zarian preempted her words with a quick, silencing kiss. Not stopping there, he peppered kisses all over her face, each one soft and light, scattering her thoughts like leaves in the wind until, eventually, her pout transformed into a smile.

He continued, kissing down her neck and tickling her with the stubble along his jaw, until Layna began to laugh. His fingers danced along her sides, finding and exploiting her ticklish spots with a gentle precision that left her squirming in his arms. Her laughter, bright and unguarded, filled the room.

Zarian held her tightly against him as her laughter melted into gentle, contented sighs. He leaned in, his lips tenderly brushing her forehead, then gliding down to caress her nose, before finally capturing her lips in a kiss so soft, so filled with love, that it washed away all trace of her frustration.

Layna gazed up at him, her eyes shining with adoration. "Is this your way of signaling that it's time for you to leave?" she whispered, her voice threaded with longing.

"Leaving you," he whispered against her lips, "is the last thing I want to do. But duty calls, even at this hour." His thumb tenderly traced her cheek. They moved to the balcony, sharing a silent farewell under the moon's watchful gaze.

He gave her one final kiss, a seal on their passion, before stepping over the railing and disappearing into the night.

Slipping into bed, the silk sheets were cool against Layna's warm skin. The memory of his lips lingered, his hands exploring the curves of her body with a hunger that matched her own. She tossed and turned restlessly, her nightgown brushing against her sensitive skin, each sensation a reminder of his touch. She was drenched in his intoxicating scent, yet his absence made her ache with desire and frustration.

Why had he stopped?

She traced her lips, remembering the pressure of his mouth against hers. Zarian's devotion was clear. Yet, when it came to crossing this final boundary, he still held himself back.

Layna wasn't naïve. She knew he was experienced—such a man as Zarian, with his handsome features and charm, and more importantly, the anonymity of his missions, would have had no lack of companionship. She tried not to dwell on those who might have come before her, always succumbing to the slithering tendrils of jealousy that twined around her sanity, pulling her down into their green, suffocating depths.

But why not me? The question haunted her amidst the residual heat of their passion.

As her body began to calm and the haze of lust cleared from her mind, her thoughts drifted to the day's events. Nizam's offer of 250,000 soldiers—an entire army lent without treaty or alliance—was staggering.

It was an outrageous move, one that would not have been made lightly. Baysaht's council must have voiced reservations about wagering so many of their soldiers.

Yet Nizam had moved forward with it. Why?

Her personal history with him added to her confusion. What did Nizam's current gesture signify? And why now? Layna's mind raced with possibilities, none of which made sense.

An irrational resentment stirred within her—a bitter feeling, not for the aid, but for the vulnerability it underscored. Alzahra's reliance on Baysaht's soldiers highlighted their weakness against Zephyria and its newfound allies.

With these thoughts, Layna eventually drifted into a fitful sleep. The night's events wove through her dreams, a flurry of desire, duty, and the deep, unfathomable game of kings and kingdoms.

Returning to his chambers, Zarian felt Layna's kisses still clinging to him. Entering the washroom, he turned on the cold water and stepped into the shower, hoping to clear the fog of lust clouding his mind.

The cold cascade was a harsh wake-up call, an icy reminder of the restraint he was supposed to uphold, both for his sake and Layna's. As the water sluiced over him, he chastised himself for his lack of control. He longed to give her everything she desired, but the fear of losing her constantly lurked in his mind, ever-present and mocking, casting a shadow over their moments together.

Dressed and somewhat centered, Zarian headed to the dungeon. Varin, battered but defiant, sat on the floor of his cell.

Jaffar reported, "He's a stubborn one, Your Majesty. Hasn't said a word yet, but the night is still young."

Zarian approached Varin, his steps echoing in the dank cell. The flickering torches cast long shadows across Varin's face, accentuating the bruises and the defiance that still lingered in his eyes.

"You've had a long night," Zarian began, crossing his arms over his chest. "It can end here if you cooperate."

Varin, slumped against the cold stone wall, lifted his head slightly, meeting Zarian's gaze. He remained silent. Despite his disheveled appearance, there was a flicker of resolve in his eyes, a stubbornness that had yet to be broken.

Zarian crouched down, his voice dropping to a dangerous whisper. "You understand the gravity of your situation. This isn't just about treason. It's about survival. Yours and Alzahra's. Speak now, and you might yet save yourself from a fate worse than this dungeon."

The silence that followed was thick. Varin's gaze faltered, darting away for a moment, but still he refused to speak, his lips pressed together tightly.

Zarian sighed and nodded to the head guard. "Keep me informed, Jaffar," he said as he straightened. Zarian exited the cell, the heavy door closing behind him with a dull thud.

As the prince retraced his steps back to his chambers, his mind was a whirlwind of thoughts. Varin's silence posed an obstacle, but it was one he was determined to overcome. The stakes were too high, the risks too great to allow one man to stand in their way.

They would break him.

Stepping into his quarters, Zarian froze, eyes widening in surprise.

Jamil was lounging casually on his bed, one arm propped behind his head as he ate a mirsham fruit.

"You're not the only one adept at scaling balconies," his fellow Medjai quipped sarcastically.

Zarian chose silence as his response, his expression guarded as he slowly unstrapped his sword and tossed it onto the sofa.

Jamil took a deep breath, the stiffness easing out of him slightly as he rose from the bed. "I want to apologize. It's been difficult for me to separate Zarian, the Medjai's crown prince, from Zarian, the man. My friend. I will do better. Let's move past this."

Unbridled relief washed over Zarian at his friend's words. "It took you long enough," he said, a genuine smile lighting up his face.

Jamil crossed the room and placed a hand on his shoulder. Without a word, Zarian pulled him into a tight embrace.

As they stepped back, Zarian punched Jamil's arm. "That's for putting your boots on my bed." Jamil chuckled, rubbing his arm lightly with a grin.

Zarian poured a glass of water for himself and offered one to Jamil. With a dramatic sigh, he began painstakingly dusting off his bed.

Jamil rolled his eyes.

"You were at the Oasis longer than I expected," Zarian said, sitting on the bed. "Did you see Soraya? How is she?"

Jamil leaned against the wooden bed frame. "She's safe and happier than I expected. She's quite adamant that you keep Layna in good spirits." The corner of his mouth quirked up. "Her exact message was, 'Ensure my sister remains happy, or else you'll answer to me.'"

Zarian chuckled affectionately, shaking his head.

"And she's thrown herself into life at the Oasis with surprising zeal, especially where our agriculture is concerned. She's brimming with ideas," Jamil added, a note of admiration creeping into his voice.

Zarian observed his friend closely. "And how is Almeer?" he asked casually.

The mention of Almeer drew a shadow over Jamil's features.

"He's been...ordinary," Jamil began begrudgingly. "He mostly spends his time with Soraya or keeps to himself. No odd contacts or other behavior. It's unlikely that he's working for Zephyria." Jamil glanced away for a moment, a flicker of frustration—or perhaps disappointment—crossing his face.

Zarian nodded thoughtfully. "I'm grateful for your change of heart," he finally said.

Jamil's mouth tightened into a hard line. "Unfortunately, our reconciliation was not the reason for my visit. Prepare yourself. The elders have confirmed it. The eclipse will occur in three days' time."

CHAPTER TWENTY-SIX

The weathered king stood on a high balcony, overlooking the rocky expanse of his kingdom. He turned slightly as his most trusted general approached.

"How is our guest adapting?" the king inquired, his voice as coarse as the rocks and pebbles that covered the mountains.

"He has exceeded all expectations, sire," the general replied, a tall man clad in battle-worn armor. "He is exceptionally well-trained and already outperforming our best soldiers."

The king raised an eyebrow. "Go on."

"Last night, I left him deep in the forest with nothing but the clothes on his back. By dawn, he had returned with a large deer, killed with his bare hands. And every morning, he runs the mountain course. He's already set the best time we've ever recorded, but I haven't told him yet. I want him to keep pushing himself."

A slow smile spread across the king's lined face. "Excellent," he murmured. "We made the right decision in allowing him to stay. He could be the weapon we need."

The general nodded in agreement, his gaze following the king's over the sprawling landscape.

As he turned to leave, the king spoke again. "Tell him he has the best time. Something tells me it would do him well to hear it."

Azhar sat alone in Jorah's old chambers, the ancient orb resting in his hands. Countless days and nights he had spent trying to unlock its mysteries. Yet, it remained inert, a silent enigma cradled within his palms.

Frustrated, he decided upon a new course of action. Perhaps under the moonlight, in the solitude of the wilderness, it might reveal its secrets.

As he headed toward the stables, his stride was purposeful, the orb secured in his cloak. The sight of the stable door slightly ajar stopped him in his tracks—an unusual occurrence at this late hour—and set his senses on edge. Sword drawn, he cautiously entered, his presence alerting the horses, their nickering the only sound in the night.

He inspected each stall carefully, tension coiling tighter in his chest with each step. The stables seemed deserted save for the horses, but his gut was screeching that something was wrong. As he approached the last stall, anticipation sharpened his focus.

Without warning, the door burst open, and a masked figure rushed out, launching an aggressive attack. The assailant aimed his dual blades with lethal intent, but Azhar was a tempest in human form. Swords clashed, metal singing against metal, echoing off the stone walls of the stable.

Azhar parried with a force that sent vibrations up the attacker's arm. He advanced, his lone blade a blur of deadly precision, cutting through the air with brutal elegance. The attacker tried to retaliate, his swords aiming for Azhar's vulnerabilities. Yet, Azhar seemed to predict each strike, his countermoves a dance of death that left no room for error.

A second attacker raced into the stables. Azhar was outnumbered, yet unyielding. He moved with a predator's grace, his attacks carving arcs of silver into the air, each one finding its mark with unerring efficiency.

The frantic whinnying and agitated snorts of the horses filled the air. The attackers were relentless, but Azhar turned their momentum against them, exploiting every falter, every second of hesitation. With a calculated maneuver, he disarmed one assailant and quickly ran him through with his sword.

He cornered the second attacker. His blade was a whisper away from victory. A final exchange, a flurry of desperate defense met with unstoppable force, until Azhar's sword found its mark and pierced through the assailant's neck.

Breathing heavily, Azhar stood victorious on the bloody stable floor. Chest heaving, he wiped the sweat from his brow, and sheathed his sword, the cold satisfaction of survival his only companion.

He approached the bodies slowly. Removing the chest plate off one corpse, he ripped its tunic down the front. The Medjai tattoo revealed itself under the moonlight, black ink mingling with crimson blood.

A cruel smile twisted Azhar's lips.

Leaving the carnage behind, he remained vigilant, the ways of the Medjai echoing in his mind—they often sent three men for a single kill.

He knew there would be one more.

His return to his chambers was cautious, every shadow a potential threat.

And there, as predicted, the third assassin awaited.

Despite his fatigue, Azhar's strikes were sharp and true, each blow fueled by a lifetime of scorn.

But in the heat of battle, Azhar found himself momentarily bested, his sword knocked from his grasp by a cunning maneuver. The clang of his weapon hitting the stone floor echoed ominously through the chambers, a sound that would have spelled death for a lesser warrior.

But Azhar was no ordinary foe.

His attacker advanced, his blade a deadly promise in the dim light. But Azhar was far from defeated. With the calm of a seasoned predator, he reached down to his boot, his movements masked by the feint of retreat.

In a fluid motion, he drew a concealed dagger. With a swift, practiced motion, Azhar's arm shot forward. The dagger found its mark, plunging deep into the assassin's chest.

The impact forced a gasp from the man's lips, his eyes widening in shock and pain as he staggered back. Azhar watched, an impassive observer to the final moments of his life. The man clutched at the dagger, a feeble attempt to stem the flow of life ebbing away. His knees buckled, and he collapsed to the floor, his final breaths a raspy whisper in the night.

Azhar waited a moment, then retrieved his dagger with calm detachment, wiping the bloodied blade on the dead man's trousers. He stood motionless over the lifeless body.

Have I made you proud now, Father?

He stepped into the dark corridor and called for a servant, his voice echoing sharply against the stone walls.

A gangly boy, no more than fifteen, hurried to his side. "Y-yes, sire?" the boy asked, his voice trembling.

"There are two bodies in the stables and one in my chambers," Azhar declared. "Take care of them. And have the men sweep the entire castle for intruders. I want no corner unchecked." Azhar glanced back into his chambers. "And bring me Lords Ebric and Garrisman. Immediately."

The boy nodded, a quick bob of his head, and rushed off, his steps echoing in the quiet corridor.

Within thirty minutes, Lords Ebric and Garrisman arrived. Their expressions were carefully neutral, but their eyes repeatedly flitted to the pool of blood on the floor, a question in their gazes they dared not voice.

The aftermath of violence lingered in the air.

"Ebric," Azhar said, "you visited the astronomers today. What have you learned?"

"Sire, I was on my way to see you when the servant came to fetch me. The astronomers have confirmed it." His eyes darted back to the bloody floor. "The eclipse will take place in three days."

A chilling smile spread across Azhar's face. "The time has come," he rejoiced, his cold smirk not quite reaching his eyes.

Addressing Lord Garrisman with a voice as sharp as a blade, he commanded, "Ride out immediately to the camp. Our full-scale assault begins at once. By the break of dawn, Alzahra shall face its reckoning." Azhar's voice grew colder still. "Instruct the generals to divide our forces in half. The first contingent will advance toward Alzahra City from the northwest, leaving a trail of destruction. Show no mercy. Let none survive in their path. Our remaining men will flank from the southwest. Alzahra will be forced to divide their defenses, and as a result, be stretched too thin to offer any real resistance on either front."

The orders were brutal, a strategy designed not just for victory, but for annihilation. Lords Ebric and Garrisman exchanged a brief look, before nodding in understanding.

As the lords left, the room felt colder. Azhar focused on the orb, its surface still dull in his hands. "Soon," he whispered, as if it could hear him. "The prophecy will unfold, and all will be as it should."

In the silence of the night, the stars were indifferent witnesses. Azhar's plan was set in motion, a grim countdown to a dawn that promised nothing but bloodshed and sorrow.

CHAPTER TWENTY-SEVEN

The council chamber was awash with mid-morning sunlight, casting long shadows across the polished floor. The air was tense as the council members took their seats around the large table.

King Khahleel stood, his gaze sweeping across the room. "I have grave news. Lord Varin has betrayed us. He is an agent for Zephyria."

A tangible shock rippled among the council members. Disbelief and outrage mingled in the air.

Before the murmurs grew, Lord Ebrahim stood, his expression grim. "To make matters worse, Zephyria launched an attack at dawn on our southeast and northeast borders. We've split our forces to protect the villages on both fronts." His voice was steady, but the underlying concern was unmistakable. "Significant casualties have been reported. I await more news from our scouts."

Lady Mirah spoke next. "We must fortify our key villages. Holding them will give us leverage to push back."

Queen Hadiyah, her brows furrowed, added, "Send messengers to our allies. Urge them to hasten their aid. Every moment counts now."

Lord Ebrahim continued, "Shahbaad sends resources but no soldiers. They have their own political tensions. And Bilkaan will secure our coast should Ezanek attack by sea."

The council turned their attention to the promise of Baysaht's 250,000 men. The sheer number brought a glimmer of hope. "Baysaht's army is mobilizing," Lord Ebrahim continued. "However, it will take days for them to join our men in the northeast. We must hope our men can hold off the Zephyrians until then." Lord Ebrahim's final words were a somber reminder. "Your Majesty, the city awaits your address in a few hours. They look to you for reassurance."

King Khahleel nodded as he addressed his council. "We face a trial that will test the very core of our kingdom. But we stand together."

The capital's city square, usually a lively hub, was tense with anticipation. A raised stand had been erected, a temporary throne for the royal family, who sat in dignified silence against the city's backdrop.

Below, Zarian stood among the crowd, scanning the sea of faces for any sign of threat. The atmosphere was charged, a collective breath held in anticipation of the king's address. Zephyria's morning assault had sown seeds of unease, leaving the citizens frightened, their murmurs a restless whisper on the wind.

King Khahleel rose, commanding silence with his presence alone. "My beloved citizens," he began, "before we discuss the war, let us first turn our attention to a rare event—an eclipse, set to grace our skies the day after next."

"It is a spectacle of nature's design, yet it comes with dangers. Our astronomers advise caution. Please, stay within your homes if you are able, and keep your eyes averted from the sky until it has passed."

"Now, the grave matter on all our minds. The war. I know it has brought worry to your hearts and doubt to your minds. But hear me now: Alzahra will stand together. We will show our enemies the might of our unity!"

Zarian's gaze found Layna. Her face was a mask of poise, every inch the future queen, a composed exterior that he knew concealed a raging storm.

"The Nahrysba Oasis has sent us 10,000 men," Khahleel continued. "Shahbaad and Janta have provided ample resources, weapons and food, and Bilkaan has secured our coast. Together, we are stronger than ever."

Murmurs of approval rippled through the crowd, but still, an undercurrent of unrest remained.

And then, Khahleel delivered the news that turned the tide of the gathering. "And now, King Nizam of Baysaht is dispatching *250,000* soldiers to aid us."

There was a moment of stunned silence.

Then the crowd erupted in applause and loud cheers.

A voice began to chant, "King Nizam!" The name was picked up, echoed by more and more voices until it became a beat, "King Nizam! King Nizam! King Nizam!"

Khahleel remained stoic, his expression betraying nothing. Yet, there was a subtle lift in his demeanor, a hint of satisfaction that his people were reassured. His speech had successfully rallied the people, lifting spirits and reaffirming their unity.

Long after the crowd dispersed, the echo of "King Nizam" still lingered, a rhythmic pulse that seemed to synchronize with Zarian's heartbeat. It reverberated through his chest, tightening a noose around his heart.

King Nizam.

King Nizam.

King Nizam.

Later in the day, Layna sought refuge in the hidden library beneath the palace. Descending the narrow stairway, the cool air of the underground chamber greeted her. Surrounded by the wisdom of the ancients, she felt a connection to her kingdom's history, a thread that tied her to the long lineage of rulers.

Some nights, when the weight of destiny felt too heavy, she would lose herself in the texts until exhaustion claimed her. Zarian often found her asleep amidst the scrolls, her face pressed against the brittle pages. Layna marveled at the history hidden here, the secrets of the ancient Medjai scattered across the continent.

She pored over the texts. Which Alzahran king or queen had first allied with the Medjai? Did they know of the prophecy? Had a distant ancestor foreseen her role centuries prior, of a descendant destined to bring about something great, perhaps, catastrophic?

The library became her world for hours. Faded ink and dead dialects presented challenges. How much knowledge had been lost to time?

Again and again, her eyes returned to the shimmering lines of the prophecy, the mention of the "earthly moon" sending uneasy shivers down her spine.

Layna sighed heavily. Like every other night, she had learned nothing useful about the eclipse. The dwindling candlelight signaled it was time to retreat.

Returning to her chambers, she looked forward to seeing Zarian. As she waited for him, she reflected on her father's address, the rallying cry around King Nizam, and the tangled web of gratitude and resentment ensnaring her heart.

That night, Zarian didn't visit Layna's chambers. His footsteps guided him instead to the dark depths of the palace dungeon. The air was thick with the scent of damp stone and the faint, unsettling tang of rust. Moisture clung to the walls, where the light from flickering torches cast shadows that danced with a life of their own. The corridors echoed with the soft drip of water.

In the heart of the dungeon, Lord Varin's labored breaths and the clinking of his heavy chains filled the cold, dark space. Draped in shadows that swallowed hope itself, he was a sight of defiant misery. The dungeon's air was thick and stale, as if the very breeze had been banished from its dank, suffocating depths.

Zarian stood before Varin, his silhouette stark against the flickering shadows. His voice resonated with authority, each word echoing off the cold stone walls. "What have you disclosed to Zephyria? Who are you working with? Are there other spies in the palace?" He fired off his questions, his imposing presence nearly filling the entirety of the cramped cell.

Varin's response was a stubborn silence, his gaze defiant even in captivity. The only sounds were the distant drip of water and the subtle shift of chains as he adjusted his position.

Zarian's patience wore thin, the muscles in his jaw tensing. He repeated his questions, his voice a notch colder, a sharper edge to his words, demanding a breach in Varin's armored silence.

Again, the disgraced master of war offered nothing. Zarian's patience began to fray at the edges. His cold, ominous voice echoed off the cell walls as he spoke, an icy rage burning behind his eyes. "The palace guards have clearly been too gentle with you. You will find none of that lenience with me. For every unanswered question, I will break a finger. Do *not* test me."

Varin scoffed. "Do you think more torture will make me talk? You overestimate your methods." He smirked at Zarian, revealing a new, bloody gap from a missing tooth giving him a gruesome, patchwork smile. He casually leaned back against the wall and waved a dismissive hand.

Undeterred by Varin's bravado, Zarian pressed on, his voice a cold command. "Who were you reporting to?"

When silence was again the response, Zarian's patience evaporated. With deliberate calmness, he firmly grasped Varin's hand. The chilling sound of his index finger snapping was a harrowing note in the stillness of the dungeon.

Varin's scream, raw and exploding with agony, reverberated off the ancient stones. Gasping for breath, he howled anew as Zarian viciously twisted the bent finger.

The prince waited until Varin's screams subsided into sharp gasps. "Are you ready to reconsider, or shall we continue?" he asked icily.

Still, Varin remained silent. Gasping for breath, he fought through the pain, a desperate attempt to protect whatever secrets he still held.

Zarian's expression hardened. "It seems you need further persuasion." He tightened his grip, clutching Varin's wrist with one hand while applying excruciating pressure with the other. The bone gave way with a sickening snap, and Varin's resolve shattered along with it. His scream pierced the heavy air, echoing through the cell.

Zarian twisted the finger until it dangled loosely. Varin's body convulsed, arms flailing, as he recoiled from the searing pain. His eyes squeezed shut, face contorted in agony, his free hand clawing desperately at the cold, unforgiving stone beneath him.

"Please, no more!" he choked out through gritted teeth, tears streaming down his face.

Zarian flicked the broken finger for good measure, drawing a strangled gasp from Varin. He loosened his grip and fixed an assessing gaze on Varin's face. "I will ask again. Who were you reporting to?"

"I don't know!" Varin gasped. "I don't know his name. He never showed his face. He would just appear like a shadow."

"What did you tell him?" Zarian pressed.

"Mostly things he already knew. About Shahbaad's resources. And Bilkaan's naval fleet," Varin managed through clenched teeth, his breath still heaving. "He...he was interested in the princess, about her activities, and about...her relationship with you."

The cold resolve in Zarian's eyes flickered, replaced with a burning intensity. "And what did you divulge about us?" he asked, his voice a lethal whisper.

Varin's resolve wavered under Zarian's fearsome gaze. "Just that...the two of you are clearly together and that she...she feels strongly for you. And you for her."

Zarian stood motionless, eyes murderous, a statue of restrained fury. Without warning, he grabbed Varin's thumb. The sound of breaking bone was a sickening crack, followed by Varin's anguished scream.

"I told him nothing more! By the moon and sun, I swear it!" Varin cried out, tears mingling with sweat as he writhed in pain.

Zarian studied him for a long moment, his expression unreadable, a muscle ticking in his cheek. Then, quietly, he asked, "And Baysaht? What did you tell him about Baysaht?"

"Nothing!" Varin panted, frantically shaking his head. "He hadn't visited for weeks before you arrested me. Please, I knew nothing of

Baysaht's involvement until it was announced that same day in the council."

Zarian roughly grabbed Varin's chin, fingers digging in painfully, his next question a whisper of steel, "Are there other spies within these walls?"

"I—I don't know," he stammered, his voice cracking under the strain. Zarian's grip tightened on his fingers, a silent warning of more pain to come. "Please!" Varin's voice rang out desperately, "I swear on my life, he told me nothing of others. I was left to grope in the dark, merely a pawn in his game!"

Zarian's angry gaze remained unyielding. "Tell me more about this man. What do you know of him? What did he offer you?"

Varin, trembling, attempted to gather his wits. "I...I don't know much, only that he works for Zephyria. He moved like a shadow. I never heard his arrival. And there were never any signs of entry." He paused, sucking in a shaky breath. "He promised me wealth. To regain the status my family once held...and a position of power after Zephyria conquered Alzahra."

Zarian's mind raced to piece together the identity of this mysterious figure. The promise of wealth and power was a classic motivator, but the efficiency and stealth of this agent spoke of a skill set that was unnervingly professional.

Varin stared at Zarian, eyes wide, braced for more pain. The prince clutched Varin's hand, the fingers jutting out at gruesome angles, and squeezed tightly. Varin screamed in agony.

Zarian grabbed his face, roughly shaking it. "I'll be taking my leave now. Answer the guards' questions, or so help me, you will pray for death." His lips peeled back in a terrifying snarl. "If I have to come back and see your sorry face again, I won't be as gentle next time."

The prince stepped back, leaving Varin's broken form slumped against the cold stone wall.

As he reached the door, Varin's voice, laced with pain yet rife with malice, cut through the silence. "It burns your very soul, doesn't it? Awaiting Nizam's arrival? For him to come claim what he has bought?"

The words halted Zarian in his tracks. He slowly turned his head, his steely gaze meeting Varin's. Despite the pain of the interrogation, Varin's eyes sparkled with a renewed defiance, a dark satisfaction in turning the knife of truth.

Zarian's expression remained impassive, but the sting of the accusation—a bitter reminder of the debt that now ensnared Alzahra—pierced him. His fingers flexed, and he resisted the urge to turn back and crush Varin's traitorous face under his boot.

Without a word, he swiftly exited the cell, the heavy door closing behind him with a resounding thud, sealing away Varin and his venomous words.

He stood there for a moment, eyes closed, shoulders slumped under an unseen weight. Inhaling deeply, he straightened and approached the head guard.

"Well done, Your Majesty," Jaffar said. "Thank you for your help. He was a tough one to break. Your methods are, uh, quite effective." Jaffar smiled nervously. "You even had me terrified out here."

Zarian did not respond immediately. "Could any of the palace guards be working for Zephyria?" he finally asked.

"Once, I'd have said no. But in light of recent betrayals," he said, glancing back at the cell door, "I find myself grappling with doubts."

"Begin quiet inquiries," Zarian instructed. "Who among the men could be motivated to turn against Alzahra? Look into personal situations, grudges, debts—anything that could be leveraged."

"It will be done," Jaffar nodded.

Zarian glanced back at Varin through the metal bars. "Get him medical attention for his fingers," he ordered reluctantly, the words tasting of ash in his mouth.

CHAPTER TWENTY-EIGHT

King Tahriq, seated at the head of a long, wooden table, surveyed the main hall of his palace. A profound transformation had taken root in the Oasis. Greenery, vibrant and lush, intertwined with the pillars of the hall, breathing new life into the ancient space. Cascades of jasmine vines spilled over edges of high alcoves, their white blooms releasing a sweet fragrance that pleasantly perfumed the air. These new plants thrived under the careful stewardship of an unexpected visitor.

As Tahriq's gaze lingered on the greenery, a begrudging warmth fluttered strangely in his chest. When the Alzahran princess first arrived seeking refuge—the *second* unwelcome visitor Zarian dared send to the sacred Oasis—his fury had been staggering.

For days, his displeasure raged like a tempest throughout the palace. The elders had remained stone-faced when he informed them, not a single one uttering a word when Tahriq assured them that the princess would be far removed from Medjai activities.

He allowed her to stay out of love for his son, yet it was clear that Zarian's decisions were increasingly guided by his heart. The crown prince's loyalties were dangerously divided, a fact that he desperately tried to conceal from the elders.

However, as days merged into weeks, Tahriq's initial ire gave way to an unexpected admiration for Soraya's strong spirit and sharp intellect. Within mere days of her arrival, she boldly made several requests for an audience with him. Tahriq swiftly rejected each one, growing increasingly irritated at her audacity.

Undeterred, the young princess had disrupted a council meeting the following week. Ignoring Jamil's insistence that she was not allowed inside, she barged in anyway. Tahriq's astonishment mirrored Jamil's, whose eyes widened into saucers, his mouth hanging open. Soraya, either oblivious or indifferent to the stunned silence, confidently approached the table with several rolled-up parchments under her arm.

Settling into a vacant seat, she unfurled her plans for agricultural advancement with an excitement that left the room momentarily paralyzed. She proposed a new irrigation method, one that promised to extend the life-giving waters of their springs further into the arid reaches of the desert. It was actually quite brilliant.

His advisers had turned to him with confused expressions, unsure how to address her proposal. After a moment's hesitation, Tahriq had approved her request, eager to be rid of her. He instructed Jamil to coordinate any resources she needed. She stood and smiled brightly, bowed, and then flounced out of the room.

Now, with the projects flourishing under her keen oversight, Tahriq felt an unexpected swell of pride and respect. The thought of his wife, Ruqi, crossed his mind, and for a fleeting moment, he imagined having a daughter like Soraya. A little girl, her laughter echoing through the stark halls, would have been a welcome presence.

Tahriq's imaginary daughter would have grown up under Ruqi's nurturing gaze and Zarian's brotherly protection. And like Soraya, his daughter, too, would have stood before him one day, her ideas and visions for their people igniting a spark of hope and change.

A sharp pang pierced through Tahriq's heart. The idea of a daughter, with dark curls and hazel eyes, a tiny version of the woman he loved so deeply, was a dream unfulfilled.

The king sighed deeply, shaking off his melancholy. How different things might have been if Soraya had captured Zarian's heart instead of her sister. An alliance through marriage with Soraya would have been straightforward and readily accepted by Khahleel.

But destiny had carved a different path—one that linked Zarian to Layna, the elder princess destined to be queen. Khahleel and his council would undoubtedly seek an alliance with a kingdom offering more than just knowledge and secrets in exchange for her hand.

And then, there was the prophecy. She was the dangerous Daughter of the Moon, and Zarian, he knew, would not fulfill his mission.

Tahriq considered the future, and a sense of foreboding clung to his heart. More pain and heartache lay ahead for his son. The thought of Zarian enduring another loss weighed heavily on him, and he longed to protect his son from losing someone else he loved.

Tahriq's contemplation was abruptly shattered as his adviser rushed in, his face taut with concern. "Your Highness, the three men we dispatched to Zephyria…they have not returned. Their delay is too long now."

Tahriq's brows drew together, worry settling deep. This was unexpected.

His son had surprised him.

With a steady, commanding voice, King Tahriq issued his orders. "Send as many men as we can spare to Alzahra City immediately. I pray it's not too late." The adviser nodded and hurried off to set the orders into motion.

In Alzahra City's royal palace, the morning light cast shadows across the council members. Lord Ebrahim stood solemnly at the table's head, thrust into the role of master of war.

"The situation is grim. We are heavily outnumbered." He paused, letting the weight of his words settle. "However, our men are holding them at bay on the southeast front, for now. At this juncture, we are heavily reliant on Baysaht's timely arrival to assist on the northeast border."

Layna maintained a composed exterior, but her hands, folded neatly on the table, clenched slightly at the mention of Baysaht.

Lord Ebrahim continued, "The medicinal plants have aided tremendously in treating our wounded and preventing infections. We are simply overwhelmed by the sheer number of injuries."

King Khahleel nodded. "Thank you, Ebrahim." Rising to signal the meeting's end, he added, "Let us prepare as best we can. Our unity and resolve will be our greatest strength." His words, though meant to inspire, felt hollow.

As the council members dispersed, Layna caught Zarian's arm, pulling him aside. "You didn't visit last night," she said quietly.

Zarian stiffened and his eyes darted to the floor. "I'm sorry, Layna. I was…preoccupied in the dungeon." He took a deep breath before meeting her gaze. "Are you alright?"

Layna's chin quivered. "I'm afraid," she confessed, her voice low as she worried her lip between her teeth. "About the war, but also about the eclipse tomorrow. I can't believe the time is here."

The vulnerability in her voice drew Zarian closer. He wrapped an arm around her and pulled her against his chest, aware of the disapproving eyes on them yet finding it difficult to care. "We'll make it through, Layna. You're strong," he assured her. He pressed a kiss against her forehead. "I'll be with you the entire time." Her posture relaxed slightly as his soothing voice eased the edges of her anxiety.

Layna looked up, her eyes searching his. "Will you come tonight? I don't want to be alone," she whispered.

"I will," he promised, tracing his thumb along her chin.

As Layna turned to leave, Zarian stood a moment longer, his promise echoing in his heart, before following her out.

Layna found bittersweet solace in the palace gardens, surrounded by colorful blooms that reminded her of Soraya. The gardens, filled with memories of her sister, offered a pale semblance of the companionship she deeply missed.

The rustling leaves whispered softly, and the sweet aroma of jasmine enveloped her, yet offered little comfort. Her thoughts were consumed with uncertainty about the eclipse. She feared for her people and her loved ones.

She feared for her own fate.

In this tranquil refuge, her parents found her, faces etched with equal parts love and concern.

Sitting beside her, her mother spoke tenderly. "I wish I had the words to ease your burdens, my child," she said softly. "The eclipse weighs heavily on us all, but naturally, your fire seems dimmer. Remember, you were born for this. Tomorrow will come and go, and the sun will shine upon us all again. Together."

Layna offered a weary smile. "I'm afraid, Mama," she admitted quietly.

Khahleel placed a gentle hand on her head. "Worry not. You have always been our shining light. And you will remain just as bright tomorrow, and the next day, and the next. I know it in my heart." He paused and gathered his thoughts. "I realize I have not said this nearly enough, but I am immeasurably proud of you—not just for your skills and intelligence, but for your compassion and kindness. You will be an incredible queen."

Layna opened her mouth to voice her fears, the what-ifs that haunted her thoughts, "Baba, if anything should happen to me—"

"None of that," Khahleel interrupted. "Nothing will happen to you."

The trio sat in comfortable silence for a beat before Hadiyah asked, "Have you heard from Soraya? I have been missing her even more lately."

Layna smiled softly. "She's doing well, keeping busy as always. She misses us, of course, but she's mostly happy. Apparently, she's convinced King Tahriq to let her oversee the agriculture there."

King Khahleel chuckled, eyes twinkling with pride. "I would expect nothing less from her, that stubborn girl. Always blooming no matter where she's planted."

After a brief silence, her father broached the subject she had been dreading. "Layna, about you and Zarian," he began hesitantly. "The council members have expressed concerns regarding your— relationship. They fear it will undermine potential alliances, ones that could offer Alzahra significant advantages in these times."

Layna's gaze dropped to her lap. She braced for a reprimand.

Her father continued, "We can discuss more after the eclipse, but know that we trust whatever decision you make for our kingdom."

For a moment, she gaped at him, uncertain she heard correctly. She stared at her father in shock who smiled warmly, tenderly patting her head.

Her mother gave her a tight smile, though she remained silent.

The support was a blessing, one she did not expect. But a whisper of doubt echoed in her mind. *Was it enough for Alzahra?*

In Zephyria's dimly lit war room, Azhar sat at the head of the table, his generals and scouts spread out before him.

One of his seasoned scouts stepped forward. "Sire, with Valtisaan's weaponry and our forces, we have breached the southwestern defenses. The enemy is in retreat. Our advance toward the palace is unrelenting," he reported, his chest puffed out. "The desert's vastness will slow us, but by midday tomorrow, we will lay siege to the capital."

Another scout brought news from the northwest. "Several Alzahran villages have been decimated, sire. But we received intelligence that Baysaht's forces are advancing. 250,000 men, maybe more. Our divided troops won't withstand their numbers, even with Valtisaan and Ezanek's aid."

The room fell silent at this revelation. Azhar felt a flicker of irritation, a dull buzzing in his ears. Baysaht's sizable force was an unexpected complication. He hadn't risked another visit to Varin so close to the eclipse.

Azhar maintained his composure, hands steepled, gaze fixed on the map spread in front of him.

"The approaching force from Baysaht…it is a massive number, sire. What are your orders?" a general asked, breaking the silence.

Azhar's cold eyes lifted, meeting the question with a steely glare. "Our men better quicken their pace and evade them," he drawled. "No delays or weaknesses. The southwestern front will continue to march to the palace."

Unease flickered across the faces of his council, a shared shock at his casual dismissal of Zephyrian lives. But no one dared voice any dissent.

"Garrisman," Azhar commanded. "Assemble thirty of our best men. Tonight, we ride for Alzahra City."

Azhar dismissed the council and returned to his chambers with determined strides. The anticipation of the coming conflict exhilarated him. He was standing on the precipice of victory.

Preparing for the journey, he carefully secured the orb within his cloak, its surface cool and unyielding. Despite countless hours of study, the orb's secrets remained locked away. Still, Azhar maintained an unwavering faith that its true powers would reveal themselves at the right time.

As night fell over Zephyria, Azhar and his chosen men descended the narrow mountain roads as quickly as the rough terrain allowed. The thunderous clatter of hooves against rock and earth shattered the silence.

After several hours, harsh mountains eventually gave way to the sprawling desert. The sound of hooves softened to a muted rumble as they transitioned onto the forgiving sands. Clouds of dust glittered under the moonlit sky.

It was then that a soft glow began to emanate from within Azhar's cloak. Perplexed, he slowed his horse to a stop. With narrowed eyes, he drew the orb from the depths of his cloak. The orb, asleep for centuries, had begun to flicker weakly.

Urging his steed to a swift gallop, Azhar clutched the glowing orb tightly. As horse and rider charged across the sands, the orb's light grew brighter with each mile closer to Alzahra.

In the quiet of her chambers, Layna paced uneasily. She sighed and glanced again at the clock, longing for Zarian's presence to anchor her anxious thoughts.

Hearing a faint movement on the balcony, she rushed through the open doors. Before Zarian could secure his footing, she was in his arms, clinging to him as if he could physically hold her fears at bay. He wrapped his muscled arms around her tightly, a fortress against the uncertainty that overwhelmed her.

"Everything will be alright," Zarian whispered, his voice a soothing wave. They moved to the divan as he continued to weave words of comfort around her.

"I just wish I knew what to expect," Layna murmured. "Everything will change tomorrow."

"If I had to guess," he said softly, "you'll gain some sort of powers. That's why the elders are so worried. But beyond these gifts, you will remain Layna, the soul who has captivated me beyond measure." Zarian watched as Layna bit her lip. "Or maybe nothing will happen, and all this worry will have been for nothing."

She chuckled weakly.

Though comforted by his words, Layna noticed a subtle stiffness in his posture. It was barely perceptible, but to her, it was as glaring as the desert's midday sun. He seemed preoccupied, his thoughts miles away, entangled possibly in the war or the prophecy.

She wanted to ask what troubled him, to offer the same comfort he had given her, time and time again, but the words remained stuck in her throat. Instead, she leaned into him, seeking peace in his proximity.

With gentle determination, Layna pressed her lips to his in a tentative kiss. It was a kiss born of a desire to forget, if only for a moment, the uncertainty of tomorrow.

The kiss deepened as their lips moved together, kindling a warmth that spread through them both. Without breaking away, Layna straddled Zarian's lap, pressing her body against his.

Zarian's hands traced deft patterns along the curve of her back. Layna's fingers tangled in his hair, pulling him closer, deepening the kiss with an urgency that left no room for distance.

Layna pressed her soft curves against Zarian's hard planes, the intensity of her movements eliciting a deep groan from him. He reluctantly broke the kiss, sighing deeply. "Layna," he rasped.

Undeterred, she kissed down his neck. Her movements were deliberate as she rolled her hips against him. Zarian's voice grew hoarse. "*Fuck*, Layna, please," he implored more forcefully, his hands tightly gripping her hips to hold her still.

Layna abruptly halted. Climbing off his lap, she stood before him, a storm brewing in her eyes. Her long-simmering frustration finally boiled over.

"Why?" she demanded, her voice thick with anger and hurt. "Why do you always deny me? Is guarding my *chastity* also part of your sacred fucking duty?" she cried, the sting of rejection sharp in her heart.

Zarian rose to his feet, towering over her, anger flashing as he met her furious gaze with his own. "No, Layna! I'm guarding my *heart*," he retorted sharply.

Layna, taken aback, could only stare. She had expected his anger but was unprepared for the sheer anguish etched into his distraught features. The fury slowly seeped out of her.

Zarian's voice trembled, straining under the weight of fears long contained, which now spilled forth in earnest. "What if Nizam arrives tomorrow to claim your hand in exchange for the *entire army* he has sent? Would you deny his proposal? Would you allow him to return to Baysaht alongside his men and risk your citizens' lives?" His questions pierced the silence between them.

"And if not tomorrow, what if he comes after the war? In one month's time? Two months' time? Your people have rallied around him. Would you risk massive unrest by rejecting him?" Zarian's voice cracked slightly as he continued.

He began pacing the room like a caged lion.

"And if not Nizam, then some other royal from a wealthy kingdom. Alzahra will need resources to rebuild, food to replace destroyed crops. Would you choose *me* over *them*, Layna?" Zarian demanded.

His questions, a cascade of his deepest fears, filled the room, making the silence that followed even more heartbreaking.

He continued pacing angrily, clutching his head in frustration. Finally, he locked his gaze on Layna, awaiting her response.

But it never came.

Layna's eyes brimmed with tears as she witnessed the distress that racked him. She wished to reassure him, to swear she was his and only his.

But her heart was not hers to give.

She was the future queen of a war-ravaged kingdom, and so, her reassurances remained stuck in her throat.

Zarian's posture slowly deflated, anger draining away, leaving behind a man laid bare by his love. "I have nothing to offer you that you don't already possess," he said, quiet in his defeat.

His eyes shone with a love so fierce, so powerful, that he would let his own kingdom, the entire world, the very *balance* burn away into nothingness for his beloved.

A resigned sigh escaped him. "I can't even hold it against you. Your selflessness, your dedication to your people, your goodness…they are the things I love most about you."

Layna's heart stopped.

Though she'd always felt his love in his actions, in his embrace, in his kisses, he had never before spoken the words aloud.

"I am deeply in love with you, Layna," he confessed, the words thick with emotion, his eyes glistening with unshed tears. "I have been for some time now. And it claws at my soul to think I may lose you to another. At least this way, I might disappear back into the shadows and live out my days. Please…please understand."

Tears streamed down Layna's cheeks as she absorbed the depth of his pain. Zarian stepped closer, tenderly wiping them away. He embraced her, kissing her forehead in a whisper of apology.

"I'm sorry, Layna. My heart can't bear another loss," he murmured. "I'm so sorry. I know you didn't ask for any of this. Not your title, not the prophecy. And I know you're afraid for tomorrow." He looked deeply into her eyes. "We'll face the eclipse together. And afterward, I promise I won't make your choice difficult." His hand caressed her cheek, a silent plea for her understanding. "Sleep now."

He pulled away, leaving Layna alone in her chambers, her heart aching with their shared sorrow.

Numb, she stood there for what felt like hours before slowly making her way to bed, her movements mechanical, a ghost haunting her own life. She wrapped herself in cold, comfortless sheets and sobbed and sobbed and sobbed until her tears ran dry.

She sought solace in sleep, but all she saw behind closed eyelids was Zarian's heartbroken face. It haunted her. His every word had resonated with the harsh ring of truth.

Sleep eluded her, a shadow just beyond reach, until finally, hours later, she drifted into a restless slumber.

Zarian headed back to his chambers, each step heavy with regret. The night air felt suffocating, and a vengeful guilt strangled his heart.

As he turned a corner, he was intercepted by a figure hastening toward him.

It was a junior palace guard, Ajmal or Amjad, Zarian could not recall exactly. He approached with urgency, breath coming in sharp gasps.

"Prince Zarian!" the young guard exclaimed, stopping before him. "I've been searching for you." He paused, catching his breath, the flicker of lantern light casting shadows across his face. "The guards are organizing a small feast for the entire palace in honor of the eclipse. We thought it would lift spirits, given the war and all." He looked at Zarian with a hopeful expression, his fingers fidgeting awkwardly at his sides. "Oh, and I assure you, there's no ale! Only water. We must remain sharp. Please join us. We would be incomplete without you."

Zarian managed a halfhearted smile. "Thank you for thinking of me," he responded politely. "But I must decline. The night holds other plans for me. Enjoy the celebration." Zarian started to walk away, then turned back. "How is your mother, by the way? I recall she was unwell."

The guard's expression shifted, the shadows playing across his face deepening. He hesitated for a beat before offering a strained smile. "She is much improved, thank you. Your concern has been a comfort to us both," he replied, not quite meeting Zarian's eyes.

"That's good to hear. Give her my best wishes." With a nod, Zarian bid the young guard good night and turned toward the solitude of his quarters.

Inside, he closed the door with a soft click, the sound echoing like a judge's gavel—final and condemning.

It found him guilty.

He trudged to his bed and sat down, head in his hands, tormented by the memory of Layna's tear-streaked face. The guilt of causing her such distress on the eve of the eclipse tore at him mercilessly. He wished he could take back his words, wished he had suppressed his insecurities for just one more day to spare her the added burden.

Sighing deeply, he rose to prepare for sleep. He poured a glass of water from the pitcher by his bedside and drank deeply, the cool liquid soothing his parched throat.

As he lay back, Layna's sorrowful image haunted him, a reminder of the pain he inflicted upon the person he loved most. Sleep quickly overcame him, dragging him into a deep, uneasy slumber.

Yet even in his dreams, Layna's tears followed.

CHAPTER TWENTY-NINE

As the first light of dawn broke over the horizon, Azhar and his men approached Alzahra City's main checkpoint. The moon, unusually large and lingering, cast an eerie glow, painting the sky an otherworldly shade of pink.

Azhar surveyed the surroundings, his gaze settling on the moon. "Listen, men, and listen well," he commanded, his voice clear over the sounds of the waking city. He quickly outlined their strategy. His men nodded, faces set in determination.

With a subtle signal, twenty of his men, disguised as commoners, approached the busy checkpoint. They moved with the unassuming gait of merchants, though their horses were laden with weapons instead of wares.

Despite the early hour, a line had already formed at the gate, mostly travelers seeking rest and merchants eager for trade. The tension among the Zephyrians was a silent undercurrent, invisible to the unsuspecting guards who watched over the throng.

In a sudden, orchestrated chaos, the tranquility shattered. The remaining ten Zephyrians thundered over the dunes toward the city walls. The furious rumble of hooves was the first warning, swiftly followed by the whistling death of arrows, arcing through the sky toward the guards. Panic ensued as arrows found their marks, throwing the city's defenders into disarray.

Caught unaware, the guards yelled orders drowned out by the panicked crowd as they scrambled to respond. The checkpoint became a scene of chaos, with civilians caught in the confusion and guards abandoning their posts to counter the Zephyrians' swift advance.

Azhar seized the moment. "Follow me," he commanded, his voice cutting through the chaos. His men urged their horses forward through the now-unguarded entrance, slipping into the city with the other people escaping the attackers.

As they rode deeper into the city, one of Azhar's men voiced his confusion. "Sire, I thought the plan was to join the others and attack the guards from behind," he blurted. "Our men will be killed."

Azhar glowered at him, and the man shrank under the weight of his glare. "The plan has changed," Azhar snarled viciously.

The Zephyrians continued toward the palace, splitting into smaller groups as they neared.

Approaching a side gate, Azhar's group was met by a young palace guard. With a nervous nod, the guard silently allowed them entrance.

"Your timing is perfect," he said. "The head guard started making inquiries. They suspect another traitor alongside Lord Varin." His fingers tapped a nervous rhythm on the hilt of his sword.

Azhar's face split into a menacing smile. "It's too late for Alzahra. You will be rewarded handsomely," he assured. "Is everything according to plan?"

"Yes," the guard confirmed. "Most of the palace will be asleep for a while longer. Only a handful didn't drink the water."

"Good," Azhar said, cold determination in his voice. He addressed his men, "Go. Kill King Khahleel and end his pitiful reign. Our little spy here will guide you." He paused, thinking for a moment. "But capture the queen alive," he added. "I will send her piece by piece to Shahbaad. It's the least I can do for old Jorah."

Turning back to the traitorous guard, he ordered, "Open the gates for my remaining men. Kill anyone in your path."

Azhar reached into his cloak and withdrew the orb. Wrapped in layers of black fabric to conceal its bright glow, it shone with a fierce, pulsing light. He looked at the eerie pink sky and took a deep breath.

It was time.

She was suspended in a void, a realm where reality blurred at the edges. Falling, plummeting through infinite darkness, her screams evaporated in the air. The sensation of freefall consumed her, a sharp tug in her gut, an eternity passed in mere moments. And then, abruptly, swift impact—her breath stolen by the sudden, jarring halt.

Blink.

She inhaled deeply, and the air was rich with sandalwood and spice. Groggily, she opened her eyes, finding herself in an unfamiliar bed, the warm glow of sunlight dancing through sheer curtains. She was laying on a bare chest, solid and warm, marked with the unmistakable Medjai tattoo. Looking upward, she saw the peaceful, sleeping face of Zarian, a tranquility in his features she had never witnessed in waking life.

Blink.

In the hush of twilight, pain throbbed through her wrist, a sharp whisper of hurt. Zarian, shadow and light, sat across her, splinting her wrist. His fury blanketed them, his expression thunderous, a muscle in his cheek still pulsing with untamed fury—yet his hands on her were as gentle as a soft desert breeze. A cut marred his cheek, a dark bloom, but it was the storm in his eyes, fierce and protective, that captured her breath. She reached out, her movements slow, tentative. Her fingers brushed against his cheek, attempting to soothe the maelstrom within him. Zarian paused, his stormy gaze locking with hers. His jaw unclenched ever so slightly, the angry muscle in his cheek stilling under her touch.

Blink.

Zarian's kiss, searching and intimate, his lips sticky sweet, enveloped her senses. Breaking away, she playfully licked the corner of his mouth, her hands tightly gripping his tunic, a teasing smile on her lips. His eyes darkened as he looked down at her, and the swirling desire within them sent a shiver through her.

Blink.

They stood in a vast room, empty and abandoned, moonlight filtering through tall windows. Here, Zarian was her trainer once more, guiding her in close combat—not with swords, but with wits and agility, teaching her to face stronger, larger adversaries. He darted behind her and secured one muscular arm across her chest, immobilizing her, while the other wrapped tightly around her waist. She quickly broke the hold, just as he taught. Turning to face him, she was pleased by the clear pride on his face.

Blink.

She awoke disoriented in a cramped room. Zarian had not returned. Did he leave her here? Her heart hammered against ribs, each beat echoing her growing anxiety. The silence suffocated her, wrapped around her lungs like a vise and squeezed. Her eyes scanned the room again and again and again as if she might conjure him with sheer force of will. But then, finally, the door opened with a gentle click. Zarian entered, the air around him alive with a delicious, spiced aroma. He was carrying bags of food, his face wary in the low light. Relief washed over her in an overwhelming rush, her heart slowly settling back into a normal rhythm.

Blink.

Her heart seized painfully; Zarian stood before her, a trickle of blood escaping the corner of his mouth, the vibrant light in his hazel eyes dimming to a haunting emptiness. The sight struck her like a physical blow, pain sharp and immediate in her chest.

Blink.

They were aboard a small rowboat. Under the sun's relentless blaze, Zarian rowed with steady, powerful strokes, the corded muscles in his arms glistening in the heat. Sweat beaded on his forehead, tracing a path down his determined face. He smiled at her, warm and weary. She raised a skein of water to his parched lips, watching hungrily as his throat bobbed as he gulped it down. She insisted again that he allow her to row, even for a few minutes, but again, he immediately refused.

Blink.

Zarian knelt, chest bared and vulnerable. He gasped for air, a desperate, futile struggle for life. He swayed, struggling to stand, only to collapse with a loud thud she felt in her bones. Blood seeped from his mouth down over his neck, staining his lips a gruesome red. She screamed and screamed and screamed.

Blink.

On a secluded rooftop under the night sky, she looked at Zarian as he moved above her, moonlight illuminating his handsome face. Arms wrapped tightly around his neck, forehead pressed against his, legs twined around hips, pulling him closer, still closer, forever closer. He buried his face in her neck, breath hot against her damp skin, his movements becoming erratic. Her back arched off the thin mattress, mouth open in a silent scream.

Blink.

Zarian, consumed by a blinding white light exploding from his eyes and mouth, his body contorted in electric pain. The light flared, brighter and hotter and hotter and brighter, an unforgiving, all-consuming, hope-shattering inferno that reduced him to nothing but charred bones. The image etched itself into her mind with cruel clarity.

Blink.

His beautiful hazel eyes, unseeing and lifeless. Zarian!

Blink.

Please, Zarian! No! Mournful eyes locked on her, he tried to speak, but all that emerged was the gurgling sound of blood.

Blink.

No! Zarian! No!

Layna awoke with a strangled scream, jerking upright as if trying to physically escape her nightmare. Her heart raced, a wild drumbeat against her chest, her skin slick with cold sweat. The terror felt so vivid, so tangibly real, that the boundary between dream and reality blurred. The room spun around her, a dizzying whirl of shadows and shapes as she fought to steady her breathing.

A noise from the balcony cut through her disorientation. Hope surged through her as the double doors swung open, flooding the dark room with blinding sunlight. Squinting against the glare, she saw a tall, muscular figure silhouetted against the brightness.

"Zarian!" Layna's voice broke with relief, a strange, panicked worry churning within her as she rose unsteadily from the bed. "I'm sorry, I'm so sorry. I love you, too!" She stumbled forward, driven by a need to affirm her choice, to cling to the reality she wished for. She wrapped her arms around him and poured out her heart. "Please forgive me for taking so long. Let's leave. Let's leave right now. I don't care where, as long as we're together."

She buried her face in his neck, seeking comfort in his familiar scent, but a momentary stutter of her heart signaled that something was wrong. His scent was foreign to her, and his embrace felt different—his body stiff, his response not the warm comfort she expected. Layna's unease deepened as his hands traveled down to her backside, tightly gripping her to the point of pain.

"Z...Zarian?" she asked hesitantly. With dawning horror, she realized it wasn't the morning light blinding her, but a bright, unnatural glow from within his cloak. Fear snaked up her spine as she met his gaze—hazel eyes like Zarian's yet frosted with a coldness she had never seen before.

As he lowered his mask, revealing his face, Layna's breath caught. This was not her Zarian.

The man before her bore a striking resemblance, a near mirror image, but there were small, subtle differences that became more pronounced the longer she looked.

Objectively, he might have been more handsome, the cut of his jaw sharper, the line of his nose straighter. But his eyes, so similar yet so fundamentally different, glinted with a cruelty that chilled her very soul.

"You're...you're his brother," she breathed in both realization and accusation.

The man's smile was malicious. "Thank you for the warm welcome, Princess. It's a pleasure to finally meet you," he rumbled, his voice filled with dark promise. "I look forward to *thoroughly* making your acquaintance."

Zarian's eyes slowly fluttered open. His mind felt blanketed by an unsettlingly deep slumber. His head pounded, each beat a hammer blow. A disorienting confusion clouded his senses.

Rising slowly, regret from the previous night consumed him like a persistent fog. He trudged to the balcony, hoping fresh air would clear his head.

The sky was an eerie pink, casting the world in a surreal light. Both the sun and full moon hung in the sky, a sight that felt ominous instead of awe-inspiring.

It was unnatural, the sun's early light mingling with the moon's pale glow, marking the day of the eclipse. Realization dawned on him, cutting through his disorientation—the eclipse was today.

He had overslept, the critical moment was near, and *Layna was alone.*

Turning, he caught sight of a horse hastily tethered to a gate—clearly out of place in the gardens below.

Panic spiked through him.

His gaze landed on the unassuming pitcher of water by his bed.

Zarian snatched up his sword and bolted through the halls, his feet slapping against the cold stone, his bare chest heaving. Dread coiled within him, a serpent preparing to strike, propelling him forward.

He had to find Layna.

The palace corridors were eerily silent, the usual morning bustle absent. The silence screamed louder than any commotion.

Something was deeply wrong.

Where there should have been sounds of servants preparing for the day, there was only a heavy, oppressive stillness, as if the palace's very soul had been paused.

He reached Layna's room and found the door unsettlingly ajar. Inside, the chaos struck him like a physical blow.

It was a scene of violence. An overturned chair, its companion pushed askew, a half-torn curtain dangling from its rod, fluttering in the breeze from the open balcony doors.

Layna had fought desperately against a much stronger assailant.

He ran back into the deserted hallway, heart pounding frantically against his ribcage. Every step felt like a race against the sands of time, each grain slipping hopelessly through his fingers.

Further down, the sight of a shattered vase halted him. The scattered fragments across the marble floor spoke of a brutal struggle.

Zarian's eyes caught sight of a door further down the corridor, haphazardly thrown open. It led to the rooftop terrace.

He flew up the narrow staircase. Time was running out, and Layna, the heart of his world, was at the center of this nightmare.

Reaching the terrace, the strange pink morning light cast ominous shadows on the cold stone floor. The terrace spread wide and desolate, a stark expanse of stone framed by the sprawling city. Two pillars stood silhouetted in the unnatural light, both haunting and strangely beautiful.

Zarian's heart stopped.

His eyes were deceiving him.

Layna was tied to one of the pillars, not with rope, but with what looked like bright, pulsating *light*.

Her arms were bound above her head, thick ropes of light winding tightly around her wrists. Two more bright cables encased her waist and knees. She was suspended, her toes frantically brushing the ground for stability.

Her beautiful face was a canvas of fear. A livid bruise spread darkly across her cheek, while her lower lip was split and oozing fresh blood. An angry red welt marred her forehead.

The sight of his love, so cruelly treated, ignited a maelstrom of fury within him, scorching through his veins with the promise of vengeance.

"Layna!" he called out, unsheathing his sword as he stepped closer.

"Zarian! Wait, it's—" Her warning was cut short as another voice, chillingly familiar, halted him in his tracks.

"Hello, brother. It certainly took you long enough," Azhar said, emerging from behind the second pillar. The morning light played off his form, casting him in a silhouette both familiar and utterly alien to Zarian.

No.

No.

It couldn't be.

Zarian's mind struggled to accept who stood before him.

Frozen in shock, he took in the sight of the man he once knew. His brother had aged, the years etching themselves in new creases around his eyes and mouth. His physique was more imposing, muscles honed from years of combat.

Bright red scratches marked his face, a vicious bite mark marred his neck, and dried blood encircled his nostrils—details that, under different circumstances, might have given Zarian a grim sense of satisfaction knowing Layna had fought back so fiercely.

His brother's eyes held a cold, ruthless gleam, a far cry from the boy he remembered from childhood.

"Zaarif?" Zarian's voice was laced with disbelief and a rising anger. "Zaarif, what have you done?"

The man before him scoffed, his voice dripping with disdain. "*Zaarif.*" He spat on the ground. "Even the name they gave me was a pale imitation of yours. Zaarif is dead. I'm *Azhar* now."

The revelation hit Zarian like a thunderclap, leaving him reeling. His brother's new identity, his betrayal, merged into a singular point of pain. His mind worked frantically.

Zaarif had been in Zephyria all this time.

"Yes, that's right!" Azhar crowed, seemingly pleased at Zarian's astonishment. "I'm the new king of Zephyria. The conqueror who brought Alzahra to its knees. The man who will harness the power of the moon's Daughter. If only Father could see me now," Azhar proclaimed, his voice laced with bitter triumph. "Well...I suppose he'll see soon enough."

Zarian, still grappling with shock, implored, "It's not too late, Zaarif. Stop this now. Let her go," he said in a desperate plea to reach the brother he once knew.

"*Let her go?* Before I've had the chance to sample her myself and discover what has so enthralled you? She must be absolutely *exquisite* to lead the righteous son astray." Azhar's words dripped with venom. "After all, I've taken your leftovers my entire life."

He clamped his hand around Layna's face with deliberate roughness, fingers digging in painfully. "In due time, my little wildcat," he sneered. "First, we need your power to reveal itself."

"Don't touch her!" Zarian's roar was visceral, torn from the depths of his soul. His fury, the raw fear for Layna's safety, vibrated through the air.

Azhar smirked in a cruel mimicry of brotherly affection. "Try and stop me, brother. I'm eager to see if you can best me now." His eyes glinted with malice, arms spread in open challenge.

Clad only in his sleeping trousers, Zarian gripped his sword tightly. Azhar, fully armed and dressed for combat, presented a stark contrast.

Zarian bent his knees and raised his sword.

He waited.

With a roar, Azhar rushed forward and Zarian raced to meet him head on. Their swords clashed loudly as the brothers locked blades, each struggling to overpower the other.

Azhar managed to knock Zarian back. His voice dripped with contempt as he said, "Is this truly your best effort, brother? At this pace, you won't survive long enough to watch me have Layna."

"Don't. Say. Her. Name," Zarian snarled through clenched teeth. His face was a mask of pure fury, veins bulging in his neck, as he circled his brother, waiting for the next attack.

When Azhar struck again, he countered the onslaught with a fearsome roar. Their movements blurred, each parry and thrust a deadly dance of steel.

Azhar's mocking laughter was cut short as Zarian launched himself forward. The loud clang of metal against metal echoed off the terrace's stone floor. Each strike Zarian delivered was met with an equally powerful counter from Azhar.

Spinning quickly, Azhar landed a long, shallow cut across Zarian's abdomen. The sight of bright blood seeping from the wound sent a jolt of fear through Layna. He was at a steep disadvantage without armor. Layna's heart ached as she watched, utterly helpless, her eyes wide with terror.

Despite the wound, Zarian continued circling, searching for an opening.

Overhead, the sky darkened, the impending eclipse casting an ominous red glow over the terrace.

Azhar continued to goad Zarian, malice coating every syllable, unleashing a lifetime's worth of resentment. "Perhaps, once I've grown bored with her, I'll leave you her head, like I did with that hound of yours. Did you ever find his body, by the way?" He chuckled darkly.

The taunt hit its mark, igniting a furious fire within Zarian. With a roar of rage, he furiously launched himself at Azhar. Their swords met with a deafening clang, but Zarian fought with a vengeance that caught Azhar off guard.

In a swift movement, Zarian disarmed Azhar, sending his sword clattering to the terrace floor. He landed a deep, searing cut across Azhar's arm, slicing through leather and flesh and muscle, drawing a furious bloom of blood. Azhar cried out in pain and grabbed his wounded arm, his face contorted in agony.

As Azhar stumbled backward, reaching for his fallen sword, Zarian made a decisive choice. He dropped his own weapon and lunged forward, pulling Azhar back in a fierce grip. Without hesitation, he delivered a powerful punch to his brother's face, splitting his lip and drawing blood.

Zarian didn't stop.

A hard jab to the stomach forced Azhar to double over in pain. Zarian tackled him to the ground, swiftly climbing atop him. A flurry of punches followed, each one landing with precision and force on Azhar's face.

"You will never lay a hand on her again!" His roar was primal, a man protecting his woman.

Azhar, cunning even in desperation, managed to seize Zarian's hand and bit fiercely, tearing off a chunk of flesh from his palm. Zarian's cry of pain halted the attack, and Azhar managed to shove him off.

As both men regained their footing, Azhar's bruised and bloodied face bore the evidence of Zarian's fury.

Layna watched with a surge of hope. Her gaze drifted upward, the sky a canvas of anticipation. The eclipse was imminent, the moon inching closer to concealing the sun, slowly tinting the world in darkness.

Azhar reclaimed his sword. His stance was unsteady, the arrogance of his earlier taunts replaced with grim silence. The brothers engaged once more, swords clashing in a deadly dance. Zarian, seemingly oblivious to the pain in his hand, easily found his rhythm and quickly disarmed Azhar again. Azhar's movements were sluggish, his defenses slowly crumbling.

"I searched for you. I wanted to bring you home!" Zarian shouted, circling his brother slowly.

"It was never my home," Azhar spat. He furiously attacked again. "Father made sure of that!"

He tried to keep up with Zarian's sword, but his steps were unsteady, his reactions slow.

With a swift maneuver, Zarian swept Azhar's legs from beneath him, pinning him to the ground, his sword a hair's breadth from sealing his fate. Yet, as he gazed down at his brother's battered face, a twisted mirror of his own, an unwanted emotion clouded his judgment.

In that brief, suspended moment, with the eclipse painting the sky in shades of prophecy, Zarian's resolve wavered.

This hesitation, a moment's mercy born of the remnants of brotherhood, opened a fatal window.

Azhar seized his chance, drawing a hidden dagger and striking with lethal precision. He jammed the dagger deep into the side of Zarian's neck and viciously pulled downward.

Zarian's sword fell from his fingers as he staggered backward, clutching the gaping wound in a futile attempt to stem the flow of blood.

Layna's screams pierced the air, a harrowing echo of heartbreak and chaos.

"Zarian! Please, Zarian! No!" Despair and denial collided in her voice, her soul reaching out to him even as the bindings of light held her fast. "No! Zarian! No!"

The sky over Alzahra City transformed into a deep red canvas. The sun, fiery monarch of day, and the moon, ethereal guardian of night, met in a rare embrace. The light dimmed and the very air held its breath. An otherworldly twilight descended. Time itself seemed to pause. The sun's bright light flared around the moon's silhouette, a ring of radiance glowing in the sky. Stars, usually hidden by daylight, twinkled into visibility.

Layna could only watch helplessly as Zarian's lifeforce drained away. He fell to his knees, his mournful eyes locking onto hers for one last, regret-filled moment. He tried to speak, but only the chilling, gurgling whisper of blood escaped his lips. His body collapsed onto the cold stone floor, a pool of blood slowly forming around his head.

Layna's wail, a sound of pure anguish, filled the sky.

Azhar dragged himself toward his brother's still form, retrieving his knife from Zarian's neck with a wet squelch. With concerted effort, he stood slowly, his expression unreadable. Casting a disdainful glance downward, he nudged Zarian's foot with a contemptuous kick.

Layna's screams, raw and unyielding, tore through the air, her grief so heavy, so profound it seemed to fracture her very being. A violent storm of emotions raged within her—anguish, despair, and an overwhelming sense of loss that burned through her heart, leaving only ashes behind.

He never knew, she thought despairingly.

He never knew that, in the end, she had chosen him.

The pain of unspoken truths and dreams unlived engulfed her. They had been denied the chance to explore their love, to build a future together.

All that remained was the echo of his name in her cries.

Her anguished screams resonated across the terrace, a lament that pierced the heavens, challenging the cruelty of fate. But even as her voice rose higher, a soul-crushing numbness crept in, a cold embrace that dulled the sharp edges of her pain. With one final, heartrending cry, Layna's strength waned, and darkness claimed her, pulling her into its depths.

And then, in the desolate silence that followed, something within her stirred—a power, ancient and untamed, called forth from the ashes of her despair.

The Daughter had awakened.

CHAPTER THIRTY

The Daughter of the Moon had awoken, and with her came the promise of vengeance.

Still bound to the pillar, her head snapped up sharply. Her eyes, once clouded with tears, now blazed with an ethereal white light, her desolation giving way to a prophecy fulfilled.

Azhar couldn't suppress a twisted laugh. "At last," he crowed. "I was beginning to suspect I had the wrong princess." He spat out a mouthful of blood and grinned darkly, his teeth stained a grisly red.

With a roar that was a battle cry, the Daughter fought fiercely against the bonds of light that constrained her. Her scream sent a pulse of energy that vibrated through the air and pushed Azhar backward.

His smile vanished as he scrambled to stay grounded, reaching within his cloak to draw forth the orb. Discarding the black cloth, he held the orb aloft as if it were both his shield and sword.

The Daughter writhed violently against the glowing shackles. The light, forged from the orb's power, flickered and strained under the weight of her fury.

She pulled harder, face contorting with exertion. Azhar's expression shifted from confidence to shock, then fear, as the bonds of light cracked. The seemingly unbreakable luminescent chains began to crumble, disintegrating into nothingness as if they were mere illusions.

Finally free, the Daughter rose up into the air, a goddess among men. Her eyes were completely white, crackling with bright energy, and her long hair billowed around her.

Azhar's bravado slipped. He pointed the orb at her, desperate to regain control. A ray of pure light shot forth. The radiant beam split into three serpentine tendrils, coiling tightly around her neck, arms, and ankles.

Bound again, the Daughter pulled against the new bonds with a terrifying cry.

Azhar motioned downward with the orb, the foretold earthly moon, which pulsed brightly with energy. Straining with effort, he managed to pull the Daughter to the ground. The bright bonds tightened further around her, painfully digging into her skin.

The stone floor beneath her feet felt cold, so different from the warmth of the blistering energy coursing through her veins.

Azhar stood before the subdued Daughter, his voice carrying on the wind. "Daughter of the Moon! I command you: kneel before your king and master." His words, laced with a force not his own, echoed around them.

The Daughter's face, a mask of pure rage, twisted as she fought his command. Her spirit clashed against the earthly moon's imposing will.

But the orb's power proved too strong.

Slowly, agonizingly, her body responded to Azhar's command. She prostrated before him, her forehead pressed against the cold, unforgiving stone.

The Daughter remained kneeling for what felt like hours as Azhar towered above her.

"*There*. Is that not better?" Azhar's voice was a caress, a smooth, dark velvet, designed to tempt and persuade. "Do you not feel the difference? Such fury resides within you—cast it aside," he murmured in a honeyed whisper, his voice somehow strangely, devastatingly familiar to her ears. It sent an unwelcome shiver down her back. "We need not be enemies. I will be your protector. Your ally. Whatever you wish me to be. Together, we will reshape the world."

He observed her hungrily, a conqueror surveying his prize.

The Daughter remained motionless, her silence a heavy shroud in the charged air.

Content with her submission, smug satisfaction curled the edges of Azhar's mouth. "We can rule together as king and queen," he assured, words coated in practiced seduction, poison disguised as promise.

He watched as her body went slack, tension slowly easing out of her. "First, we'll return to Zephyria. Together, we'll learn to master your powers. Then, we'll take kingdom by kingdom and unite the entire continent under our reign."

The Daughter remained kneeling, her body relaxed and pliant, her breathing slow and deep. Pleased with her obedience, Azhar eased some of the oppressive force from the orb. The light binding her flickered in response.

Her rage simmered beneath an illusion of obedience. The Daughter listened to Azhar's grand delusions, each word stoking the fire of defiance within her.

Azhar eased more of the orb's force. With a sudden surge of energy, she bolted upright with a loud cry. She stood proud and defiant.

Undefeated and untamed.

Azhar recoiled, his expression twisting into fury.

"I would have been gentle with you, but it seems you need a firm hand!" he shouted angrily. The orb pulsed ominously in his hand, mirroring his wrath. "If it is force you desire, then so be it! One way or another, you will bend to my will!"

The Daughter's gaze was a silent scream of revulsion. Her white, crackling eyes narrowed into thin slits, and her lip curled in disgust as a shiver of abhorrence rippled through her.

With a piercing cry, she unleashed a force so strong that the very air around her trembled. The ethereal shackles binding her erupted into fragments of light, scattering into oblivion.

Panicking, Azhar raised the orb once more. A vibrant beam burst forth, attempting to bind her again.

But this time, the Daughter was ready.

She lifted her hand, and a powerful ray of light shot out from her palm to meet the orb's assault.

Azhar grimaced, the veins on his forehead pulsing as he unleashed more power from the orb. Its light flared into a blinding brilliance.

The Daughter stumbled back, overwhelmed by the sheer force of the beam. She tried to summon more of her own light, but the orb's power outmatched hers.

Azhar pushed forward, and the light from the earthly moon blazed brighter still.

The Daughter staggered back, her light wavering against the earthly moon's assault. Her legs buckled and she collapsed, her trembling hand barely managing to intercept the orb's searing beam. Light engulfed her, pinning her in place, sapping her strength.

It grew hotter and brighter, brighter and hotter, until it blazed so fiercely, it blinded her.

As she shielded her eyes, her gaze landed on Zarian's lifeless, bloodied body.

A spark of recognition flickered deep within her.

She knew him.

Fragments of time crashed through her mind—memories that weren't hers, but felt devastatingly familiar.

He offered her a pastry from his plate, his lips curving into a soft smile.

He held her, his hands steady as she sobbed into his chest, her burdens too heavy to bear alone.

He kissed her as if he'd die without her, right here, on this very terrace.

She stared at his broken body, Azhar's light bearing down, and something shattered inside her.

She *knew* him. He had been *hers*.

She rose quickly and regained her balance, the fury in her eyes burning brighter than the orb's light. Her hands shot forward, palms open against the onslaught. The light pouring from her doubled, surging brighter than the orb's brilliance.

Their energies collided, a swirling maelstrom of light where neither side yielded. The Daughter's beam fought against the orb's rays in a dance of power that lit up the terrace.

Slowly, thin streams of blood trickled from the Daughter's nostrils and eyes, painting her face with the brutal toll of her struggle.

Azhar, straining under the orb's weight, staggered backward as the beam from her hands surged in brilliance.

With an inhuman bellow, the Daughter amplified her assault. The light around her flickered wildly and enveloped her in a bright, brilliant aura.

A loud crack vibrated through the air.

Sharp fragments scattered to the floor. The Daughter's light had shattered the orb, and it crumbled, along with Azhar's hold over her.

Azhar stumbled back, his confidence dissolving into fear. "Impossible! That's impossible!" he screamed, his face a mask of pure terror as she advanced.

She raised her hand, directing a piercing beam of light into his chest. Azhar's anguished wail tore through the air, a sound vibrating with pure agony as energy engulfed him, his body stiffening under the electric flow. She intensified the beam, her anger and sorrow fueling its power. He began to convulse, light exploding from his eyes and mouth in a horrific spectacle.

Blood seeped from the empty cavities that once held his eyes, while his lips burned away, erased by the Daughter's all-consuming fury.

As she channeled more power, Azhar's form blurred, engulfed by the blinding light, until he was no longer visible, his very essence devoured by her might.

The light receded as suddenly as it had exploded, leaving behind nothing but a heap of charred bones on the stone floor.

Breathing heavily, the Daughter stood over the remnants of her foe. As the battle subsided and her light dimmed, the sky began to normalize. The moon, having bestowed its powers upon its Daughter, continued its slow descent toward the horizon.

Her eyes, still aglow with the fierce, white light, dimmed slightly. The Daughter turned her gaze again toward Zarian's lifeless body. With slow, deliberate steps, she moved toward him. The crackling energy that surrounded her faded into a solemn hush.

Kneeling beside him, she laid a gentle hand on his chest, where his heart lay silent, his skin deathly cold to her touch. From her glowing eyes, a single tear fell, mingling with the blood trailing down her cheeks. With her other hand, she tenderly cupped the deep wound in his neck. A soft light slowly emanated from her palms.

Closing her eyes, she channeled a serene, healing energy, so different from the destructive force she wielded moments before. The energy flowed from her, like glowing tendrils of mist, wrapping Zarian in a cocoon of light. Under the soft radiance, the marks of battle slowly began to mend, the fabric of his being knit back together.

Minutes stretched on, the air filled with the silent prayer of her light.

The shallow gash across his abdomen closed first, followed by the gaping wound in his neck. Her light grew brighter, healing, mending, cleansing, until even the blood coating his skin evaporated into thin air.

The Daughter waited, patient and sure, her hand clenching and unclenching on his chest.

There was only silence. She took a shaky breath, her fingertips digging into his chest.

A second tear rolled down her cheek.

She waited.

And then, miraculously, a heartbeat—faint but undeniable—pulsed under her touch.

One beat, two beats, a stutter and a long pause.

And then, blessedly, a third beat.

Zarian's eyes snapped open, a sharp, desperate intake of breath fracturing the silence. His body convulsed, arching violently off the ground as life forcefully reclaimed him. Gasping for air, he blinked at the figure above him haloed by light.

"Layna?" His voice was a rasp, disbelief and fear mingling in his gaze.

A gentle smile broke across the Daughter's face, softening her divine fury into a moment of pure, human joy.

Before she could speak, a distant noise caught her attention. Her head jerked toward the horizon. As she stood, the light from her fingertips crackled loudly once more. Without a backward glance, she dashed across the terrace and leaped into the air.

Instead of plummeting, she soared *up*—higher and higher until she was a mere speck in the sky silhouetted against the sun. Aloft, her hair billowed around her, a halo fit for a goddess.

From the skies, she beheld the entirety of Alzahra City and the vast desert stretching beyond. Her enhanced vision, surpassing any mere human's, allowed her to see miles away, where the Zephyrian horde approached from the southeast.

There was no obstacle between the enemy and her beloved city.

With a swift motion, she raised her hands skyward, then sharply brought them down. Miles away, the desert floor heeded her command. Beneath the army, the sands erupted in a vicious dance, swirling into a chaotic whirlwind that veiled the sky.

The ground tore open, revealing a gaping chasm that plunged into darkness. The earth itself split apart, exposing an abyss so terrifying, so dark, it whispered of a passage to the underworld itself.

The Zephyrian forces panicked, confusion turning to terror as the ground crumbled beneath them. Horses neighed in fright, soldiers shouted in shock, all before being consumed by the desert's gaping maw.

The chasm stretched across the desert, a sight of awe and horror. Its edges were sharp and sudden, plunging everything into its shadowy depths.

For a moment, the world held its breath, the vast emptiness swallowing all life that had existed moments before.

Then, as swiftly as it had opened, the earth closed over the abyss. The sands shifted back with a rumble, sealing away the Zephyrian horde as if it had never existed. The desert became a seamless expanse once more.

As the Daughter lowered her hands, her body trembled with the sheer magnitude of energy she had commanded. Blood streamed anew from her nostrils, thick crimson torrents against her skin, yet there was a new mastery in her bearing.

The Daughter slowly descended back to the terrace, landing gently on the stone floor. She walked toward Zarian, who stood frozen in silent awe, his eyes wide.

As she closed the distance between them, her white eyes flickered—once, twice, thrice—before returning to their normal state.

"Zarian?" Layna whispered, dazed, before her strength gave way, and she collapsed into unconsciousness.

CHAPTER THIRTY-ONE

Zarian sat, a statue of disbelief, in the sunlight, Layna's fragile form cradled delicately in his arms. The world around him felt surreal, reality woven with strands of the unimaginable. The rise and fall of her chest against him was a comforting rhythm, tethering him to the present.

Yet, his mind was steeped in confusion.

He tried to grasp at his flickering memories, piecing them together like fragments of a dream. His body carried an odd weakness, the lingering echo of a life just returned.

He had died, had he not?

The memory was clear and sharp—the cold bite of the blade in his neck, the triumph in his brother's eyes, the world fading to nothing as his eyes locked onto Layna's anguished face.

The memory of his own death, a moment suspended between time and eternity, clashed violently with the reality of his renewed breath.

How could it be?

He remembered the pain, the sense of finality as Azhar delivered the fatal blow. He remembered Layna's harrowing screams, her body still bound by light, her bruised face streaked with tears.

He remembered his failure.

He remembered the blackness, the absence of anything and everything.

But in the next moment, he drew what felt like his first breath anew. He had opened his eyes and gazed upon Layna—yet it was not the Layna he knew. Hovering above him, she was a vision both magnificent and terrifying, her eyes ablaze with white light, smears of blood painting a frightful contrast on her face.

But then, she had smiled at him.

And in that gentle curve of her lips, Zarian saw *his* Layna shimmer through. She was not completely lost to him, not erased by the power that had transformed her. His Layna was still there, somewhere inside the frightening goddess before him. He remembered the cool relief that washed over him, the slight dimming of his fear.

Zarian's mind replayed the moment she had leaped from the terrace—it had practically stopped his heart once more. But instead of falling, she ascended into the sky, her form etched against the backdrop of the sun in a magnificent display of power.

How long had she remained suspended there? He strained to recall, but the memory eluded him, blurred at the edges like a dream.

What wonders had she wrought in the sky?

He had watched in silent awe as she returned to the terrace. The white fire in her eyes faded, and she was Layna once again—*his* Layna.

Clutching her close, he anchored himself in her presence, her face a guiding light in the murky darkness of his thoughts. Her breaths, a soft rhythm against the silence, brought him peace. He was alive and—somehow, against all conceivable odds—he breathed alongside her.

He kept his gaze steady on Layna, trying his best to ignore the charred remains nearby. His mind recoiled from the implications that threatened to overwhelm his already frayed senses.

For now, he focused on their survival and the warmth of Layna in his arms.

Numbness enveloped Zarian, a protective shroud against the reality unraveling around him. Time lost meaning as he sat on the terrace, cradling Layna in his arms, the world reduced to the space they occupied. He sat counting her breaths for hours, or perhaps only moments, until Jamil breached his bubble of isolation, snapping Zarian back to some semblance of awareness.

Zarian's gaze lifted to meet Jamil's, instantly wary of the three men behind him. He tightened his hold on Layna as he drew her closer to his chest, prepared to shield her from any threat, real or perceived.

With gentle insistence, Jamil helped him stand, his voice laced with concern as he suggested someone else carry Layna to safety. Zarian didn't speak but refused to relinquish his hold.

He could not bear to let her out of his arms.

The memory of his failure, of seeing Layna in peril while he could do nothing but die, haunted him. He clutched her close. Her weight in his arms, though a struggle in his weakened state, was one he would carry willingly.

And so, Zarian carried her.

Flanked by Jamil and the other Medjai, he walked through the halls of a palace ravaged by conflict. The corridors were littered with bodies—palace guards who died defending their people, servants caught in the attack, and the Zephyrian invaders who had breached the sanctuary of the palace. Zarian felt a deep, aching gratitude in his chest that Layna, unconscious in his arms, was spared the sight.

Each step toward the infirmary was harder than the last. His body, barely his own, cried for rest, a plea that became harder and harder to ignore.

After what felt like a lifetime, they finally reached the infirmary, and Jamil quickly signaled the healers. Zarian gently laid Layna on an empty bed, her form so light, yet carrying the weight of his entire world.

Then, as if his strength was tethered to her, it waned the moment she left his arms. He sank to the floor, his body surrendering to exhaustion.

Waking with a start, Zarian found himself in an unfamiliar bed. The rough sheets scratched uncomfortably against his skin, and the fresh, earthy scent of herbs bombarded his senses. Blinking rapidly against the bright light, his eyes focused on the gray ceiling.

A sense of ownership slowly returned to him; his limbs felt like his own again, his mind clear of the hazy fog that had shrouded it.

Bolting upright, he scanned his surroundings—a frantic search that calmed only upon seeing Layna asleep in the bed next to his, her chest rising and falling gently. A curtain partially separated their beds from the rest of the infirmary.

His knees buckled as he leaped out of bed.

Steadying himself, he stood beside her. He noted the healers' handiwork. The remnants of blood and battle were cleansed from her face, her swollen lip now a healing scab, and the bruises that painted her skin in hues of pain were now fading to the purplish blue of recovery.

Exhaustion shadowed her features, making her seem more fragile than he had ever seen her. He reached out, hesitating for a moment before allowing his fingertips to brush against her warm cheek, grounding himself in the reality that she was alive.

He quickly surveyed himself, realizing he was still wearing sleep trousers, his upper body bare. In disbelief, he ran his hands over his abdomen and his neck. Despite the uncomfortable tightness of his skin, there wasn't even a single scar to mark what had transpired.

Zarian turned back to Layna just as Jamil appeared at the infirmary doorway. Relief washed over his friend's face.

"You're awake," Jamil noted, a smile breaking through his concern as he approached with a pitcher of water.

"Has she awoken yet?" Zarian asked urgently, his voice rough as if it had been dragged over broken glass. His gaze flickered to Layna's still form before returning to Jamil.

Jamil's smile faltered as he poured Zarian a glass of water. "No, not yet," he replied gently. Zarian drank deeply, the water soothing his parched throat, but his thoughts remained fixed on Layna.

"How long?" Zarian asked between gulps.

"A little over a day," Jamil responded, nodding toward a pile of clothes on the chair between the beds. "You can change in there." He pointed to a nearby door. Zarian glanced at the clothes, then back at Layna. Jamil stepped closer. "It's alright. I'll watch over her." Nodding, Zarian headed to get dressed.

Returning in under three minutes, he took a seat beside Jamil. "What happened?" His eyes never strayed long from Layna's slumbering form.

Jamil took a deep breath. "Your father sent us—about fifty Medjai—to the palace. He said you'd need our help. He didn't give details, just said it was urgent."

"When we arrived, the palace was eerily quiet. Practically deserted. We split up immediately, searching for any signs of the enemy or the royal family."

"We found about twenty Zephyrians scattered throughout. They had already killed the few guards and servants who were awake. We overpowered them easily." His eyes dropped to his lap, shoulders slumping slightly. "But we were too late. They had already murdered the king."

Pain darkened Zarian's features as he glanced at Layna. His heart ached at the thought of the painful loss she would face upon waking.

She *would* awaken, he told himself.

She had to.

With a silent apology in his eyes, Jamil continued, "We were able to rescue the queen. She was terrified, of course, but unharmed. After that, we searched for you and Layna. I found you both on the terrace. Sarnab, Kharteen, and Dhil were with me."

Zarian's expression grew pensive, his mind racing. "I think the water was spiked with something. That's why I felt so disoriented, why I woke so late."

The two Medjai shared a knowing look. "*Neendakhi*," they said simultaneously. Zarian sighed deeply, cradling his head in his hands.

"That makes sense," Jamil remarked. "We found a palace guard in the gardens, stabbed to death. He must have drugged the water and opened the gates for the Zephyrians. It seems they disposed of him as soon as he served his purpose. A fitting end for a traitor." Jamil leaned closer to Zarian. "Now, your turn. What happened?"

A young healer entered, arms full of fresh supplies. Seeing Zarian awake, he hurried over and greeted the two men. He began checking Zarian's vitals, his hands moving with practiced motions as he conducted a swift but thorough examination.

Zarian, for his part, endured the scrutiny with resigned patience. Once satisfied, the healer gave Zarian a nod of approval and left them to their privacy.

The prince inhaled deeply. "I awoke much later than expected. I noticed a horse tied up right in the middle of the gardens. That was the first sign. That, along with my disorientation and headache, I just knew something was wrong. I rushed to Layna's room, but I was too late." His voice cracked as he continued, "She had been captured. I found her restrained on the terrace…by Zaarif."

Jamil's mouth fell open. "*Zaarif?* But how?"

"Azhar," Zarian corrected, a hard edge in his voice. "The new king of Zephyria, that was Zaarif." He paused, letting Jamil absorb this revelation. "And he had the orb. He used it to bind Layna to the pillar." Zarian's eyes clouded over, the weight of painful memories pulling him back.

"We fought," he said simply, looking down at his lap. "Then, at the eclipse's peak, the prophecy unfolded. The Daughter of the Moon was unleashed." He hesitated. "She—she dealt with Azhar. She did what I couldn't. She used her light against him. The bones on the terrace are his." Jamil winced and placed a hand on Zarian's shoulder.

Zarian continued, omitting his own death and miraculous revival, his mind still grappling with that reality. "She levitated into the sky, using her power fiercely, but it was all a haze to me." His eyes met Jamil's. "When she returned to the terrace, she was Layna again, but she collapsed. The power was too much."

Concern washed over his features as he looked at Layna. "I could do nothing but hold her," he whispered.

"You did everything you could," Jamil reassured, squeezing Zarian's shoulder. "All that matters is that you're both safe." He paused, thinking. "I can't believe that Azhar was Zaarif. All this time. Do you think your father knew?"

"He must have known," Zarian snapped, voice brimming with resentment. "He concealed Zaarif's whereabouts for years. He knew, and still he chose silence. Leaving me in the dark at such a pivotal moment…it's unfathomable."

"I am truly sorry, brother." Jamil paused and looked at him closely, observing, not for the first time, the absence of any visible wounds. "You mentioned that you and Zaarif fought?"

"Yes," Zarian replied flatly, his gaze dropping to the floor, a shadow of pain flickering across his face.

Jamil watched his friend closely for several heartbeats but didn't press further. Instead, he rose to his feet. "The queen will be coming soon to see Layna. She's shown incredible strength through all of this. Managing a war-torn kingdom while grieving her husband."

His gaze flickered between Zarian and Layna. "I must return to the Oasis. I'll inform your father of what has happened. And…I'll bring Soraya back. She should be here." Zarian, lost in thought, didn't respond. "Will you be alright?" Jamil pressed, a deep crease forming between his brows.

Zarian nodded. "Thank you, Jamil. For everything."

Days passed, but Layna remained deeply asleep. Zarian, steadfast and unwavering, barely left her bedside, his vigil a constant through the days and nights that followed. The world outside continued its relentless march, but time stood still for him, each tick of the clock stretching into eternity.

He watched her, hope and despair battling within him, clinging to the slightest movement, a twitch of her hand or a flutter beneath her eyelids, as signs she might return to him.

Soraya arrived at the palace in time for her father's funeral. It was a modest affair. Historically, royal funerals were grand public events, a celebration of the monarch's legacy, but a private event felt more appropriate given the recent tragedies.

With heavy hearts, Hadiyah and Soraya arranged the somber ceremony. Soraya, speaking both for herself and for Layna, shared a heartfelt tribute to their father. Both mother and daughter lit the funeral pyre, standing together in tears until the flames died.

During the funeral, Zarian stayed by Layna's side in the infirmary, tightly gripping her hand, silently urging her to open her eyes. His heart ached knowing she would deeply regret missing her beloved father's farewell.

After the funeral, the queen and Lord Ebrahim, with Burhani's assistance, assumed the mantle of leadership, working tirelessly to begin healing and rebuilding Alzahra.

Word soon arrived at the palace, a whisper of victory from the northeast: Baysaht's forces defeated the second Zephyrian faction.

Yet, an eerie silence hung over the fate of the southeastern troops. No tales of battles won or lost reached their ears—it was as if the very sands had conspired to keep their fate a secret.

Rumors fluttered like uneasy birds through the palace and markets. Wandering souls spoke of a fantastical event—the desert itself rising in fury, sands parted by the hand of a vengeful goddess, swallowing the southeastern army whole.

These storytellers, with wide eyes and trembling voices, were met with disbelief. Laughter and dismissal followed their accounts, their stories too wild to be taken as anything but the ramblings of those touched by the desert's hot sun.

In the quiet infirmary, a week passed—a week since the eclipse turned the world on its head. Layna lay still, a silent witness to the passage of time. Her ordeal had demanded a steep toll, leaving her trapped in the murky depths of a coma.

On the seventh day, amidst hushed whispers and the soft creaking of the infirmary doors, a subtle change stirred the air.

Layna's eyes fluttered open.

Tinga noticed first, her voice filled with joy and disbelief. "She's awake! Come, healer, quickly!" Her urgency brought the room to life, stirring the healers into swift action.

Zarian gently helped Layna sit up as she struggled to shake off her week-long sleep. In that moment, everyone in the room—family and palace staff alike—bowed deeply in unison.

The new queen of Alzahra had finally awoken.

The significance of their bows crashed forcefully into Layna's slowly returning consciousness. "No, no, no," she whispered, her voice rough with disuse, as her eyes welled with tears.

She denied the reality they confirmed—the reality of her father's death.

Soraya and Zarian held her tightly, Tinga gently stroking her hair, her loved ones offering whispered words of comfort. As she surrendered to her grief, the weight of her new reality settled upon her.

Queen Layna had awakened to a world forever changed.

CHAPTER THIRTY-TWO

Three days after Layna's awakening, the healers deemed her fit to leave the infirmary. They subjected her to numerous examinations, before finally confirming that aside from noticeable weight loss, she appeared remarkably well.

However, Layna had a blank space in her memory regarding the events of the eclipse. During a final examination, a young healer cautiously asked, "Your Majesty, what is the last thing you remember before waking here?"

Layna paused, reaching back through the fog of lost time. The room faded around her, the memory plunging her back into a moment steeped in fear.

"I was bound to the pillar," she recounted, her gaze distant. "On the terrace, under a red sky."

Zarian watched Layna closely, noting the furrows of worry creasing her brow. She wore a new vulnerability, the trauma and grief leaving a deep mark on her spirit. The fiery spark that defined her seemed muted, dimmed by unseen shadows behind her eyes.

Her mental state was fragile, like a vessel weathered by a tempest. Seeing her like this—her inner light barely a flicker—gutted Zarian. At times, she flinched at the sight of him before recognition slowly settled in. Though rare, those moments cut deeper than any pain he'd ever known.

He resolved to be her anchor, to help rekindle her fire, and to stand by her as she navigated the path back to herself.

Zarian walked Layna back to her chambers, his hand gently resting on her lower back. As they neared her chambers, he halted, turning to face her.

"Please consider it again," Zarian implored. "You can move to a different set of chambers. A new space might shield you from painful memories, somewhere you can feel safe and secure."

Layna shook her head. "So much has already changed," she said. "He took my father! I won't let him take anything else." She caressed Zarian's cheek in gratitude. "I appreciate your concern, truly."

Together, they stepped into her chambers. The soft, warm glow of the late afternoon sun filtered through the open balcony doors. Tinga and the servants had meticulously restored the room to its former elegance, erasing any signs of chaos from the attack. Every piece of furniture, every drape, and even the smallest trinkets were placed exactly as before.

They settled on the plush sofa as they had done countless times. "I need you to tell me everything," Layna said. "I know you've been holding back because of my mental state. But I can't keep wandering aimlessly in this fog until my memory returns. Please. It's time."

And so, Zarian told her.

He recounted her bright white eyes, her massive display of power, and her ascension to the sky. Once more, he held back the truth of his own death and miraculous return. She was not yet ready to shoulder that revelation, he told himself.

Their conversation flowed for hours, a cathartic release of words and emotions. He told her of the seven days she remained unconscious, how he kept vigil by her bedside. He spoke of his pain, his fear, and the fierce hope that she would open her eyes and look at him once more.

Never in his life had he wished for anything more fervently.

Layna listened, eyes filled with love and tears, absorbing every detail.

As the night deepened and the candlelight waned, Zarian noticed her fatigue. "You should sleep," he coaxed gently. "The healers made it clear that rest is paramount for your recovery. Your mind needs to heal before your memories can return."

Layna's initial protest faded at the sincerity in his voice. Nodding, she let him guide her to bed.

"Soraya insisted on staying with you," Zarian said, drawing the covers over her. "She'll be here when you wake." Layna nodded and closed her eyes.

Zarian lingered a moment longer before quietly exiting the room, the door closing softly behind him.

In the days following her emergence from the coma, Layna and Zarian tried to weave the fragile threads of their lives back into normalcy. Yet, this fleeting peace was interrupted by the arrival of the Medjai elders, accompanied by King Tahriq.

The air in the great hall was thick with anticipation, as if the very stones of the palace held their breath. Seven elders in pristine robes, most with long white beards, stood before Layna, Zarian, Lord Ebrahim and Hadiyah.

Zarian greeted his father with a cold rigidity. Once, he would have knelt before King Tahriq and received a warm embrace upon rising. This time, however, he remained resolutely upright, offering only the barest nod in acknowledgment, his feet firmly planted by Layna's side.

The elders silently took their positions before Layna, their sharp gazes fixed unerringly on her. Their probing eyes seemed to wait with bated breath for any sign of the power that had shaken their world.

Unease crawled up Layna's spine under their blatant appraisal. She stiffened, fingers fidgeting nervously under their gaze.

Zarian's eyes flicked down to her hands. He edged closer, until the length of his arm pressed against hers. The warmth of his touch grounded her. Layna's posture softened as she stood straighter, her hands relaxing at her sides.

The elders' sharp gazes flickered from Layna to Zarian, their expressions shifting from intense scrutiny to staunch disapproval. Deep frowns creased their lined, weathered faces.

Despite their disdain, Zarian remained undeterred. He locked eyes with the head elder, his chin raised in defiance, an unspoken challenge passing between them.

After a tense moment, the head elder relented. "Let us begin," Zanjeel declared, waving his hand dismissively. "We will only speak with the princess and our prince."

Hadiyah opened her mouth to protest, but Layna gently laid a hand on her shoulder. "It's alright, Mama," she reassured quietly. Hadiyah took a deep breath before giving a terse nod. With a final, lingering glance at the elders, she turned to leave, Lord Ebrahim following close behind. The senior adviser stopped in front of Zarian, locking eyes with him. A brief, silent exchange passed between the two men, and Zarian gave a subtle nod of understanding. Satisfied, Lord Ebrahim followed Hadiyah out of the hall.

The remaining group quickly took their seats. Zarian recounted the ordeal to the elders, piecing together the events as best as he could recall. He again omitted the tale of his death and rebirth, for reasons he did not quite understand. He had kept the full extent of what occurred a closely guarded secret, not breathing a word to anyone.

As he handed the fragmented remnants of the orb to the elders, he watched as their expressions turned grave. Brows furrowed, eyes darkened, and lips tightened into thin lines at the sight of the shattered orb. The old men exchanged worried glances.

The head elder cleared his throat. "So, she remembers nothing? Nothing at all?" he inquired, his gaze shifting between Zarian and Layna.

"Nothing," Layna confirmed, her voice marked with frustration.

The elder's nod was grave. His sharp eyes remained fixed on Layna. "Since that day, have you felt *any* hint of the powers returning? Even the slightest trace?"

Layna held his penetrating gaze, her voice unwavering, "No, there has been nothing."

Still, the elders were not convinced, insisting on conducting their own tests.

What followed was an intrusive, lengthy examination that Zarian watched with growing anger. The elders subjected Layna to a barrage of stimuli—loud sounds, blinding lights, and even physical pain. One elder, Hilder, made a small incision on her palm to observe any unusual healing response.

Zarian's tolerance dwindled rapidly. He hovered nearby, fists clenched tightly and mouth set in a grim line. When he could bear it no longer, he intervened, his voice vibrating with barely contained rage. "Enough," he commanded, his deep voice echoing through the hall.

The elders, taken aback by his interruption, shot him scowling looks of displeasure. Zanjeel watched him with a calculating gaze, his eyes sharp like a hawk.

Next, the elders shepherded Layna and Zarian back to the terrace. Layna's steps were hesitant as she climbed the narrow flight of stairs.

The terrace's vast expanse unfolded before them, the scene of her transformation starkly unchanged. The sun bore down on the group, but its warmth was useless against the cold apprehension coiling in her belly.

Her heart raced and her head swam. A pounding drum began to beat painfully behind her eyes. As she gazed at the twin pillars, a strong wave of nausea threatened to overwhelm her.

Zarian cast a worried glance in her direction. He placed a reassuring hand on her back, drawing soothing circles until her breathing returned to normal.

Zarian's eyes fell to the floor where the stones were still stained with soot. He swallowed hard, his chest heavy with grief.

He had buried his brother's bones in the desert alone.

He didn't notice Tahriq's mournful, watery gaze upon him.

One of the elders, Zarqi, swept his gaze across the terrace, pausing at the pillars. Contemplation crossed his weathered features. "Perhaps," he mused aloud, "we should bind her to the pillar once again. It might serve as a catalyst to reawaken any dormant powers."

The suggestion hung ominously in the air.

Layna's breath hitched, dread gripping her at the thought of being helpless once more. The idea of revisiting such vulnerability, bound and exposed, sent a chilling wave through her veins.

Her fears, however, were unfounded.

Zarian quickly stepped in front of her, his eyes lethal with cold resolve. "You will not subject her to that again," he growled. "Find another method for your evaluations." He stood unyielding, a physical shield against any threat.

Zanjeel regarded him with disapproval. "Prince Zarian," he reprimanded sternly, "we are quite disappointed with your behavior. Your defiance raises questions about your loyalty. We begin to suspect you serve *another* instead of our order." His sharp gaze flicked to Layna before boring again into Zarian.

The prince did not respond. Instead, he rested his hand on the hilt of his sword, eyes aflame with silent threat.

Incensed, Zanjeel's eyes darted angrily to King Tahriq, seeking an intervention, a command to compel the prince to step aside.

But Tahriq remained silent, gaze fixed firmly on the terrace floor. The elders awaited his order, but none came. Tahriq's scowl deepened, yet he offered no reprimand or support to either side.

The elders found themselves in a deadlock. They were painfully aware that Zarian could strike down all seven of them before they drew their next breath.

Their authority met its match in a man fiercely guarding the woman he loved.

And so, the elders were forced to continue without restraining Layna. They subjected her to more tests across the terrace. At one point, they placed the fragmented shards of the orb in her hands, urging her to meditate. Yet, their efforts were fruitless, and the shattered pieces remained inert in her grasp.

Next, they burned incense, its thick smoke swirling around Layna. The pungent aroma was overpowering, eliciting nothing but a fit of coughing—a decidedly human reaction.

Their examination stretched into the depths of the night, under the silent watch of the moon. The elders hoped the moon's presence might coax the Daughter's powers to reveal themselves.

They even ventured to the hidden library, sifting through texts and reciting ancient chants in forgotten tongues over her. Layna listened to the cadence of the unfamiliar words, but the rituals bore no fruit.

No sign of the Daughter's abilities surfaced.

The extraordinary had given way to the ordinary, leaving the elders baffled, and Zarian barely restraining himself at every turn.

After nearly two full days of exhaustive trials, there were still no signs of the powers that had once surged through the princess.

The elders convened, murmuring among themselves in hushed deliberation.

They finally turned to Layna and Zarian, their expressions solemn. "It appears," Zanjeel began, "that the power which once resided within the princess has departed. She was destined to wield such extraordinary strength for but a single day."

Layna exhaled deeply, the tension knotting her shoulders slowly unfurling. Beside her, Zarian's hand found hers, his grip firm, their fingers intertwining in a silent exchange of relief.

As the elders prepared to depart, King Tahriq sought a moment alone with his son in the courtyard.

Tahriq opened and closed his mouth several times, struggling to find the words to bridge the insurmountable gap between them.

Yet, the apology that was needed remained stubbornly unspoken.

"It seems your heart is here," Tahriq finally said, eyes flicking to Layna who stood a few paces away by the fountain.

"It is." Zarian crossed his arms over his chest, his gaze stoic as he regarded his father.

Tahriq chose his next words with care. "Then in your current state, you are of no use to the Medjai. You would be a liability on missions. I command you to remain here and guard our interests in Alzahra," he decreed, his eyes glistening in the sunlight.

Zarian studied his father. Though gratitude flickered briefly in his heart, it was overshadowed by the pain of Tahriq's secrets.

The chasm between them was not so easily bridged.

With a small, almost imperceptible nod, Zarian accepted his new charge. Without another word, he turned on his heel, leaving his father standing alone.

CHAPTER THIRTY-THREE

In the wake of the eclipse's world-altering events, Lord Ebrahim and Hadiyah focused on diplomacy, acting swiftly to shape the narrative of Alzahra's trial. Emissaries were dispatched across the continent to request support.

Amidst these efforts, another goal emerged—planning Layna's coronation. The palace buzzed with activity to solidify her position as the new monarch. Every detail was scrutinized, from the intricate designs of her gown to the flawless orchestration of the event. The security measures were meticulously planned. The decorations, the ceremonial crown, the positioning of the royal family—all were examined with careful precision.

Stories of the Moon Queen, as she had come to be known, spread like light through darkness, captivating and terrifying the continent in equal measure. Eyewitnesses in Alzahra City during the eclipse painted a picture of a deity among mortals, a woman shrouded in ethereal light who commanded the heavens.

These rumors of an awe-inspiring, fearsome figure had an unexpected benefit. Kingdoms near and far, intrigued and frightened by her alleged might, hastened to align themselves with Alzahra.

The palace's official position was of vehement denial, dismissing the fantastical stories as mere rumors.

Still, in a show of solidarity—or perhaps in hopes of favor from the infamous Moon Queen—once-neutral kingdoms sent convoys laden with aid. Supplies and resources vital for Alzahra's reconstruction poured in from kingdoms across the continent. Caravans arrived bearing food, medical supplies, construction materials, and skilled laborers. The palace, scarred by recent conflict, began to see signs of repair, mirrored by the recovery of villages that had suffered during Zephyria's attack. The influx of grain, stone, and healing herbs revitalized the kingdom, breathing new life into its wounded heart.

Yet, amidst the awe and alliances, shadows crept at the edges. Whispers of witchcraft and dark pacts circulated. Accusations flew, brazen and fearful, suggesting such power could only come from forbidden knowledge. Some even accused the Moon Queen of consorting with demons to gain her powers.

These suspicions seeded doubt and fear, giving rise to factions within Alzahra itself. Voices, emboldened by suspicion and superstition, clamored for her to step down. They painted her as volatile, her presence a cause for unease.

A new faction arose, the Children of the Pure, and challenged Layna's legitimacy not based on her lineage, but on the unfathomable source of her rumored powers. In the heart of Alzahra City, where unity should have been strongest, fractures appeared, casting splintering shadows over the kingdom's future.

The very power that had saved them now posed a question none could easily answer:

Could they trust a queen touched by the moon?

And so, the council hastened to plan Layna's coronation, hoping to quell the discord threatening to divide their society. The palace raced against time and dissent, hoping the ceremony would usher in a new era of stability.

In the aftermath of the eclipse, Layna and Zarian grappled with their new realities.

Layna mourned her father, deprived of the chance to say goodbye. His counsel, unwavering support, and the legacy he left behind now rested on her narrow shoulders. Every corner of the palace whispered memories of him. At times, she half expected to see him at breakfast or in the council chambers, before the brutal reality of his death slammed into her again.

Meanwhile, Zarian contended again with the loss of a sibling. Not the twisted man Azhar had become, but the brother he remembered from childhood—Zaarif, with his genuine smile and heart full of dreams. Zaarif, who once shared his laughter and hopes, before fate corrupted him into someone unrecognizable.

On the surface, things seemed normal, but an underlying tension, a formality of sorts, crept between them. This distance was caused, perhaps, by Layna's lingering trauma and grief, or the looming pressure of her coronation, or possibly, the secret burden Zarian still harbored about his rebirth.

Weeks passed, until the awaited moment was upon them—Coronation Day. Tinga dressed Layna in Alzahra's royal colors: an exquisite ceremonial burgundy gown, its long sleeves embellished with golden embroidery and gems. The bodice was tightly laced, and the skirt puffed out dramatically.

In her chambers, Layna stood quietly at her balcony, lost in thought. A soft knock at the door interrupted her reverie. She instinctively knew it was Zarian coming to check on her.

He entered, clad in a formal navy tunic. The sight coaxed a small smile onto her face, remembering the simpler, carefree times at the royal ball.

It seemed like a lifetime ago.

"You look breathtaking," he marveled, his quiet strength wrapping around her like a warm embrace. "How do you feel?" His eyes searched hers intently, as they so often did now, looking for what she assumed was reassurance that she was still the woman he loved.

"I'm nervous," she admitted quietly. "Today, of all days, I wish Baba were here. I know that doesn't make sense. There would be no need for a coronation if he were still here." She paused, swallowing the lump in her throat. "But he would have known how to lead Alzahra through this." A deep sigh escaped her, carrying the weight of her grief and uncertainty. "I don't feel ready. How can I be the queen Alzahra needs when I feel so lost? I am a shadow of myself. And my people are afraid of me." Her shoulders slumped inwards, eyes closing in weariness.

Zarian gently tilted her face, forcing her eyes to meet his. "The rumors will pass. And you're stronger than you know. You have a kind heart and a wise soul—the very qualities that made your father a great king. You *are* ready for this. You will be an exceptional queen." The deep timbre of his voice soothed the edges of her anxiety as it often did.

So much remained unspoken between them, a sea of words and feelings pushed aside by the whirlwind of tragedies. They had barely had a moment to breathe, let alone discuss their relationship amidst the demands of this new world.

For now, they found peace in the present, in the healing silence that enveloped them as they stood together.

For Layna, this moment of peace was enough, for now, to anchor her in the promise of their tomorrow.

She hoped it was enough for Zarian, too.

Layna inhaled deeply, steeling herself for the day ahead, and stepped out from her chambers with Zarian by her side. As they reached the main foyer, they were greeted by her mother, Soraya, Lord Ebrahim, and Burhani, each immaculately dressed in their ceremonial garments. Soraya enveloped her in a tight embrace, careful not to disturb Layna's intricately braided bun.

Together, they exited the palace, flanked by palace guards. Layna's gaze swept over their faces, not recognizing a single one. These were new recruits, handpicked and trained under Zarian's careful scrutiny.

The group moved forward, stepping into the light of a day that would mark a new chapter for Alzahra. A large carriage awaited them in the courtyard. The ride to the city center was quick, the streets a blur of colors.

Before the eclipse, Layna's presence would have sparked celebration, her name on the lips of a cheering crowd, her path lined with adoring subjects, flower petals strewn in celebration.

Her people had always loved her.

But now, as she emerged from the carriage, she was met with uneasy stares, a strange mix of fealty and fear, the aftermath of rumors that had wrapped both awe and suspicion around her.

The tension was tangible, threading thickly through the assembly. Whispers of the Moon Queen and her powers carried on the wind, though none were bold enough to openly jeer.

The coronation ceremony was brief by design, intending to limit Layna's exposure. Lord Ebrahim formally declared her the new queen, his voice steady as he recited the sacred oath of monarchs.

Layna, her voice clear and unwavering, repeated the words and pledged to uphold Alzahra's laws and always act in the best interests of its people. Her binding promise to the kingdom resonated through the silent crowd, sealing her fate as their ruler.

Lord Ebrahim placed the heirloom crown on her head. Sparkling in the sunlight, it was made of finely wrought gold. Embedded within the delicate filigree were gleaming red rubies, their rich, red depths winking in the light.

Below in the crowd, Zarian watched Layna. Immense pride welled up inside him. She was the leader Alzahra needed.

Yet mingled with that pride was an unnamable sense of loss, a lump in his throat, and a burning in his eyes he struggled to conceal.

Lord Ebrahim concluded the ceremony with, "All hail Queen Layna!" His call for celebration was taken up by the crowd, their voices initially hesitant, but soon unified in their shouts of reverence.

Yet, as echoes of "Queen Layna" rang out, a shift occurred—the chant transformed, morphing into a moniker that carried a different weight.

"Moon Queen! Moon Queen! Moon Queen!"

After the coronation, the return to the palace was somber. Layna, now officially queen, headed toward her father's private office—a room brimming with memories and the weight of responsibility that now rested on her shoulders.

A room that was now hers.

The crown on her head felt oppressively heavy. Layna yearned to cast it off and ease the pressure at the base of her skull, yet she resisted.

Her kingdom needed her.

Her mother needed her.

Poor Hadiyah, thrust into managing the kingdom so soon after becoming a widow. She deserved space and time to finally mourn and process her own grief.

As Layna sat reviewing her father's notes, the door swung open, and Zarian strode in.

They had avoided discussing their future together—Zarian giving her time to heal and Layna delaying making a decision.

He no longer visited her at night, fearing that seeing him climb over the balcony would re-traumatize her and dredge up painful memories.

How Layna wished to return to the woman she once was—the one who had captured Zarian's heart. She wanted to laugh again, to smile again, to experience the joy of a newly blossoming love again.

Zarian approached her with purpose, his handsome face determined. He walked around the large desk, firmly grasped her hands, and pulled her up from the chair. Her heart thudded as his warm hands cradled her face.

Warm hazel eyes locked onto hers, and he seemed on the cusp of voicing long-held thoughts, something exceedingly important.

But the moment shattered when the door swung open abruptly.

Layna and Zarian both snapped their heads to the doorway as a servant entered hastily. The man froze, cheeks flushing at the sight of his new queen and Zarian in such an intimate manner. Quickly averting his gaze, he shifted awkwardly on his feet.

Layna recognized him as a courier. The servant cleared his throat, overcoming his initial embarrassment, eyes sparkling eagerly as a broad grin spread across his face.

"Your Majesty! It's here! You've received a letter from Prince—er, King Nizam!" he announced, his voice brimming with enthusiasm.

With a flourish, he presented her with a crisp envelope sealed with the regal emblem of Baysaht. Emblazoned upon it in exquisite precision was her new title: *Queen Layna*. Below it, in smaller font, was King Nizam's name.

With furrowed brows, Layna traced her fingertips over the intricate, embossed lettering, and her eyes flashed white.

THE STORY CONTINUES

Continue Layna and Zarian's story in **Book 2** *of the Moon & Sands trilogy:*

THE MOON'S FURY

EXTRAS

Can't wait for the next book?

Follow the author on Instagram for sneak peeks, artwork, and more!

@leenakazakbooks

ACKNOWLEDGEMENTS

To my best friend: I can't find the words to truly thank you for all you've done for me; I'm not sure those words even exist. This tale has been eight years in the making, and you've been my greatest support throughout it. I've constantly pestered you with drafts, revisions, and new scenes, and you've always met my excitement with your own. Every time (*and there were many times*) when I doubted myself, calling the story awful and boring, you knew just what to say to reassure me (*anything is boring if you read it ten thousand times*). Besides the story, you've been my unwavering rock through every single moment in my life, no matter how minuscule or insignificant. I feel eternally blessed to have you as my friend. Thank you for everything that you do and for always being just a text message away.

To my sister: Wow. Eight years later, here we are. I'll try to keep this cool and casual since I know you despise super lengthy emotional rants. Eight years ago, when I was struggling with my life and trauma, you were there for me in ways I never expected. We mended our relationship and started afresh, and I can't thank God enough. Thank you for reading through this, giving me your unfiltered feedback and comments, and keeping me grounded. Most importantly, thank you for all the time you spent with the kids so I could rest my brain and focus on writing and editing. I love you exactly as you are, with your rough edges and brutal honesty. You are the most incredible, selfless, and deserving person that I know. And if you don't believe me, you can ask the kids.

To my husband: I feel like my life began after I met you. Thank you for loving me so perfectly, so completely, so deeply. To quote Zarian, you healed parts of me I didn't even know were broken. Thank you for being an incredible partner (*I know I don't make it easy*) and always thinking of me in everything you do. You make my happiness your priority, above anything and everything else, and I love you immensely for it. I can't express how much it means to me to be able to turn my anxious mind off around you, knowing I can depend on you to take care of things. Thank you for never making me feel like my overwhelming emotions are a burden. No feeling of mine is too small for you. Your patience and love for me are as deep and endless as the fabled springs of the Oasis. I feel so lucky and blessed to be your wife. Being with you makes everything brighter. *You* are my home.

To my family: If you suspect I wrote this, take the blue pill. Fine, in all seriousness, I wouldn't be the person I am without your love and support. From planning weddings to our family game nights to our group chats, I treasure the traditions we have forged together. Thank you for carving time in your busy lives to read my story. Thank you for all your support in bringing this book to the world and for your words of encouragement. I am incredibly proud of this debut novel and extremely excited to share the next part of my journey with you. I hope you are, too! Now, take the blue pill.